THE GHOST

ROBERT HARRIS

THE GHOST

HUTCHINSON

LONDON

Published by Hutchinson 2007

2 4 6 8 10 9 7 5 3 1

First published in Great Britain in 2007 by
Hutchinson
Random House, 20 Vauxhall Bridge Road,
London SW1V 2SA

www.rbooks.co.uk

Addresses for companies within The Random House Group Limited can be found at:
www.randomhouse.co.uk/offices.htm

The Random House Group Limited Reg. No. 954009

A CIP catalogue record for this book is available from the British Library

ISBN 9780091796259 (trade paperback)

Typeset in 13 on 18pt Spectrum by Palimpsest Book Production Limited,
Grangemouth, Stirlingshire
Printed and bound in Australia by
Griffin Press

To Gill

Author's Note

I would like to thank Andrew Crofts for permission to use the quotes from his excellent handbook, *Ghostwriting* (A & C Black, 2004). Two other successful ghostwriters, Adam Sisman and Luke Jennings, were kind enough to share their experiences with me. Philippe Sands QC generously provided advice about international law. Rose Styron spent several days showing me round Martha's Vineyard: I could not have had a more gracious and well-informed guide. My publisher in the USA, David Rosenthal, and my agent, Michael Carlisle, gave me great help with the American aspects of this novel – although each, of course, is as unlike his fictional counterpart as it is possible to be.

Robert Harris

Cap Bénat, 26 July 2007

I am not I: thou art not he or she:
they are not they.

EVELYN WAUGH,
Brideshead Revisited

One

Of all the advantages that ghosting offers, one of the greatest must be the opportunity that you get to meet people of interest.

Andrew Crofts, Ghostwriting

The moment I heard how McAra died I should have walked away. I can see that now. I should have said, 'Rick, I'm sorry, this isn't for me, I don't like the sound of it,' finished my drink and left. But he was such a good storyteller, Rick — I often thought *he* should have been the writer and I the literary agent — that once he'd started talking there was never any question I wouldn't listen, and by the time he had finished, I was hooked.

The story, as Rick told it to me over lunch that day, went like this:

McAra had caught the last ferry from Woods Hole, Massachusetts, to Martha's Vineyard two Sundays earlier. I worked out afterwards it must have been January the twelfth. It was touch and go whether the ferry would sail at all. A gale had been blowing since mid-afternoon and the last few crossings had been cancelled. But towards nine o'clock the wind eased slightly and at nine forty-five the master decided it was safe to cast off. The boat was crowded: McAra was lucky to get a space for his car. He parked below decks and then went upstairs to get some air.

No one saw him alive again.

The crossing to the island usually takes forty-five minutes, but on this particular night the weather slowed the voyage considerably: docking a two-hundred-foot vessel in a fifty-knot wind, said Rick, is nobody's idea of fun. It was nearly eleven when the ferry made land at Vineyard Haven and the cars started up – all except one: a brand new tan-coloured Ford Escape SUV. The purser made a loudspeaker appeal for the owner to return to his vehicle as he was blocking the drivers behind him. When he still didn't show, the crew tried the doors, which turned out to be unlocked, and freewheeled the big Ford down to the quayside. Afterwards they searched the ship with care: stairwells, bar, toilets, even the lifeboats – nothing. They called the terminal at Woods Hole to check if anyone had disembarked before the boat sailed or had perhaps been accidentally left behind – again: nothing. That was when an official of the Massachusetts Steamship Authority finally contacted the Coast Guard station in Falmouth to report a possible man overboard.

A police check on the Ford's licence plate revealed it to be registered to one Martin S. Rhinehart of New York City, although Mr Rhinehart was eventually tracked down to his ranch in California. By now it was about midnight on the East Coast, nine p.m. on the West.

'This is *the* Marty Rhinehart?' I interrupted.

'This is he.'

Rhinehart immediately confirmed over the telephone to the police that the Ford belonged to him. He kept it at his house on Martha's Vineyard for the use of himself and his guests in the summer. He also confirmed that, despite the time of year, a group of people were staying there at the moment. He said he would get his assistant to call the house and find out if anyone had borrowed the car. Half an hour later she rang back to say that someone was indeed missing, a person by the name of McAra.

There was nothing now that could be done until first light. Not that it mattered. Everyone knew that if a passenger had gone overboard it would be a search for a corpse. Rick is one of those irritatingly fit Americans in his early forties who looks about nineteen and does terrible things to his body with bicycles and canoes. He knows that sea: he once spent two days paddling a kayak the entire sixty miles round the island. The ferry from Woods Hole plies the strait where Vineyard Sound meets Nantucket Sound, and that is dangerous water. At high tide you can see the force of the currents sucking the huge channel buoys over on to their sides. Rick shook his head. In January, in a gale, in *snow*? No one could survive more than five minutes.

A local woman found the body early the next morning, thrown up on the beach about four miles down the island's coast at Lambert's Cove. The driver's licence in the wallet confirmed him to be Michael James McAra, aged fifty, from Balham in south London. I remember feeling a sudden shot of sympathy at the mention of that dreary, unexotic suburb: he certainly was a long way from home, poor devil. His passport named his mother as his next-of-kin. The police took his corpse to the little morgue in Vineyard Haven and then drove over to the Rhinehart residence to break the news and to fetch one of the other guests to identify him.

It must have been quite a scene, said Rick, when the volunteer guest finally showed up to view the body: 'I bet the morgue attendant is still talking about it.' There was one patrol car from Edgartown with a blue flashing light, a second car with four armed guards to secure the building, and a third vehicle, bomb-proof, carrying the instantly recognisable man who, until eighteen months earlier, had been the Prime Minister of Great Britain and Northern Ireland.

*

The lunch had been Rick's idea. I hadn't even known he was in town until he rang me the night before. He insisted we meet at his club. It was not *his* club, exactly — he was actually a member of a similar mausoleum in Manhattan, whose members had reciprocal dining rights in London — but he loved it all the same. At lunchtime only men were admitted. Each wore a dark blue suit and was over sixty: I hadn't felt so young since I left university. Outside, the winter sky pressed down on London like a great grey tombstone. Inside, yellow electric light from three immense candelabra glinted on dark polished tables, plated silverware and rubied decanters of claret. A small card placed between us announced that the club's annual backgammon tournament would be taking place that evening. It was like the Changing of the Guard or the Houses of Parliament — a foreigner's image of England.

'I'm amazed this hasn't been in the papers,' I said.

'Oh, but it has. Nobody's made a secret of it. There've been obituaries.'

And now I came to think of it, I *did* vaguely remember seeing something. But I had been working fifteen hours a day for a month to finish my new book, the autobiography of a footballer, and the world beyond my study had become a blur.

'What on earth was an ex-prime minister doing identifying the body of a man from Balham who fell off the Martha's Vineyard ferry?'

'Michael McAra,' announced Rick, with the emphatic delivery of a man who has flown three thousand miles to deliver this punchline, '*was helping him write his memoirs.*'

And this is where, in that parallel life, I express polite sympathy for the elderly Mrs McAra ('such a shock to lose a child at that age'), fold my heavy linen napkin, finish my drink, say goodbye, and step out into the chilly London street with the whole of my undistinguished career stretching safely ahead of me. Instead I excused myself, went to the club's lavatory and studied an unfunny *Punch* cartoon while urinating thoughtfully.

'You realise I don't know anything about politics?' I said when I got back.

'You voted for him, didn't you?'

'Adam Lang? Of course I did. Everybody voted for him. He wasn't a politician; he was a craze.'

'Well, that's the point. Who's interested in politics? In any case, it's a professional ghostwriter he needs, my friend, not another goddamned politico.' He glanced around. It was an iron rule of the club that no business could be discussed on the premises – a problem for Rick, seeing as he never discussed anything else. 'Marty Rhinehart paid ten million dollars for these memoirs on two conditions. First, it'd be in the stores within two years. Second, Lang wouldn't pull any punches about the War on Terror. From what I hear, he's nowhere near meeting either requirement. Things got so bad around Christmas, Rhinehart gave him the use of his vacation house on the Vineyard so that Lang and McAra could work without any distractions. I guess the pressure must have gotten to McAra. The state medical examiner found enough booze in his blood to put him four times over the driving limit.'

'So it was an accident?'

'Accident? Suicide?' He casually flicked his hand. 'Who'll ever know? What does it matter? It was the book that killed him.'

'That's encouraging,' I said.

While Rick went on with his pitch, I stared at my plate and imagined the former prime minister looking down at his assistant's cold white face in the mortuary — staring down at his ghost, I suppose one could say. How did it feel? I am always putting this question to my clients. I must ask it a hundred times a day during the interview phase: How did it feel? *How did it feel?* And mostly they can't answer, which is why they have to hire me to supply their memories: by the end of a successful collaboration I am more them than they are. I rather enjoy this process, to be honest: the brief freedom of being someone else. Does that sound creepy? If so, let me add that real craftsmanship is required. I not only extract from people their life stories, I impart a shape to those lives which was often invisible; sometimes I give them lives they never even realised they had. If that isn't art, what is?

I said, 'Should I have heard of McAra?'

'Yes, so let's not admit you haven't. He was some kind of aide when Lang was prime minister. Speechwriting, policy research, political strategy. When Lang resigned, McAra stayed with him, to run his office.'

I grimaced. 'I don't know, Rick,' I said.

Throughout lunch I'd been half watching an elderly television actor at the next table. He'd been famous when I was a child for playing the single parent of teenage girls in a sitcom. Now, as he rose unsteadily and started to shuffle towards the exit, he looked as though he'd been made up to act the role of his own corpse. That was the type of person whose memoirs I ghosted: people who had fallen a few rungs down the celebrity ladder, or who had a few rungs left to climb, or who were just about clinging to the top and were desperate to cash in while there was still time. I was abruptly overwhelmed by the ridiculousness of the whole idea that I might collaborate on the memoirs of a prime minister.

'I don't know—' I began again, but Rick interrupted me.

'Rhinehart Inc. are getting frantic. They're holding a beauty parade at their London office tomorrow morning. Maddox himself is flying over from New York to represent the company. Lang's sending the lawyer who negotiated the original deal for him – the hottest fixer in Washington, a very smart guy by the name of Sidney Kroll. I've other clients I could put in for this, so if you're not up for it, just tell me now. But from the way they've been talking, I think you're the best fit.'

'Me? You're kidding.'

'No. I promise you. They need to do something radical – take a risk. It's a great opportunity for you. And the money will be good. The kids won't starve.'

'I don't have any kids.'

'No,' said Rick with a wink, 'but I do.'

*

We parted on the steps of the club. Rick had a car waiting outside with its engine running. He didn't offer to drop me anywhere, which made me suspect he was off to see another client, to whom he would make exactly the same pitch he had just made to me. What is the collective noun for a group of ghosts? A train? A town? A haunt? At any rate, Rick had plenty of us on his books. Take a look at the bestseller lists: you would be amazed how much of it is the work of ghosts, novels as well as non-fiction. We are the phantom operatives who keep publishing going, like the unseen workers beneath Walt Disney World. We scuttle along the subterranean tunnels of celebrity, popping up here and there, dressed as this character or that, preserving the seamless illusion of the Magic Kingdom.

'See you tomorrow,' he said, and dramatically, in a puff of exhaust fumes, he was gone: Mephistopheles on a fifteen per cent commission. I stood for a minute, undecided, and if I had been in another part of London it is still just possible things might have gone differently. But I was in that narrow zone where Soho washes up against Covent Garden: a trash-strewn strip of empty theatres, dark alleys, red lights, snack bars and bookshops – so many book-shops you can start to feel ill just looking at them, from the tiny little rip-off specialist dealers in Cecil Court to the cut-price behe-moths of Charing Cross Road. I often drop into one of the latter, to see how my titles are displayed, and that was what I did that afternoon. Once I was inside, it was only a short step across the scuffed red carpet of the Biography & Memoir department, and suddenly I had gone from 'Celebrity' to 'Politics'.

I was surprised by how much they had on the former prime minister – an entire shelf, everything from the early hagiography, *Adam Lang: Statesman for Our Time*, to a recent hatchet job entitled *Would You Adam and Eve It? The Collected Lies of Adam Lang*, both by the same author. I took down the thickest biography and opened it at the photographs: Lang as a toddler, feeding a bottle of milk to a lamb beside a dry-stone wall, Lang as Lady Macbeth in a school play, Lang dressed as a chicken in a Cambridge University Footlights revue, Lang as a distinctly stoned-looking merchant banker in the seven-ties, Lang with his wife and young children on the doorstep of a new house, Lang wearing a rosette and waving from an open-topped bus on the day he was elected to parliament, Lang with his colleagues, Lang with world leaders, with pop stars, with soldiers in the Middle East. A bald customer in a scuffed leather coat browsing the shelf next to me stared at the cover. He held his nose with one hand and mimed flushing a toilet with the other.

I moved around the corner of the bookcase and looked up McAra, Michael in the index. There were only five or six innocuous references – no reason in other words why anyone outside the party or the government need ever have heard of him, so to hell with you, Rick, I thought. I flicked back to the photograph of the prime minister seated smiling at the cabinet table, with his Downing Street staff arrayed behind him. The caption identified McAra as the burly figure in the back row. He was slightly out of focus – a pale, unsmiling, dark-haired smudge. I squinted more closely at him. He looked exactly the sort of unappealing inadequate that is congenitally drawn to politics and makes people like me stick to the sports pages. You'll find a McAra in any country, in any system, standing behind any leader with a political machine to operate: a greasy engineer in the boiler room of power. And this was the man who had been entrusted to ghost a ten-million-dollar memoir? I felt professionally affronted. I bought myself a small pile of research material and headed out of the bookshop with a growing conviction that maybe Rick was right; perhaps I was the man for the job.

It was obvious the moment I got outside that another bomb had gone off. At Tottenham Court Road people were surging up above ground from all four exits of the tube station like storm water from a blocked drain. A loudspeaker said something about 'an incident at Oxford Circus'. It sounded like an edgy romantic comedy: *Brief Encounter* meets the War on Terror. I carried on up the road, unsure of how I would get home – taxis, like false friends, tending always to vanish at the first sign of trouble. In the window of one of the big electrical shops the crowd watched the same news bulletin relayed simultaneously on a dozen televisions: aerial shots of Oxford Circus, black smoke gushing out of the underground station, thrusts of orange flame. An electronic ticker-tape running across the bottom of the screen announced a suspected suicide bomber, many dead and injured, and gave an emergency number to call. Above the rooftops a helicopter tilted and circled. I could smell the smoke — an acrid, eye-reddening blend of diesel and burning plastic.

It took me two full hours to walk home, lugging my heavy bag of books — up to Marylebone Road and then westwards towards Paddington. As usual, the entire tube system had been shut down to check for further bombs; so had the main railway stations. The traffic on either side of the wide street was stalled and, on past form, would remain so until evening. (If only Hitler had known he didn't need a whole air force to paralyse London, I thought: just a revved-up teenager with a bottle of bleach and a bag of weedkiller.) Occasionally a police car or an ambulance would mount the kerb, roar along the pavement and attempt to make progress up a side street.

I trudged on towards the setting sun.

It must have been six when I reached my flat. I had the top two floors of a high, stuccoed house in what the residents call Notting Hill and the Post Office stubbornly insists is North Kensington. Used syringes glittered in the gutter; at the halal butchers opposite they did the slaughtering on the premises. It was grim. But from the attic extension which served as my office I had a view across west London which would not have disgraced a skyscraper: rooftops, railway yards, motorway and sky — a vast urban-prairie sky, sprinkled with the lights of aircraft descending towards Heathrow. It was this view which had sold me the apartment, not the estate agent's gentrification patter – which was just as well, as the rich bourgeoisie have no more returned to this area than they have to downtown Baghdad.

Kate had already let herself in and was watching the news. Kate: I had forgotten she was coming over for the evening. She was my . . . ? I never knew what to call her. To say she was my girlfriend was absurd: no one the wrong side of thirty has a *girlfriend*. Partner wasn't right either, as we didn't live under the same roof. Lover? How could one keep a straight face? Mistress? Do me a favour. Fiancée? Certainly not. I suppose I ought to have realised it was ominous that forty thousand years of human language had failed to produce a word for our relationship. (Kate isn't her real name, by the way, but I don't see why she should be dragged into all this. In any case, it suits her better than the name she does have: she looks like a Kate, if you know what I mean – sensible but sassy, girlish but always willing to be one of the boys. She works in television, but let's not hold that against her.)

'Thanks for the concerned phone call,' I said. 'I'm dead actually, but don't worry about it.' I kissed the top of her head, dropped the books on to the sofa and went into the kitchen to pour myself a whisky. 'The entire tube is down. I've had to walk all the way from Covent Garden.'

'Poor darling,' I heard her say. 'And you've been shopping.'

I topped up my glass with water from the tap, drank half, then topped it up again with whisky. I remembered I was supposed to have reserved a table at a restaurant. When I went back into the living room she was removing one book after another from the carrier bag. 'What's all this?' she said, looking up at me. 'You're not interested in *politics.*' And then she realised what was going on, because she was smart — smarter than I was. She knew what I did for a living; she knew I was meeting an agent; and she knew all about McAra. 'Don't tell me they want *you* to ghost his book?' She laughed. 'You cannot be serious.' She tried to make a joke of it — 'You *cannot* be serious' in an American accent, like that tennis player a few years ago — but I could see her dismay. She hated Lang; felt personally betrayed by him. She used to be a party member. I had forgotten that, too.

'It'll probably come to nothing,' I said, and drank some more whisky.

She went back to watching the news, only now with her arms tightly folded, always a warning sign. The tickertape announced that the death toll was seven, and likely to rise.

'But if you're offered it you'll do it?' she asked, without turning to look at me.

I was spared having to reply by the newsreader announcing that they were cutting live to New York to get the reaction of the former prime minister, and suddenly there was Adam Lang, at a podium marked 'Waldorf-Astoria', where it looked as though he had been addressing a lunch. 'You will all by now have heard the tragic news from London,' he said, 'where once again the forces of fanaticism and intolerance . . .'

Nothing he uttered that night warrants reprinting. It was almost a parody of what a politician might say after a terrorist attack. Yet watching him, you would have thought his own wife and children had been eviscerated in the blast. This was his genius: to refresh and elevate the clichés of politics by the sheer force of his perform-ance. Even Kate was briefly silenced. Only when he had finished and his largely female, mostly elderly, audience was rising to applaud did she mutter, 'What's he doing in New York anyway?'

'Lecturing?'

'Why can't he lecture here?'

'I suppose because no one here would pay him a hundred thousand dollars a throw.'

She pressed mute.

'There was a time,' said Kate slowly, after what felt like a very long silence, 'when princes taking their countries to war were supposed to risk their lives in battle – you know, lead by example. Now they travel around in bomb-proof cars with armed bodyguards and make fortunes three thousand miles away, while the rest of us are stuck with the consequences of their actions. I just don't understand you,' she went on, turning to look at me properly for the first time. 'All the things I've said about him over the past few years – "war criminal" and the rest of it – and you've sat there nodding and agreeing. And now you're going to write his propaganda for him, and make him richer. Did none of it ever mean anything to you at all?'

'Hold on a minute,' I said. 'You're a fine one to talk. You've been trying to get an interview with him for months. What's the difference?'

'What's the difference? Christ!' She clenched her hands – those slim white hands I knew so well – and raised them in frustration, half-claw, half-fist. The sinews stood out in her arms. *'What's the difference?* We want to hold him to account – that's the difference! To ask him proper questions! About torturing and bombing and lying! Not "How does it feel?" *Christ!* This is a complete bloody waste of time.'

She got up then and went into the bedroom to collect the bag she always brought on the nights she planned to stay. I heard her filling it noisily with lipstick, toothbrush, perfume spray. I knew if

I went in I could retrieve the situation. She was probably expecting it: we'd had worse rows. I'd have been obliged to concede that she was right, acknowledge my unsuitability for the task, affirm her moral and intellectual superiority in this as in all things. It needn't even have been a verbal confession: a meaningful hug would probably have been enough to get me a suspended sentence. But the truth was, at that moment, given a choice between an evening of her smug left-wing moralising and the prospect of working with a so-called war criminal, I preferred the war criminal. So I simply carried on staring at the television.

Sometimes I have a nightmare in which all the women I have ever slept with assemble together. It's a respectable rather than a huge number — were it a drinks party, say, my living room could accommodate them quite comfortably. And if, God forbid, this gathering were ever to occur, Kate would be the undisputed guest of honour. She is the one for whom a chair would be fetched, who would have her glass refilled by sympathetic hands, who would sit at the centre of a disbelieving circle as my moral and physical flaws were dissected. She was the one who had stuck it the longest.

She didn't slam the door as she left but closed it very carefully. That was stylish, I thought. On the television screen the death toll had just increased to eight.

Two

A ghost who has only a lay knowledge of the subject will be able to keep asking the same questions as the lay reader, and will therefore open up the potential readership of the book to a much wider audience.

Ghostwriting

Rhinehart Publishing UK consisted of five ancient firms acquired during a vigorous bout of corporate kleptomania in the nineties. Wrenched out of their Dickensian garrets in Bloomsbury, upsized, downsized, rebranded, renamed, reorganised, modernised and merged, they had finally been dumped in Hounslow, in a steel-and-smoked-glass office block with all its pipes on the outside. It nestled among the pebbledash housing estates like an abandoned spacecraft after a fruitless mission to find intelligent life.

I arrived, with professional punctuality, five minutes before noon, only to discover the main door locked. I had to buzz for entry. A noticeboard in the foyer announced that the terrorism alert was ORANGE/HIGH. Through the darkened glass I could see the security men in their dingy aquarium checking me on a monitor. When I finally got inside I had to turn out my pockets and pass through a metal-detector.

Quigley was waiting for me by the lifts.

'Who're you expecting to bomb you?' I asked. 'Random House?'

'We're publishing Lang's memoirs,' replied Quigley in a stiff voice. 'That alone makes us a target, apparently. Rick's already upstairs.'

'How many've you seen?'

'Five. You're the last.'

I knew Roy Quigley fairly well — well enough to know he disapproved of me. He must have been about fifty, tall and tweedy. In a happier era he would have smoked a pipe and offered tiny advances to minor academics over long lunches in Soho. Now his midday meal was a plastic tray of salad taken at his desk overlooking the M4 and he received his orders direct from the head of sales and marketing, a girl of about sixteen. He had three children in private schools he couldn't afford. As the price of survival he'd actually been obliged to start taking an interest in popular culture: to wit, the lives of various footballers, supermodels and foul-mouthed comedians, whose names he pronounced carefully and whose customs he studied in the tabloids with scholarly detachment, as if they were remote Micronesian tribespeople. I'd pitched him an idea the year before, the memoirs of a TV magician who had — of course! — been abused in childhood, but who had used his skill as an illusionist to conjure up a new life, etc., etc. He'd turned it down flat. The book had gone straight to number one: *I Came, I Sawed, I Conquered*. He still bore a grudge.

'I have to tell you,' he said, as we rose to the penthouse floor, 'that I don't think you're the right man for this assignment.'

'Then it's a good job it's not your decision, Roy.'

Oh yes, I had Quigley's measure right enough. His title was UK Group Editor-in-Chief, which meant he had all the authority of a dead cat. The man who really ran the global show was waiting for us in the boardroom: John Maddox, chief executive of Rhinehart

Inc., a big, bull-shouldered New Yorker with alopecia. His bald head glistened under the strip lighting like a massive varnished egg. As a young man he'd acquired a wrestler's physique in order (according to *Publishers Weekly*) to tip out the window anyone who stared too long at his scalp. I made sure my gaze never rose further than his superhero chest. Next to him was Lang's Washington attorney, Sidney Kroll, a bespectacled forty-something with a delicate pale face, floppy raven hair and the limpest, dampest handshake I'd been offered since Dippy the Dolphin bobbed up from his pool when I was twelve.

'And Nick Riccardelli I think you know,' said Quigley, completing the introductions with just a hint of a shudder. My agent, who was wearing a shiny grey shirt and a thin red leather tie, winked up at me.

'Hi, Rick,' I said.

I felt nervous as I took my seat beside him. The room was lined, Gatsby-like, with immaculate unread hardcover books. Maddox sat with his back to the window. He laid his massive, hairless hands on the glass-topped table, as if to prove he had no intention of reaching for a weapon just yet, and said, 'I gather from Rick you're aware of the situation and that you know what we're looking for. So perhaps you could tell us exactly what you think you'd bring to this project.'

'Ignorance,' I said brightly, which at least had the benefit of shock value, and before anyone could interrupt I launched into the little speech I'd rehearsed in the taxi coming over. 'You know my track record. There's no point my trying to pretend I'm something I'm not. I'll be completely honest. I don't read political memoirs. So what?' I shrugged. 'Nobody does. But actually that's not my problem.' I pointed at Maddox. 'That's *your* problem.'

'Oh please,' said Quigley quietly.

'And let me be even more recklessly honest,' I went on. 'Rumour has it you paid ten million dollars for this book. As things stand, how much of that d'you think you're going to see back? Two million? Three? That's bad news for you, and that's especially bad news,' I said, turning to Kroll, 'for your client. Because for him this isn't about money. This is about reputation. This is Adam Lang's opportunity to speak directly to history, to get his case across. The last thing he needs is to produce a book that nobody reads. How will it look if his life story ends up on the remainder tables? But it doesn't have to be this way.'

I know in retrospect what a huckster I sounded. But this was pitch-talk, remember — which, like declarations of undying love in a stranger's bedroom at midnight, shouldn't necessarily be held against you the next morning. Kroll was smiling to himself, doodling on his yellow pad. Maddox was staring hard at me. I took a breath.

'The fact is,' I continued, 'a big name alone doesn't sell a book. We've all learned that the hard way. What sells a book — or a movie, or a song — is *heart*.' I believe I may even have thumped my chest at this point. 'And that's why political memoir is *the* black hole of publishing. The name outside the tent may be big but everyone knows that once they're inside they're just going to get the same old tired show, and who wants to pay twenty-five dollars for that? You've got to put in some heart, and that's what I do for a living. And whose story has more heart than the guy who starts from nowhere and ends up running a country?'

I leaned forwards. 'You see, here's the joke: a leader's autobiography ought to be *more* interesting than most memoirs, not *less*. So I see my ignorance about politics as an advantage. I *cherish* my ignorance, quite frankly. Besides, Adam Lang doesn't need any help from me with the politics of this book – he's a political genius. What he does need, in my humble opinion, is the same thing a movie star needs, or a baseball player, or a rock star: an experienced collaborator who knows how to ask him the questions which will draw out his heart.'

There was a silence. I was trembling. Rick gave my knee a reassuring pat under the table. 'Nicely done.'

'What utter balls,' said Quigley.

'Think so?' asked Maddox, still looking at me. He said it in a neutral voice, but if I had been Quigley, I would have detected danger.

'Oh, John, *of course*,' said Quigley, with all the dismissive scorn of four generations of Oxford scholars behind him. 'Adam Lang is a world historical figure, and his autobiography is going to be a world publishing event. A piece of history, in fact. It shouldn't be approached like a . . .' he ransacked his well-stocked mind for a suitable analogy but finished lamely '. . . a feature for a celebrity magazine.'

There was another silence. Beyond the tinted windows the traffic was backing up along the motorway. Rainwater rippled the gleam of the stationary headlights. London still hadn't returned to normal after the bomb.

'It seems to me,' said Maddox, in the same slow, quiet voice, his big pink mannequin's hands still resting on the table, 'that I have entire warehouses full of "world publishing events" that I somehow can't figure out how to get off my hands. And a heck of a lot of people read celebrity magazines. What do you think, Sid?'

For a few seconds Kroll merely carried on smiling to himself and doodling. I wondered what he found so funny. 'Adam's position on this is very straightforward,' he said eventually. (*Adam*: he tossed the first name as casually into the conversation as he might a coin into a beggar's cap.) 'He takes this book very seriously – it's his testament, if you will. He wants to meet his contractual obligations. And he wants it to be a commercial success. He's therefore more than happy to be guided by you, John, and by Marty also, within reason. Obviously, he's still very upset by what happened to Mike, who was irreplaceable.'

'Obviously.' We all made the appropriate noises.

'Irreplaceable,' he repeated. 'And yet – *he has to be replaced.*' He looked up, pleased with his drollery, and at that instant I knew there was no horror the world could offer – no war, no genocide, no famine, no childhood cancer – to which Sidney Kroll would not see the funny side. 'Adam can certainly appreciate the benefits of trying someone entirely different. In the end, it all comes down to a personal bond.' His spectacles flashed in the strip lights as he scrutinised me. 'Do you work out, maybe?' I shook my head. 'Pity. Adam likes to work out.'

Quigley, still reeling from Maddox's put-down, attempted a comeback. 'Actually, I know quite a good writer on the *Guardian* who uses a gym.'

'Maybe,' said Rick, after an embarrassed pause, 'we could run over how you see this working practically.'

'First off, we need it wrapped up in a month,' said Maddox. 'That's Marty's view as well as mine.'

'A month?' I repeated. 'You want a book in a month?'

'A completed manuscript does exist,' said Kroll. 'It just needs some work.'

'A lot of work,' said Maddox grimly. 'Okay. Taking it backwards: we publish in June, which means we ship in May, which means we edit and we print in March and April, which means we have to have the manuscript in house at the end of February. The Germans, French, Italians and Spanish all have to start translating right away. The newspapers need to see it for the serial deals. There's a television tie-in. Publicity tour's got to be fixed well in advance. We need to book space in the stores. So the end of February – that's it, period. What I like about your résumé,' he said, consulting a sheet of paper on which I could see all my titles listed, 'is that you're obviously experienced and above all you're fast. You deliver.'

'Never missed once,' said Rick, putting his arm round my shoulders and squeezing me. 'That's my boy.'

'And you're a Brit. The ghost definitely has to be a Brit, I think. To get the jolly old tone right.'

'We agree,' said Kroll. 'But everything will have to be done in the States. Adam's completely locked in to a lecture tour there right now, and a fundraising programme for his foundation. I don't see him coming back to the UK till March at the earliest.'

'A month in America, that's fine – yes?' Rick glanced at me eagerly. I could feel him willing me to say yes, but all I was thinking was, *A month, they want me to write a book in a month . . .*

I nodded slowly. 'I suppose I can always bring the manuscript back here to work on.'

'The manuscript stays in America,' said Kroll flatly. 'That's one of the reasons Marty made the house on the Vineyard available. It's a secure environment. Only a few people are allowed to handle it.'

'Sounds more like a bomb than a book!' joked Quigley. Nobody laughed. He rubbed his hands unhappily. 'You know, I will need to see it myself at some point. I am supposed to be editing it.'

'In theory,' said Maddox. 'Actually we need to talk about that later.' He turned to Kroll. 'There's no room in this schedule for revisions. We'll need to revise as we go.'

As they carried on discussing the timetable I studied Quigley. He was upright but motionless, like one of those victims in the movies who gets stuck with a stiletto while standing in a crowd and dies without anyone noticing. His mouth opened and closed ever so slightly, as if he had a final message to impart. Yet even at the time I realised he'd asked a perfectly reasonable question. If he was the editor, why shouldn't he see the manuscript? And why did it have to be held in a 'secure environment' on an island off the eastern seaboard of the USA? I felt Rick's elbow in my ribs and realised Maddox was talking to me.

'How soon can you get over there? Assuming we go with you rather than one of the others — how fast can you move?'

'It's Friday today,' I said. 'Give me a day to get ready. I could fly Sunday.'

'And start Monday? That would be great.'

Rick said, 'You won't find anyone who can move quicker than that.'

Maddox and Kroll looked at one another and I knew then that I had the job. As Rick said afterwards, the trick is always to put yourself in their position. 'It's like interviewing a new cleaner. Do you want someone who can give you the history of cleaning, and the theory of cleaning, or do you want someone who'll just get down and clean your fucking house? They chose you because they think you'll clean their fucking house.'

'We'll go with you,' said Maddox. He stood and reached over and shook my hand. 'Subject to reaching a satisfactory agreement with Rick here, of course.'

Kroll added, 'You'll also have to sign a non-disclosure agreement.'

'No problem,' I said, also getting to my feet. That didn't bother me. Confidentiality clauses are standard procedure in the ghosting world. 'I couldn't be happier.'

And I couldn't have been. Everyone except Quigley was smiling and suddenly there was a kind of boys-together, locker-room-after-the-match kind of feeling in the air. We chatted for a minute or so, and that was when Kroll took me to one side and said, very casually, 'I've something here you might care to take a look at.'

He reached under the table and pulled out a bright yellow plastic bag with the name of some fancy Washington clothes store printed on it in curly black copperplate. My first thought was that it must be the manuscript of Lang's memoirs, and that all the stuff about a 'secure environment' had been a joke. But when he saw my expression, Kroll laughed and said, 'No, no, it's not *that*. It's just a book by another client of mine. I'd really appreciate your opinion if you get a chance to look at it. Here's my number.' I took his card and slipped it into my pocket. Quigley still hadn't said a word.

'I'll give you a call when we've settled the deal,' said Rick.

'Make them howl,' I told him, squeezing his shoulder.

Maddox laughed. 'Hey! Remember!' he called as Quigley showed me out of the door. He struck his big fist against his blue-suited chest. 'Heart!'

As we went down in the lift, Quigley stared at the ceiling. 'Was it my imagination or did I just get fired in there?'

'They wouldn't let you go, Roy,' I said, with all the sincerity I could muster, which wasn't much. 'You're the only one left who can remember what publishing used to be like.'

'"Let you go",' he said bitterly. 'Yes, that's the modern euphemism, isn't it? As if it's a favour. You're clinging to the edge of a cliff and someone says, "Oh, I'm terribly sorry, we're going to have to let you go."'

A couple on their lunch break got in at the fourth floor and Quigley was silent until they got off to go to the restaurant on the second. When the doors closed, he said, 'There's something not right about this project.'

'Me, you mean?'

'No. Before you.' He frowned. 'I can't quite put my finger on it. The way no one's allowed to see anything, for a start. And that fellow Kroll makes me shiver. And poor old Mike McAra, of course. I met him when we signed the deal two years ago. He didn't strike me as the suicidal type. Rather the reverse. He was the sort who specialised in making other people want to kill themselves, if you know what I mean.'

'Hard?'

'Hard, yes. Lang would be smiling away, and there would be this thug next to him with eyes like a snake's. I suppose you've got to have someone like that when you're in Lang's position.'

We reached the ground floor and stepped out into the lobby. 'You can pick up a taxi round the corner,' said Quigley, and for that one small, mean gesture – leaving me to walk in the rain rather than calling me a cab on the company's account – I hoped he'd rot. 'Tell me,' he said suddenly, 'when did it become fashionable to be stupid? That's the thing I really don't understand. The Cult of the Idiot. The Elevation of the Moron. Our two biggest-selling novelists – the actress with the tits and that ex-army psycho – have never written a word of fiction, did you know that?'

'You're talking like an old man, Roy,' I told him. 'People have been complaining that standards are slipping ever since Shakespeare started writing comedies.'

'Yes, but now it's really happened, hasn't it? It was never like this before.'

I knew he was trying to goad me – the ghostwriter to the stars off to produce the memoirs of an ex-prime minister – but I was too full of myself to care. I wished him well in his retirement and set off across the lobby swinging that damned yellow plastic bag.

*

It must have taken me half an hour to find a ride back into town. I had only a very hazy idea of where I was. The roads were wide, the houses small. There was a steady, freezing drizzle. My arm was aching from carrying Kroll's manuscript. Judging by the weight, I reckoned it must have been close on a thousand pages. Who was his client? Tolstoy? Eventually I stopped at a bus shelter in front of a greengrocer and a funeral parlour. Wedged into its metal frame was the card of a minicab firm.

The journey home took almost an hour and I had plenty of time to take out the manuscript and study it. The book was called *One Out of Many*. It was the memoir of some ancient US senator, famous only for having kept on breathing for about a hundred and fifty years. By any normal measure of tedium it was off the scale – up, up and away, beyond boring into some oxygen-starved stratosphere of utter nullity. The car was overheated and smelled of stale takeaways. I began to feel nauseous. I put the manuscript back into the bag and wound down the window. The fare was forty pounds.

I had just paid the driver and was crossing the pavement towards my flat, head down into the rain, searching for my keys, when I felt someone touch me lightly on the shoulder. I turned and walked into a wall, or was hit by a truck – that was the feeling: some great iron force slammed into me and I fell backwards, into the grip of a second man. (I was told afterwards there were two of them, both in their twenties. One had been hanging round the entrance to the basement flat, the other appeared from nowhere and grabbed me from behind.) I crumpled, felt the gritty wet stone of the gutter against my cheek and gasped and sucked and cried like a baby. My fingers must have clasped the plastic bag with involuntary tight-ness, because I was conscious, through this much greater pain, of a smaller and sharper one – a flute in the symphony – as a foot trod on my hand, and something was torn away.

Surely one of the most inadequate words in the English language is 'winded', suggestive as it is of something light and fleeting – a graze, perhaps, or a touch of breathlessness. But I hadn't been *winded*. I had been whumped and whacked and semi-asphyxiated, knocked to the ground and humiliated. My solar plexus felt as though it had been stuck with a knife. Sobbing for air, I was convinced I had been stabbed. I was aware of people taking my arms and pulling me up into a sitting position. I was propped against a tree, its hard bark jabbing into my spine, and when at last I managed to gulp some oxygen into my lungs, I immediately started patting my stomach blindly, feeling for the gaping wound I knew must be there, imagining my intestines strewn around me. But when I inspected my moist fingers for blood, there was only dirty London rainwater. It must have taken a minute for me to realise that I wasn't going to die – that I was, essentially, intact – and then all I wanted was to get away from these good-hearted folk who had gathered around me, and were producing mobile phones and asking me about calling the police and an ambulance.

The prospect of having to wait ten hours to be examined in casualty, followed by half a day spent hanging around the local police station to make a statement, was enough to propel me out of the gutter, up the stairs and into my flat. I locked the door, peeled off my outer clothes, and went and lay on the sofa, trembling. I didn't move for perhaps an hour, as the cold shadows of that January afternoon gradually gathered in the room. Then I went into the kitchen and was sick in the sink, after which I poured myself a very large whisky.

I could feel myself moving now out of shock and into euphoria. Indeed, with a little alcohol inside me I felt positively merry. I checked my inside jacket pocket and then my wrist: I still had my wallet and my watch. The only thing that had gone was the yellow plastic bag containing Senator Alzheimer's memoirs. I laughed out loud as I pictured the thieves running down Ladbroke Grove and stopping in some alleyway to check their haul: *'My advice to any young person seeking to enter public life today . . .'* It wasn't until I'd had another drink that I realised this could be awkward. Old Alzheimer might not mean anything to me, but Sidney Kroll might view matters differently.

I took out his card. Sidney L. Kroll of Brinkerhof Lombardi Kroll, attorneys, M Street, Washington DC. After thinking about it for ten minutes or so, I went back and sat on the sofa and called his cell phone. He answered on the second ring: 'Sid Kroll.'

I could tell by his inflexion he was smiling.

'Sidney,' I said, trying to sound natural using his first name, 'you'll never guess what's happened.'

'Some guys just stole my manuscript?'

For a moment I couldn't speak. 'My God,' I said, 'is there nothing you don't know?'

'What?' His tone changed abruptly. 'Jesus,' he said, 'I was kidding. Is that *really* what happened? Are you okay? Where are you now?'

I explained what had happened. He said not to worry. The manuscript was *totally* unimportant. He'd only given it to me because he thought it might be of interest to me in a professional capacity. He'd get another sent over. What was I going to do? Was I going to call the police? I said I would if he wanted, but as far as I was concerned, bringing in the police was generally more trouble than it was worth. I preferred to view the episode as just another round on the gaudy carousel of urban life: 'You know, *que será será*, bombed one day, mugged the next.'

He agreed. 'It was a real pleasure to meet with you today. It's great that you're on board. Cheerio,' he said, just before he hung up, and there was that little smile in his voice again. *Cheerio.*

I went into the bathroom and opened my shirt. A livid red horizontal mark was branded into my flesh, just above my stomach and below my ribcage. I stood in front of the mirror for a better look. It was three inches long and half an inch wide, and curiously sharp-edged. That wasn't caused by flesh and bone, I thought. I'd say that was a knuckleduster. That looked *professional*. I started to feel strange again and went back to the sofa.

When the phone rang it was Rick, to tell me the deal was done. 'What's up?' he said, interrupting himself. 'You don't sound right.'

'I just got mugged.'

'No!'

Once more I described what had happened. Rick made appropriately sympathetic noises, but the moment he learned I was well enough to work, the anxiety left his voice. As soon as he could, he brought the conversation round to what really interested him.

'So you're still fine to fly to the States on Sunday?'

'Of course, I'm just a bit shocked, that's all.'

'Okay, well, here's another shock for you. For one month's work, on a manuscript that's supposedly already written, Rhinehart Inc.

are willing to pay you two hundred and fifty thousand dollars, plus expenses.'

'*What?*'

If I hadn't already been sitting on the sofa I would have fallen on to it. They say every man has his price. A quarter of a million dollars for four weeks' work was roughly ten times mine.

'That's fifty thousand dollars paid weekly for the next four weeks,' said Rick, 'plus a bonus of fifty if you get the job done on time. They'll take care of air fares and accommodation. *And* you'll get a collaborator credit.'

'On the title page?'

'Do me a favour! In the acknowledgements. But it'll still be noticed in the trade press. I'll see to that. Although for now your involvement is strictly confidential. They were very firm about that.' I could hear him chuckling down the phone, and imagined him tilting back in his chair. 'Oh yes, a whole new wide world is opening up for you, my boy!'

He was right there.

Three

If you are painfully shy or find it hard to get others into a relaxed and confident state, then ghosting might not be for you.

Ghostwriting

American Airlines Flight 109 was due to leave Heathrow for Boston at 10.30 on Sunday morning. Rhinehart biked round a one-way business-class ticket on Saturday afternoon, along with a contract and the privacy agreement. I had to sign both while the messenger waited. I trusted Rick to have got the contract straight and didn't even bother to read it; the non-disclosure undertaking I scanned quickly in the hall. It's almost funny in retrospect: *'I shall treat all confidential information as being strictly private and confidential, and shall take all steps necessary to prevent it from being disclosed or made public to any third party or relevant person . . . I shall not use or disclose or permit the disclosure by any person of the confidential information for the benefit of any third party . . . Neither I nor the relevant persons shall by any means copy or part with possession of the whole or any part of the confidential information without prior permission of the Owner . . .'* I signed without a qualm.

I've always liked to be able to disappear quickly. It used to take me about five minutes to put my London life into cold storage. All my bills were paid by direct debit. There were no deliveries to cancel – no milk, no papers. My cleaner, whom I hardly ever saw in any case, would look in twice a week and retrieve all the mail from downstairs. I had cleared my desk of work. I had no appointments. My neighbours I had never spoken to. Kate had likely gone for good. Most of my friends had long since entered the kingdom of family life, from whose distant shores, in my experience, no traveller e'er returned. My parents were dead. I had no siblings. I could have died myself and, as far as the world was concerned, my life would have gone on as normal. I packed one suitcase with a week's change of clothes, a sweater and a spare pair of shoes. I put my laptop and mini disc-recorder into my shoulder bag. I would use the hotel laundry. Anything else I needed, I would buy on arrival.

I spent the rest of the day and all that evening up in my study, reading through my books on Adam Lang and making a list of questions. I don't want to sound too Jekyll and Hyde about this, but as the day faded – as the lights came up in the big tower blocks across the railway marshalling yard, and the red, white and green stars winked and fell towards the airport – I could feel myself beginning to get into Lang's skin. He was a few years older, but apart from that our backgrounds were similar. The resemblances hadn't struck me before: an only child, born in the Midlands, educated at the local grammar school, a degree from Cambridge, a passion for student drama, a complete lack of interest in student politics.

I went back to look at the photographs. *'Lang's hysterical performance as a chicken in charge of a battery farm for humans at the 1972 Cambridge Footlights Revue earned him plaudits.'* I could imagine us both chasing the same girls, taking a bad show to the Edinburgh Fringe in the back of some beat-up Volkswagen van, sharing digs, getting stoned. And yet somehow, metaphorically speaking, I had stayed a chicken, while he had gone on to become prime minister. This was the point at which my normal powers of empathy deserted me, for there seemed nothing in his first twenty-five years that could explain his second. But there would be time enough, I reasoned, to find his voice.

I double-locked the door before I went to bed that night and dreamed I was following Adam Lang through a maze of rainy red-brick streets. When I got into a minicab and the driver turned round to ask me where I wanted to go, he had McAra's lugubrious face.

*

Heathrow the next morning looked like one of those bad science-fiction movies set in the near future after the security forces have taken over the state. Two armoured personnel carriers were parked outside the terminal. A dozen men with Rambo machine guns and bad haircuts patrolled inside. Vast lines of passengers queued to be frisked and X-rayed, carrying their shoes in one hand and their pathetic toiletries in a clear plastic bag in the other. Travel is sold as freedom, but we were about as free as lab rats. This is how they'll manage the next Holocaust, I thought, as I shuffled forward in my stockinged feet: they'll simply issue us with air tickets and we'll do whatever we're told.

Once I was through security I headed across the fragrant halls of duty free towards the American Airlines lounge, intent only on a courtesy cup of coffee and the Sunday morning sports pages. A satellite news channel was burbling away in the corner. No one was watching. I fixed myself a double espresso and was just turning to the football reports in one of the tabloids when I heard the words 'Adam Lang'. Three days earlier, like everyone else in the lounge, I would have taken no notice, but now it was as if my own name was being called out. I went and stood in front of the screen and tried to make sense of the story.

To begin with, it didn't seem that important. It sounded like old news. Four British citizens had been picked up in Pakistan a few years back — 'kidnapped by the CIA', according to their lawyer — taken to a secret military installation in eastern Europe and tortured. One had died under interrogation, the other three had been imprisoned in Guantanamo. The new twist, apparently, was that a Sunday paper had obtained a leaked Ministry of Defence document which seemed to suggest that Lang had ordered an SAS unit to seize the men and hand them over to the CIA. Various expressions of outrage followed, from a human rights lawyer, and a spokesman for the Pakistan government. File footage showed Lang wearing a garland of flowers round his neck on a visit to Pakistan while he was prime minister. A spokeswoman for Lang was quoted as saying the former prime minister knew nothing of the reports and was refusing to comment. The British government had consistently rejected demands to hold an inquiry. The programme moved on to the weather, and that was it.

I glanced around the lounge. Nobody else had stirred. Yet for some reason I felt as if someone had just run an ice pack down my spine. I pulled out my cell phone and called Rick. I couldn't remember whether he had gone back to America or not. It turned out he was sitting about a mile away, in the British Airways lounge, waiting to board his flight to New York.

'Did you just see the news?' I asked him.

Unlike me, Rick was a news addict.

'The Lang story? Sure.'

'D'you think there's anything in it?'

'How the hell do I know? Who cares if there is? At least it's keeping his name on the front pages.'

'D'you think I should ask him about it?'

33

'Who gives a shit?' Down the line I heard a loudspeaker announcement howling in the background. 'They're calling my flight. I got to go.'

'Just before you do,' I said quickly, 'can I just run something past you? When I was mugged on Friday — somehow it didn't make much sense, the way they left my wallet and only ran off with a manuscript. But looking at this news — well, I was just wondering: you don't think they thought I was carrying Lang's memoirs?'

'But how'd they know that?' said Rick in a puzzled voice. 'You'd only just met Maddox and Kroll. I was still negotiating the deal.'

'Well, maybe someone was watching the publishers' offices, and then followed me when I left. It *was* a bright yellow plastic bag, Rick. I might as well have been carrying a flare.' And then another thought came to me, so alarming I didn't know where to begin. 'While you're on — what do you know about Sidney Kroll?'

'Young Sid?' Rick gave a chuckle of admiration. 'My, but he's a piece of work, isn't he? He's going to put honest crooks like me out of business. He cuts his deals for a flat fee rather than commission, and you won't find an ex-president or a cabinet member who doesn't want him on their team. Why?'

'It's not possible, is it,' I said hesitantly, voicing the thought more or less as it developed, 'that he gave me that manuscript because he thought — if anyone was watching — he thought it would look as though I was leaving the building carrying Adam Lang's book?'

'Why the hell would he do that?'

'I don't know. For the fun of it? To see what would happen?'

'To see if you'd get mugged?'

'Okay, all right, it sounds mad, but just think it through for a minute. Why are the publishers so paranoid about this manuscript?

Even Quigley hasn't been allowed to see it. Why won't they let it out of America? Maybe it's because they think someone over here is desperate to get hold of it.'

'So?'

'So perhaps Kroll was using me as bait – sort of a tethered goat – to test who was after it, find out how far they'd be willing to go.'

Even as the words were leaving my mouth I knew I was sounding ridiculous.

'But Lang's book is a boring crock of shit!' said Rick. 'The only people they want to keep it away from at this point are their shareholders! *That's* why it's under wraps.'

I was starting to feel a fool. I would have let the subject go, but Rick was enjoying himself too much.

'A tethered goat!' I could have heard his shout of laughter from the other terminal even without the phone. 'Let me get this straight. According to your theory, someone must have known Kroll was in town, known where he was Friday morning, known what he'd come to discuss . . .'

'All right,' I said. 'Let's leave it.'

'. . . *known* he might just give Lang's manuscript to a new ghost, known who you were when you came out of the meeting, known where you lived. Because you said they were waiting for you, didn't you? Wow. This must've been some operation. Too big for a newspaper. This must've been a *government*—'

'Forget it,' I said, finally managing to cut him off. 'You'd better catch your flight.'

'Yeah, you're right. Well, you have a safe trip. Get some sleep on the plane. You're sounding weird. Let's talk next week. And don't worry about it.'

He rang off.

I stood there holding my silent phone. It was true. I was sounding weird. I went into the men's room. The bruise where I'd been punched on Friday had ripened, turned black and purple, and was fringed with yellow, like some exploding supernova in an astronomy textbook.

A short time later they announced the Boston flight was boarding, and once we were in the air my nerves steadied. I love that moment when a drab grey landscape flickers out of sight beneath you, and the plane tunnels up through the cloud to burst into the sunshine. Who can be depressed at ten thousand feet when the sun is shining and the other poor saps are still stuck on the ground? I had a drink. I watched a movie. I dozed for a while. But I must admit I also scoured that business-class cabin for every Sunday newspaper I could find, ignored the sports pages for once, and read all that had been written about Adam Lang and those four suspected terrorists.

*

We made our final approach to Logan Airport at one in the afternoon, local time.

As we came in low over Boston Harbor the sun we had been chasing all day seemed to travel over the water alongside us, striking the downtown skyscrapers one after the other: erupting columns of white and blue, gold and silver, a firework display in glass and steel. O my America! I thought, my new-found-land – my land where the book market is five times the size of the United Kingdom's – shine thy light on me! As I queued for immigration I was practically humming 'The Star-Spangled Banner'. Even the guy from the Department of Homeland Security – embodying the rule that

the folksier an institution's name, the more Stalinist its function —
couldn't dent my optimism. He sat frowning behind his glass screen
at the very notion of anyone flying three thousand miles to spend
a month on Martha's Vineyard in mid-winter. When he discovered
I was a writer, he couldn't have treated me with greater suspicion
if I had been wearing an orange jumpsuit.

'What kind of books you write?'

'Autobiographies.'

This obviously baffled him. He suspected mockery, but wasn't
quite sure. 'Autobiographies, huh? Don't you have to be famous to
do that?'

'Not any more.'

He stared hard at me, then slowly shook his head, like a weary
St Peter at the Pearly Gates, confronted by yet another sinner trying
to wheedle his way into Paradise. 'Not any more,' he repeated, with
an expression of infinite distaste. He picked up his metal stamp and
punched it twice. He let me in for thirty days.

When I was through immigration I turned on my phone. It
showed a welcoming message from Lang's personal assistant,
someone named Amelia Bly, apologising for not providing a driver
to collect me from the airport. Instead she suggested I take a bus
to the ferry terminal at Woods Hole, and promised a car would
meet me when I landed at Martha's Vineyard. I bought a *New York
Times* and a *Boston Globe* and checked them while I waited for the bus
to leave to see if they had the Lang story, but either it had broken
too late for them or they weren't interested.

The bus was almost empty and I sat up front near the driver as
we pushed south through the tangle of freeways, out of the city
and into open country. It was a few degrees below freezing and the
sky was clear, but there had been snow not long before. It was piled

in banks next to the road and clung to the higher branches in the forests which stretched away on either side in great rolling waves of white and green. New England is basically Old England on steroids – wider roads, bigger woods, larger spaces; even the sky seemed huge and glossy. I had a pleasing sense of gaining time, imagining a gloomy, wet Sunday night in London, in contrast to this sparkling afternoon winterland. But gradually it began to darken here as well. I guess it must have been almost six when we reached Woods Hole and pulled up at the ferry terminal, and by then there was a moon and stars.

Oddly enough, it wasn't until I saw the sign for the ferry that I remembered to spare a thought for McAra. Not surprisingly, the dead-man's-shoes aspect of the assignment wasn't one I cared to dwell on, especially after my mugging. But as I wheeled my suitcase into the ticket office to pay my fare, and then stepped back out again into the bitter wind, it was only too easy to imagine my predecessor going through similar motions a mere three weeks earlier. He had been drunk, of course, which I wasn't. I looked around. There were several bars just across the car park. Perhaps he had gone into one of those? I wouldn't have minded a drink myself. But then I might sit on exactly the same bar stool as he had, and that would be ghoulish, I thought, like taking one of those tours of murder scenes in Hollywood. Instead I joined the passenger queue and tried to read the *Times* Sunday magazine, turning to the wall for protection from the wind. There was a wooden board with painted lettering: 'CURRENT NATIONWIDE THREAT LEVEL IS ELEVATED'. I could smell the sea but it was too dark to see it.

The trouble is, once you start thinking about a thing, you can't always make yourself stop. Most of the cars waiting to board the ferry had their engines running so the drivers could use their heaters in the cold, and I found myself checking for a tan-coloured Ford Escape SUV. Then, when I actually got on the boat, and climbed the clanging metal stairwell to the passenger deck, I wondered whether this was the way McAra had come. I told myself to leave it, that I was working myself up for nothing. But I suppose that ghosts and ghostwriters go naturally together. I sat in the fuggy passenger cabin and studied the plain, honest faces of my fellow travellers, and then, as the boat shuddered and cast off from the terminal, I folded my paper and went out on to the open top deck.

It's amazing how cold and darkness conspire to alter everything. The Martha's Vineyard ferry on a summer's evening I imagine must be delightful. There's a big stripy funnel straight out of a storybook, and rows of blue plastic seats facing outwards, running the length of the deck, where families no doubt sit in their shorts and T-shirts, the teenagers looking bored, the dads jumping about with excitement. But on this January night the deck was deserted, and the north wind blowing down from Cape Cod sliced through my jacket and shirt and chilled my skin to gooseflesh. The lights of Woods Hole slipped away. We passed a marker buoy at the entrance to the channel swinging frantically this way and that as if it was trying to free itself from some underwater monster. Its bell tolled in time with the waves like a funeral chime and the spray flew as vile as witch's spit.

I jammed my hands in my pockets, hunched my shoulders up around my neck and crossed unsteadily to the starboard side. The handrail was only waist-high and for the first time I appreciated how easily McAra might have gone over. I actually had to brace to keep from slipping myself. Rick was right. The line between accident and suicide isn't always clearly defined. You could kill yourself without ever really making up your mind. The mere act of leaning out too far and imagining what it might be like could tip you over. You'd hit that heaving icy black water with a smack that would take you ten feet under, and by the time you came up the ship might be a hundred yards away. I hoped McAra had absorbed enough booze to blunt the horror, but I doubted if there was a drunk in the world who wouldn't be sobered by total immersion in a sea only half a degree above freezing.

And nobody would have heard him fall! That was the other thing. The weather wasn't nearly as bad as it had been three weeks earlier, and yet, as I glanced around, I could see not a soul on deck. I really started shivering then; my teeth were chattering like some fairground clockwork novelty.

I went down to the bar for a drink.

*

We rounded the West Chop lighthouse and came into the ferry terminal at Vineyard Haven just before seven, docking with a rattle of chains and a thump which almost sent me flying down the stairs. I hadn't been expecting a welcoming committee, which was fine, because I didn't get one, just an elderly local taxi driver holding a torn-out page from a notebook on which my name was misspelled. As he heaved my suitcase into the back, the wind lifted a big sheet of clear plastic and sent it twisting and flapping over the ice in the car park. The sky was packed white with stars.

I'd bought a guide book to the island, so I had a vague idea of what I was in for. In summer the population is a hundred thousand, but when the vacationers have closed up their holiday homes and migrated west for the winter, it drops to fifteen. These are the hardy, insular natives: the folks who call the mainland 'America'.

There are a couple of highways, one set of traffic lights, and dozens of long sandy tracks leading to places with names like Squibnocket Pond and Job's Neck Cove. My driver didn't utter a word the whole journey, just scrutinised me in the mirror. As my eyes met his rheumy glance for the twentieth time I wondered if there was a reason why he resented picking me up. Perhaps I was keeping him from something. It was hard to imagine what. The streets around the ferry terminal were mostly deserted, and once we were out of Vineyard Haven and on to the main highway there was nothing to see but darkness.

By then I'd been travelling for seventeen hours. I didn't know where I was, or what landscape I was passing through, or even where I was going. All attempts at conversation had failed. I could see nothing except my reflection in the cold darkness of the window. I felt as though I'd come to the edge of the earth, like some seventeenth-century English explorer who was about to have his first encounter with the native Wampanoags. I gave a noisy yawn and quickly clamped the back of my hand to my mouth.

'Sorry,' I explained to the disembodied eyes in the rear-view mirror. 'Where I come from it's after midnight.'

He shook his head. At first I couldn't make out whether he was sympathetic or disapproving; then I realised he was trying to tell me it was no use talking to him: he was deaf. I went back to staring out of the window.

After a while we came to a crossroads and turned left into what I guessed must be Edgartown, a settlement of white clapboard houses with white picket fences, small gardens and verandas, lit by ornate Victorian streetlamps. Nine out of ten were dark but in the few windows which shone with yellow light I glimpsed oil paintings of sailing ships and whiskered ancestors. At the bottom of the hill, past the Old Whaling Church, a big, misty moon cast a silvery light over shingled roofs and silhouetted the masts in the harbour. Curls of wood smoke rose from a couple of chimneys. I felt as though I was driving on to a film set for *Moby Dick*. The headlights picked out a sign to the Chappaquiddick ferry, and not long after that we pulled up outside the Lighthouse View Hotel.

Again, I can picture the scene in summer: buckets and spades and fishing nets piled up on the veranda, rope sandals left by the door, a dusting of white sand trailed up from the beach — that kind of thing. But out of season the big old wooden hotel creaked and banged in the wind like a sailing boat stuck on a reef. I suppose the management must have been waiting till spring to strip the blistered paintwork and wash the crust of salt off the windows. The sea was pounding away nearby in the darkness. I stood with my suitcase on the wooden deck and watched the lights of the taxi disappear around the corner with something close to nostalgia.

Inside the lobby, a girl dressed up as a Victorian maid with a white lace mob cap handed me a message from Lang's office. I would be picked up at ten the next morning, and should bring my passport to show to security. I was starting to feel like a man on a mystery tour: as soon as I reached one location, I was given a fresh set of instructions to proceed to the next. The hotel was empty, the restaurant dark. I was told I could have my choice of rooms so I picked one on the second floor with a desk I could work at and photographs of Old Edgartown on the wall: John Coffin House, *circa* 1890; the whale ship *Splendid* at Osborn Wharf, *circa* 1870. After the receptionist had gone, I put my laptop, list of questions and the stories I had torn out of the Sunday newspapers on the desk and then stretched out on the bed.

I fell asleep at once and didn't wake until two in the morning, when my body clock, still adjusted to London time, went off like Big Ben. I spent ten minutes searching for a minibar, before realising there wasn't one. On impulse, I called Kate's home number. What exactly I was going to say to her I had no idea. In any case there was no answer. I meant to hang up but instead found myself rambling to her answering service. She must have left for work very early. Either that, or she hadn't come home the night before. That was something to think about, and I duly thought about it. The fact that I had no one to blame but myself didn't make me feel any better. I took a shower and afterwards I got back into bed, turned off the lamp, and pulled the damp sheets up under my chin. Every few seconds the slow pulse of the lighthouse filled the room with a faint red glow. I must have lain there for hours, eyes wide open, fully awake and yet disembodied, and in this way passed my first night on Martha's Vineyard.

*

The landscape which dissolved out of the dawn the next morning was flat and alluvial. Across the road beneath my window was a creek, then reed beds, and beyond those a beach and the sea. A pretty Victorian lighthouse with a bell-shaped roof and a wrought-iron balcony looked across the straits to a long, low spit of land about a mile away. That, I realised, must be Chappaquiddick. A squadron of hundreds of tiny white sea birds, in a formation as tight as a school of fish, soared and flicked and dived above the shallow waves.

I went downstairs and ordered a huge breakfast. From the little shop next to reception I bought a copy of *The New York Times*. The story I was looking for was entombed deep in the world news section, and then re-interred to ensure maximum obscurity far down the page:

LONDON (AP) – Former British premier Adam Lang authorized the illegal use of British special forces troops to seize four suspected al-Qaeda terrorists in Pakistan and then hand them over for interrogation by the CIA, according to newspaper reports here Sunday.

The men – Nasir Ashraf, Shakeel Qazi, Salim Khan and Faruk Ahmed – all British citizens, were seized in the Pakistani city of Peshawar five years ago. All four were allegedly transferred out of the country to a secret location, and tortured. Mr Ashraf is reported to have died under interrogation. Mr Qazi, Mr Khan and Mr Ahmed were subsequently detained at Guantanamo for three years. Only Mr Ahmed presently remains in US custody.

According to documents obtained by the London *Sunday Times*, Mr Lang personally endorsed "Operation Tempest", a secret mission to kidnap the four men by the UK's elite Special Air Services (SAS). Such an operation would have been illegal under both UK and international law.

The British Ministry of Defence last night refused to comment on either the authenticity of the documents or the existence of "Operation Tempest". A spokeswoman for Mr Lang said that he had no plans to issue a statement.

I read it through three times. It didn't seem to add up to much. Or did it? It was hard to tell any more. One's moral bearings were no longer as fixed as they used to be. Methods my father's generation would have considered beyond the pale, even when fighting the Nazis – torture, for example – were now apparently acceptable civilised behaviour. I decided that the ten per cent of the population who worry about these things would be appalled by the report, assuming they ever managed to locate it; the remaining ninety would probably just shrug. We had been told that the Free World was taking a walk on the dark side. What did people expect?

I had a couple of hours to kill before the car was due to collect me, so I took a walk over the wooden bridge to the lighthouse, and then strolled into Edgartown. In daylight it seemed even emptier than it had the previous night. Squirrels chased undisturbed along the side-walks and scampered up into the trees. I must have passed two dozen of those picturesque nineteenth-century whaling captain's houses, and it didn't look as if one was occupied. The widow's walks on the fronts and sides were deserted. No black-shawled women stared mournfully out to sea, waiting for their menfolk to come home – presumably because the menfolk were all on Wall Street. The restaurants were closed; the little boutiques and galleries stripped bare of stock. I had wanted to buy a windproof jacket but there was no place open. The windows were filled with dust and the husks of insects. 'Thanks for a great season!!!' read the cards. 'See you in the spring!'

It was the same in the harbour. The primary colours of the port were grey and white – grey sea, white sky, grey shingle roofs, white clapboard walls, bare white flagpoles, jetties weathered blue-grey and green-grey, on which perched matching grey-and-white gulls. It was as if Martha Stewart had colour-coordinated the whole place, Man and Nature. Even the sun, now hovering discreetly over Chappaquiddick, had the good taste to shine pale white.

I put my hand up to shield my eyes and squinted at the distant strand of beach with its isolated holiday houses. That was where

Senator Edward Kennedy's career had taken its disastrous wrong turn. According to my book, the whole of Martha's Vineyard had been a summer playground for the Kennedys, who liked to sail over for the day from Hyannisport. There was a story of how Jack, when he was president, had wanted to moor his boat at the private jetty of the Edgartown Yacht Club, but had decided to sail away when he saw the massed ranks of the members, Republicans to a man, lined up with their arms folded, watching him, daring him to land. It was the summer before he was shot.

The few yachts moored now were shrouded for winter. The only movement was a solitary fishing boat with an outboard motor heading for the lobster traps. I sat for a while on a bench and waited to see if anything would happen. Gulls swooped and cried. On a nearby yacht the wind rattled the cables against a metal mast. There was hammering in the distance as property was renovated for the summer. An old guy walked a dog. Apart from that, nothing occurred in almost an hour which could possibly have distracted an author from his work. It was a non-writer's idea of a writer's paradise. I could see why McAra might have gone insane.

Four

The ghost will also be under pressure from the publishers to dig up something controversial that they can use to sell serial rights and to generate publicity at the time of publication.

Ghostwriting

It was my old friend the deaf taxi-driver who picked me up from the hotel later that morning. Because I'd been booked into a hotel in Edgartown, I'd naturally assumed that Rhinehart's property must be somewhere in the port itself. There were some big houses overlooking the harbour, with gardens sloping down to private moorings, that looked to me to be ideal billionaire real estate — which shows how ignorant I was about what serious wealth can buy. Instead, we drove out of town for about ten minutes, following signs to West Tisbury, into flat, thickly wooded country, and then, before I'd even noticed a gap in the trees, swung left down an unmade sandy track.

Until that moment I was unfamiliar with scrub oak. Maybe it looks good in full leaf. But in winter I doubt if nature has a more depressing vista to offer in its entire flora department than mile after mile of those twisted, dwarfish, ash-coloured trees. A few curled brown leaves were the only evidence they might once have been alive. We rocked and bounced down a narrow forest road for almost three miles and the only creature we saw was a run-over skunk, until at last we came to a closed gate, and there materialised from this petrified wilderness a man carrying a clipboard and wearing the unmistakable dark Crombie overcoat and polished black Oxfords of a British plainclothes copper.

I wound down my window and handed him my passport. His big, sullen face was brick-coloured in the cold, his ears terracotta: not a policeman happy with his lot. He looked as if he'd been assigned to guard one of the Queen's granddaughters in the Caribbean for a fortnight, only to find himself diverted here at the last minute. He scowled as he checked my name against the list on his clipboard, wiped a big drop of clear moisture from the end of his nose, and walked around inspecting the taxi. I could hear surf performing its continuous, rolling somersault on a beach some-where. He returned and gave me back my passport, and said – or at least I thought he said: he muttered it under his breath – 'Welcome to the madhouse.'

I felt a sudden twist of nerves, which I hope I concealed, because the first appearance of a ghost is important. I try never to show anxiety. I strive always to look professional. It's dress code: chameleon. Whatever I think the client is likely to be wearing, I endeavour to wear the same. For a footballer, I might put on a pair of trainers; for a pop singer, a leather jacket. For my first ever meeting with a former prime minister, I had decided against a suit – too formal: I would have looked like his lawyer or accountant – and selected instead a pale blue shirt, a conservative striped tie, a sports jacket and a pair of grey trousers. My hair was neatly brushed, my teeth cleaned and flossed, my deodorant rolled on. I was as ready as I would ever be. *The madhouse?* Did he really say that? I looked back at the policeman but he had moved out of sight.

The gate swung clear, the track curved, and a few moments later I had my first glimpse of the Rhinehart compound: four wooden cube-shaped buildings – a garage, a storeroom, a couple of cottages for the staff – and up ahead the house itself. It was only two storeys high, but as wide as a stately home, with a long, low roof and a pair of big square brick chimneys of the sort you might see in a crematorium. The rest of the building was made entirely of wood, but although it was new it had already weathered to a silvery-grey, like garden furniture left out for a year. The windows on this side were as tall and thin as gun-slits, and what with these, and the greyness, and the blockhouses further back, and the encircling forest, and the sentry at the gate, it all somehow resembled a holiday home designed by Albert Speer; the Wolf's Lair came to mind.

Even before we drew up, the front door opened and another police guard – white shirt, black tie, zippered grey jacket – welcomed me unsmilingly into the hall. He quickly searched my shoulder bag while I glanced around. I'd met plenty of rich people in the course of my work, but I don't think I'd ever been inside a billionaire's house before. There were rows of African masks on the smooth white walls, and lighted display cabinets filled with wood carvings and primitive pottery of crude figures with giant phalluses and torpedo breasts – the sort of thing a naughty child might do while the teacher's back was turned. It was entirely lacking in any kind of skill or beauty or aesthetic merit. The first Mrs Rhinehart, I discovered afterwards, was on the board of the Metropolitan Museum of Modern Art; the second was a Bollywood actress, fifty years his junior, whom Rhinehart had been advised by his bankers to marry in order to break into the Indian market.

From somewhere inside the house I heard a woman with a

British accent shouting, 'This is absolutely bloody *ridiculous!*' Then a door slammed, and an elegant blonde in a dark blue jacket and skirt, carrying an A4 black and red hardcover notebook, came clicking down the corridor on high heels.

'Amelia Bly,' she said with a fixed smile. She was probably forty-five but at a distance could have passed for ten years younger. She had beautiful large, clear blue eyes, but wore too much make-up, as if she worked on a cosmetics counter in a department store and had been obliged to demonstrate all the products at once. She exuded a sweet and opulent smell of perfume. I presumed she was the spokeswoman mentioned in that morning's *Times*. 'Adam's in New York unfortunately and won't be back till later this afternoon.'

'Actually, forget I said that: it's *fucking* ridiculous!' shouted the unseen woman.

Amelia expanded her smile a fraction further, creating tiny fissures in her smooth pink cheeks.

'Oh dear. I'm so sorry. I'm afraid poor Ruth's having one of those days.'

Ruth. The name resonated briefly like a warning drumbeat or the clatter of a thrown spear among the African tribal art. It had never occurred to me that Lang's wife might be here. I had assumed she would be at home in London. She was famous for her in-dependence, among other things.

'If this is a bad time . . .' I said.

'No, no. She definitely wants to meet you. Come and have a cup of coffee. I'll fetch her. How's the hotel?' she added over her shoulder. 'Quiet?'

'As the grave.'

I retrieved my bag from the Special Branch man and followed her into the interior of the house, trailing in her cloud of scent.

She had very nice legs, I noticed; her thighs swished nylon as she walked. She showed me into a room full of cream leather furniture, poured me some coffee from a jug in the corner, then disappeared. I stood for a while at the French windows with my mug, looking out over the back of the property. There were no flower beds – presumably nothing delicate would grow in this desolate spot – just a big lawn that expired about a hundred yards away into sickly brown undergrowth. Beyond that was a lake, as smooth as a sheet of steel under an immense aluminium sky. To the left, the land rose slightly to the dunes that marked the edge of the beach. I couldn't hear the ocean: the glass doors were too thick – bullet-proof, I later discovered.

An urgent burst of Morse from the passage signalled the return of Amelia Bly.

'I'm so sorry. I'm afraid Ruth's a little busy at the moment. She sends her apologies. She'll catch you later.' Amelia's smile had hardened somewhat. It looked as natural as her nail polish. 'So, if you've finished your coffee, I'll show you where we work.'

She insisted that I went first up the stairs.

The house, she explained, was arranged so that all the bedrooms were on the ground floor, with the living space above, and the moment we ascended into the huge open sitting room, I understood why. The wall facing the coast was entirely made of glass. There was nothing man-made within sight, just ocean, lake and sky. It was primordial: a scene unchanged for ten thousand years. The soundproofed glass and under-floor heating created the effect of a luxurious time-capsule that had been propelled back to the Neolithic age.

'Quite a place,' I said. 'Don't you get lonely at night?'

'We're in here,' said Amelia, opening a door.

I followed her into a big study, adjoining the sitting room, which was presumably where Marty Rhinehart worked on holiday. There was a similar view from here, except that this angle favoured the ocean more than the lake. The shelves were full of books on German military history, their swastika-ed spines whitened by exposure to the sun and the salinated air. There were two desks – a little one in the corner at which a secretary sat typing at a computer, and a larger one, entirely clear except for a photograph of a powerboat and a model of a yacht. The sour old skeleton that was Marty Rhinehart crouched over the wheel of his boat – living disproof of the old adage that you can't be too thin or too rich.

'We're a small team,' said Amelia. 'Myself, Alice here' – the girl in the corner looked up – 'and Lucy who's with Adam in New York. Jeff the driver's also in New York – he'll be bringing the car back this afternoon. Six protection officers from the UK – three here and three with Adam at the moment. We badly need another pair of hands, if only to handle the media, but Adam can't bring himself to replace Mike. They were together so long.'

'And how long have you been with him?'

'Eight years. I worked in Downing Street. I'm on attachment from the Cabinet Office.'

'Poor Cabinet Office.'

She flashed her nail-polish smile. 'It's my husband I miss the most.'

'You're married? I notice you're not wearing a ring.'

'I can't, sadly. It's far too large. It bleeps when I go through airport security.'

'Ah.' We understood one another perfectly.

'The Rhineharts also have a live-in Vietnamese couple, but they're so discreet, you'll hardly notice them. She looks after the house and he does the garden. Dep and Duc.'

'Which is which?'

'Duc is the man. Obviously.'

She produced a key from the pocket of her well-cut jacket and unlocked a big gunmetal filing cabinet, from which she withdrew a box file.

'This is not to be removed from this room,' she said, laying it on the desk. 'It is not to be copied. You can make notes, but I must remind you that you've signed a confidentiality agreement. You have six hours to read it before Adam gets in from New York. I'll have a sandwich sent up to you for lunch. Alice – come on. We don't want to cause him any distractions, do we?'

After they'd gone, I sat down in the leather swivel chair, took out my laptop, switched it on, and created a document entitled 'Lang MS'. Then I loosened my tie, unfastened my wristwatch and laid it on the desk beside the file. For a few moments I allowed myself to swing back and forth in Rhinehart's chair, savouring the ocean view and the general sensation of being world dictator. Then I flipped open the lid of the file, pulled out the manuscript and started to read.

*

All good books are different but all bad books are exactly the same. I know this to be a fact because in my line of work I read a lot of bad books – books so bad they aren't even published, which is quite a feat, when you consider what is published.

And what they all have in common, these bad books, be they novels or memoirs, is this: *they don't ring true*. I'm not saying that a good book *is* true necessarily, just that it *feels* true for the time you're reading it. A publishing friend of mine calls it the Seaplane

Test, after a movie he once saw about people in the City of London that opened with the hero arriving for work in a seaplane he landed on the Thames. From then on, my friend said, there was no point in watching.

Adam Lang's memoir failed the Seaplane Test.

It wasn't that the facts in it were wrong necessarily — I wasn't in a position to judge at that stage — it was rather that the whole book somehow felt false, as if there was a hollow at its centre. It consisted of sixteen chapters, arranged chronologically: 'Early Years', 'Into Politics', 'Challenge for the Leadership', 'Changing the Party', 'Victory at the Polls', 'Reforming Government', 'Northern Ireland', 'Europe', 'The Special Relationship', 'Second Term', 'The Challenge of Terror', 'The War on Terror', 'Sticking the Course', 'Never Surrender', 'Time to Go' and 'A Future of Hope'. Each chapter was between ten and twenty thousand words long and hadn't been written so much as bolted together from speeches, official minutes, communiqués, memoranda, interview transcripts, office diaries, party manifestos and newspaper articles. Occasionally, Lang permitted himself a private emotion ('I was overjoyed when our third child was born') or a personal observation ('the American president was much taller than I had expected') or a sharp remark ('as Foreign Secretary, Richard Rycart often seemed to prefer presenting the foreigners' case to Britain rather than the other way round') but not very often, and not to any great effect. And where was his wife? She was barely mentioned.

A crock of shit, Rick had called it. But actually this was worse. Shit, to quote Gore Vidal, has its own integrity. This was a crock of nothing. It was strictly accurate and yet overall it was a lie — it had to be, I thought. No human being could pass through life and feel so little. Especially Adam Lang, whose political stock-in-trade was emotional empathy. I skipped ahead to the chapter called 'The War on Terror'. If there was going to be anything to interest American readers it must surely be here. I skimmed it, searching for words like 'rendition', 'torture', 'CIA'. I found nothing, and certainly no mention of Operation Tempest. What about the war in the Middle East? Surely some mild criticism here of the US president, or the Defense Secretary, or the Secretary of State; some hint of betrayal or let-down; some behind-the-scenes scoop or previously classified document? No. Nowhere. Nothing. I took a gulp, literally and metaphorically, and began reading again from the top.

At some point the secretary, Alice, must have brought me in a tuna sandwich and a bottle of mineral water, because later in the afternoon I noticed them at the end of the desk. But I was too busy to stop, and besides I wasn't hungry. In fact I was beginning to feel nauseous, as I shuffled those sixteen chapters, scanning the sheer white cliff-face of featureless prose for any tiny handhold of interest I could cling to. No wonder McAra had thrown himself off the Martha's Vineyard ferry. No wonder Maddox and Kroll had flown to London to try to rescue the project. No wonder they were paying me fifty thousand dollars a week. All these seemingly bizarre events were rendered entirely logical by the direness of the manuscript. And now it would be *my* reputation which would come spiralling down, strapped into the back seat of Adam Lang's kamikaze seaplane. I would be the one pointed out at publishing parties – assuming I was ever invited to another publishing party – as the ghost who had collaborated on the biggest flop in literary history. In a sudden shaft of paranoid insight I fancied I saw my real role in the operation: that of designated fall guy.

I finished the last of the six hundred and twenty-one pages in mid-afternoon ('Ruth and I look forward to the future, whatever it may hold') and when I laid down the manuscript I pressed my hands to my cheeks and opened my mouth and eyes wide, in a reasonable imitation of Edvard Munch's *The Scream*.

That was when I heard a cough in the doorway and looked up to see Ruth Lang watching me. To this day I don't know how long she'd been there. She raised a thin black eyebrow.

'As bad as that?' she said.

*

She was wearing a man's thick, shapeless white sweater, so long in the sleeves that only her chewed fingernails were visible, and once we got downstairs she pulled on top of this a pale blue cagoule, disappearing for a while as she tugged it over her head, her pale face emerging at last with a frown. Her short dark hair stuck up in Medusa's spikes.

It was she who had proposed a walk. She said I looked as though I needed one, which was true enough. She found me her husband's windproof jacket, which fitted perfectly, and a pair of waterproof boots belonging to the house, and together we stepped out into the blustery Atlantic air. We followed the path around the edge of the lawn and climbed up on to the dunes. To our right was the lake, with a jetty, and next to that a rowing boat which had been hauled above the reed beds and laid upside down. To our left was the grey ocean. Ahead of us, bare white sand stretched for a couple of miles, and when I looked behind, the picture was the same, except that a policeman in an overcoat was following about fifty yards distant.

'You must get sick of this,' I said, nodding to our escort.

'It's been going on so long I've stopped noticing.'

We pressed on into the wind. Close up, the beach didn't look so idyllic. Strange pieces of broken plastic, lumps of tar, a dark blue

canvas shoe stiff with salt, a wooden cable drum, dead birds, skele-
tons and bits of bone — it was like walking along the side of a six-lane
highway. The big waves came in with a roar and receded like passing
trucks.

'So,' said Ruth, 'how bad is it?'

'You haven't read it?'

'Not all of it.'

'Well,' I said, politely, 'it needs some work.'

'How much?'

The word Hiroshima floated briefly into my mind. 'It's fixable,'
I said, which I suppose it was: even Hiroshima was fixed eventually.
'It's the deadline that's the trouble. We absolutely have to do it in
four weeks, and that's less than two days for each chapter.'

'Four weeks!' She had a deep, rather dirty laugh. 'You'll never
get him to sit still for as long as that!'

'He doesn't have to write it, as such. That's what I'm being paid
for. He just has to talk to me.'

She had pulled up her hood. I couldn't really see her face. Only
the sharp white tip of her nose was visible. Everyone said she was
smarter than her husband, and that she'd loved their life at the top
even more than he had. If there was an official visit to some foreign
country, she usually went with him: she refused to be left at home.
You only had to watch them on TV together to see how she bathed
in his success. Adam and Ruth Lang: The Power and the Glory.
Now she stopped and turned to face the ocean, her hands thrust
deep in her pockets. Along the beach, as if playing Grandma's footsteps, the policeman also stopped.

'You were my idea,' she said.

I swayed in the wind. I almost fell over. 'I was?'

'Yes. You were the one who wrote Christy's book for him.'

It took me a moment to work out who she meant. Christy Costello. I hadn't thought of him in a long while. He was my first bestseller. The intimate memoirs of a seventies rock star. Drink, drugs, girls, a near-fatal car crash, surgery, and finally rehab and redemp in the arms of a good woman. It had everything. You could give it at Christmas to your grungy teenager or your church-going granny, and each would be equally happy. It sold three hundred thousand copies in hardcover in the UK alone.

'You know *Christy*?' It seemed so unlikely.

'We stayed at his house on Mustique last winter. I read his memoirs. They were by the bed.'

'Now I'm embarrassed.'

'No? Why? They were brilliant, in a horrible kind of a way. Listening to his scrambled stories over dinner and then seeing how you'd turned them into something resembling a life – I said to Adam then: "This is the man you need to write your book."'

I laughed. I couldn't stop myself. 'Well,' I said, 'I hope your husband's recollections aren't quite as hazy as Christy's.'

'Don't count on it,' she said. She pulled back her hood and took a deep breath. She was better-looking in the flesh than she was on television. The camera hated her almost as much as it loved her husband. It didn't catch her amused alertness, the animation of her face. 'God, I miss home,' she said. 'Even though the kids are away at university. I keep telling him – it's like being married to Napoleon on St Helena.'

'Then why don't you go back to London?'

She didn't say anything for a while, just stared at the ocean, biting her lip. Then she looked at me, sizing me up. 'You did sign that confidentiality agreement?'

'Of course.'

'You're sure?'

'Check with Sid Kroll's office.'

'Because I don't want to read about this in some gossip column next week, or in some cheap little kiss-and-tell book of your own a year from now.'

'Whoa,' I said, taken aback by her venom. 'I thought you just said I was your idea. I didn't ask to come here. And I haven't kissed anyone.'

She nodded. 'All right. Then I'll tell you why I can't go home, between you and me. Because there's something not quite right with him at the moment, and I'm a bit afraid to leave him.'

Boy, I thought. This just gets better and better.

'Yes,' I replied diplomatically. 'Amelia told me he was very upset by Mike's death.'

'Oh she did, did she? Quite when *Mrs Bly* became such an expert about my husband's emotional state I'm not sure.' If she had hissed and sprung claws she couldn't have made her feelings plainer. 'Losing Mike certainly made it worse, but it isn't just that. It's losing power – that's the real trouble. Losing power, and now having to sit down and relive everything, year by year. While all the time the press are going on and on about what he did and didn't do. He can't get free of the past, you see. He can't move on.' She gestured help-lessly at the sea, the sand, the dunes. 'He's stuck. We're both stuck.'

As we walked back to the house, she put her arm through mine. 'Oh dear,' she said. 'You must be starting to wonder what you've let yourself in for.'

★

There was a lot more activity in the compound when we got back. A dark green Jaguar limousine with a Washington licence plate was parked at the entrance, and a black minivan with darkened windows was drawn up behind it. As the front door opened I could hear several telephones ringing at once. A genial grey-haired man in a cheap brown suit was sitting just inside, drinking a cup of tea, talking to one of the police guards. He jumped up smartly when he saw Ruth Lang. They were all quite scared of her, I noticed.

'Afternoon, ma'am.'

'Hello, Jeff. How was New York?'

'Bloody chaos, as usual. Like Piccadilly Circus in the rush hour.' He had a crafty London accent. 'Thought for a while I wouldn't get back in time.'

Ruth turned to me. 'They like to have the car ready in position when Adam lands.' She began the long process of wriggling out of her cagoule just as Amelia Bly came round the corner, a cell phone wedged between her elegant shoulder and her sculpted chin, her nimble fingers zipping up an attaché case.

'That's fine, that's fine. I'll tell him.' She nodded to Ruth and carried on speaking – 'On Thursday he's in Chicago' – then looked at Jeff and tapped her wristwatch.

'Actually, I think *I'll* go to the airport,' said Ruth, suddenly pulling her cagoule back down. 'Amelia can stay here and polish her nails or something. Why don't you come?' she added to me. 'He's keen to meet you.'

Score one to the wife, I thought. But no: in the finest traditions of the British civil service, Amelia bounced off the ropes and came back punching. 'Then I'll travel in the back-up car,' she said, snapping her cell phone shut and smiling sweetly. 'I can do my nails in there.'

Jeff opened one of the Jaguar's rear doors for Ruth, while I went round and nearly broke my arm tugging at the other. I slid into the leather seat and the door closed behind me with a gaseous thump.

'She's armoured, sir,' said Jeff into the rear-view mirror as we pulled away. 'Weighs two and a half tons. Yet she'll still do a hundred with all four tyres shot out.'

'Oh do shut up, Jeff,' said Ruth, good-humouredly. 'He doesn't want to hear all that.'

'The windows are an inch thick and don't open, in case you were thinking of trying. She's air-tight against chemical and biological attack, with oxygen for an hour. Makes you think, doesn't it? At this precise moment, sir, you're probably safer than you've ever been in your life, or ever will be again.'

Ruth laughed again and made a face. 'Boys with their toys!'

The outside world seemed muffled, distant. The forest track ran smooth and quiet as rubber. Perhaps this is what it feels like being carried in the womb, I thought: this wonderful feeling of complete security. We ran over the dead skunk and the big car didn't register the slightest tremor.

'Nervous?' asked Ruth.

'No. Why? Should I be?'

'Not at all. He's the most charming man you'll ever meet. My own Prince Charming!' And she gave her deep-throated, mannish laugh again. 'God,' she said, staring out of the window, 'will I be glad to see the back of these trees. It's like living in an enchanted wood.'

I glanced over my shoulder at the unmarked minivan following close behind. I could see how this was addictive. I was getting used to it already. Being forced to give it up after it had become a habit would be like letting go of Mummy. But thanks to terrorism, Lang would never have to give it up – never have to stand in line for public transport; never even drive himself. He was as pampered and cocooned as a Romanov before the revolution.

We came out of the forest on to the main road, turned left, and almost immediately swung right through the airport perimeter. I stared out of the window in surprise at the big runway.

'We're here already?'

'In summer Marty likes to leave his office in Manhattan at four,' said Ruth, 'and be on the beach by six.'

'I suppose he has a private jet,' I said, in an attempt at know-ingness.

'Of course he has a private jet.'

She gave me a look which made me feel like a hick who'd just used his fish knife to butter his roll. *Of course he has a private jet.* You don't own a thirty-million-dollar house and travel to it by bus. The man must have a carbon footprint the size of a yeti's. I realised then that just about everybody the Langs knew these days had a private jet. Indeed, here came Lang himself, in a corporate Gulfstream, dropping out of the darkening sky and skimming in low over the gloomy pines. Jeff put his foot down and a minute later we pulled up outside the little terminal. There was a self-important cannonade of slamming doors as we piled inside – me, Ruth, Amelia, Jeff and one of the protection officers. Inside, a patrolman from the Edgartown police force was already waiting. Behind him on the wall I could see a faded photograph of Bill and Hillary Clinton being greeted on the tarmac at the start of some scandal-shrouded pres-idential vacation.

The private jet taxied in from the runway. It was painted dark blue and had HALLINGTON written in gold letters by the door. It looked bigger than the usual CEO's phallic symbol, with a high tail and six windows either side, and when it came to a stop and the engines were cut the silence over the deserted airfield was un-expectedly profound.

The door opened, the steps were lowered, and out came a couple of Special Branch men. One headed straight for the terminal building. The other waited at the foot of the steps, going through the motions of checking the empty tarmac, glancing up and around and behind him. Lang himself seemed in no hurry to disembark. I could just about make him out in the shadows of the interior, shaking hands with the pilot and a male steward, then finally – almost reluctantly, it seemed to me – he came out and paused at the top of the steps. He was holding his own briefcase, which was not something he had done when he was prime minister. The wind lifted the back of his jacket and plucked at his tie. He smoothed down his hair. He glanced around as if he was trying to remember what he was supposed to do. It was on the edge of becoming embar-rassing when suddenly he caught sight of us watching him through the big glass window. He pointed and waved and grinned, in exactly the way that he had in his heyday, and the moment – whatever it was – had passed. He came striding eagerly across the concourse, transferring his briefcase from one hand to the other, trailed by a third Special Branch man and a young woman pulling a suitcase on wheels.

We left the window just in time to meet him as he came in through the arrivals gate.

'Hi, darling,' he said, and stooped to kiss his wife. His skin had a slightly orange tint. I realised he was wearing make-up.

She stroked his arm. 'How was New York?'

'Great. They gave me the Gulfstream Four – you know, the transatlantic one, with the beds and the shower. Hi, Amelia. Hi, Jeff.' He noticed me. 'Hello,' he said. 'Who are you?'

'I'm your ghost,' I said.

I regretted it the instant I said it. I'd conceived it as a witty, self-deprecatory, break-the-ice kind of a line. I'd even practised my delivery in the mirror before I left London. But somehow out there, in that deserted airport, amid the greyness and the quietness, it hit precisely the wrong note. He flinched.

'Right,' he said doubtfully, and although he shook my hand, he also drew his head back slightly, as if to inspect me from a safer distance.

Christ, I thought, he thinks I'm a lunatic.

'Don't worry,' Ruth told him. 'He isn't always such a jerk.'

Five

It is essential for the ghost to make the subject feel completely comfortable in his or her company.

Ghostwriting

'Brilliant opening line,' said Amelia as we drove back to the house. 'Did they teach you that at ghost school?'

We were sitting together in the back of the minivan. The secretary who'd just flown in from New York — her name was Lucy — and the three protection officers occupied the seats in front of us. Through the windscreen I could see the Jaguar immediately ahead carrying the Langs. It was starting to get dark. Pinned by two sets of headlights, the scrub oaks loomed and writhed.

'It was particularly tactful,' she went on, 'given that you're replacing a dead man.'

'All right,' I groaned. 'Stop.'

'But you do have one thing going for you,' she said, turning her large blue eyes on me, and speaking quietly so that no one else could hear. 'Almost uniquely among all members of the human race, you seem to be trusted by Ruth Lang. Now why's that, do you suppose?'

'There's no accounting for taste.'

'True. Perhaps she thinks you'll do what she tells you.'

'Perhaps she does. Don't ask me.' The last thing I needed was to get stuck in the middle of this cat fight. 'Listen, Amelia — can I call you Amelia? As far as I'm concerned, I'm helping write a book. I don't want to get caught up in any palace intrigues.'

'Of course not. You just want to do your job and get out of here.'

'Now you're mocking me again.'

'You make it so easy.'

After that I shut up for a while. I could see why Ruth didn't like her. She was a shade too clever and several shades too blonde for comfort, especially from a wife's point of view. In fact it struck me as I sat there, passively inhaling her Chanel, that she might be having an affair with Lang. That would explain a lot. He'd been noticeably cool towards her at the airport, and isn't that always the surest sign? In which case, no wonder they were so paranoid about confidentiality. There could be enough material here to keep the tabloids happy for weeks.

We were halfway down the track when Amelia said: 'You haven't told me what you thought of the manuscript.'

'Honestly? I haven't had so much fun since I read the memoirs of Leonid Brezhnev.' She didn't smile. 'I don't understand how it happened,' I went on. 'You people were running the country not that long ago. Surely one of you had English as a first language?'

'Mike . . .' she began, and then stopped. 'But I don't want to speak ill of the dead.'

'Why make them an exception?'

'All right then: Mike. The problem was, Adam passed it all over to Mike to deal with right at the beginning, and poor Mike was simply swamped by it. He disappeared to Cambridge to do the research and we barely saw him for a year.'

'Cambridge?'

'Cambridge – where the Lang Papers are stored. You've really done your homework, haven't you? Two thousand boxes of documents. Two hundred and fifty metres of shelving. One million separate papers, or thereabouts – nobody's ever bothered to count.'

'McAra went through all that?' I was incredulous. My idea of a rigorous research schedule was a week with a tape recorder sitting opposite my client, fleshed out by whatever tissue of inaccuracies Google had to offer.

'No,' she said irritably. 'He didn't go through every box, obviously, but enough so that when he finally did emerge, he was completely overwrought and exhausted. I think he simply lost sight of what he was supposed to be doing. That seems to have triggered a clinical depression, though none of us noticed it at the time. He didn't even sit down with Adam to go over it all until just before Christmas. And of course by then it was far too late.'

'I'm sorry,' I said, twisting in my seat so that I could see her properly. 'You're telling me that a man who's being paid ten million dollars to write his memoirs within two years turns the whole project over to someone who knows nothing about producing books, and who is then allowed to wander off on his own for twelve months?'

Amelia put a finger to her lips, and gestured with her eyes to the front of the car. 'You're very loud, for a ghost.'

'But surely,' I whispered, 'a former prime minister must recognise how important his memoirs are to him.'

'If you want the honest truth, I don't think Adam ever had the slightest intention of producing this book within two years. And he thought that that would be fine. So he let Mike take it over as a kind of reward for sticking by him all the way through. But then, when Marty Rhinehart made it clear he was going to hold him to the original contract, and when the publishers actually read what Mike had produced . . .' Her voice trailed off.

'Couldn't he just have paid the money back, and started all over again?'

'I think you know the answer to that question better than I do.'

'He wouldn't have got nearly such a large advance.'

'Two years after leaving office? He wouldn't have got even half.'

'And nobody saw this coming?'

'I raised it with Adam every so often. But history doesn't really interest him – it never has, not even his own. He was much more concerned with getting his foundation established.'

I sat back in my seat. I could see how easily it all must have happened: McAra, the party hack turned Stakhanovite of the archive, blindly riveting together his vast and useless sheets of facts; Lang, always a man for the bigger picture – 'the future not the past': wasn't that one of his slogans? – being feted around the American lecture circuit, preferring to live, not relive, his life; and then the horrible realisation that the great memoir project was in trouble, followed, I assumed, by recriminations, the sundering of old friendships, and suicidal anxiety.

'It must have been rough on all of you.'

'It was. Especially after they discovered Mike's body. I offered to go and do the identification, but Adam felt it was his responsibility. It was an awful thing to go through. Suicide leaves everyone feeling guilty. So please, if you don't mind, no more jokes about ghosts.'

I was on the point of asking her about the rendition stories in the weekend papers when the brake lights of the Jaguar glowed, and we came to a stop.

'Well, here we are again,' she said, and for the first time I detected a hint of weariness in her voice. 'Home.'

It was fairly dark by this time — half past five or thereabouts — and the temperature had dropped with the sun. I stood beside the minivan and watched as Lang ducked out of his car and was swept through the door by the usual swirl of bodyguards and staff. They had him inside so quickly, one might have thought an assassin with a telescopic sight had been spotted in the woods. Immediately, all along the façade of the big house, the windows started lighting up, and it was possible, briefly, to imagine that this was a focus of real power, and not merely some lingering parody of it. I felt very much an outsider, unsure of what I was supposed to do, and still twisting with embarrassment over my gaffe at the airport. So I lingered outside in the cold for a while. To my surprise, the person who realised I was missing and who came out to fetch me was Lang.

'Hi, man!' he called from the doorway. 'What on earth are you doing out here? Isn't anybody looking after you? Come and have a drink.'

He touched my shoulder as I entered and steered me down the passage towards the room where I'd had coffee that morning. He'd already taken off his jacket and tie and pulled on a thick grey sweater.

'I'm sorry I didn't get a chance to say hello properly at the airport. What would you like?'

'What are you having?' Dear God, I prayed, let it be something alcoholic.

'Iced tea.'

'Iced tea would be fine.'

'You're sure? I'd sooner have something stronger, but Ruth would kill me.' He called to one of the secretaries: 'Luce, ask Dep to bring us some tea, would you, sweetheart? So,' he said, plonking himself down in the centre of the sofa and flinging out his arms to rest along its back, 'you have to be me for a month, God help you.' He swiftly crossed his legs, his right ankle resting on his left knee. He drummed his fingers, wiggled his foot and inspected it for a moment, then returned his cloudless gaze to me.

'I hope it will be a fairly painless procedure, for both of us,' I said, and hesitated, unsure how to address him.

'Adam,' he said. 'Call me Adam.'

There always comes a moment, I find, in dealing with a very famous person face to face, when you feel as if you're in a dream, and this was it for me: a genuine out-of-body experience. I beheld myself as if from the ceiling, conversing in an apparently relaxed manner with a world statesman in the home of a media billion-aire. He was actually going out of his way to be nice to me. He *needed* me. What a lark, I thought.

'Thank you,' I said. 'I have to tell you I've never met an ex-prime minister before.'

'Well,' he smiled, 'I've never met a ghost, so we're even. Sid Kroll says you're the man for the job. Ruth agrees. So how exactly are we supposed to go about this?'

'I'll interview you. I'll turn your answers into prose. Where necessary, I might have to add linking passages, trying to imitate your voice. I should say, incidentally, that anything I write you'll be able to correct afterwards. I don't want you to think I'll be putting words in your mouth that you wouldn't actually want to use.'

'And how long will this take?'

'For a big book, I'd normally do fifty or sixty hours of inter-views. That would give me about four hundred thousand words, which I'd then edit down to a hundred thousand.'

'But we've already got a manuscript.'

'Yes,' I said, 'but frankly, it's not really publishable. It's research notes, it's not a book. It doesn't have any kind of voice.' Lang pulled a face. He clearly didn't see the problem. 'Having said that,' I added quickly, 'the work won't be entirely wasted. We can ransack it for facts and quotations, and I don't mind the structure, actually — the sixteen chapters — although I'd like to open differently, find something more intimate.'

The Vietnamese housekeeper brought in our tea. She was dressed entirely in black — black silk trousers and a collarless black shirt. I wanted to introduce myself but when she handed me my glass, she avoided meeting my gaze.

'You heard about Mike?' asked Lang.

'Yes,' I said. 'I'm sorry.'

Lang glanced away, towards the darkened window. 'We should put something nice about him in the book. His mother would like it.'

'That should be easy enough.'

'He was with me a long time. Since before I became prime minister. He came up through the party. I inherited him from my predecessor. You think you know someone pretty well, and then . . .' He shrugged and stared into the night.

I didn't know what to say, so I didn't say anything. It's in the nature of my work to act as something of a confessor figure, and I have learnt over the years to behave like a shrink — to sit in silence and give the client time. I wondered what he was seeing out there. After about half a minute he appeared to remember I was still in the room.

'Right. How long do you need from me?'

'Full time?' I sipped my drink and tried not to wince at the sweet taste. 'If we work really hard we should be able to break the back of it in a week.'

'A week?' Lang performed a little facial mime of alarm.

I resisted the temptation to point out that ten million dollars for a week's work wasn't exactly the national minimum wage. 'I may need to come back to you to plug any holes, but if you can give me till Friday, I'll have enough to rewrite most of this draft. The important thing is that we start tomorrow, and get the early years out of the way.'

'Fine. The sooner we get it done the better.' Suddenly Lang was leaning forwards, a study in frank intimacy, his elbows on his knees, his glass between his hands. 'Ruth's going stir crazy out here. I keep telling her to go back to London while I finish the book, see the kids, but she won't leave me. I love your work, I have to say.'

I almost choked on my tea. 'You've read some of it?' I tried to imagine what footballer, or rock star, or magician, or reality game show contestant might have come to the attention of a prime minister.

'Sure,' he said, without a flicker of doubt. 'There was some fellow we were on holiday with . . .'

'Christy Costello?'

'Christy Costello! Brilliant. If you can make sense out of his life, you might even be able to make sense out of mine.' He jumped up and shook my hand. 'It's good to meet you, man. We'll make a start first thing tomorrow. I'll get Amelia to fix you a car to take you back to your hotel.' And then he suddenly started singing:

> *Once in a lifetime*
> *You get to have it all*
> *But you never knew you had it*
> *Till you go and lose it all.*

He pointed at me. 'Christy Costello, "Once in a Lifetime", nineteen seventy' — he wobbled his hand speculatively, his head cocked, his eyes half closed in concentration — 'seven?'

'Eight.'

'Nineteen seventy-eight! Those were the days! I can feel it all coming back.'

'Save it for tomorrow,' I said.

★

'How did it go?' enquired Amelia as she showed me to the door.

'Pretty well, I think. It was all very friendly. He kept calling me "man".'

'Yes,' she said, 'he always does that when he can't remember someone's name.'

'Tomorrow,' I said, 'I'll need a private room where I can do the interviewing. I'll need a secretary to transcribe his answers as we go along – every time we break I'll bring the fresh tapes out to her. I'll need my own copy of the existing manuscript on disk – yes, I know,' I said, holding up my hand to cut off her objections, 'I won't take it out of the building. But I'm going to have to cut and paste it into the new material, and also try to rewrite it so that it sounds vaguely like it was produced by a human being.'

She was writing all this down in her black and red book. 'Anything else?'

'How about dinner?'

'Good night,' she said firmly, and closed the door.

One of the policemen gave me a ride back to Edgartown. He was as morose as his colleague on the gate. 'I hope you get this book done soon,' he said. 'Me and the lads are getting pretty brassed off stuck out here.'

He dropped me at the hotel and said he'd pick me up again in the morning. I had just opened the door to my room when my cell phone rang. It was Kate.

'Are you okay?' she said. 'I got your message. You sounded a bit – odd.'

'Did I? Sorry. I'm fine now.' I fought back the impulse to ask her where she'd been when I called.

'So? Have you met him?'

'I have. I've just come from him.'

'And?' Before I could answer, she said: 'Don't tell me: *charming*.'

I briefly held the phone away from my ear and gave it the finger.

'You certainly pick your moments,' she went on. 'Did you see yesterday's papers? You must be the first recorded instance of a rat actually boarding a sinking ship.'

'Yes, of course I saw them,' I said defensively, 'and I'm going to ask him about it.'

'When?'

'When the moment arises.'

She made an explosive noise which somehow managed to combine hilarity, fury, contempt and disbelief. 'Well, yes, *do* ask him. Ask him why he illegally kidnaps British citizens in another country and hands them over to be tortured. Ask him if he knows about the techniques the CIA uses to simulate drowning. Ask him what he plans to say to the widow and children of the man who died of a heart attack—'

'Hold on,' I interrupted, 'you lost me after drowning.'

'I'm seeing someone else,' she said.

'Good,' I said, and hung up.

After that there didn't seem much else to do except go down to the bar and get drunk.

It was decorated to look like the kind of place Captain Ahab might fancy dropping into after a hard day at the harpoon. The seats and tables were made out of old barrels. There were antique seine nets and lobster traps hanging on the roughly planked walls, along with schooners in bottles and sepia photographs of deep-sea anglers standing proudly beside the suspended corpses of their prey: the fishermen would now all be as dead as their fish, I thought, and such was my mood the notion pleased me. A big television above the bar was showing an ice hockey game. I ordered a beer and a bowl of clam chowder and sat where I could see the screen. I know nothing about ice hockey, but sport is a great place to lose your-self for a while, and I'll watch anything available.

'You're English?' said a man at a table in the corner. He must have heard me ordering. He was the only other customer in the bar.

'And so are you,' I said.

'Indeed I am. Are you here on holiday?'

He had a clipped, hello-old-chap-fancy-a-round-of-golf sort of a voice. That, and the striped shirt with the frayed plain collar, the double-breasted blazer, the tarnished brass buttons, and the blue silk handkerchief in the top pocket, all flashed bore, bore, bore as clearly as the Edgartown lighthouse.

'No. Working.' I resumed watching the game.

'So what's your line?' He had a glass of something clear with ice and a slice of lemon in it. Vodka and tonic? Gin and tonic? I was desperate not to be trapped into conversation with him.

'Just this and that. Excuse me.'

I got up and went to the lavatory and washed my hands. The face in the mirror was that of a man who'd slept six hours out of the past forty. When I returned to the table my chowder had arrived. I ordered another drink, but pointedly didn't offer to buy one for my compatriot. I could feel him watching me.

'I hear Adam Lang's on the island,' he said.

I looked at him properly then. He was in his middle-fifties, slim but broad-shouldered. Strong. His iron-grey hair was slicked straight back off his forehead. There was something vaguely military about him, but also unkempt and faded, as if he relied on food parcels from a veterans' charity. I answered in a neutral tone: 'Is he?'

'So I hear. You don't happen to know his whereabouts, do you?'

'No. I'm afraid not. Excuse me again.'

I started to eat my chowder. I heard him sigh noisily, and then the clink of ice as his glass was set down.

'Cunt,' he said, as he passed my table.

Six

I have often been told by subjects that by the end of the research process, they feel as if they have been in therapy.

Ghostwriting

There was no sign of him when I came down to breakfast the next morning. The receptionist told me there was no other guest apart from me in residence. She was equally firm that she hadn't seen a British man in a blazer. I'd already been awake since four – an improvement on two, but not much – and was groggy enough and hungover enough to wonder if I hadn't hallucinated the whole encounter. I felt better after some coffee. I crossed the road and walked around the lighthouse a couple of times to clear my head and by the time I returned to the hotel the minivan had arrived to take me to work.

I'd anticipated that my biggest problem on the first day would be physically getting Adam Lang into a room and keeping him there for long enough to start interviewing him. But the strange thing was that when we reached the house *he* was already waiting for *me*. Amelia had decided we should use Rhinehart's office, and we found the former prime minister, wearing a dark green tracksuit, sprawled in the big chair opposite the desk, one leg draped over the arm. He was flicking through a history of World War II which he'd obviously just taken down from the shelf. A mug of tea stood on the floor beside him. His trainers had sand on their soles: I guessed he must have gone for a run on the beach.

'Hi, man,' he said, looking up at me. 'Ready to start?'

'Good morning,' I said. 'I just need to sort out a few things first.'

'Sure. Go ahead. Ignore me.'

He went back to his book while I opened my shoulder bag and carefully unpacked the tools of the ghosting trade: a Sony Walkman digital tape recorder with a stack of MD-R 74 mini-discs and a mains lead (I've learned the hard way not to rely soley on batteries); a metallic silver Panasonic Toughbook laptop computer, which is not much larger than a hardcover novel, and considerably lighter; a couple of small black Moleskine notebooks and three brand-new Jetstream rollerball pens, made by the Mitsubishi Pencil Co.; and finally two white plastic adaptors, one a British multipoint plug and one a converter to fit an American socket. It's a superstition with me always to use the same items, and to lay them out in the proper sequence. I also had a list of questions, culled from the books I'd bought in London and my reading of McAra's first draft the previous day.

'Did you know,' said Lang suddenly, 'that the Germans had jet fighters in 1944? Look at that.' He held up the page to show the photograph. 'It's a wonder we won.'

'We have no floppy disks,' said Amelia, 'only these flashdrives. I've loaded the manuscript on to this one for you.' She handed me an object the size of a small plastic cigarette lighter. 'You're welcome to copy it on to your own computer, but I'm afraid that if you do, your laptop must stay here, locked up overnight.'

'And apparently Germany declared war on America, not the other way round.'

'Isn't this all a bit paranoid?'

'The book contains some potentially classified material which has yet to be approved by the Cabinet Office. More to the point, there's also a very strong risk of some news organisation using unscrupulous methods to try to get hold of it. Any leak would jeopardise our newspaper serialisation deals.'

Lang said: 'So you've actually got my whole book on that?'

'We could get a hundred books on that, Adam,' said Amelia, patiently.

'Amazing.' He shook his head. 'You know the worst thing about my life?' He closed the book with a snap and replaced it on the shelf. 'You get so out of touch. You never go in a shop. Everything's done for you. You don't carry any money – if I want some money, even now, I have to ask one of the secretaries or one of the protection boys to get it for me. I couldn't do it myself anyway, I don't know my . . . what're they called? I don't even know that.'

'PIN?'

'You see? I just don't have a clue. I'll give you another example. The other week, Ruth and I went out to dinner with some people in New York. They've always been very generous to us, so I say, "Right, tonight, this is on me." So I give my credit card to the manager and he comes back a few minutes later, all embarrassed, and he shows me the problem. There's still a strip where the signature's supposed to be.' He threw up his arms and grinned. 'The card hadn't been activated.'

'This,' I said, excitedly, 'is exactly the sort of detail we need to put in your book. Nobody knows this sort of thing.'

Lang looked startled. 'I can't put that in. People would think I was a complete idiot.'

'But it's human detail. It shows what it's like to be you.' I knew this was my moment. I had to get him to focus on what we needed right from the start. I came round from behind the desk and confronted him. 'Why don't we try to make this book unlike any other political memoir that's ever been written? Why don't we try to tell the truth?'

He laughed. 'Now that would be a first.'

'I mean it. Let's tell people what it really feels like to be prime minister. Not just the policy stuff – any old bore can write about that.' I almost cited McAra, but managed to swerve away at the last moment. 'Let's stick to what no one except you knows – the day-to-day experience of actually leading a country. What do you feel like in the mornings? What are the strains? What's it like to be so cut off from ordinary life? What's it like to be hated?'

'Thanks a lot.'

'What fascinates people isn't policy – who cares about policy? What fascinates people is always people – the detail of another person's life. But because the detail is naturally all so familiar to you, you can't sort out what it is the reader wants to know. It has to be drawn out of you. That's why you need me. This shouldn't be a book for political hacks. This should be a book for everyone.'

'The people's memoir,' said Amelia drily, but I ignored her, and so, more importantly, did Lang, who was looking at me quite differently now: it was as if some electric light bulb marked 'self-interest' had started to glow behind his eyes.

'Most former leaders couldn't get away with it,' I said. 'They're too stiff. They're too awkward. They're too *old*. If they take off their jacket and tie and put on a' – I gestured at his outfit '– put on a tracksuit, say, they look phoney. But you're different. And that's why you should write a different kind of political memoir, for a different age.'

Lang was staring at me. 'What do you think, Amelia?'

'I think you two were made for one another. I'm beginning to feel like a gooseberry.'

'Do you mind,' I asked, 'if I start recording? Something useful might come out of this. Don't worry – the tapes will all be your property.'

Lang shrugged and gestured towards the Sony Walkman. As I pressed RECORD, Amelia slipped out and closed the door quietly behind her.

'The first thing that strikes me,' I said, bringing a chair round from behind the desk so that I could sit facing him, 'is that you aren't really a politician at all, in the conventional sense, even though you've been so amazingly successful.' This was the sort of tough questioning I specialised in. 'I mean, when you were growing up, no one would have expected you to become a politician, would they?'

'Jesus, no,' said Lang. 'Not at all. I had absolutely no interest in politics, either as a child or as a teenager. I thought people who were obsessed by politics were weird. I still do, as a matter of fact. I liked playing football. I liked theatre and the movies. A bit later on I liked going out with girls. I never dreamed I might become a politician. Most student politicians struck me as complete nerds.'

Bingo! I thought. We'd only been working two minutes and already we had a potential opening for the book right there:

When I was growing up I had no interest in politics. In fact I thought people who were obsessed by politics were weird.
    I still do . . .

'So what changed? What turned you on to politics?'

'Turned on is about right,' said Lang, with a laugh. 'I'd left Cambridge and drifted for a year, really, hoping that a play I'd been involved in might get taken up by a theatre in London. But it didn't happen and so I ended up working in a bank, living in this grotty basement flat in Lambeth, feeling very sorry for myself, because all my friends from Cambridge were working in the BBC, or getting paid a fortune to do voice-overs on adverts, or what have you. And I remember it was a Sunday afternoon – raining, I was still in bed – and someone starts knocking on the door . . .'

It was a story he must have told a thousand times, but you wouldn't have guessed it, watching him that morning. He was sitting back in his chair, smiling at the memory, going over the same old words, using the same rehearsed gestures – he was miming knocking on a door – and I thought what an old trouper he was: the sort of pro who'd always make an effort to put on a good show, whether he had an audience of one or one million.

'. . . and this person just wouldn't go away. Knock knock knock. And, you know, I'd had a bit to drink the night before and what have you, and I'm moaning and groaning. I've got the pillow over my head. But it starts up again: knock knock knock. So eventually – and by now I'm swearing quite a bit, I can tell you – I get out of bed, I pull on a dressing gown, and I open the door. And there's this girl – this gorgeous girl. She's wringing wet from the rain, but she completely ignores that, and launches into this speech about the local elections. Bizarre. I have to say I didn't even know there *were* any local elections, but at least I have the sense to pretend that I'm very interested, and so I invite her in, and make her a cup of tea, and she dries off. And that's it – I'm in love. And it quickly becomes clear that the best way of getting to see her again is to take one of her leaflets and turn up the next

Tuesday evening, or whenever it is, and join the local party. Which I do.'

'And this is Ruth?'

'This is Ruth.'

'And if she'd been a member of a different political party?'

'I'd have gone along and joined it just the same. I wouldn't have *stayed* in it,' he added quickly. 'I mean obviously this was the start of a long political awakening for me – bringing out values and beliefs that were already present, but were simply dormant at that time. No, I couldn't have stayed in just *any* party. But everything would have been different if Ruth hadn't knocked on that door that afternoon, and kept knocking.'

'And if it hadn't been raining.'

'If it hadn't been raining I would have found some other excuse to invite her in,' said Lang with a grin. 'I mean, come on, man – I wasn't *completely* hopeless.'

I grinned back, shook my head, and jotted 'opening??' in my notebook.

*

We worked all morning without a break, except for when a tape was filled. Then I would briefly hurry downstairs to the room Amelia and the secretaries were using as a temporary office, and hand it over to be transcribed. This happened a couple of times, and always on my return I'd find Lang sitting exactly where I'd left him. At first I thought this was a testament to his powers of concentration. Only gradually did I realise it was because he had nothing else to do.

I took him carefully through his early years, focusing not so much on the facts and dates (McAra had assembled those dutifully enough) as on the impressions and physical objects of his childhood: the semi-detached home on a housing estate in Leicester; the personalities of his father (a builder) and his mother (a teacher); the quiet, apolitical values of the English provinces in the sixties, where the only sounds to be heard on a Sunday were church bells and the chimes of ice cream vans; the muddy Saturday morning games of football at the local park and the long summer afternoons of cricket down by the river; his father's Austin Atlantic and his own first Raleigh bike; the comics – the *Eagle* and the *Victor* – and the radio comedies – *I'm Sorry, I'll Read That Again* and *The Navy Lark*; the 1966 World Cup Final and *Z Cars* and *Ready, Steady, Go!*; *The Guns of Navarone* and *Carry On Doctor* at the local ABC; Millie singing 'My Boy Lollipop' and Beatles singles played at 45 rpm on his mother's Dansette Capri.

Sitting there in Rhinehart's study, the minutiae of English life nearly half a century earlier seemed as remote as bric-a-brac in a Victorian *trompe l'oeil* – and, you might have thought, about as relevant. But there was cunning in my method, and Lang, with his genius for empathy, grasped it at once, for this was not just his childhood we were itemising, but mine and that of everyone who was born in England in the fifties and who grew to maturity in the seventies.

'What we need to do,' I told him, 'is to persuade the reader to identify emotionally with Adam Lang. To see beyond the remote figure in the bomb-proof car. To recognise in him the same things they recognise in themselves. Because if I know nothing else about this business, I know this: once you have the reader's sympathy, they'll follow you anywhere.'

'I get it,' he said, nodding emphatically. 'I think that's brilliant.'

And so we swapped memories for hour after hour, and I will

not say we began to *concoct* a childhood for Lang exactly — I was always careful not to depart from the known historical record — but we certainly pooled our experiences, to such an extent that a few of my memories inevitably became blended into his. You may find this shocking. I was shocked myself, the first time I heard one of my clients on television weepily describing a poignant moment from his past which was actually from *my* past. But there it is. People who succeed in life are rarely reflective. Their gaze is always on the future: that's why they succeed. It's not in their nature to remember what they were feeling, or wearing, or who was with them, or the scent of freshly cut grass in the churchyard on the day they were married, or the tightness with which their first baby squeezed their finger. That's why they need ghosts — to flesh them out, as it were.

As it transpired, I only collaborated with Lang for a short while, but I can honestly say I never had a more responsive client. We decided that his first memory would be when he tried to run away from home at the age of three and he heard the sound of his father's footsteps coming up behind him and the hardness of his muscled arms as he scooped him back to the house. We remembered his mother ironing, and the smell of wet clothes on a wooden frame drying in front of a coal fire, and how he liked to pretend that the clothes-horse was a house. His father wore a vest at table and ate pork dripping and kippers; his mother liked the occasional sweet sherry and had a book called *A Thing of Beauty* with a red and gold cover. Young Adam would look at the pictures for hours; that was what first gave him his interest in the theatre. We remembered Christmas pantomimes he had been to (I made a note to look up exactly what was playing in Leicester when he was growing up) and his stage debut in the school nativity play.

'Was I a wise man?'

'That sounds a little smug.'

'A sheep?'

'Not smug enough.'

'A guiding star?'

'Perfect!'

By the time we broke for lunch, we had reached the age of seventeen, when his performance in the title role of Christopher Marlowe's *Dr Faustus* had confirmed him in his desire to become an actor. McAra, with typical thoroughness, had already dug out the review in the *Leicester Mercury*, December 1971, describing how Lang had 'held the audience spellbound' with his final speech, as he glimpsed eternal damnation.

While Lang went off to play tennis with one of his bodyguards I dropped by the downstairs office to check on the transcription. An hour's interviewing generally yields between seven and eight thousand words, and Lang and I had been at it from nine till nearly one. Amelia had set both secretaries on the task. Each was wearing headphones. Their fingers skimmed the keyboards, filling the room with a soothing rattle of plastic. With a bit of luck I would have about a hundred double-spaced pages of material to show for that morning's work alone. For the first time since arriving on the island, I felt the warm breath of optimism.

'This is all new to me,' said Amelia, who was bent over Lucy's shoulder, reading Lang's words as they unfurled across the screen. 'I've never heard him mention any of this before.'

'The human memory is a treasure house, Amelia,' I said, deadpan. 'It's merely a matter of finding the right key.'

I left her peering at the screen and went into the kitchen. It was about as large as my London flat, with enough polished granite to furnish a family mausoleum. A tray of sandwiches had been laid out. I put one on a plate, and wandered around the back of the house until I came to a solarium – I suppose that's what you would call it – with a big sliding glass door leading to an outside swimming pool. The pool was covered with a grey tarpaulin, depressed by rainwater, on which floated a brown scum of rotting leaves. There were two silvered wooden cube-shaped buildings at the far end, and beyond those the scrub oak and the white sky. A small, dark figure – so bundled up against the cold he was almost spherical – was raking leaves and piling them into a wheelbarrow. I presumed he must be the Vietnamese gardener, Duc. I really must try to see this place in summer, I thought.

I sat down on a lounger, releasing a faded odour of chlorine and sun tan lotion, and called Rick in New York. He was in a rush, as usual.

'How's it going?'

'We had a good morning. The man's a pro.'

'Great. I'll call Maddox. He'll be glad to hear it. The first fifty thousand just came in, by the way. I'll wire it over. Speak to you later.'

The line went dead.

I finished my sandwich and went back upstairs, still clutching my silent phone. I had had an idea, and my new-born confidence gave me the courage to act on it. I went into the study and closed the door. I plugged Amelia's flashdrive into my laptop, then I attached a cable from my computer to the cell phone and dialled up the internet. How much easier my life would be, I reasoned – how much quicker the job would be done – if I could work on the book in my hotel room each night. I told myself I was doing no harm. The risks were minimal. The machine rarely left my side. If necessary it was small enough to fit under my pillow while I slept.

The moment I was on line, I addressed an email to myself, attached the manuscript file, and pressed SEND.

The upload seemed to take an age. Amelia started calling my name from downstairs. I glanced at the door and suddenly my fingers were thick and clumsy with anxiety. 'Your file has been transferred,' said the female voice which for some reason is favoured by my internet service provider. 'You have email,' she announced a fraction later.

Immediately I yanked the cable out of the laptop and I had just removed the flashdrive when somewhere in the big house a klaxon started. At the same time there was a hum and a rattle above the window behind me and I spun round to see a heavy metal shutter dropping from the ceiling. It descended very quickly, blocking first the view of the sky, then the sea and the dunes, flattening the winter afternoon to dusk, crushing the last sliver of light to blackness. I groped for the door, and when I flung it open the unfiltered sound of the siren was strong enough to vibrate my stomach.

The same process was happening in the living room: one, two, three shutters, falling like steel curtains. I stumbled in the gloom, cracking my knee against a sharp edge. I dropped my phone. As I stooped to retrieve it the klaxon stalled on a rising note and died with a moan. I heard heavy footsteps coming up the steps, and then a sabre of light flashed into the big room, catching me in a furtive crouch, my arms flung up to shield my face: a parody of guilt.

'Sorry, sir,' came a policeman's puzzled voice from the darkness. 'Didn't realise there was anyone up here.'

*

It was a drill. They held it once a week. 'Lockdown', I think they called it. Rhinehart's security people had installed the system to protect him against terrorist attack, kidnap, hurricanes, unionised labour, the Securities and Exchange Commission, or whatever passing nightmare presently stalked the restless nights of the *Fortune* 500. As the shutters rose and the pale wash of Atlantic light was released back into the house, Amelia came into the living room to apologise for not having warned me. 'It must have made you jump.'

'You could say that.'

'But then I did rather lose track of you.' There was an edge of suspicion to her manicured voice.

'It's a big house. I'm a big boy. You can't keep an eye on me all the time.' I tried to sound relaxed, but I knew I radiated unease.

'A word of advice.' Her glossy pink lips parted in a smile, but her big, clear blue eyes were as cold as crystal. 'Don't go wandering round too much on your own. The security boys don't like it.'

'Gotcha.' I smiled back.

There was a squeak of rubber soles on polished wood and Lang came hurtling up the stairs at a tremendous rate, taking them two or three at a time. He had a towel around his neck. His face was flushed, his thick and wavy hair damp and darkened by sweat. He seemed angry about something.

'Did you win?' asked Amelia.

'Didn't play tennis in the end.' He blew out his breath, dropped into the nearby sofa, bent forward and started vigorously towelling his head. 'Gym.'

Gym? I looked at him in amazement. Hadn't he already been for a run before I arrived? What was he in training for? The Olympics?

I said, in a jovial way, designed to show Amelia how unfazed I was, 'So – are you ready to get back to work?'

He glanced up at me furiously and snapped: 'You call what we're doing *work*?'

It was the first time I'd ever seen a flash of bad temper from him, and it struck me with the force of a revelation that all this running and pressing and lifting had nothing whatever to do with training; he wasn't even doing it for enjoyment. It was simply what his metabolism demanded. He was like some rare marine specimen fished up from the depths of the ocean, which could only live under extreme pressure. Deposited on the shore, exposed to the thin air of normal life, Lang was in constant danger of expiring from sheer boredom.

'Well, I certainly call it work,' I said stiffly. 'For both of us. But if you think it's not intellectually demanding enough for you, we can stop now.'

I thought I might have gone too far, but then with a great effort of self-control – so great, you could practically see the intricate machinery of his facial muscles, all the little levers and pulleys and cables, working together – he managed to hoist a tired grin back on to his face. 'All right, man,' he said tonelessly. 'You win.' He flicked me with his towel. 'I was only kidding. Let's get back to it.'

Seven

Quite often, particularly if you are helping them write a memoir or autobiography, the author will dissolve into tears when they're telling the story . . . Your job under these circumstances is to pass the tissues, keep quiet and keep recording.

Ghostwriting

'Were your parents at all political?'

We were once again in the study, in our usual positions. He was sprawled out in the armchair, still wearing his tracksuit, the towel still draped round his neck. He exuded a faint aroma of sweat. I sat opposite with my notebook and list of questions. The mini-disc recorder was on the desk beside me.

'Not at all, no. I'm not sure my father even voted. He said they were all as bad as one another.'

'Tell me about him.'

'He was a builder. Self-employed. He was in his fifties when he met my mother. He'd already got two teenaged sons by his first wife – she'd run off and left him some while before. Mum was a teacher, twenty years younger than him. Very pretty, very shy. The story was he came to do some repair work on the school roof, and they got talking, and one thing led to another, and they got married. He built them a house and the four of them moved in. I came along the following year, which was a shock to him, I think.'

'Why?'

'He thought he was through with babies.'

'I get the impression, reading what's already been written, that you weren't that close to him.'

Lang took his time before answering. 'He died when I was sixteen. He'd already retired by then, because of bad health, and my stepbrothers had grown up, married, moved out. And so that was the only time I remember him being around a lot. I was just getting to know him, really, when he had his heart attack. I mean, I got on all right with him. But if you're saying was I closer to my mother – then yes, obviously.'

'And your stepbrothers? Were you close to them?'

'God, no!' For the first time since lunch, Lang gave a shout of laughter. 'Actually, you'd better scrub that. We can leave them out, can't we?'

'It's your book.'

'Leave them out, then. They both went into the building trade, and neither of them ever missed an opportunity to tell the press they wouldn't be voting for me. I haven't seen them for years. They must be about seventy now.'

'How exactly did he die?'

'Sorry?'

'Sorry – your father. I wondered how he died. Where did he die?'

'Oh, in the garden. Trying to move a paving slab that was too heavy for him. Old habits . . .' He looked at his watch.

'Who found him?'

'I did.'

'Could you describe that?' It was hard going – far harder than the morning session.

'I'd just come home from school. It was a really beautiful spring day, I remember. Mum was out doing something for one of her charities. I got a drink from the kitchen and went out into the back garden, still in my school uniform, thinking I'd kick a ball around or something. And there he was, in the middle of the lawn. Just a graze on his face where he'd fallen. The doctors told us he was probably dead before he hit the ground. But I suspect they always say that, to make it easier for the family. Who knows? It can't be an easy thing, can it – dying?'

'And your mother?'

'Don't all sons think their mothers are saints?' He looked at me for confirmation. 'Well, mine was. She gave up teaching when I was born, and there was nothing she wouldn't do for anyone. She came from a very strong Quaker family. Completely selfless. She was so proud when I got into Cambridge, even though it meant she was left alone. She never once let on how ill she was – didn't want to spoil my time there, especially when I started acting and was so busy. That was typical of her. I'd no idea how bad things were until the end of my second year.'

'Tell me about that.'

'Right.' Lang cleared his throat. 'God. I knew she hadn't been well, but – you know, when you're nineteen, you don't take much notice of anything apart from yourself. I was in Footlights. I had a couple of girlfriends. Cambridge was paradise for me. I used to call her every Sunday night, and she always sounded fine, even though she was living on her own. Then I got home and she was – I was shocked – she was . . . a skeleton basically. There was a tumour on her liver. I mean, maybe now they could do something – but then . . .' He made a helpless gesture. 'She was dead in a month.'

'What did you do?'

'I went back to Cambridge at the start of my final year and I – I lost myself in life, I suppose you could say.'

He was silent.

'I had a similar experience,' I said.

'Really?' His tone was expressionless. He was looking out at the ocean, at the Atlantic breakers rolling in, his thoughts seemingly far away over the horizon.

'Yes.' I don't normally talk about myself in a professional situation, or in any situation for that matter. But sometimes a little self-revelation can help to draw a client out. 'I lost my parents at about that age. And didn't you find, in a strange way, despite all the sadness, that it made you stronger?'

'Stronger?' He turned away from the window and frowned at me.

'In the sense of being self-reliant. Knowing that the worst thing that could possibly happen to you had happened, and you'd survived it. That you could function on your own.'

'You may be right. I've never really thought about it. At least not until just lately. It's strange. Shall I tell you something?' He leaned forwards. 'I saw two dead bodies when I was in my teens and then – despite being prime minister, with all that entails: having to order men into battle and visit the scene of bomb blasts and what have you – I didn't see another corpse for thirty-five years.'

'And who was that?' I asked stupidly.

'Mike McAra.'

'Couldn't you have sent one of the policemen to identify him?'

'No.' He shook his head. 'No, I couldn't. I owed him that, at least.' He paused again, then abruptly grabbed his towel and rubbed his face. 'This is a morbid conversation,' he declared. 'Let's change the subject.'

I looked down at my list of questions. There was a lot I wanted to ask him about McAra. It was not that I intended to use it in the book, necessarily: even I recognised that a post-resignation trip to the morgue to identify an aide's body was hardly going to sit well in a chapter entitled 'A Future of Hope'. It was rather to satisfy my own curiosity. But I also knew I didn't have the time to indulge myself: I had to press on. And so I did as he requested and changed the subject.

'Cambridge,' I said. 'Let's talk about that.'

I'd always expected that the Cambridge years, from my point of view, were going to be the easiest part of the book to write. I'd been a student there myself, not long after Lang, and the place hadn't changed much. It never changed much: that was its charm. I could do all the clichés – bikes, scarves, gowns, punts, cakes, gas fires, choirboys, riverside pubs, porters in bowler hats, Fenland winds, narrow streets, the thrill of walking on stones once trodden by Newton and Darwin, etc., etc. And it was just as well, I thought, looking at the manuscript, because once again my memories would have to stand in for Lang's. He had gone up to read economics, briefly played football for his college's second eleven, and had won a reputation as a student actor. Yet although McAra had dutifully assembled a list of every production the ex-prime minister had ever appeared in, and even quoted from a few of the revue sketches Lang had performed for Footlights, there was – again – something thin and rushed about it all. What was missing was passion. Naturally, I blamed it on McAra. I could well imagine how little sympathy that stern party functionary would have had with all these dilet-tantes and their adolescent posturings in bad productions of Brecht and Ionescu. But Lang himself seemed oddly evasive about the whole period.

'It's so long ago,' he said. 'I can hardly remember anything about it. I wasn't much good, to be honest. Acting was basically an opportunity to meet girls – don't put that in, by the way.'

'But you *were* very good,' I protested. 'When I was in London I read interviews with people who said you were good enough to become a professional.'

'I suppose I wouldn't have minded,' Lang conceded, 'at one stage. Except you don't change things by being an actor. Only politicians can do that.' He looked at his watch again.

'But Cambridge,' I persisted. 'It must have been hugely important in your life, coming from your background.'

'Yes. I enjoyed my time there. I met some great people. It wasn't the real world, though. It was fantasy land.'

'I know. That was what I liked about it.'

'So did I. Just between the two of us: I *loved* it.' Lang's eyes gleamed at the memory. 'To go out on to a stage and pretend to be someone else! And to have people applaud you for doing it! What could be better?'

'Great,' I said, baffled by his change of mood. 'This is more like it. Let's put that in.'

'No.'

'Why not?'

'Why not?' Lang sighed. 'Because these are the memoirs of a *prime minister*.' He suddenly pounded his hand hard against the side of his chair. 'And all my political life, whenever my opponents have been really stuck for something to hit me with, they've always said I was a *fucking actor*.' He sprang up and started striding up and down. '"Oh, Adam Lang,"' he drawled, performing a pitch-perfect caricature of an upper-class Englishman, '"have you noticed the way he changes his voice to suit whatever company he's in?" "Aye"' – and now he

96

was a gruff Scotsman – '"you can't believe anything the wee bastard says. The man's a performer, just piss and wind in a suit!"' And now he became pompous, judicious, hand-wringing: '"It is Mr Lang's tragedy that an actor can only be as good as the part he is given, and finally this prime minister has run out of lines." You'll recognise that last one from your no doubt extensive researches.'

I shook my head. I was too astonished by his tirade to speak.

'It's from the editorial in *The Times* on the day I announced my resignation. The headline was "Kindly leave the stage".' He carefully resumed his seat and smoothed back his hair. 'So no, if you don't mind, we won't dwell on my years as a student actor. Leave it exactly the way that Mike wrote it.'

For a little while neither of us spoke. I pretended to adjust my notes. Outside, one of the policemen struggled along the top of the dunes, head-first into the wind, but the soundproofing of the house was so efficient he looked like a mime artist. I was remembering Ruth Lang's words about her husband: *There's something not quite right with him at the moment, and I'm a bit afraid to leave him.* Now I could see what she meant. I heard a click and leaned across to check the recorder.

'I need to change discs,' I said, grateful for the opportunity to get away. 'I'll just take this down to Amelia. I won't be a minute.'

Lang was brooding again, staring out of the window. He made a small, slightly dismissive gesture with his hand to signal that I should go. I went downstairs to where the secretaries were typing. Amelia was standing by a filing cabinet. She turned around as I came in. I suppose my face must have given me away.

'What's happened?' she said.

'Nothing.' But then I felt an urge to share my unease. 'Actually, he seems a bit on edge.'

'Really? That's not like him. In what way?'

97

'He just blew up at me over nothing. I guess it must be too much exercise at lunchtime,' I said, trying to make a joke out of it. 'Can't be good for a man.'

I gave the disc to one of the secretaries – Lucy I think it was – and picked up the latest transcripts. Amelia carried on looking at me, her head tilted slightly.

'What?' I said.

'You're right. There is something troubling him, isn't there? He took a call just after you finished your session this morning.'

'From whom?'

'It came through on his mobile. He didn't tell me. I wonder . . . Alice, darling – do you mind?'

Alice got up and Amelia slipped into position in front of the computer screen. I don't think I ever saw fingers move so rapidly across a keyboard. The clicks seemed to merge into one continuous purr of plastic, like the sound of a million dominoes falling. The images on the screen changed almost as quickly. And then the clicks slowed to a few staccato taps as Amelia found what she was looking for.

'Shit!'

She tilted the screen towards me, then sat back in her chair in disbelief. I bent to read it.

The web page was headed 'Breaking News':

January 27, 2:57 PM (ET)

NEW YORK (AP) – Former British Foreign Secretary Richard Rycart has asked the International Criminal Court in The Hague to investigate allegations that the former British Prime Minister Adam Lang ordered the illegal handover of suspects for torture by the CIA.

Mr Rycart, who was dismissed from the Cabinet by Mr Lang four years ago, is currently the United Nations' Special Envoy for Humanitarian Affairs, and an outspoken critic of US foreign policy. Mr Rycart maintained at the time he left the Lang government that he was sacked for being insufficiently pro-American.

In a statement issued from his office in New York, Mr Rycart said he had passed a number of documents to the ICC some weeks ago. The documents – details of which were leaked to a British newspaper at the weekend – allegedly show that Mr Lang, as prime minister, personally authorized the seizure of four British citizens in Pakistan five years ago.

Mr Rycart went on: "I have repeatedly asked the British government, in private, to investigate this illegal act. I have offered to give testimony to any inquiry. Yet the government have consistently refused even to acknowledge the existence of Operation Tempest. I therefore feel I have no alternative except to present the evidence in my possession to the ICC."

'The little shit,' whispered Amelia.

The telephone on the desk started ringing. Then another on a small table beside the door chimed in. Nobody moved. Lucy and Alice looked at Amelia for instructions, and as they did, Amelia's mobile, which she had in a little leather pouch on her belt, set up its own electronic warble. For the briefest of moments I saw her panic – it must have been one of the very few occasions in her life when she didn't know what to do – and in the absence of any guidance, Lucy started reaching for the phone on the desk.

'Don't!' shouted Amelia, then added, more calmly, 'Leave it. We need to work out a line to take.' By now a couple of other phones were trilling away in the recesses of the house. It was like noon in a clock factory. She took out her mobile and examined the incoming number. 'The pack is on the move,' she said, and turned it off. For a few seconds she drummed her fingertips on the desk. 'Right. Unplug all the phones,' she instructed Alice, with something of her old confidence back in her voice, 'then start surfing the main news sites on the web to see if you can discover anything else Rycart might be saying. Lucy – find a television and monitor all the news channels.' She looked at her watch. 'Is Ruth still out walking? Shit! She is, isn't she?'

She grabbed her black and red book and clattered off down the corridor on her high heels. Unsure of what I was supposed to do, or even exactly what was happening, I decided I'd better follow her. She was calling for one of the Special Branch men. 'Barry! Barry!' He stuck his head out of the kitchen. 'Barry, please find Mrs Lang and get her back here as soon as you can.' She started climbing the stairs to the living room.

Once again, Lang was sitting motionless, exactly where I had left him. The only difference was that he had his own small mobile phone in his hand. He snapped it shut as we came in.

'I take it from all the telephone calls that he's issued his statement,' he said.

Amelia spread her hands wide in exasperation. 'Why didn't you tell me?'

'Tell you before I'd told Ruth? I don't think that would have been very good politics, do you? Besides, I felt like keeping it to myself for a while. Sorry,' he said to me, 'for losing my temper.'

I was touched by his apology. That was graciousness in adversity, I thought. 'Don't worry about it,' I said.

'And have you?' asked Amelia. 'Told her?'

'I wanted to break it to her face to face. Obviously, that's no longer an option, so I just called her.'

'And how did she take it?'

'How do you think?'

'The little shit,' repeated Amelia.

'She should be back any minute.'

Lang got to his feet and stood looking out of the window with his hands on his hips. I smelt again the sharp tang of his sweat. It made me think of an animal at bay. 'He wanted very much to let me know there was nothing personal,' said Lang, with his back to us. 'He wanted very *very* much to tell me that it was only because of his well-known stand on human rights that he felt he couldn't keep quiet any longer.' He snorted at his own reflection. 'His well-known stand on human rights . . . Dear God.'

Amelia said, 'Do you think he was taping the call?'

'Who knows? Probably. Probably he's going to broadcast it. Anything's possible with him. I just said, "Thank you very much, Richard, for letting me know," and hung up.' He turned round, frowning. 'It's gone unnervingly quiet down there.'

'I've had the phones unplugged. We need to work out what we're going to say.'

'What did we say at the weekend?'

'That we hadn't seen what was in *The Sunday Times* and had no plans to comment.'

'Well, at least we now know where they got their story.' Lang shook his head. His expression was almost admiring. 'He really is after me, isn't he? A leak to the press on Sunday, preparing the ground for a statement on Tuesday. Three days of coverage instead of one, building up to a climax. This is straight out of the textbook.'

'Your textbook.'

Lang acknowledged the compliment with a slight nod and returned his gaze to the window. 'Ah,' he said. 'Here comes trouble.'

A small and determined figure in a blue cagoule was striding down the path from the dunes, moving so rapidly that the policeman behind her had to break into an occasional loping run to keep up. The pointed hood was pulled down low to protect her face and her chin was pressed to her chest, giving Ruth Lang the appearance of a medieval knight in a polyester visor, heading into battle.

'Adam, we've really got to put out a statement of our own,' said Amelia. 'If you don't say anything, or if you leave it too long, you'll look . . .' She hesitated. 'Well, they'll draw their own conclusions.'

'All right,' said Lang. 'How about this?' Amelia uncapped a small silver pen and opened her notebook. '"Responding to Richard Rycart's statement, Adam Lang made the following remarks: 'When a policy of offering one hundred per cent support to the United States in the global war on terror was popular in the United Kingdom, Mr Rycart approved of it. When it became unpopular, he disapproved of it. And when, due to his own administrative incompetence, he was asked to leave the Foreign Office, he suddenly developed a passionate interest in upholding the so-called human rights of suspected terrorists. A child of three could see through his infantile tactics in seeking to embarrass his former colleagues.'" End point. End paragraph.'

Amelia had stopped writing midway through Lang's dictation. She was staring at the former prime minister, and if I didn't know it was impossible, I'd swear the Ice Queen had the beginnings of a tear in one eye. He stared back at her. There was a gentle tap on the open door and Alice came in, holding a sheet of paper.

'Excuse me, Adam,' she said. 'This just came over AP.'

Lang seemed reluctant to break eye contact with Amelia, and I knew then – as surely as I had ever known anything – that their relationship was more than merely professional. After what seemed an embarrassingly long interlude he took the paper from Alice and started to read it. That was when Ruth came into the study. By this time I was starting to feel like a member of an audience who has left his seat in the middle of a play to find a lavatory and somehow wandered on to the stage: the principal actors were pretending I wasn't there, and I knew I ought to leave, but I couldn't think of an exit line.

Lang finished reading and gave the paper to Ruth. 'According to the Associated Press,' he announced, 'sources in The Hague – whoever they may be – say the prosecutor's office of the International Criminal Court will be issuing a statement in the morning.'

'Oh, Adam!' cried Amelia. She put her hand to her mouth.

'Why weren't we given some warning of this?' demanded Ruth. 'What about Downing Street? Why haven't we heard from the embassy?'

'The phones are disconnected,' said Lang. 'They're probably trying to get through now.'

'Never mind *now!*' shrieked Ruth. 'What fucking use is *now?* We needed to know about this a week ago! What are you people doing?' she said, turning her fury on Amelia. 'I thought the whole point of *you* was to maintain liaison with the Cabinet Office. You're not telling me they didn't know this was coming?'

'The ICC prosecutor is very scrupulous about not notifying a suspect if he's under investigation,' said Amelia. 'Or the suspect's government, for that matter. In case they start destroying evidence.'

Her words seemed to stun Ruth. It took her a beat to recover. 'So that's what Adam is now? A suspect?' She turned to her husband. 'You need to talk to Sid Kroll.'

'We don't actually know what the ICC are going to say yet,' Lang pointed out. 'I should talk to London first.'

'Adam,' said Ruth, addressing him very slowly, as if he had suffered an accident and might be concussed, 'if it suits them, they will hang you out to dry. You need a lawyer. Call Sid.'

Lang hesitated, then turned to Amelia. 'Get Sid on the line.'

'And what about the media?'

'Issue a holding statement,' said Ruth. 'Just a sentence or two.'

Amelia pulled out her mobile and started scrolling through the address book. 'D'you want me to draft something?'

'Why doesn't *he* do it?' said Ruth, pointing at me. 'He's supposed to be the writer.'

'Fine,' said Amelia, not quite concealing her irritation, 'but it needs to go out immediately.'

'Hang on a minute,' I said.

'I should sound confident,' Lang said to me, 'certainly not defensive — that would be fatal. But I shouldn't be cocky, either. No bitterness. No anger. But don't say I'm pleased at this opportunity to clear my name, or any balls like that.'

'So,' I said, 'you're not defensive but you're not cocky, you're not angry but you're not pleased?'

'That's it.'

'Then what exactly are you?'

Surprisingly, under the circumstances, everybody laughed.

'I told you he was funny,' said Ruth.

Amelia abruptly held up her hand and waved us to be quiet. 'I have Adam Lang for Sidney Kroll,' she said. 'No, he won't hold.'

★

I went downstairs with Alice and stood behind her shoulder while she sat at a keyboard, patiently waiting for the ex-prime minister's words to flow from my mouth. It wasn't until I started contemplating what Lang should say that I realised I hadn't asked him the crucial question: had he actually ordered the seizure of those four men? That was when I knew that of course he must have done, otherwise he'd simply have denied it outright at the weekend, when the original story broke. Not for the first time, I felt seriously out of my depth.

'I have always been a passionate . . .' I began. 'No – scrub that – I have always been a strong – no, *committed* – supporter of the work of the International Criminal Court.' (Had he been? I'd no idea. I assumed he had. Or, rather, I assumed he'd always pretended he had.) 'I have no doubt that the ICC will quickly see through this politically motivated piece of mischief-making.' I paused. I felt it needed one more line: something broadening and statesmanlike. What would I say if I were him? 'The international struggle against terror,' I said, in a sudden burst of inspiration, 'is too important to be used for the purposes of personal revenge.'

Lucy printed it off, and when I took it back up to the study I felt a curious bashful pride, like a schoolboy handing in his homework. I pretended not to see Amelia's outstretched hand, and showed it first to Ruth (at last I was learning the etiquette of this exile's court). She nodded her approval and slid it across the desk to Lang, who was listening on the telephone. He glanced at it silently, beckoned for my pen, and inserted a single word. He tossed the statement back to me and gave me the thumbs-up.

Into the telephone he said: 'That's great, Sid. And what do we know about these three judges?'

'Am I allowed to see it?' said Amelia, as we went downstairs.

Handing it over, I noticed that Lang had added 'domestic' to the final sentence: 'The international struggle against terror is too important to be used for the purposes of *domestic* personal revenge.' The brutal antithesis of 'international' and 'domestic' made Rycart appear even more petty.

'Very good,' said Amelia. 'You could be the new Mike McAra.'

I gave her a look. I think she meant it as a compliment. It was always hard to tell with her. Not that I cared. For the first time in my life I was experiencing the adrenalin of politics. Now I saw why Lang was so restless in retirement. I guessed this was how sport must feel, when played at its hardest and fastest. It was like tennis on Centre Court at Wimbledon. Rycart had fired his serve low across the net, and we had lunged for it, got our racket to it, and shot the ball right back at him, with added spin.

One by one the telephones were reconnected. Immediately they began ringing, demanding attention, and I heard the secretaries feeding my words to the hungry reporters — '*I have always been a committed supporter of the work of the International Criminal Court.*' I watched my sentences emailed to the news agencies. And within a couple of minutes, on the computer screen and on television, I started seeing and hearing them all over again. ('In a statement issued in the last few minutes, the former prime minister says . . .') The world had become our echo chamber.

In the middle of all this, my own phone rang. I jammed the receiver to one ear and had to put my finger in the other to hear who was calling. A faint voice said: 'Can you hear me?'

'Who is this?'

'It's John Maddox, from Rhinehart in New York. Where the hell are you? Sounds like you're in a madhouse.'

'You're not the first to call it that. Hold on, John. I'll try to find somewhere quieter.' I walked out into the passage and kept following it round to the back of the house. 'Is that better?'

'I've just heard the news,' said Maddox. 'This can only be good for us. We should start with this.'

'What?' I was still walking.

'This war crimes stuff. Have you asked him about it?'

'Haven't had much chance, John, to be honest.' I tried not to sound too sarcastic. 'He's a little tied up right now.'

'Okay, so what've you covered so far?'

'The early years – childhood, university . . .'

'No, no,' said Maddox impatiently. 'Forget all that crap. *This* is what's interesting. Get him to focus on this. And he mustn't talk to anyone else about it. We need to keep this absolutely exclusive to the memoirs.'

I'd ended up in the solarium, where I'd spoken to Rick at lunchtime. Even with the door closed I could still hear the faint noise of the telephones ringing on the other side of the house. The notion that Lang would be able to avoid saying anything about illegal kidnapping and torture until the book came out was a joke. Naturally I didn't put it in quite those terms to the chief executive of the third largest publishing house in the world. 'I'll tell him, John,' I said. 'It might be worth your while speaking to Sidney Kroll. Perhaps Adam could say that his lawyers have instructed him not to talk.'

'Good idea. I'll call Sid now. In the meantime, I want you to accelerate the timetable.'

'Accelerate?' In the empty room my voice sounded thin and hollow.

'Sure. Accelerate. As in speed things up. Right at this moment, Lang is hot. People are starting to get interested in him again. We can't afford to let this opportunity slip.'

'Are you now saying you want the book in *less* than a month?'

'I know it's tough. And it'll probably mean settling for just a polish on a lot of the manuscript rather than a total rewrite. But what the hell? No one's going to read most of that stuff anyway. The earlier we go, the more we'll sell. Think you can do it?'

No, was the answer. No, you bald-headed bastard, you psychopathic prick – have you seriously read this junk? You must be out of your fucking mind. 'Well, John,' I said mildly, 'I can try.'

'Good man. And don't worry about your own deal. We'll pay you just as much for two weeks' work as we would for four. I tell you, if this war crimes thing comes off, it could be the answer to our prayers.'

By the time he hung up, two weeks had somehow ceased to be a figure plucked at random from the air and had become a firm deadline. I would no longer conduct forty hours of interviews with Lang, ranging over his whole life: I would get him to focus specifically on the War on Terror, and we would begin the memoir with that. The rest I would do my best to improve, rewriting where I could.

'What if Adam isn't keen on this?' I asked, in what proved to be our final exchange.

'He will be,' said Maddox. 'And if he isn't, then you can just remind *Adam*' – his tone implied we were just a pair of faggoty Englishmen, conspiring to rob a red-blooded American – 'of his contractual obligation to produce a book that gives us a full and frank account of the War on Terror. I'm relying on you. Okay?'

It's a melancholy place to be, a solarium when there's no sun. I could see the gardener in exactly the same spot where he had been working the day before, stiff and clumsy in his thick outdoor clothes, still piling leaves in his wheelbarrow. No sooner had he cleared away one lot of detritus than the wind blew in more. I permitted myself a brief moment of despair, leaning back against the wall, my head tilted to the ceiling, pondering the fleeting nature of summer days and of human happiness. I tried to call Rick but his assistant said he was out for the afternoon, so I left a message asking him to ring me back. Then I went in search of Amelia.

She wasn't in the office, where the secretaries were still fielding calls, or the passage, or the kitchen. To my surprise, one of the policemen told me she was outside. It must have been after four by now, and getting cold. She was standing in the turning circle in front of the house. In the January gloom, the tip of her cigarette glowed bright red as she inhaled, then faded to nothing.

'I wouldn't have guessed you were a smoker,' I said.

'I only ever allow myself one. And then only at times of great stress or great contentment.'

'Which is this?'

'Very funny.'

She had buttoned her jacket against the chilly dusk, and was smoking in that curious *noli me tangere* way that a certain kind of woman does, with one arm held loosely against her waist and the other – the one with the hand holding the cigarette – slanted across her breast. The fragrant smell of the burning tobacco in the open air made me crave a cigarette myself. It would have been my first in more than a decade, and it would have started me back on forty a day for sure – but still, at that moment, if she'd offered me one, I would have taken it.

She didn't.

'John Maddox just called,' I said. 'Now he wants the book in two weeks instead of four.'

'Christ. Good luck.'

'I don't suppose there's the faintest chance of my sitting down with Adam for another interview today, is there?'

'What do you think?'

'In that case, could I have a lift back to my hotel? I'll do some work there instead.'

She exhaled smoke through her nose and studied me. 'You're not planning to take that manuscript out of here, are you?'

'Of course not!' My voice always rises an octave when I tell a lie. I could never have become a politician: I'd have sounded like Donald Duck. 'I just want to write up what we did today, that's all.'

'Because you do realise how serious this is getting, don't you?'

'Of course. You can check my laptop if you want.'

She paused just long enough to convey her suspicion. 'All right,' she said, finishing her cigarette. 'I'll trust you.' She dropped the stub on to the drive and extinguished it delicately with the pointed toe of her shoe, then stooped and retrieved it. I imagined her at school, similarly removing the evidence: the head girl who was never caught smoking. 'Collect your stuff. I'll get one of the boys to take you into Edgartown.'

We walked back into the house and parted in the corridor. She headed back to the ringing telephones. I climbed the stairs to the study, and as I came closer I could hear Ruth and Adam Lang shouting at one another. Their voices were muffled, and the only words I heard distinctly came at the tail-end of her final rant: *'Spending the rest of my bloody life here!'* The door was ajar. I hesitated. I didn't want to interrupt, but on the other hand I didn't want to hang around and be caught looking as if I were eavesdropping. In the end I knocked lightly, and after a pause I heard Lang say wearily, 'Come.'

He was sitting at the desk. His wife was at the other end of the room. They were both breathing heavily, and I sensed that something momentous – some long-pent-up explosion – had just occurred. I could understand now why Amelia had fled outside to smoke.

'Sorry to interrupt,' I said, gesturing towards my belongings. 'I wanted to . . .'

'Fine,' said Lang.

'I'm going to call the children,' said Ruth bitterly. 'Unless of course you've already done it.'

Lang didn't look at her: he looked at me. And, oh, what layers of meaning there were to be read in those glaucous eyes! He invited me, in that long instant, to see what had become of him: stripped of his power, abused by his enemies, hunted, homesick, trapped between his wife and his mistress. You could write a hundred pages about that one brief look, and still not get to the end of it.

'Excuse me,' said Ruth, and pushed past me quite roughly, her small, hard body banging into mine. At the same moment, Amelia appeared in the doorway, holding a telephone.

'Adam,' she said, 'it's the White House. They have the President of the United States on the line for you.' She smiled at me and ushered me towards the door. 'Would you mind? We need the room.'

*

It was pretty well dark by the time I got back to the hotel. There was just enough light in the sky to show up the big black storm clouds massing over Chappaquiddick, rolling in from the Atlantic.

The girl in reception, in her little lace mob cap, said there was a run of bad weather on the way.

I went up to my room and stood in the shadows for a while, listening to the creaking of the old inn sign and the relentless boom-and-hiss, boom-and-hiss of the surf beyond the empty road. The lighthouse switched itself on at the precise moment when the beam was pointing directly at the hotel and the sudden eruption of red into the room jerked me out of my reverie. I turned on the desk lamp and took my laptop out of my shoulder bag. We had travelled a long way together, that laptop and I. We had endured rock stars who believed themselves messiahs with a mission to save the planet. We had survived footballers whose monosyllabic grunts would make a silverback gorilla sound as if he were reciting Shakespeare. We had put up with soon-to-be-forgotten actors who had egos the size of a Roman emperor's, and entourages to match. I gave the machine a comradely pat. Its once shiny metal case was scratched and dented: the honourable wounds of a dozen campaigns. We had got through those. We would somehow get through even this.

I hooked it up to the hotel telephone, dialled my internet service provider and, while the connection was going through, went into the bathroom for a glass of water. The face that stared back at me from the mirror was a deterioration even on the spectre of the previous evening. I pulled down my lower eyelids and examined the yolky whites of my eyes, before moving on to the greying teeth and hair, and the red filigrees of my cheeks and nose. Martha's Vineyard in midwinter seemed to be ageing me. It was Shangri-La in reverse.

From the other room I heard the familiar announcement: 'You have email.'

I saw at once that something was wrong. There was the usual queue of a dozen junk messages, offering me everything from penis enlargement to *The Wall Street Journal*, plus an email from Rick's office confirming the payment of the first part of the advance. Just about the only thing that wasn't listed was the email I had sent myself that afternoon.

For a few moments, I stared stupidly at the screen, then I opened the separate filing cabinet on the laptop's hard drive which automatically stores every piece of email, incoming and outgoing. And there, sure enough, to my immense relief, at the top of the 'Email you have sent' queue was one entitled 'No subject', to which I had attached the manuscript of Adam Lang's memoirs. But when I opened the blank email and clicked on the box labelled 'download', all I received was a message saying, 'That file is not currently available'. I tried a few more times, always with the same result.

I took out my mobile and called the internet company.

I shall spare you a full account of the sweaty half-hour that followed – the endless selecting from lists of options, the queuing, the listening to muzak, the increasingly panicky conversation with the company's representative in Uttar Pradesh, or wherever the hell he was speaking from.

The bottom line was that the manuscript had vanished, and the company had no record of its ever having existed.

I lay down on the bed.

I am not very technically minded, but even I was beginning to grasp what must have happened. Somehow, Lang's manuscript had been wiped from the memory of my internet service provider's computers. For which there were two possible explanations. One was that it hadn't been uploaded properly in the first place – but that couldn't be right, because I had received those two messages while I was still in the office: 'Your file has been transferred' and 'You have email'. The other was that the file had since been deleted. But how could that have happened? Deletion would imply that someone had direct access to the computers of one of the world's biggest internet conglomerates, and was able to cover their tracks at will. It would also imply — had to imply — that my emails were all being monitored.

Rick's voice floated into my mind — *'Wow. This must've been some operation. Too big for a newspaper. This must've been a* government' — followed swiftly by Amelia's — *'You do realise how serious this is getting, don't you?'*

'But the book is crap!' I cried out loud, despairingly, at the portrait of the Victorian whaling master hanging opposite the bed. 'There's nothing in it that's worth all this trouble!'

The stern old Victorian seadog stared back at me, unmoved. I had broken my promise, his expression seemed to say, and something out there — some nameless force — knew it.

Eight

Authors are often busy people and hard to get hold of; sometimes they are temperamental. The publishers consequently rely on the ghosts to make the process of publication as smooth as possible.

Ghostwriting

There was no question of my doing any more work that night. I didn't even turn on the television. Oblivion was all I craved. I switched off my mobile, went down to the bar and, when that closed, sat up in my room emptying a bottle of Scotch until long past midnight, which no doubt explains why for once I slept right through the night.

I was woken by the bedside telephone. The harsh metallic tone seemed to vibrate my eyeballs in their dusty sockets, and when I rolled over to answer it I felt my stomach keep on rolling, wobbling away from me across the mattress and on to the floor like a balloon taut full of some noxious, viscous liquid. The revolving room was very hot; the air-conditioning turned up to maximum. I realised I'd gone to sleep fully dressed, and had left all the lights burning.

'You need to check out of your hotel immediately,' said Amelia. 'Things have changed.' Her voice pierced my skull like a knitting needle. 'There's a car on its way.'

That was all she said. I didn't argue; I couldn't. She'd gone.

I once read that the ancient Egyptians used to prepare a pharaoh for mummification by drawing his brain out through his nose with a hook. At some point in the night a similar procedure had seemingly been performed on me. I shuffled across the carpet and pulled back the curtains to unveil a sky and sea as grey as death. Nothing was stirring. The silence was absolute, unbroken even by the cry of a gull. A storm was coming in all right: even I could tell that.

But then, just as I was about to turn away, I heard the distant sound of an engine. I squinted down at the street beneath my window and saw a couple of cars pull up. The doors of the first opened and two men got out — young, fit-looking, wearing ski jackets, jeans and boots. The driver stared up at my window and instinctively I took a step backwards. By the time I risked a second look he had opened the rear of the car and was bent over it. When he straightened he was holding what at first, in my paranoid state, I took to be a machine gun. Actually it was a television camera.

I started to move quickly then, or at least as quickly as my condition would allow. I opened the window wide to let in a blast of freezing air. I undressed, showered in lukewarm water, and shaved. I put on clean clothes and packed. By the time I got down to reception it was eight forty-five — an hour after the first ferry from the mainland had docked at Vineyard Haven — and the hotel looked as though it was staging an international media convention. Whatever you might say against Adam Lang, he was certainly doing wonders for the local economy: Edgartown hadn't been this busy since Chappaquiddick. There must have been thirty people hanging around, drinking coffee, swapping stories in half a dozen languages, talking on their mobiles, checking equipment. I'd spent enough time around reporters to be able to tell one type from another. The television correspondents were dressed as though they were going to a funeral; the news agency hacks were the ones who looked like gravediggers.

I bought a copy of *The New York Times* and went into the restaurant, where I drank three glasses of orange juice straight off, before turning my attention to the paper. Lang wasn't buried in the international section any longer. He was right up there on the front page:

WAR CRIMES COURT
TO RULE ON BRITISH
EX-PREMIER

~

ANNOUNCEMENT
DUE TODAY

~

Former Foreign Sec.
Alleges Lang OK'd
Use of Torture by CIA

Lang had issued a 'robust' statement, it said (I felt a thrill of pride). He was 'embattled', 'coping with one blow after another' – beginning with 'the accidental drowning of a close aide earlier in the year'. The affair was 'an embarrassment' for the British and American governments. 'A senior administration official insisted, however, that the White House remained loyal to a man who was formerly its closest ally. "He was there for us and we'll be there for him," the official added, speaking only after a guarantee of anonymity.'

But it was the final paragraph that really made me choke into my coffee:

The publication of Mr Lang's memoirs, which had been scheduled for June, has been brought forward to the end of April. John Maddox, chief executive of Rhinehart Publishing Inc., which is reported to have paid $10 million for the book, said that the finishing touches were now being put to the manuscript. "This is going to be a world publishing event," Mr Maddox told *The New York Times* in a telephone interview yesterday. "Adam Lang will be giving the first full inside scoop by a leader on the west's War on Terror."

I folded the newspaper, rose and walked with dignity through the lobby, carefully stepping around the camera bags, the two-foot zoom lenses and the hand-held mikes in their woolly grey windproof prophylactics. Between the members of the Fourth Estate, a cheerful, almost a party atmosphere prevailed, as might have existed among eighteenth-century gentlefolk off for a good day out at a hanging.

'The news room says the press conference in The Hague is now at ten o'clock Eastern,' someone shouted.

I passed unnoticed and went out on to the veranda where I put a call through to my agent. His assistant answered – Brad, or Brett, or Brat: I forget his name; Rick changed staff almost as quickly as he changed his wives.

I asked to speak to Mr Ricardelli.

'He's away from the office right now.'

'Where is he?'

'On a fishing trip.'

'*Fishing?*'

'He'll be calling in occasionally to check his messages.'

'That's nice. Where is he?'

'The Bouma National Heritage Rainforest Park.'

'Christ. Where's that?'

'It was a spur-of-the-moment thing—'

'Where is it?'

Brad, or Brett, or Brat hesitated.

'Fiji.'

*

The minivan took me up the hill out of Edgartown, past the book-shop and the little cinema and the whaling church. When we reached the edge of town we followed the signs left to West Tisbury rather than right to Vineyard Haven, which at least implied that I was being taken back to the house, rather than to be deported for breaching the Official Secrets Act. I sat behind the police driver, my suitcase on the seat beside me. He was one of the younger ones, dressed in their standard non-uniform uniform of grey zippered jacket and black tie. His eyes sought mine in the mirror and he observed that it was all a very bad business. I replied briefly that it was, indeed, a bad business, and then pointedly stared out of the window to avoid having to talk.

We were quickly into the flat countryside. A deserted cycle track ran beside the road. Beyond it stretched the drab forest. My frail body might be on Martha's Vineyard but my mind was in the South Pacific. I was thinking of Rick in Fiji, and all the elaborate and humil-iating ways I could fire him when he got back. The rational part of me knew I would never do it – why shouldn't he go fishing? – but the irrational was to the fore that morning. I suppose I was afraid, and fear distorts one's judgement even more than alcohol and exhaustion. I felt duped, abandoned, aggrieved.

'After I've dropped you off, sir,' said the policeman, undeterred by my silence, 'I've got to pick up Mr Kroll from the airport. You can always tell it's a bad business when the lawyers start turning up.' He broke off and leaned in close to the windscreen. 'Oh fuck, here we go again.'

Up ahead it looked as though there had been a traffic accident. The vivid blue lights of a couple of patrol cars flashed dramatically in the gloomy morning, illuminating the nearby trees like sheet lightning in a Wagner opera. As we came closer I could see a dozen or more cars and vans pulled up on either side of the road. People were standing around aimlessly, and I assumed, in that lazy way the brain sometimes assembles information, that they had been in a pile-up. But as the minivan slowed and indicated to turn left, the bystanders started grabbing things from beside the road and came running at us. 'Lang! Lang! Lang!' a woman shouted over a bullhorn. 'Liar! Liar! Liar!' Images of Lang in an orange jumpsuit, gripping prison bars with bloodied hands, danced in front of the windscreen: 'WANTED! WAR CRIMINAL! ADAM LANG!'

The Edgartown police had blocked the track down to the Rhinehart compound with traffic cones and quickly pulled them out of the way to let us through, but not before we'd come to a stop. Demonstrators surrounded us and a fusillade of thumps and kicks raked the side of the van. I glimpsed a brilliant arc of white light illuminating a figure — a man, cowled like a monk. He turned away from his interviewer to stare at us and I recognised him dimly from somewhere. But then he vanished behind a gauntlet of contorted faces, pounding hands, and dripping spit.

'They're always the really violent bastards,' said my driver, 'peace protesters.' He put his foot down, the rear tyres slithered uselessly, then bit, and we shot forwards into the silent woods.

*

Amelia met me in the passage. She stared contemptuously at my single piece of luggage as only a woman could.

'Is that really everything?'

'I travel light.'

'Light? I'd say *gossamer*.' She sighed. 'Right. Follow me.'

My suitcase was one of those ubiquitous pull-alongs, with an extendable handle and small wheels. It made an industrious hum on the stone floor as I trailed after her down the passage and around to the back of the house.

'I tried to call you several times last night,' she said, without turning round, 'but you didn't answer.'

Here it comes, I thought.

'I forgot to charge my mobile.'

'Oh? What about the phone in your room? I tried that as well.'

'I went out.'

'Until midnight?'

I winced behind her back. 'What did you want to tell me?'

'This.'

She stopped outside a door, opened it, and stood aside to let me go in. The room was in darkness, but the heavy curtains didn't quite meet in the middle, and there was just enough light for me to make out the shape of a double bed. It smelled of stale clothes and old ladies' soap. She crossed the floor and briskly pulled back the curtains.

'You'll be sleeping in here from now on.'

It was a plain room, with sliding glass doors that opened directly on to the lawn. Apart from the bed, there was a desk with an Anglepoise lamp, an armchair covered in something beige and thickly woven, and a wall-length built-in wardrobe with mirrored doors. I could also see into a white-tiled en suite bathroom. It was neat and functional; dismal.

I tried to make a joke of it. 'So this is where you put the granny, is it?'

'No, this is where we put Mike McAra.'

She slid back one of the doors to the closet, revealing a few jackets and shirts on hangers. 'I'm afraid we haven't had a chance to clear it yet, and his mother's in a home for the elderly so she doesn't have the space to store it. But as you say yourself, you travel light. And besides, it will only be for a few days, now that publication has been brought forward.'

I've never been particularly superstitious, but I do believe that certain places have an atmosphere, and from the moment I stepped into that room, I didn't like it. The thought of touching McAra's clothes filled me with something close to panic.

'I always make it a rule not to sleep in a client's house,' I said, attempting to keep my voice light and offhand. 'I often find, at the end of a working day, it's vital to get away.'

'But now you can have constant access to the manuscript. Isn't that what you want?' She gave me her smile, and for once there was genuine merriment in it. She had me exactly where she wanted me, literally and figuratively. 'Besides, you can't keep running the media gauntlet. Sooner or later they'll discover who you are, and then they'll start pestering you with questions. That would be horrid for you. This way you can work in peace.'

'Isn't there another room I could use?'

'There are only six bedrooms in the main house. Adam and

Ruth have one each. I have one. The girls share. The duty policemen have the use of one for the overnight shift. And the guest block is entirely taken over by Special Branch. Don't be squeamish: the sheets have been changed.' She consulted her elegant gold watch. 'Look,' she said, 'Sidney Kroll will be arriving any minute. We're due to get the ICC announcement in less than thirty minutes. Why don't you settle in here, and then come up and join us? Whatever's decided will affect you. You're practically one of us now.'

'I am?'

'Of course. You drafted the statement yesterday. That makes you an accomplice.'

After she'd gone I didn't unpack. I couldn't face it. Instead I sat gingerly on the end of the bed and stared out of the window at the wind-blasted lawn, the low scrub and the immense sky. A small blaze of brilliant white light was travelling quickly across the grey expanse, swelling as it came closer. A helicopter. It passed low over-head, shaking the heavy glass doors, and then, a minute or two later, reappeared, hovering a mile away, just above the horizon, like a sinister and portentous comet. It was a sign of how serious things had become, I thought, if some hard-pressed news manager on a trimmed budget was willing to hire a chopper in the hope of catching a fleeting shot of the former British prime minister. I pictured Kate, smugly watching the live coverage in her office in London, and was seized by a fantastic desire to run out and start twirling, like Julie Andrews at the start of *The Sound of Music*: Yes, darling, it's me! I'm here with the war criminal! I'm an *accomplice*!

I sat there for a while, until I heard the noise of the minivan pulling up outside the front of the house, followed by a commo-tion of voices in the hall, and then a small army of footsteps thudding up the wooden staircase: I reckoned that must be the sound of a thousand dollars an hour in legal fees on the hoof. I gave Kroll and his client a couple of minutes for handshakes, condolences and general expressions of confidence, then wearily left my dead man's room and went up to join them.

*

Kroll had flown in by private jet from Washington with two young paralegals, an exquisitely pretty Mexican woman he introduced as Encarnacion, and a black guy from New York called Josh. They sat on either side of him, their laptops open, on a sofa which placed their backs to the ocean view. Adam and Ruth Lang had the couch opposite, Amelia and I an armchair each. A cinema-sized flat screen TV next to the fireplace was showing the aerial shot of the house, as relayed live from the helicopter we could hear buzzing faintly outside. Occasionally the news station cut to the waiting journalists in the large, chandeliered room in The Hague where the press conference was due to be held. Each time I saw the empty podium with its ICC logo in tasteful UN blue – laurel boughs and scales of justice – I felt a little more sick with nerves. But Lang himself seemed cool. He was jacketless, wearing a white shirt and a dark blue tie. It was the sort of high-pressure occasion his metabolism was built for.

'So here's the score,' said Kroll, when we'd all taken our places. 'You're not being charged. You're not being arrested. None of this is going to amount to a hill of beans, I promise you. All that the prosecutor is asking for right now is permission to launch a formal investigation. Okay? So when we go out of here you walk tall, you look cool, and you have peace in your heart, because it's all going to be fine.'

'The President told me he thought they might not even let her investigate,' said Lang.

'I always hesitate to contradict the leader of the free world,' said Kroll, 'but the general feeling in Washington this morning is they'll have to. Our Madam Prosecutor is quite a savvy operator, it seems. The British government have consistently refused to hold an investigation of their own into Operation Tempest – that gives her a legal pretext to look into it herself. And by leaking her case just before going into the Pre-Trial Chamber, she's put a lot of pressure on those three judges to at least give her permission to move to the investigation stage. If they tell her to drop it, they know damn well that everyone will just say they're scared to go after a major power.'

'That's crude smear tactics,' said Ruth. She was wearing black leggings and another of her shapeless tops. Her shoeless feet were tucked beneath her on the sofa, her back was turned to her husband.

Lang shrugged. 'It's politics.'

'Exactly my point,' said Kroll. 'Treat it as a political problem, not a legal one.'

Ruth said, 'We need to get out our version of what happened. Refusing to comment isn't enough any more.'

I saw my chance. 'John Maddox—' I began.

'Yeah,' said Kroll, cutting me off, 'I talked to John, and he's right. We really have to go for this whole story now in the memoirs. It's the perfect platform for you to respond, Adam. They're very excited.'

'Fine,' said Lang.

'As soon as possible you need to sit down with our friend here' – I realised Kroll had forgotten my name – 'and go over the whole thing in detail. But you'll need to make sure it's all cleared with me first. The test we have to apply is to imagine what every word might sound like if it's read out while you're standing in the dock.'

'Why?' said Ruth. 'I thought you said none of this was going to amount to anything.'

'It won't,' said Kroll smoothly, 'especially if we're careful not to give them any extra ammunition.'

'This way we get to present it the way we want,' said Lang. 'And whenever I'm asked about it, I can refer people to the account in my memoirs. Who knows? It might even help sell a few copies.' He looked around. We all smiled. 'Okay,' he said, 'to come back to today. What am I actually likely to be investigated for?'

Kroll gestured to Encarnacion.

'Either crimes against humanity,' she said carefully, 'or war crimes.'

There was a silence. Odd the effect such words can have. Perhaps it was the fact that it was she who had said them: she looked so innocent. We stopped smiling.

'Unbelievable,' said Ruth eventually, 'to equate what Adam did or didn't do with the Nazis.'

'That's precisely why the United States doesn't recognise the court,' said Kroll. He wagged his finger. 'We warned you what would happen. An international war crimes tribunal sounds very noble in principle. But you go after all these genocidal maniacs in the Third World, and sooner or later the Third World is going to come right back after you, otherwise it looks like discrimination. They kill three thousand of us, we kill one of them, and suddenly we're all war criminals together. It's the worst kind of moral equivalence. Well, they can't drag America into their phoney court, so who can they drag? It's obvious: our closest ally – you. Like I say, it's not legal, it's political.'

'You should make exactly that point, Adam,' said Amelia, and she wrote something in her black and red notebook.

'Don't worry,' he said grimly, 'I will.'

'Go ahead, Connie,' said Kroll. 'Let's hear the rest of it.'

'The reason we can't be sure which route they'll choose at this stage is that torture is outlawed both by Article Seven of the 1998 Rome Statute, under the heading of crimes against humanity, and also under Article Eight, that is war crimes. Article Eight also categorises as a war crime' – she consulted her laptop – '"wilfully depriving a prisoner of war or other protected person of the rights of fair and regular trial" and "unlawful deportation or transfer or unlawful confinement". *Prima facie*, sir, you could be accused under either Seven or Eight.'

'But I haven't ordered that anyone should be tortured!' said Lang. His voice was incredulous, outraged. 'And I haven't deprived anyone of a fair trial, or illegally imprisoned them. Perhaps – *perhaps* – you could make that charge against the United States, but not Great Britain.'

'That's true, sir,' agreed Encarnacion. 'However, Article Twenty-Five, which deals with individual criminal responsibility, states that' – and once again her cool dark eyes flickered to the computer screen – '"a person shall be criminally responsible and liable for punishment if that person facilitates the commission of such a crime, aids, abets or otherwise assists in its commission or its attempted commission, including the means for its commission".'

Again, there was a silence, which was filled by the distant drone of the helicopter.

'That's rather sweeping,' said Lang quietly.

'It's absurd, is what it is,' cut in Kroll. 'It means that if the CIA fly a suspect for interrogation somewhere in a private plane, the owners of that private plane are technically guilty of facilitating a crime against humanity.'

'But legally——' began Lang.

'It's not legal, Adam,' said Kroll, with just a hint of exasperation, 'it's political.'

'No, Sid,' said Ruth. She was concentrating hard, frowning at the carpet and shaking her head emphatically. 'It's legal as well. The two are inseparable. That passage your young lady just read out makes it perfectly obvious why the judges will have to allow an investigation, because Richard Rycart has produced documentary evidence which suggests that Adam did in fact do all those things: aided, abetted and facilitated.' She looked up. 'That is legal jeopardy – isn't that what you call it? And that leads inescapably to political jeopardy. Because in the end it will all come down to public opinion, and we're unpopular enough back home as it is, without this.'

'Well, if it's any comfort, Adam's certainly not in jeopardy as long as he stays here, among his friends.'

The armoured glass vibrated slightly. The helicopter was coming in again for a closer look. Its searchlight filled the room. But on the television screen all that could be seen in the big picture window was a reflection of the sea.

'Wait a minute,' said Lang, raising his hand to his head and clutching his hair, as if he were glimpsing the situation for the first time. 'Are you saying that I can't leave the United States?'

'Josh,' said Kroll, nodding to his other assistant.

'Sir,' said Josh gravely, 'if I may, I would like just to read you the opening of Article Fifty-Eight, which covers arrest warrants.' He fixed his solemn gaze on Adam Lang. '"At any time after the initiation of an investigation, the Pre-Trial Chamber shall, on the application of the Prosecutor, issue a warrant of arrest of a person if, having examined the application and the evidence or other information submitted by the Prosecutor, it is satisfied that there are reasonable grounds to believe that the person has committed a crime within the jurisdiction of the Court, and the arrest of the person appears necessary to ensure the person's appearance at trial."'

'Jesus,' said Lang. 'What are "reasonable grounds"?'

'It won't happen,' said Kroll.

'You keep saying that,' said Ruth irritably, 'but it could.'

'It won't but it could,' said Kroll, spreading his hands. 'Those two statements aren't incompatible.' He permitted himself one of his private smiles and turned to Adam. 'Nevertheless, as your attorney, until this whole thing is resolved, I do strongly advise you not to travel to any country that recognises the jurisdiction of the International Criminal Court. All it would take is for two of these three judges to decide to grandstand to the human rights crowd, go ahead and issue a warrant, and you could be picked up.'

'But just about every country in the world recognises the ICC,' said Lang.

'America doesn't.'

'And who else?'

'Iraq,' said Josh, 'China, North Korea, Indonesia.'

We waited for him to go on; he didn't.

'And that's *it*?' said Lang. 'Everywhere else *does*?'

'No, sir. Israel doesn't. And some of the nastier regimes in Africa.'

Amelia said, 'I think something's happening.'

She aimed the remote at the television.

★

And so we watched as the Spanish Chief Prosecutor – all massive black hair and bright red lipstick, as glamorous as a film star in the silvery strobe of camera flashes – announced that she had that morning been granted the power to investigate the former British prime minister, Adam Peter Benet Lang, under Articles Seven and Eight of the 1998 Rome Statute of the International Criminal Court.

Or rather the others all watched her, while I watched Lang. '*AL — intense concentration,*' I jotted in my notebook, pretending to take down the words of the Chief Prosecutor but really studying my client for any insights I could use later. '*Reaches hand out for R: she doesn't respond. Glances at her. Lonely, puzzled. Withdraws hand. Looks back at screen. Shakes head. CP says "Was this just single incident or part of systematic pattern of criminal behaviour?" — AL flinches. Angry. CP: "Justice must be equal for rich & poor, powerful & weak alike." Shouts at screen, "What about the terrorists?"*'

I had never witnessed any of my authors at a real crisis in their lives before, and scrutinising Lang, I gradually began to realise that my favourite catch-all question — '*How did it feel?*' — was in truth a crude tool, vague to the point of uselessness. In the course of those few minutes, as the legal procedure was explained, a rapid succession of emotions swept across Lang's craggy face, as fleeting as cloud shadows passing over a hillside in spring — shock, fury, hurt, defiance, dismay, shame . . . How were these to be disentangled? And if he didn't know precisely what he felt now, even as he was feeling it, how could he be expected to know it in ten years' time? Even his reaction at this moment I would have to manufacture for him. I would have to simplify it to make it plausible. I would have to draw on my own imagination. In a sense, I would have to lie.

The Chief Prosecutor finished her statement, briefly answered a couple of shouted questions, then left the podium. Halfway out of the room, she stopped to pose for the cameras again, and there was another blizzard of phosphorus as she turned to give the world the benefit of her magnificent aquiline profile, and then she was gone. The screen reverted to the aerial shot of Rhinehart's house, in its setting of woods, pond and ocean, as the world waited for Lang to appear.

Amelia dipped the sound. Downstairs, the phones started ringing.

'Well,' said Kroll, breaking the silence, 'there was nothing in *that* we weren't expecting.'

'Yes,' said Ruth. '*Well done.*'

Kroll pretended not to notice.

'We should get you to Washington, Adam, right away. My plane's waiting at the airport.'

Lang was still staring at the screen. 'When Marty said I could use his vacation house, I never realised how cut off this place was. We should never have come. Now we look as though we're hiding.'

'Exactly my feeling. You can't just hole up here, at least not today. I've made some calls. I can get you in to see the House Majority Leader at lunchtime and we can have a photo op with the Secretary of State this afternoon.'

Lang finally dragged his eyes away from the television. 'I don't know about doing all that. It could look as though I'm panicking.'

'No it won't. I've already spoken to them. They send their best wishes: they want to do everything they can to help. They'll both say the meetings were fixed weeks ago, to discuss the Adam Lang Foundation.'

'But that sounds false, don't you think?' Lang frowned. 'What are we supposed to be discussing?'

'Who cares? Aids. Poverty. Climate change. Mideast peace. Africa. Whatever you like. The point is to say: it's business as usual, I have my agenda, it's the big stuff, and I'm not going to be diverted from it by these clowns pretending to be judges in The Hague.'

Amelia said, 'What about security?'

'The Secret Service will take care of it. We'll fill in the blanks in the schedule as we go along. The whole town will turn out for you. I'm waiting to hear back from the Vice President, but that would be a private meeting.'

'And the media?' said Lang. 'We'll need to respond soon.'

'On the way to the airport, we'll pull over and say a few words. I can make a statement, if you like. All you have to do is stand next to me.'

'No,' said Lang firmly. 'No. Absolutely not. That really will make me look guilty. I'll have to talk to them myself. Ruth, what do you think about going to Washington?'

'I think it's a terrible idea. I'm sorry, Sid, I know you're working hard for us, but we've got to consider how this will play in Britain. If Adam goes to Washington he'll look like America's whipping boy, running crying home to Daddy.'

'So what would you do?'

'Fly back to London.' Kroll began to object but Ruth talked over him. 'The British people may not like him much at the moment, but if there's one thing they hate more than Adam, it's interfering foreigners telling them what to do. The government will have to support him.'

Amelia said, 'The British government are going to cooperate fully with the investigation.'

'Oh really?' said Ruth, in a voice as sweet as cyanide. 'And what makes you think that?'

'I'm not thinking it, Ruth, I'm reading it. It's on the television. Look.'

We looked. The headline was running across the bottom of the screen. 'BREAKING NEWS: BRITISH GOVT "WILL COOPERATE FULLY" WITH WAR CRIMES PROBE.'

'How dare they?' cried Ruth. 'After all we've done for them!'

Josh said, 'With respect, ma'am, as signatories to the ICC, the British government have no choice. They're obliged under international law to "cooperate fully". Those are the precise words of Article Eighty-Six.'

'And what if the ICC eventually decides to arrest me?' asked Lang quietly. 'Do the British government "cooperate fully" with that as well?'

Josh had already found the relevant place on his laptop. 'That's covered by Article Fifty-Nine, sir. "A State Party which has received a request for a provisional arrest or for arrest and surrender shall immediately take steps to arrest the person in question."'

'Well, I think that settles it,' said Lang. 'Washington it is.'

Ruth folded her arms. The gesture reminded me of Kate: a warning of storms to come. 'I still say it will look bad,' she said.

'Not as bad as being led away in handcuffs from Heathrow.'

'At least it would show you had some guts.'

'Then why the hell don't you just fly back without me?' snapped Lang. Like his outburst of the previous afternoon, it wasn't so much the display of temper that was startling as the way it suddenly erupted. 'If the British government want to hand me over to this kangaroo court, then fuck them! I'll go where people want me. Amelia, tell the boys we're leaving in five minutes. Get one of the girls to pack me an overnight bag. And you'd better pack one for yourself.'

'Oh, but why don't you share a suitcase?' said Ruth. 'It will be so much more convenient.'

At that, the very air seemed to congeal. Even Kroll's little smile froze at the edges. Amelia hesitated, then nervously smoothed down her skirt, picked up her notebook, and rose in a hiss of silk. As she walked across the room towards the stairs, she kept her gaze fixed straight ahead. Her throat was flushed a tasteful pink, her lips compressed. Ruth waited until she had gone, then slowly uncoiled her feet from beneath her and carefully pulled on her flat, wooden-soled shoes. She, too, left without a word. Thirty seconds later, a door slammed downstairs.

Lang flinched and sighed. He got up and collected his jacket from the back of a chair and shrugged it on. That was the signal for us all to move. The paralegals snapped their laptops shut. Kroll stood and stretched, spreading his fingers wide: he reminded me of a cat, arching its back and briefly unsheathing its claws. I put away my notebook.

'I'll see you tomorrow,' said Lang, offering me his hand. 'Make yourself comfortable. I'm sorry to abandon you. At least all this coverage should improve sales.'

'That's true,' I said. I cast around for something to say that would lighten the atmosphere. 'Perhaps Rhinehart's publicity department have arranged the whole thing.'

'Well, tell them to stop it, will you?' He smiled, but his eyes looked bruised and puffy.

'What are you going to say to the media?' asked Kroll, putting his arm across Lang's shoulders.

'I don't know. Let's talk about it in the car.'

As Lang turned to leave, Kroll gave me a wink. 'Happy ghosting,' he said.

Nine

What if they lie to you? 'Lie' is probably too strong a word. Most of us tend to embroider our memories to suit the picture of ourselves that we would like the world to see.

Ghostwriting

I could have gone down to see them off. Instead I watched them leave on television. I always say you can't beat sitting in front of a TV screen if you're after that authentic, first-hand experience. For example, it's curious how helicopter news shots impart to even the most innocent activity the dangerous whiff of criminality. When Jeff the chauffeur brought the armoured Jaguar round to the front of the house and left the engine running, it looked for all the world as if he were organising a Mafia getaway just before the cops arrived. In the cold New England air, the big car seemed to float on a sea of exhaust fumes.

I had the same disorientating feeling that I'd experienced the previous day, when Lang's statement started pinging back at me from the ether. On the television I could see one of the Special Branch men opening the rear passenger door, and standing there, holding it open, while down in the corridor I could hear Lang and the others preparing to leave. 'All right, people?' Kroll's voice floated up the staircase. 'Is everybody ready? Okay. Remember:

happy, happy faces. Here we go.' The front door opened, and moments later on the screen I glimpsed the top of the ex-prime minister's head as he took the few hurried steps to the car. He ducked out of sight, just as his attorney scuttled after him, round to the Jaguar's other side. At the bottom of the picture it said 'ADAM LANG LEAVES MARTHA'S VINEYARD HOUSE'. They know everything, I thought, these satellite boys, but they've never heard of tautology.

Behind them, the entourage debouched in rapid single file from the house and headed for the minivan. Amelia was in the lead, her hand clutched to her immaculate blonde hair to protect it against the rotors' down-draught; then came the secretaries, followed by the paralegals, and finally a couple of bodyguards.

The long, dark shapes of the cars, their headlights gleaming, pulled out of the compound and set off through the ashy expanse of scrub oak towards the West Tisbury highway. The helicopter tracked them, whirling away the few winter leaves and flattening the sparse grass. Gradually, for the first time that morning, as the noise of its rotors faded, something like peace returned to the house. It was as if the eye of a great electrical storm had finally moved on. I wondered where Ruth was, and whether she was also watching the coverage. I got up and stood at the top of the stairs and listened for a while, but all was quiet, and by the time I returned to the television, the coverage had shifted from aerial to ground level, and Lang's limousine was pulling out of the woods.

A lot more police had arrived at the end of the track, courtesy of the Commonwealth of Massachusetts, and a line of them was keeping the demonstrators safely corralled on the opposite side of the highway. For a moment the Jaguar appeared to be accelerating toward the airport, but then its brake lights glowed and it stopped. The minivan swerved to a halt behind it. And suddenly, there was Lang, coatless, seemingly as oblivious to the cold as he was to the chanting crowd, striding over to the cameras, trailed by three Special Branch men. I hunted around for the remote control in the chair where Amelia had been sitting – her scent still lingered on the leather – pointed it at the screen, and pumped up the volume.

'I apologise for keeping you waiting so long in the cold,' Lang began. 'I just wanted to say a few words in response to the news from The Hague.' He paused and glanced at the ground. He often did that. Was it genuine, or merely contrived, to give an impression of spontaneity? With him, one never knew. The chant of 'Lang! Lang! Lang! Liar! Liar! Liar!' was clearly audible in the background.

'These are strange times,' he said, and hesitated again, 'strange times' – and now at last he looked up – 'when those who have always stood for freedom, peace and justice are accused of being criminals, while those who openly incite hatred, glorify slaughter and seek the destruction of democracy are treated by the law as if *they* are victims.'

'Liar! Liar! Liar!'

'As I said in my statement yesterday, I have always been a strong supporter of the International Criminal Court. I believe in its work. I believe in the integrity of its judges. And that is why I do not fear this investigation. Because I know in my heart I have done nothing wrong.'

He glanced across at the demonstrators. For the first time he appeared to notice the waving placards: his face, the prison bars, the orange jumpsuit, the bloodied hands. The line of his mouth set firm.

'I refuse to be intimidated,' he said, with an upward tilt of his chin. 'I refuse to be made a scapegoat. I refuse to be distracted from my work combating Aids, poverty and global warming. For that reason, I propose to travel now to Washington to carry on my schedule as planned. To everyone watching in the United Kingdom and throughout the world, let me make one thing perfectly clear. As long as I have breath in my body, I shall fight terrorism wherever it has to be fought, whether it be on the battlefield, or – if necessary – in the courts. Thank you.'

Ignoring the shouted questions – 'When are you going back to Britain, Mr Lang?' 'Do you support torture, Mr Lang?' – he turned and strode away, the muscles of his broad shoulders flexing beneath his handmade suit, his trio of bodyguards fanned out behind him. A week ago I would have been impressed, as I had been by his speech in New York after the London suicide bomb, but now I was surprised at how unmoved I felt. It was like watching some great actor in the last phase of his career, emotionally overspent, with nothing left to draw on but technique.

I waited until he was safely back in his gas- and bomb-proof cocoon, and then I switched off the television.

*

With Lang and the others gone, the house seemed not merely empty but desolate, bereft of purpose. I came down the stairs and passed the lighted showcases of tribal erotica. The chair by the front door where one of the bodyguards always sat was vacant. I reversed my steps and followed the corridor round to the secretaries' office. The small room, normally clinically neat, looked as if it had been abandoned in a panic, like the cipher room of a foreign embassy in a surrendering city. A profusion of papers, computer disks and old editions of *Hansard* and the *Congressional Record* was strewn across the desk. It occurred to me then that I had no copy of Lang's manuscript to work on, but when I tried to open the filing cabinet, it was locked. Beside it, a basket full of waste from the paper-shredder overflowed.

I looked into the kitchen. An array of butcher's knives was laid out on a chopping block; there was fresh blood on some of the blades. I called a hesitant 'Hello?' and stuck my head round the door of the pantry, but the housekeeper wasn't there.

I had no idea which was my room, and I therefore had no option but to work my way along the corridor, trying one door after another. The first was locked. The second was open, the room beyond it exuding a rich, sweet odour of heavy aftershave; a track-suit was thrown across the bed: it was obviously the bedroom used by Special Branch during the night shift. The third door was locked and I was about to try the fourth when I heard the sound of a woman weeping. I could tell it was Ruth: even her sobs had a combative quality. *'There are only six bedrooms in the main house,'* Amelia had said. *'Adam and Ruth have one each.'* What a set-up this was, I thought, as I crept away: the ex-prime minister and his wife sleeping in separate rooms, with his mistress just along the corridor. It was almost French.

Gingerly, I tried the handle of the next room. This one wasn't locked, and the aroma of worn clothes and lavender soap, even more than the sight of my old suitcase, established it immediately as McAra's former berth. I went in and closed the door very softly. The big mirrored closet took up the whole of the wall dividing my room from Ruth's, and when I slid back the glass door a fraction, I could just make out her muffled wailing. The door scraped on its runner, and I guess she must have heard, for all at once the crying stopped, and I imagined her startled, raising her head from her damp pillow and staring at the wall. I drew away. On the bed I noticed that someone had put a box of A4 paper, stuffed so full the top didn't fully fit. A yellow Post-it note said, 'Good luck! Amelia.' I sat on the counterpane and lifted the lid. 'MEMOIRS', proclaimed the title page, 'by Adam Lang'. So she hadn't forgotten me after all, despite the exquisitely embarrassing circumstances of her departure. You could say what you liked about Mrs Bly, but the woman was a pro.

I recognised I was now at a decisive point. Either I continued to hang around at the fringes of this floundering project, pathetically hoping that at some point someone would help me. Or — and I felt my spine straightening as I contemplated the alternative — *or* I could seize control of it myself, try to knock these six hundred and twenty-one ineffable pages into some kind of publishable shape, take my two hundred and fifty grand, and head off to lie on a beach somewhere for a month until I had forgotten all about the Langs.

Put in those terms, it wasn't a choice. I steeled myself to ignore both McAra's lingering traces in the room, and Ruth's more corporeal presence next door. I took the manuscript from its box and placed it on the table next to the window, opened my shoulder bag and took out my laptop and the transcripts from yesterday's interviews. There wasn't a lot of room to work, but that didn't bother me. Of all human activities, writing is the one for which it is easiest to find excuses not to begin — the desk's too big, the desk's too small, there's too much noise, there's too much quiet, it's too hot, too cold, too early, too late. I had learned over the years to ignore them all, and simply to start. I plugged in my laptop, switched on the Anglepoise, and contemplated the blank screen and its pulsing cursor.

A book unwritten is a delightful universe of infinite possibilities. Set down one word, however, and immediately it becomes earthbound. Set down one sentence and it's halfway to being just like every other bloody book that's ever been written. But the best must never be allowed to drive out the good. In the absence of genius there is always craftsmanship. One can at least try to write something which will arrest the reader's attention — which will encourage them, after reading the first paragraph, to take a look at the second, and then the third. I picked up McAra's manuscript to remind myself of how not to begin a ten-million-dollar autobiography:

Chapter One

Early Years

Langs are Scottish folk originally, and proud of it. Our name is a derivation of 'long', the Old English word for tall, and it is from north of the border that my forefathers hail. It was in the sixteenth century that the first of the Langs . . .

God help us! I ran my pen through it, and then zigzagged a thick blue line through all the succeeding paragraphs of Lang ancestral history. If you want a family tree, go to a garden centre — that's what I advise my clients. Nobody else is interested. Maddox's instruction was to begin the book with the war crimes allegations, which was fine by me, although it could only serve as a kind of long prologue. At some point, the memoir proper would have to begin, and for this I wanted to find a fresh and original note — something which would make Lang sound like a normal human being. The fact that he wasn't a normal human being was neither here nor there.

From Ruth Lang's room came the sound of footsteps, and then her door opened and closed. I thought at first she might be coming to investigate who was moving around next door, but instead I heard her walking away. I put down McAra's manuscript and turned my attention to the interview transcripts. I knew what I wanted. It was there in our first session:

I remember it was a Sunday afternoon. Raining. I was still in bed. And someone starts knocking on the door . . .

If I tidied up the grammar, the account of how Ruth had canvassed Lang for the local elections and so drawn him into politics would make a perfect opening. Yet McAra, with his characteristic tone-deafness for anything of human interest, had failed even to mention it. I rested my fingers on the keys of my laptop, then started to type:

Chapter One

Early Years

I became a politician out of love. Not love for any particular party or ideology, but love for a woman who came knocking on my door one wet Sunday afternoon . . .

You may object that this was corny, but don't forget that (a) corn sells by the ton, (b) that I only had two weeks to rework an entire manuscript, and (c) that it sure as hell was a lot better than starting with the derivation of the name Lang. I was soon rattling away as fast as my two-finger typing would permit me:

She was wringing wet from the pouring rain, but she didn't seem to notice.
Instead, she launched into a passionate speech about the local elections.
Until that point, I'm ashamed to say, I didn't even know there were any
local elections, but I had the good sense to pretend that I did . . .

I looked up. Through the window I could see Ruth marching determinedly across the dunes, into the wind, on yet another of her brooding, solitary walks, with only her trailing bodyguard for company. I watched till she was out of sight, then went back to my work.

*

I carried on for a couple of hours, until about one o'clock or so, and then I heard a very light tapping of fingertips on wood. It made me jump.

'Mister?' came a timid female voice. 'Sir? You want lunch?'

I opened the door to find Dep, the Vietnamese housekeeper, in her black silk uniform. She was about fifty, as tiny as a bird. I felt that if I sneezed I would have blown her from one end of the house to the other.

'That would be very nice. Thanks.'

'Here, or in kitchen?'

'The kitchen would be great.'

After she'd shuffled away on her slippered feet, I turned to face my room. I knew I couldn't put it off any longer. Treat it like writing, I said to myself: go for it. I unzipped my suitcase and laid it on the bed. Then, taking a deep breath, I slid open the doors to the closet and began removing McAra's clothes from their hangers, piling them over my arm – cheap shirts, off-the-peg jackets, chain-store trousers, and the sort of ties you buy at the airport: nothing handmade in *your* wardrobe, was there, Mike? He had been a big fellow, I realised, as I felt all those supersized collars and great hooped waistbands: much larger than I am. And, of course, it was exactly as I'd dreaded: the feel of the unfamiliar fabric, even the clatter of the metal hangers on their chrome-plated rail, was enough to breach the barrier of a quarter of a century's careful defences and plunge me straight back into my parents' bedroom, which I'd steeled myself to clear three months after my mother's funeral.

It's the possessions of the dead that always get to me. Is there anything sadder than the clutter they leave behind? Who says that all that's left of us is love? All that was left of McAra was *stuff*. I heaped it over the armchair, then reached up to the shelf above the clothes rail to pull down his suitcase. I'd expected it would be empty, but as I took a hold of the handle, something slid around inside. Ah, I thought. At last. The secret document.

The case was huge and ugly, made of moulded red plastic, too bulky for me to manage easily, and it hit the floor with a thud. It seemed to reverberate through the quiet house. I waited a moment, then gently laid the suitcase flat on the floor, knelt in front of it and pressed the catches. They flew up with a loud and simultaneous snap.

It was the kind of luggage that hasn't been made for more than a decade, except perhaps in the less fashionable parts of Albania. Inside it had a hideously patterned shiny plastic lining, from which dangled frilly elastic bands. The contents consisted of a single large padded envelope addressed to M. McAra Esq., care of a post office box number in Vineyard Haven. A label on the back showed that it had come from The Adam Lang Archive Centre in Cambridge,

England. I opened it and pulled out a handful of photographs and photocopies, together with a compliments slip from Dr Julia Crawford-Jones, PhD, Director.

One of the photographs I recognised at once: Lang in his chicken outfit, from the Footlights Revue in the early seventies. There were a dozen other production stills showing the whole cast; a set of photographs of Lang punting, wearing a straw boater and a striped blazer; and three or four of him at a riverside picnic, apparently taken on the same day as the punting. The photocopies were of various Footlights programmes and theatre reviews from Cambridge, plus a lot of local newspaper reports of the Greater London Council elections of May 1977, and Lang's original party membership card. It was only when I saw the date on the card that I rocked back on my heels. It was from 1975.

I started to re-examine the package with more care after that, beginning with the election stories. At first glance I thought they'd come from the London *Evening Standard*, but I saw now they were from the news sheet of a political party – Lang's party – and that he was actually pictured in a group as an election volunteer. It was hard to make him out in the poorly reproduced photocopy. His hair was long. His clothes were shabby. But that was him, all right, one of a team knocking on doors in a council estate. 'Canvasser: A. Lang.'

I was more irritated than anything. It certainly didn't strike me as sinister. Everybody tends to heighten their own reality. We start with a private fantasy about our lives and perhaps one day, for fun, we turn it into an anecdote. No harm is done. Over the years, the anecdote is repeated so regularly it becomes accepted as a fact. Quite soon, to contradict this fact would be embarrassing. In time, we probably come to believe it was true all along. And by these slow accretions of myth, like a coral reef, the historical record takes shape.

I could see how it would have suited Lang to pretend he'd only gone into politics because he'd fancied a girl. It flattered him, by making him look less ambitious, and it flattered her, by making her look more influential than she probably was. Audiences liked it. Everyone was happy. But now the question arose: what was I supposed to do?

It's not an uncommon dilemma in the ghosting business, and the etiquette is simple: you draw the discrepancy to the author's attention, and leave it up to them to decide how to resolve it. The collaborator's responsibility is not to insist on the absolute truth: if it were, our end of the publishing industry would collapse under the dead weight of reality. Just as the beautician doesn't tell her client that she has a face like a sack of toads, so the ghost doesn't confront the autobiographer with the fact that half their treasured reminiscences are false. Don't dictate, facilitate: that is our motto. Obviously, McAra had failed to observe this sacred rule. He must have had his suspicions about what he was being told, ordered up a parcel of research from the archives, and then removed the ex-prime minister's most polished anecdote from his memoirs. What an amateur! I could imagine how well that must have been received. No doubt it helped explain why relations had become so strained.

I turned my attention back to the Cambridge material. There was a strange kind of innocence about these faded *jeunesse dorée*, stranded in that lost but happy valley that lay somewhere between the twin cultural peaks of hippydom and punk. Spiritually, they looked far closer to the sixties than the seventies. The girls had long lacy dresses in floral print, with plunging necklines, and big straw hats to keep off the sun. The men's hair was as long as the women's. In the only colour picture, Lang was holding a bottle of champagne in one hand and what looked very much like a joint in the other; a girl seemed to be feeding him strawberries, while in the background a bare-chested man gave a thumbs-up sign.

The biggest of the cast photographs showed eight young people grouped together, under a spotlight, their arms outstretched, as if they had just finished some show-stopping song-and-dance routine in a cabaret. Lang was on the far right-hand side, wearing his striped blazer, a bow tie and a straw boater. There were two girls in leotards, fishnet tights and high heels: one with short blonde hair, the other dark frizzy curls, possibly a redhead (it was impossible to tell from the monochrome photo): both pretty. Two of the men apart from Lang I recognised: one was now a famous comedian, the other an actor. A third man looked older than the others: a postgraduate researcher, perhaps. Everyone was wearing gloves.

Glued to the back was a typed slip listing the names of the performers, along with their colleges: G. W. Syme (Caius), W. K. Innes (Pembroke), A. Parke (Newnham), P. Emmett (St John's), A. D. Martin (King's), E. D. Vaux (Christ's), H. C. Martineau (Girton), A. P. Lang (Jesus).

There was a copyright stamp – *Cambridge Evening News* – in the bottom left-hand corner, and scrawled diagonally next to it in blue biro was a telephone number, prefixed by the British international dialling code. No doubt McAra, indefatigable fact-hound that he was, had hunted down one of the cast, and I wondered which of them it was, and if he or she could remember the events depicted in the photographs. Purely on a whim, I took out my mobile and dialled the number.

Instead of the familiar two-beat British ringing tone, I heard the single sustained note of the American. I let it ring for a long while. Just as I was about to give up, a man answered, cautiously.

'Richard Rycart.'

The voice, with its slight colonial twang — *'Richard Roicart'* — was unmistakably that of the former Foreign Secretary. He sounded suspicious. 'Who is this?' he asked.

I hung up at once. In fact, I was so alarmed, I actually threw the phone on to the bed. It lay there for about thirty seconds, and then started to ring. I darted over and grabbed it — the incoming number was listed as 'withheld' — and quickly switched it off. For half a minute I was too stunned to move.

I told myself not to rush to any conclusions. I didn't know for certain that McAra had written down the number, or even rung it. I checked the package to see when it had been dispatched. It had left the United Kingdom on January the third — nine days before McAra died.

It suddenly seemed vitally important for me to get every remaining trace of my predecessor out of that room. Hurriedly, I stripped the last of his clothes from the closet, upending the drawers of socks and underpants into his suitcase (I remember he wore thick knee-length socks and baggy white Y-fronts: this boy was old-fashioned all the way through). There were no personal papers that I could find — no diary or address book, letters or even books — and I presumed they must have been taken away by the police imme-diately after his death. From the bathroom I removed his blue plastic disposable razor, toothbrush, comb and the rest of it, and then the job was done: all tangible effects of Michael McAra, former aide to the Right Honourable Adam Lang, were crammed into a suitcase and ready to be dumped. I dragged it out into the corridor and around to the solarium. It could stay there until the summer, for all I cared: just as long as I didn't have to see it again. It took me a moment to recover my breath.

And yet, even as I headed back towards his — my — our —

room, I could sense his presence, loping along clumsily at my heels. 'Fuck off, McAra,' I muttered to myself. 'Just fuck off and leave me alone to finish this book and get out of here.' I stuffed the photographs and photocopies back into their original envelope and looked around for somewhere to hide it, then I stopped and asked myself why I should want to conceal it. It wasn't exactly top secret. It had nothing to do with war crimes. It was just a young man, a student actor, more than thirty years earlier, on a sunlit river bank, drinking champagne with his friends. There could be any number of reasons why Rycart's number was on the back of that photo. But still, somehow, it demanded to be hidden, and in the absence of any other bright idea, I'm ashamed to say I resorted to the cliché of lifting the mattress and stuffing it underneath.

'Lunch, sir,' called Dep softly from the corridor. I wheeled round. I wasn't sure if she'd seen me, but then I wasn't sure it mattered: compared to what else she must have witnessed in the house over the past few weeks, my own strange behaviour would surely have seemed small beer.

I followed her into the kitchen. 'Is Mrs Lang around?' I said.

'No, sir. She go Vineyard Haven. Shopping.'

She had fixed me a club sandwich. I sat on a tall stool at the breakfast bar and compelled myself to eat it, while she wrapped things in tin foil and put them back in one of Rhinehart's array of six stainless-steel fridges. I considered what I should do. Normally I would have forced myself back to my desk and continued writing all afternoon. But for just about the first time in my career as a ghost, I was blocked. I'd wasted half the morning composing a charmingly intimate reminiscence of an event which hadn't happened – *couldn't* have happened, because Ruth Lang hadn't arrived to start her career in London until 1976, by which time her future husband had already been a party member for a year.

Even the thought of tackling the Cambridge section, which once I'd regarded as words in the bank, now led me to confront a blank wall. Who was he, this happy-go-lucky, girl-chasing, politically allergic would-be actor? What suddenly turned him into a party activist, trailing around council estates, if it wasn't meeting Ruth? It made no sense to me. That was when I realised I had a fundamental problem with our former prime minister. He was not a psychologically credible character. In the flesh, or on the screen, playing the part of a statesman, he seemed to have a strong personality. But somehow, when one sat down to think about him, he vanished. This made it almost impossible for me to do my job: unlike any number of show-business and sporting weirdos I had worked with in the past, when it came to Lang, I simply couldn't make him up.

I took out my cell phone and considered calling Rycart. But the more I reflected on how the conversation might go, the more reluctant I became to initiate it. What exactly was I supposed to say? 'Oh, hello, you don't know me, but I've replaced Mike McAra as Adam Lang's ghost. I believe he may have spoken to you a day or two before he was washed up dead on a beach.' I put the phone back in my pocket, and suddenly I couldn't rid my mind of the image of McAra's heavy body rolling back and forth in the surf. Did he hit rocks, or was he run straight up on to soft sand? What was the name of the place where he'd been found? Rick had mentioned it when we had lunch at his club in London. Lambert something-or-other.

'Excuse me, Dep,' I said to the housekeeper.

She straightened from the fridge. She had such a sweetly sympathetic face.

'Sir?'

'Do you happen to know if there's a map of the island I could
borrow?'

Ten

It is perfectly possible to write a book for someone, having done nothing but listen to their words; but extra research often helps to provide more material and descriptive ideas.

Ghostwriting

It looked to be about ten miles away, on the north-western shore of the Vineyard. Lambert's Cove: that was it.

There was something beguiling about the names of the locations all around it: Blackwater Brook, Uncle Seth's Pond, Indian Hill, Old Herring Creek Road. It was like a map from a children's adventure story, and in a strange way that was how I conceived of my plan: as a kind of amusing excursion. Dep suggested I borrow a bicycle – oh yes, Mr Rhinehart, he keep many, many bicycles, for use of guests – and something about the idea of that appealed to me as well, even though I hadn't ridden a bike for years, and even though I knew, at some deeper level, no good would come of it. More than three weeks had passed since the corpse had been recovered. What would there be to see? But curiosity is a powerful human impulse – some distance below sex and greed, I grant you, but far ahead of altruism – and I was simply curious.

The biggest deterrent was the weather. The receptionist at the hotel in Edgartown had warned me that the forecast was for a

storm, and although it still hadn't broken yet, the sky was beginning to sag with the weight of it, like a soft grey sack waiting to
split apart. But the appeal of getting out of the house for a while
was overpowering and I couldn't face going back to McAra's old
room and sitting in front of my computer. I took Lang's windproof
jacket from its peg in the cloakroom, and followed Duc the gardener
along the front of the house to the weathered wooden cubes that
served as staff accommodation and outbuildings.

'You must have to work hard here,' I said, 'to keep it looking
so good.'

Duc kept his eyes on the ground.

'Soil bad. Wind bad. Rain bad. Salt bad. Shit.'

After that, there didn't seem much else to say on the horti-
cultural front, so I kept quiet. We passed the first two cubes. He
stopped in front of the third and unlocked the big double doors.
He dragged back one of them and we went inside. There must have
been a dozen bicycles parked in two racks, but my gaze went straight
to the tan-coloured Ford Escape SUV which took up the other half
of the garage. I had heard so much about it, and had imagined it
so often when I was coming over on the ferry, that it was quite a
shock to encounter it unexpectedly.

Duc saw me looking at it. 'You want to borrow?' he asked.

'No, no,' I said quickly. First the dead man's job, then his bed,
then a ride in his car – who could tell where it might end? 'A bike
will be fine. It will do me good.'

The gardener wore an expression of deep scepticism as he
watched me go, wobbling off uncertainly on one of Rhinehart's
expensive mountain bikes. He obviously thought I was mad, and
perhaps I *was* mad – island madness, don't they call it? I raised my
hand to the Special Branch man in his little wooden sentry's hut,

half hidden in the trees, and that was very nearly a painful mistake, as it made me swerve towards the undergrowth. But then I somehow steered the machine back into the centre of the track, and once I got the hang of the gears (the last bike I'd owned only had three, and two of those didn't work) I found I was moving fairly rapidly over the hard, compacted sand.

It was eerily quiet in that forest, as if there had been some great volcanic catastrophe that had bleached the vegetation white and brittle and poisoned the wild animals. Occasionally, in the distance, a wood pigeon emitted one of its hollow, klaxon cries, but that served more to emphasise the silence than to break it. I pedalled on up the slight gradient until I reached the T-junction where the track joined the highway.

The anti-Lang demonstration had dwindled to just one man on the opposite side of the road. He had obviously been busy over the past few hours, erecting some kind of installation – low wooden boards on which had been mounted hundreds of terrible images, torn from magazines and newspapers, of burned children, tortured corpses, beheaded hostages and bomb-flattened neighbourhoods. Interspersed among this collage of death were long lists of names, some handwritten poems and letters. It was all protected against the elements by sheets of polythene. A banner ran across the top, as over a stall at a church jumble sale: 'FOR AS IN ADAM ALL DIE, EVEN SO IN CHRIST SHALL ALL BE MADE ALIVE'. Beneath it was a flimsy shelter made of wooden struts and more polythene, containing what looked like a card table and a folding chair. Sitting patiently at the table was the man whom I'd briefly glimpsed that morning and couldn't remember. But I recognised him now all right. He was the military type from the hotel bar who'd called me a cunt.

I came to an uncertain halt and checked left and right for traffic, conscious all the while of him staring at me from only twenty feet away. And he must have recognised me, because I saw to my horror that he had got to his feet. 'Just one moment!' he shouted, in that peculiar clipped voice, but I was so anxious not to become embroiled in his madness that, even though there was a car coming, I teetered out into the road and began pedalling away from him, standing up to try to get up some speed. The car hit its horn. There was a blur of light and noise, and I felt the wind of it as it passed, but when I looked back the protester had given up his pursuit, and was standing in the centre of the road, staring after me, arms akimbo.

After that, I cycled hard, conscious I would soon start to lose the light. The air in my face was cold and damp, but the pumping of my legs kept me warm enough. I passed the entrance to the airport, and followed the perimeter of the state forest, its fire lanes stretching wide and high through the trees like the shadowy aisles of cathedrals. I couldn't imagine McAra doing this – he didn't look the cycling type – and I wondered again what I thought I would achieve, apart from getting drenched. I toiled on past the white clapboard houses and the neat New England fields, and it didn't take much effort to visualise it still peopled by women in stern black bonnets, and by men who regarded Sunday as the day to put on a suit rather than take one off.

Just out of West Tisbury I stopped by Scotchman's Lane to check directions. The sky was really threatening now, and a wind was getting up. I almost lost the map. In fact, I almost turned back. But I'd come so far, it seemed stupid to give up now, so I eased myself back on to the thin, hard saddle and set off again. About two miles later the road forked and I parted from the main highway, turning left towards the sea. The track down to the cove was similar to the approach to the Rhinehart place – scrub oak, ponds, dunes – the only difference being that there were more houses here. Mostly, they were vacation homes, shuttered up for the winter, but a couple of chimneys fluttered thin streamers of brown smoke, and from one window I heard a radio playing classical music. A cello concerto. That was when it started to rain at last – hard, cold pellets of moisture, almost hail, that exploded on my hands and face and carried the smell of the sea in them. One moment they were plopping sporadically in the pond and rattling in the trees around me, and the next it was as if some great aerial dam had broken and the rain started to sweep down in torrents. Now I remembered why I disliked cycling: bicycles don't have roofs, they don't have windscreens and they don't have heaters.

The spindly, leafless scrub oaks offered no hope of shelter, but it was impossible to carry on cycling – I couldn't see where I was going – so I dismounted and pushed my bike, until I came to a low picket fence. I tried to prop the bike against it, but the machine fell over with a clatter, its back wheel spinning. I didn't bother to pick it up but ran up the cinder path, past a flagpole, to the veranda of the house. Once I was out of the rain, I leaned forward and shook my head vigorously to get the water out of my hair, and immediately a dog started barking and scratching at the door behind me. I'd assumed the house was empty – it certainly looked it – but a hazy white moon of a face appeared at the dusty window, blurred by the mosquito shutter, and a moment later the door opened and the dog flew out at me.

I dislike dogs almost as much as they dislike me, but I did my best to seem charmed by the hideous, yapping white furball, if only to appease its owner, an old-timer of not far off ninety to judge by the liver spots, the stoop and the still-handsome skull poking through the papery skin. He was wearing a well-cut sports jacket over a buttoned-up cardigan, and had a plaid scarf round his neck. I made a stammering apology for disturbing his privacy, but he soon cut me off.

'You're British?' he said, squinting at me.

'I am.'

'That's okay. You can shelter. Sheltering's free.'

I didn't know enough about America to be able to tell from his accent where he was from, or what he might have done. But I guessed he was a retired professional, and fairly well off – you had to be, living in a place where a shack with an outside lavatory would cost you half a million dollars.

'British, eh?' he repeated. He studied me through rimless spectacles. 'You anything to do with this feller Lang?'

'In a way,' I said.

'Seems intelligent. Why'd he want to get himself mixed up with that damn fool in the White House?'

'That's what everyone would like to know.'

'War crimes!' he said, with a roll of his head, and I caught a glimpse of two flesh-coloured hearing aids, one in either ear. 'We could all have been charged with those! And maybe we ought to have been. I don't know. I guess I'll just have to put my trust in a higher judgement.' He chuckled sadly. 'I'll find out soon enough.'

I didn't know what he was talking about. I was just glad to be standing where it was dry. We leaned on the weathered handrail and stared out together at the rain while the dog skittered dementedly on its claws around the veranda. Through a gap in the trees I could just make out the sea – vast and grey, with the white lines of the incoming waves moving remorselessly down it, like interference on an old monochrome TV.

'So, what brings you to this part of the Vineyard?' asked the old man.

There seemed no point in lying.

'Someone I knew was washed up on the beach down there,' I said. 'I thought I'd take a look at the spot. To pay my respects,' I added, in case he thought I was a ghoul.

'Now *that* was a funny business,' he said. 'You mean the British guy a few weeks ago? No *way* should that current have carried him this far west. Not at this time of year.'

'What?' I turned to look at him. Despite his great age, there was still something youthful about his sharp features and keen manner. His thin white hair was combed straight back off his forehead. He looked like an antique boy scout.

'I've known this sea most of my life. Hell, a guy tried to throw *me* off that damn ferry when I was still at the World Bank, and I can tell you this: if he'd succeeded, I wouldn't have floated ashore in Lambert's Cove!'

I was conscious of a drumming in my ears, but whether it was my blood or the downpour hitting the shingle roof I couldn't tell.

'Did you mention this to the police?'

'The police? Young man, at my age, I have better things to do with what little time I have left than spend it with the police! Anyway, I told all this to Annabeth. She was the one who was dealing with the police.' He saw my blank expression. 'Annabeth Wurmbrand,' he said. 'Everybody knows Annabeth – Mars Wurmbrand's widow. She has the house nearest the ocean.' At my failure to react, he became slightly testy. 'She's the one who told the police about the lights.'

'The lights?'

'The lights on the beach on the night the body was washed up. Nothing happens round here that she doesn't see. Kay used to say she was always happy leaving Mohu in the fall, knowing she could be sure Annabeth would keep an eye on things all winter.'

'What kind of lights were these?'

'Flashlights, I guess.'

'Why wasn't this reported in the media?'

'In the media?' He gave another of his grating chuckles. 'Annabeth's never spoken to a reporter in her life! Except maybe an editor from *The World of Interiors*. It took her a decade even to trust Kay, because of the *Post*.'

That started him off talking about Kay's big old place up on Lambert's Cove Road that Bill and Hillary used to like so much, and where Lady Di had stayed, of which only the chimneys now remained, but by then I had stopped listening. It seemed to me the rain had eased somewhat and I was anxious to get away. I interrupted.

'Do you think you could point me in the direction of Mrs Wurmbrand's house?'

'Sure,' he said. 'But there's not much point in going there.'

'Why not?'

'She fell downstairs two weeks ago. Been in a coma ever since. Poor Annabeth. Ted says she's never going to regain consciousness. So that's another one gone. Hey!' he shouted, but by then I was halfway down the steps from the veranda.

'Thanks for the shelter,' I called over my shoulder, 'and the talk. I've got to get going.'

He looked so forlorn, standing there alone under his dripping roof, with the Stars and Stripes hanging like a dishrag from its slick pole, that I almost turned back.

'Well, tell your Mr Lang to keep his spirits up!' He gave me a trembling military salute and turned it into a wave. 'You take care now.'

I righted my bike and set off down the track. I wasn't even

noticing the rain any more. About a quarter of a mile down the slope, in a clearing close to the dunes and the lake, was a big, low house, surrounded by a wire fence and discreet signs announcing it was private property. There were no lamps lit, despite the darkness of the storm. That, I surmised, must be the residence of the comatose widow. Could it be true? She had seen *lights*? Well, it was certainly the case that from the upstairs windows one would have a good view of the beach. I leaned the bike against a bush and scrambled up the little path, through sickly, yellowish vegetation and lacy green ferns, and as I came to the crest of the dune the wind seemed to push me away, as if this too were a private domain and I had no business trespassing.

I'd already glimpsed what lay beyond the dunes from the old guy's house, and as I'd cycled down the track, I'd heard the boom of the surf getting progressively louder. But it was still a shock to clamber up and suddenly be confronted by that vista – that seam-less grey hemisphere of scudding clouds and heaving ocean, the waves hurtling in and smashing against the beach in a continuous, furious detonation. The low sandy coast ran away in a curve to my right for about a mile and ended in the jutting outcrop of Makonikey Head, misty through the spray. I wiped the rain out of my eyes to try to see better, and I thought of McAra alone on this immense shore – face down, glutted with salt water, his cheap winter clothes stiff with brine and cold. I imagined him emerging out of the bleak dawn, carried in on the tide from Vineyard Sound, scraping the sand with his big feet, being washed out again, and then returning, slowly creeping higher up the beach until at last he grounded. And then I imagined him dumped over the side of a dinghy and dragged ashore by men with flashlights, who'd come back a few days later and thrown a garrulous old witness down her architect-designed stairs.

A few hundred yards along the beach a pair of figures emerged from the dunes and started walking towards me, dark and tiny and frail amid all that raging nature. I glanced in the other direction. The wind was whipping spouts of water from the surface of the waves and flinging them ashore, like the outlines of some amphibious invading force: they made it halfway up the beach and then dissolved.

What I ought to do, I thought, staggering slightly in the wind, is give all this to a journalist: some tenacious reporter from *The Washington Post*, some noble heir to the tradition of Woodward and Bernstein. I could see the headline. I could write the story in my mind.

WASHINGTON (AP) – The death of Michael McAra, aide to former British premier Adam Lang, was a covert operation that went tragically wrong, according to sources within the intelligence community.

Was that so implausible? I took another look at the figures on the beach. It seemed to me they had quickened their pace and were heading towards me. The wind slashed rain in my face and I had to wipe it away. I ought to get going, I thought. By the time I looked again they were closer still, stumbling determinedly up the expanse of sand. One was short, the other tall. The tall one was a man, the short one a woman.

The short one was Ruth Lang.

*

I was amazed that she should have turned up. I waited until I was sure it was her, then I went halfway down the beach to meet her. The noise of the wind and the sea wiped out our first exchanges.

She had to take my arm and pull me down slightly, so that she could shout in my ear. '*I said*,' she repeated, and her breath was almost shockingly hot against my freezing skin, '*Dep told me you were here!*' The wind whipped her blue nylon hood away from her face and she tried to fumble for it at the nape of her neck, then gave up. She shouted something but just at that moment a wave exploded against the shore behind her. She smiled helplessly, waited until the noise had subsided, then cupped her hands and shouted, 'What are you doing?'

'Oh, just taking the air.'

'No – really.'

'I wanted to see where Mike McAra was found.'

'Why?'

I shrugged. 'Curiosity.'

'But you didn't even know him.'

'I'm starting to feel as if I did.'

'Where's your bike?'

'Just behind the dunes.'

'We came to fetch you back before the storm started.' She beckoned to the policeman. He was standing about five yards away, watching us – soaked, bored, disgruntled. 'Barry,' she shouted to him, 'bring the car round, will you, and meet us on the road. We'll wheel the bike up and find you.' She spoke to him as if he were a servant.

'Can't do that, Mrs Lang, I'm afraid,' he yelled back. 'Regulations say I have to stay with you at all times.'

'Oh, for God's sake!' she said, scornfully. 'Do you seriously think there's a terrorist cell at Uncle Seth's Pond? Go and get the car before you catch pneumonia.'

I watched his square, unhappy face, as his sense of duty warred with his desire for dryness. 'All right,' he said eventually. 'I'll meet you in ten minutes. But please don't leave the path or speak to anyone.'

'We won't, Officer,' she said, with mock humility. 'I promise.'

He hesitated, then began jogging back the way he'd come.

'They treat us like children,' complained Ruth, as we climbed up the beach. 'I sometimes think their orders aren't to protect us so much as to spy on us.'

We reached the top of the dune and automatically we both turned round to stare at the sea. After a second or two, I risked a quick glance at her. Her pale skin was shiny with rain, her short dark hair flattened and glistening like a swimmer's cap. Her flesh looked hard, like alabaster in the cold. People used to say they couldn't understand what her husband saw in her, but at that moment I could – there was a tautness about her; a quick, nervous energy: she was a force.

'To be honest, I've come back here a couple of times myself,' she said. 'Usually I bring a few flowers and wedge them under a stone. Poor Mike. He hated to be away from the city. He hated country walks. He couldn't even swim.'

She quickly brushed her cheeks with her hand. Her face was too wet for me to tell whether she was crying or not.

'It's a hell of a place to end up,' I said.

'Oh no. No it's not. When it's sunny, it's rather wonderful. It reminds me of Cornwall.'

She scrambled down the little footpath to the bike, and I followed her. To my surprise, she suddenly mounted it and pedalled away, coming to a stop about a hundred yards up the track, at the edge of the wood. When I reached her she gazed at me intently, her dark brown eyes almost black in the fading afternoon light. 'Do you think his death was suspicious?'

The directness of the question took me unawares. 'I'm not sure,'

I said. It was all I could do to stop myself telling her right then what I'd heard from the old man. But I sensed this was neither the time nor the place. I wasn't sufficiently sure of my facts, and it seemed crass, somehow, to pass unverified gossip on to a grieving friend. Besides, I was a little scared of her: I didn't want to be on the receiving end of one of her scathing cross-examinations. So all I said was: 'I don't know enough about it, to be honest. Presumably the police have investigated the whole thing pretty thoroughly.'

'Yes. Of course.'

She got off the bike and handed it to me and we started ascending through the scrub oak towards the road. It was much calmer away from the sea. The downpour had almost stopped and the rain had released rich, cold smells of earth and wood and herbs. I could hear the ticking of the rear wheel as we walked.

'The police were very active at first,' she said, 'but it's all gone quiet lately. I think the inquest was adjourned. Anyway, they can't be that concerned − they released Mike's body last week and the embassy have flown it back to the UK.'

'Oh?' I tried not to sound too surprised. 'That seems very quick.'

'Not really. It's been three weeks. They did an autopsy. He was drunk and he drowned. End of story.'

'But what was he doing on the ferry in the first place?'

She gave me a sharp look. 'That I don't know. He was a grown man. He didn't have to account for his every move.'

We walked on in silence and the thought occurred to me that McAra could easily have left the island for the weekend to visit Richard Rycart in New York. That would explain why he'd written down Rycart's number, and also why he hadn't told the Langs where he was going. How could he? *So long, guys, I'm just off to the United Nations to see your bitterest political enemy . . .'*

164

We passed the house where I'd sought shelter from the downpour. I kept an eye out for the old man. But the white clapboard property appeared as deserted as when I'd first seen it – so freezing, locked and abandoned, in fact, that I half wondered if I might not have imagined the whole encounter.

Ruth said, 'The funeral's in London on Monday. He's being buried in Streatham. His mother's too ill to attend. I've been thinking that perhaps I ought to go. One of us should put in an appearance, and it doesn't seem likely to be my husband.'

'I thought you said you didn't want to leave him.'

'It rather looks as though he's left me, wouldn't you say?'

She didn't talk any more after that, but started fumbling around for her hood again, even though she didn't really need it. I found it for her with my free hand and she pulled it up roughly, without thanking me, then walked on, slightly ahead, staring at the ground.

Barry was waiting for us at the end of the track in the minivan, reading a Harry Potter novel. The engine was running and the headlights were on. Occasionally, the big windscreen wiper scraped noisily across the glass. He put aside his book with obvious reluctance, got out, opened up the rear door and pushed the seats forward. Between us we manoeuvred the bike into the back of the van, then he returned to his place behind the wheel and I climbed in beside Ruth.

We took a different route to the one I'd cycled, the road twisting up a hill away from the sea. The dusk was damp and gloomy, as if one of the massive storm clouds had failed to rupture but had gradually subsided to earth like a deflated airship and settled over the island. I could understand why Ruth said the landscape reminded her of Cornwall. The minivan's headlights fell on wild, almost moorland country and in the wing mirror I could just make out the luminous white horses flecking the waters of Vineyard Sound. The heater was turned up full and I had to keep rubbing a porthole in the condensation to see where we were going. I could feel my clothes drying, sticking to my skin, releasing the same faintly unpleasant odour of sweat and dry-cleaning fluid I had smelled in McAra's room.

Ruth didn't speak for the whole of the journey. She kept her back turned slightly towards me and stared out of the window. But just as we passed the lights of the airport, her cold, hard hand moved across the seat and grasped mine. I didn't know what she was thinking, but I could guess, and I returned her pressure: even a ghost can show a little human sympathy from time to time. In the driver's mirror, Barry's eyes stared into mine. As we indicated to turn right into the wood, the images of death and torture, and the words 'FOR AS IN ADAM ALL DIE', flickered briefly in the darkness, but as far as I could see the little polythene hut was empty. We rocked down the track towards the house.

Eleven

There may be occasions on which the subject will tell the ghost something that contradicts something else they have said, or something that the ghost already knows about them. If that happens it is important to mention it immediately.

Ghostwriting

The first thing I did when we got back was run a hot bath, tipping in half a bottle of organic bath oil (pine, cardamom and ginger) which I found in the bathroom cabinet. While that was filling I drew the curtains in the bedroom and peeled off my damp clothes. Naturally, a house as modern as Rhinehart's didn't have anything so crudely useful as a radiator, so I left them where they fell, went into the bathroom and stepped into the large tub.

Just as it's worth getting really hungry occasionally, simply to savour the taste of food, so the pleasure of a hot bath can only truly be appreciated if you've been chilled by the rain for hours. I groaned with relief, let myself slide right down until only my nostrils were above the aromatic surface, and lay there like some basking alligator in its steamy lagoon for several minutes. I suppose that's why I didn't hear anyone knock on my bedroom door, and only became aware that someone was next door when I broke the surface and heard them moving around.

'Hello?' I called.

'Sorry,' Ruth called back. 'I did knock. It's me. I was just bringing you some dry clothes.'

'That's all right,' I said. 'I can manage.'

'You need something that's been properly aired, or you'll catch your death. I'll get Dep to clean the others.'

'Really, there's no need.'

'Dinner's in an hour. Is that okay?'

'That's fine,' I said, surrendering. 'Thank you.'

I listened for the click of the door as she left. Immediately I rose from the bath and grabbed a towel. On the bed, she had laid out a freshly laundered shirt belonging to her husband (it was handmade, with his monogram, APBL, on the pocket), a sweater and a pair of jeans. Where my own discarded clothes had been there was only a wet mark on the floor. I lifted the mattress – the package was still there – then let it fall.

There was something disconcerting about Ruth Lang. You never knew where you were with her. Sometimes she could be aggressive for no reason – I hadn't forgotten her behaviour during our first conversation, when she virtually accused me of planning to write a kiss-and-tell memoir about her and Lang – and then at others she was bizarrely overfamiliar, holding hands or dictating what you should wear. It was as if some tiny mechanism was missing from her brain: the bit that told you how to behave naturally with other people.

I drew my towel more tightly around me, knotted it at my waist, and sat down at the desk. I'd been struck before by how strangely absent she was from her husband's autobiography. That was one of the reasons I'd wanted to begin the main part of the book with the story of their meeting – until I discovered that Lang had made it up. She was there, naturally enough, on the dedication page –

To Ruth,

and my kids,

and the people of Britain

— but then one had to wait another fifty pages until she actually appeared in person. I leafed through the manuscript until I reached the passage.

It was at the time of the London elections that I first got to know Ruth Capel, one of the most energetic members of the local association. I would like to be able to say that it was her political commitment that first drew me to her, but the truth is that I found her immensely attractive — small, intense, with very short dark hair, and piercing dark eyes. She was a North Londoner, the only child of two university lecturers, and had been passionately interested in politics almost from the time she could speak — unlike me! She was also, as my friends never tired of pointing out, much cleverer than I was! She had gained a First at Oxford in politics, philosophy and economics, and then done a year's postgraduate research in post-colonial government as a Fulbright Scholar. As if that were not enough to intimidate me, she had also come top in the Foreign Office entrance examinations, although she later left to work for the party's foreign affairs team in parliament.

Nevertheless, the Lang family motto has always been 'Nothing ventured, nothing gained', and I managed to arrange for us to go canvassing together. It was then a relatively easy matter, after a hard evening's knocking on doors and handing out leaflets, to suggest a casual drink in a local pub. At first, other members of the campaign team used to join us on these excursions, but gradually they became aware that Ruth and I wanted to spend time alone together. A year after the elections, we began sharing a flat, and when Ruth became pregnant with our first child, I asked her to marry me. Our wedding took place at Marylebone registry office in June 1979, with Andy Martin, one of my old friends from Footlights, acting as my best man. For our honeymoon, we borrowed Ruth's parents' cottage near Hay-on-Wye. After two blissful weeks, we returned to London, ready for the very different political fray following the election of Margaret Thatcher.

That was the only substantial reference to her.

I slowly worked my way through the succeeding chapters, underlining the places where she was mentioned. Her 'lifelong knowledge of the party' was 'invaluable' in helping Lang gain his safe parliamentary seat. 'Ruth saw the possibility that I might become party leader long before I did' was the promising opening of Chapter Three, but how or why she reached this prescient conclusion wasn't explained.. She surfaced to give 'characteristically shrewd advice' when he had to sack a colleague. She shared his hotel suites at party conferences. She straightened his tie on the night he became prime minister. She went shopping with the wives of other world leaders on official visits. She even gave birth to his children ('my kids have always kept my feet firmly on the ground'). But for all that, hers was a phantom presence in the memoirs, which puzzled me, because she certainly wasn't a phantom presence in his life. Perhaps this was why she had been keen to hire me: she guessed I would want to put in more about her.

When I checked my watch I realised I'd already spent an hour going over the manuscript, and it was time for dinner. I contemplated the clothes she had laid out on the bed. I'm what the English would call 'fastidious' and the Americans 'tight-assed': I don't like eating food that's been on someone else's plate, or drinking from the same glass, or wearing clothes that aren't my own. But these were cleaner and warmer than anything I possessed, and she had gone to the trouble of fetching them, so I put them on – rolling up the shirtsleeves because I had no cufflinks – and went upstairs.

*

There was a log fire burning in the stone hearth, and someone, presumably Dep, had lit candles all around the room. The security lights in the grounds had also been turned on, illuminating the gaunt white outlines of trees and the greenish-yellow vegetation bending in the wind. As I came up into the room, a gust of rain slashed across the huge picture window. It was like the lounge of some luxurious boutique hotel out of season, which had only two guests.

Ruth was sitting on the same sofa, in the same position she had adopted that morning, with her legs drawn up beneath her, reading *The New York Review of Books*. Arranged in a fan on the low table in front of her was an array of magazines, and beside them – a harbinger of things to come, I hoped – a long-stemmed glass of what looked like white wine. She glanced up approvingly.

'A perfect fit,' she said. 'And now you need a drink.' She leaned her head over the back of the sofa – I could see the cords of muscle standing out in her neck – and called in her mannish voice in the direction of the stairs. 'Dep!' And then to me: 'What will you have?'

'What are you having'

'Biodynamic white wine,' she said, 'from the Rhinehart Vinery in Napa Valley.'

'He doesn't own a distillery, I suppose?'

'It's delicious. You must try it. Dep,' she said to the housekeeper, who had appeared at the top of the stairs, 'bring the bottle, would you, and another glass?'

I sat down opposite her. She was wearing a long red wrap-around dress and on her normally scrubbed-clean face was a trace of make-up. There was something touching about her determination to put on a show, even as the bombs, so to speak, were falling all around her. All we needed was a wind-up gramophone and we could have played the plucky English couple in a Noël Coward play, keeping up brittle appearances while the world went smash around us. Dep poured me some wine and left the bottle.

'We'll eat in twenty minutes,' instructed Ruth, 'because first,' she said, picking up the remote control and jabbing it fiercely at the television, 'we must watch the news. Cheers,' she said, and raised her glass.

'Cheers,' I replied, and did the same.

I drained the glass in thirty seconds. White wine. What *is* the point of it? I picked up the bottle and studied the label. Apparently the vines were grown in soil treated in harmony with the lunar cycle, using manure buried in a cow's horn and flower heads of yarrow fermented in a stag's bladder. It sounded like the sort of suspicious activity for which people quite rightly used to be burned as witches.

'You like it?' asked Ruth.

'Subtle and fruity,' I said, 'with a hint of bladder.'

'Pour us some more then. Here comes Adam. Christ, it's the lead story. I think I may have to get drunk for a change.'

The headline behind the newsreader's shoulder read 'LANG: WAR CRIMES'. I didn't like the fact that they weren't bothering to use a question mark any more. The familiar scenes from the morning unfolded: the press conference at The Hague, Lang leaving the Vineyard house, the statement to reporters on the West Tisbury highway. Then came shots of Lang in Washington, first greeting members of Congress in a warm glow of flashbulbs and mutual admiration, and then, more sombrely, with the Secretary of State. Amelia Bly was clearly visible in the background: the official wife. I didn't dare look at Ruth.

'Adam Lang,' said the Secretary of State, 'has stood by our side in the War against Terror, and I am proud to stand by his side this afternoon, and to offer him, on behalf of the American people, the hand of friendship. Adam. Good to see you.'

'Don't grin,' said Ruth.

'Thank you,' said Adam, grinning and shaking the proffered hand. He beamed at the cameras. He looked like an eager student collecting a prize on speech day. 'Thank you very much. It's good to see you.'

'Oh, for fuck's sake!' shouted Ruth.

She pointed the remote and was about to press it when Richard Rycart appeared, passing through the lobby of the United Nations, surrounded by the usual bureaucratic phalanx. At the last minute he seemed to swerve off his planned course and walked over to the cameras. He was a little older than Lang, just coming up to sixty. He'd been born in Australia, or Rhodesia, or some part of the Commonwealth, before coming to England in his teens. He had a cascade of iron-grey hair which flooded dramatically over his collar, and was well aware − judging by the way he positioned himself − of which was his best side: his left. His tanned and hook-prowed profile reminded me slightly of a Sioux Indian chief.

'I watched the announcement in The Hague today,' he said,

'with great shock and sadness.' I sat forward. This was definitely the voice I'd heard on the phone earlier in the day: that residual singsong accent was unmistakable. 'Adam Lang was and is an old friend of mine . . .'

'You hypocritical bastard,' said Ruth.

'. . . and I regret that he's chosen to bring this down to a personal level. This isn't about individuals. This is about justice. This is about whether there's to be one law for the rich white western nations and another for the rest of the world. This is about making sure that every political and military leader, when they make a decision, know that they will be held to account by international law. Thank you.'

A reporter shouted: 'If you're called to testify, sir, will you go?'

'Certainly I'll go.'

'I bet you will, you little shit,' said Ruth.

The news bulletin moved on to a report about a suicide bombing in the Middle East, and she turned off the television. At once her mobile phone started ringing. She glanced at it.

'It's Adam, calling to ask how I think it went.' She turned that off, as well. 'Let him sweat.'

'Does he always ask your advice?'

'Always. And he always used to take it. Until just lately.'

I poured us some more wine. Very slowly, I could feel it starting to have an effect.

'You were right,' I said. 'He shouldn't have gone to Washington. It did look bad.'

'We should never have come *here*,' she said, gesturing with her wine to the room. 'I mean – look at it. And all for the sake of the Adam Lang Foundation. Which is what, exactly? Just a high-class displacement activity for the recently unemployed.' She leaned forward to take her glass. 'Shall I tell you the first rule of politics?'

'Please.'

'Never lose touch with your base.'

'I'll try not to.'

'Shut up. I'm being serious. You can reach beyond it, by all means – you've got to reach beyond it, if you're going to win. But never, ever lose touch with it altogether. Because once you do, you're finished. Imagine if those pictures tonight had been of him arriving in London – flying back to fight these ridiculous people and their absurd allegations. It would've looked magnificent! Instead of which . . . God!' She shook her head and gave a sigh of anger and frustration. 'Come on. Let's eat.'

She pushed herself off the sofa, spilling a little wine in the process. It spattered the front of her red woollen dress. She didn't seem to notice, and I had a horrible premonition that she was going to get drunk. (I share the serious drinker's general prejudice that there's nothing more irritating than a man drunk, except a woman drunk: they somehow manage to let everybody down.) But when I offered to top her up, she covered her glass with her hand.

'I've had enough.'

The long table by the window had been laid for two, and the sight of Nature raging silently beyond the thick screen heightened the sense of intimacy: the candles, the flowers, the crackling fire. It felt slightly overdone. Dep brought in two bowls of clear soup and for a while we clinked our spoons against Rhinehart's porcelain in self-conscious silence.

'How is it going?' she said eventually.

'The book? It's not, to be honest.'

'Why's that – apart from the obvious reason?'

I hesitated.

'Can I talk frankly?'

'Of course.'

'I find it difficult to understand him.'

'Oh?' She was drinking iced still water now. Over the rim of her glass, her dark eyes gave me one of her double-barrelled-shotgun looks. 'In what way?'

'I can't understand why this good-looking eighteen-year-old lad who goes to Cambridge without the slightest interest in politics, and who spends his time acting and drinking and chasing girls, suddenly ends up—'

'Married to me?'

'No, no, not that. Not that at all.' (Yes, is what I meant: yes, yes, that; of course.) 'No. I don't understand why, by the time he's twenty-two or twenty-three, he's suddenly a member of a political party. Where's that coming from?'

'Didn't you ask him?'

'He told me he joined because of you. That you came and canvassed him, and that he was attracted to you, and that he followed you into politics out of love, essentially. To see more of you. I mean, *that* I can relate to. It *ought* to be true.'

'But it isn't?'

'Well, you know it isn't. He was a party member for at least a year before he even met you.'

'Was he?' She wrinkled her forehead and sipped some more water. 'But that story he always tells about what drew him into politics—I do have a distinct memory of that episode, because I canvassed in the London elections of seventy-seven, and I definitely knocked on his door, and after that was when he started showing up at party meetings regularly. So there has to be a grain of truth in it.'

'A grain,' I conceded. 'Maybe he'd joined in seventy-five, hardly showed any interest for two years, and then he met you and became more active. It still doesn't answer the basic question of what took him into a political party in the first place.'

'Is it really that important?'

Dep arrived to clear away the soup plates, and during the pause in our conversation I considered Ruth's question.

'Yes,' I said, when we were alone again, 'oddly enough I think it is important.'

'Why?'

'Because even though it's a tiny detail, it still means he isn't quite who we think he is. I'm not even sure he's quite who *he* thinks he is — and that's really difficult, if you've got to write the guy's memoirs. I just feel I don't know him at all. I can't catch his voice.'

Ruth frowned at the table, and made minute adjustments to the placing of her knife and fork. She said, without looking up, 'How do you know he joined in seventy-five?'

I had a moment's alarm that I'd said too much. But there seemed no reason not to tell her. 'Mike McAra found Adam's original party membership card in the Cambridge archives.'

'Christ,' she said, 'those archives! They've got everything, from his infant school reports to our laundry bills. Typical Mike, to ruin a good story by too much research.'

'He also dug out some obscure party newsletter that shows Adam canvassing in seventy-seven.'

'That must be after he met me.'

'Maybe.'

I could tell something was troubling her. Another volley of rain burst against the window and she put the tips of her fingers to the heavy glass, as if she wanted to trace the raindrops. The effect of the lighting in the garden made it look like the ocean bed: all waving fronds and thin grey tree trunks, rising like the spars of sunken boats. Dep came in with the main course – steamed fish, noodles, and some kind of obscure pale green vegetable that resembled a weed: probably *was* a weed. I ostentatiously poured the last of the wine into my glass and studied the bottle.

Dep said, 'You want another, sir?'

'I don't suppose you have any whisky, do you?'

The housekeeper looked to Ruth for guidance.

'Oh, bring him some bloody whisky,' said Ruth.

Dep returned with a bottle of fifty-year-old Chivas Regal Royal Salute, and a cut-glass tumbler. Ruth started to eat. I mixed myself a Scotch and water.

'This is delicious, Dep!' called Ruth. She dabbed her mouth with the corner of her napkin, and then inspected the smear of lipstick on the white linen with surprise, as if she thought she might have started bleeding. 'Coming back to your question,' she said to me, 'I don't think you should try to find mystery where there is none. Adam always had a social conscience – he inherited that from his mother – and I know that after he left Cambridge and moved to London he became very unhappy. I believe he was actually clinically depressed.'

'Clinically depressed? He may have had treatment for it? Really?' I tried to keep the excitement out of my voice. If this was true, it was the best piece of news I'd received all day. Nothing sells a memoir quite so well as a good dose of misery. Childhood sexual abuse, grinding poverty, quadriplegia: in the right hands, these are money in the bank. There ought to be a separate section in book-shops labelled *Schadenfreude*.

'Put yourself in his place.' Ruth continued eating, gesturing with her laden fork. 'His mother and father were both dead. He'd left university, which he'd loved. Many of his acting friends had agents and were getting offers of work. But he wasn't. I think he was lost, and I think he turned to political activity to compensate. He might not want to put it in those terms – he's not one for self-analysis – but that's my reading of what happened. You'd be surprised how many people end up in politics because they can't succeed in their first choice of a career.'

'So meeting you must have been a very important moment for him.'

'Why do you say that?'

'Because you had genuine political passion. And knowledge. And contacts in the party. You must have given him the focus to really go forward.' I felt as if a mist were clearing. 'Do you mind if I make a note of this?'

'Go ahead. If you think it's useful.'

'Oh, it is.' I put my knife and fork together – I'm not really a fish and weed man – took out my notebook and opened it to a new page. I was imagining myself in Lang's place again – in my early twenties, orphaned, alone, ambitious, talented, but not quite talented enough, looking for a path to follow, taking a few tentative steps into politics, and then meeting a woman who suddenly made the future possible.

'Marrying you was a real turning-point.'

'I was certainly a bit different to his Cambridge girlfriends, all those Jocastas and Pandoras. Even when I was a girl I was always more interested in politics than ponies.'

'Didn't you ever want to be a proper politician in your own right?' I asked.

'Of course. Didn't you ever want to be a proper writer?'

It was like being struck in the face. I'm not sure if I didn't put down my notebook.

'Ouch,' I said.

'I'm sorry. I didn't mean to be rude. But you must see that we're in the same boat, you and I. I've always understood more about politics than Adam. And you know more about writing. But in the end, he's the star, isn't he? And we both know our job is to service the star. It's his name on the book that's going to sell it, not yours. It was the same for me. It didn't take me long to realise that he could go all the way in politics. He had the looks and the charm. He was a great speaker. People liked him. Whereas I was always a bit of an ugly duckling, with this brilliant gift for putting my foot in it. As I've just demonstrated.' She put her hand on mine again. It was warm now, fleshier. 'I'm so sorry. I've hurt your feelings. I suppose even ghosts must have feelings, just like the rest of us.'

'If you prick us,' I said, 'we bleed.'

'You've finished eating? In that case, why don't you show me this research that Mike dug out? It might jog my memory. I'm interested.'

*

I went down to my room and retrieved McAra's package. By the time I returned upstairs, Ruth had moved back over to the sofa. Fresh logs had been thrown on the fire and the wind in the chimney was roaring, sucking up orange sparks. Dep was clearing away the dishes. I just managed to rescue my tumbler and the bottle of Scotch.

'Would you like dessert?' asked Ruth. 'Coffee?'

'I'm fine.'

'We're finished, Dep. Thank you.' She moved up slightly, to indicate that I should sit next to her, but I pretended not to notice and took my former place opposite her, across the table. I was still smarting from her crack about my not being a proper writer.

180

Perhaps I'm not. I've never composed poetry, it's true. I don't write sensitive explorations of my adolescent angst. I have no opinion on the human condition, except perhaps that it's best not examined too closely. I see myself as the literary equivalent of a skilled lathe-operator, or a basket-weaver; a potter, maybe: I make mildly diverting objects that people want to buy.

I opened the envelope and took out the photocopies of Lang's membership card, and the articles about the London elections. I slid them across to her. She crossed her legs at the ankles, leaned forwards to read, and I found myself staring into the surprisingly deep and shadowy valley of her cleavage.

'Well, there's no arguing with that,' she said, putting the membership card to one side. 'That's his signature all right.' She tapped the report on the canvassers in 1977. 'And I recognise some of these faces. I must have been off that night, or campaigning with a different group. Otherwise I would have been in the picture with him.' She looked up. 'What else have you got there?'

There didn't seem much point in hiding anything, so I passed over the whole package. She inspected the name and address, and then the postmark, and glanced across at me. 'What was Mike up to, then?'

She opened the neck of the envelope and held it apart with her thumb and forefinger, and peered inside cautiously, as if there might be something in the padded interior that would bite her. Then she upended it and tipped the contents out over the table. I watched her intently, as she sorted through the photographs and programmes – studied her pale, clever face for any hint of a clue as to why this might have been so important to McAra. I saw the hard lines soften as she picked out a photograph of Lang in his striped blazer on a dappled river bank.

'Oh, look at him,' she said. 'Isn't he pretty?'

She held it up next to her cheek.

'Irresistible,' I said.

She inspected the picture more closely. 'My God, look at them. Look at his *hair*. It was another world, wasn't it? I mean, what was happening while this was being taken? Vietnam. The Cold War. The first miners' strike in Britain since 1926. The military coup in Chile. And what do they do? They get a bottle of champagne and they go punting!'

'I'll drink to that.'

She picked up one of the photocopies.

'Listen to this,' she said, and started to read:

> The girls they all will miss us
> As the train it pulls away.
> They'll blow a kiss and say 'Come back
> To Cambridge town some day.'
> We'll throw a rose neglectfully and turn and sigh farewell
> Because we know the chance they've got
> Is a snowball's chance in hell.
> Cheer oh, Cambridge, suppers, bumps and Mays,
> Trinners, Fenner's, cricket, tennis
> Footlights shows and plays.
> We'll take a final, farewell stroll
> Along dear old KP,
> And a final punt up old man Cam
> To Grantchester for tea.

She smiled and shook her head. 'I can't even understand half of it. It's in Cambridge code.'

'Bumps are college boat races,' I said. 'Actually, you had those at Oxford as well, but you were probably too busy with the miners' strike to notice. Mays are May balls – they're at the beginning of June, obviously.'

'Obviously.'

'Trinners is Trinity College. Fenner's is the university cricket ground.'

'And KP?'

'King's Parade.'

'They wrote it to send the place up,' she said. 'But now it sounds nostalgic.'

'That's satire for you.'

'And what's this telephone number?'

I should have known that nothing would escape her. She showed me the photograph with the number written on the back. I didn't reply. I could feel my face beginning to flush. Of course, I ought to have told her earlier. Now I'd made myself look guilty.

'Well?' she insisted.

I said quietly, 'It's Richard Rycart's.'

It was almost worth it just for her expression. She looked as though she'd swallowed a hornet. She put her hand to her throat.

'*You've* been calling Richard Rycart?' she gasped.

'*I* haven't. It must have been McAra.'

'That's not possible.'

'Who else could have written down that number?' I held out my cell phone. 'Try it.'

She stared at me for a while, as if we were playing a game of truth or dare, then she reached over, took my phone and entered the fourteen digits. She raised it to her ear and stared at me again. About thirty seconds later a flicker of alarm passed across her face.

She fumbled to press the disconnect button and put the phone back on the table.

'Did he answer?' I asked.

She nodded. 'It sounded as though he was in a restaurant.'

The phone began to ring, throbbing along the surface of the table as if had come alive.

'What should I do?' I asked.

'Do what you want. It's your phone.'

I turned it off. There was a silence, broken only by the roaring and cracking of the log fire.

She said, 'When did you discover this?'

'Earlier today. When I moved into McAra's room.'

'And then you went to Lambert's Cove, to look at where his body came ashore?'

'That's right.'

'And why did you do that?' Her voice was very quiet. 'Tell me honestly.'

'I'm not sure.' I paused. 'There was a man there,' I blurted out. I couldn't keep it to myself any longer. 'An old-timer, who's familiar with the currents in Vineyard Sound. He says there's no way, at this time of year, that a body from the Woods Hole ferry would wash up at Lambert's Cove. And he also said another woman, who has a house just behind the dunes, had seen flashlights on the beach during the night when McAra went missing. But then she fell downstairs and is in a coma. So she can't tell the police anything.' I spread my hands. 'That's all I know.'

She was looking at me with her mouth slightly open.

'That,' she said slowly, 'is *all* you know. *Jesus.*' She started feeling around on the sofa, patting the leather with her hands, then turned her attention to the table, searching under the photographs. 'Jesus. Shit.' She flicked her fingers at me. 'Give me your phone.'

'Why?' I asked, handing it over.

'Isn't it obvious? I need to call Adam.' She held it outstretched in her palm, inspected it, and quickly started entering his number with her thumb. She got about halfway through, then stopped.

'What?' I said.

'Nothing.' She was looking beyond me, over my shoulder, chewing the inside of her lip. Her thumb was poised over the keypad, and for a long moment it stayed there, until at last she put the phone back down on the table.

'You're not going to call him?'

'Maybe. In a while.' She stood. 'I'm going for a walk first.'

'But it's nine o'clock at night,' I protested. 'It's pouring with rain.'

'It'll clear my head.'

'I'll come with you.'

'No. Thanks, but I need to think things through on my own. You stay here and have another drink. You look as though you need one. Don't wait up.'

*

It was the poor bloody copper I felt sorry for. No doubt he'd been downstairs, with his feet up in front of the television, looking forward to a quiet night in. And suddenly here was Lady Macbeth again, off on yet another of her ceaseless walks, this time in the middle of an Atlantic storm. I stood at the window and watched them cross the lawn, towards the silently raging vegetation. She was in the lead, as usual, her head bowed, as if she'd lost something precious and was retracing her steps, searching the ground, trying to find it. The floodlights spread her shadow four ways. The Special Branch man was still pulling on his coat.

I suddenly felt overwhelmingly tired. My legs were stiff from cycling. I felt shivery with an incipient cold. Even Rhinehart's whisky had lost its allure. She had said not to wait up, and I decided I wouldn't. I put the photographs and photocopies away in the envelope and went downstairs to my room. When I took off my clothes and switched off the light, sleep seemed to swallow me instantly – to suck me down through the mattress and into its dark waters, as if it were a strong current and I an exhausted swimmer.

I surfaced at some point to find myself alongside McAra, his large, clumsy body turning in the water, like a dolphin's. He was fully clothed, in a thick black raincoat, and heavy, rubber-soled shoes. *I'm not going to make it*, he said to me, *you go on without me.*

I sat up in alarm. I'd no idea how long I'd been asleep. The room was in darkness, apart from a vertical strip of light to my left.

'Are you awake?' said Ruth softly, knocking on the door.

She had opened it a few inches and was standing in the corridor.

'I am now.'

'I'm sorry.'

'It doesn't matter. Hold on.'

I went into the bathroom and put on the white towelling robe that was hanging on the back of the door, and when I returned to the bedroom and let her in I saw that she was wearing an identical robe to mine. It was too big for her. She looked unexpectedly small and vulnerable. Her hair was soaking wet. Her bare feet had left a trail of damp prints from her room to mine.

'What time is it?' I said.

'I don't know. I just spoke to Adam.' She seemed stunned, trembling. Her eyes were open very wide.

'And?'

She glanced along the corridor. 'Can I come in?'

Still groggy from my dream, I turned on the bedside light. I stood aside to let her pass and closed the door after her.

'The day before Mike died, he and Adam had a terrible row,' she said, without preliminaries. 'I haven't told anyone this before, not even the police.'

I massaged my temples and tried to concentrate.

'What was it about?'

'I don't know, but it was furious — terminal — and they never spoke again. When I asked Adam about it he refused to discuss it. It's been the same every time I've broached it since. In the light of what you've found out today, I felt I had to have it out with him once and for all.'

'What did he say?'

'He was having dinner with the Vice President. At first, that bloody woman wouldn't even go in and give him the phone.'

She sat on the edge of the bed and put her face in her hands. I didn't know what to do. It seemed incongruous to remain standing, towering over her, so I sat down next to her. She was shaking from head to toe: it could have been fear, or anger, or maybe it was just the cold.

'He said to begin with he couldn't talk,' she went on, 'but I said he bloody well had to talk. So he took the phone into the men's room. When I told him Mike had been in touch with Rycart just before he died, he didn't even pretend to be surprised.' She turned to me. She looked stricken. 'He *knew*.'

'He said that?'

'He didn't need to. I could tell by his voice. He said we shouldn't say any more over the telephone. We should talk when he gets back. Dear God help us — what has he got himself mixed up in?'

Something seemed to give way in her and she sagged towards me, her arms outstretched. Her head came to rest against my chest and I thought for a moment she might have fainted, but then I realised she was clinging to me, holding on so fiercely I could feel her bitten fingertips through the thick material of the robe. My hands hovered an inch or two above her, moving back and forth uncertainly, as if she was giving off some kind of magnetic field. Finally, I stroked her hair and tried to murmur words of reassurance I didn't really believe.

'I'm afraid,' she said in a muffled voice. 'I've never been frightened in my life before. But I am now.'

'Your hair's wet,' I said gently. 'You're drenched. Let me get you a towel.'

I extricated myself and went into the bathroom. I looked at myself in the mirror. I felt like a skier at the top of an unfamiliar black run. When I returned to the bedroom, she'd taken off her robe and had got into bed, pulling up the sheet to cover her breasts.

'Do you mind?' she said.

'Of course not,' I said.

I turned off the light and climbed in beside her, and lay on the cold side of the bed. She rolled over and put her hand on my chest and pressed her lips very hard against mine, as if she were trying to give me the kiss of life.

Twelve

The book is not a platform for the ghost to air their own views on anything at all.

Ghostwriting

When I woke the next morning I expected to find her gone. That's the usual protocol in these situations, isn't it? The business of the night transacted, the visiting party retreats to their own quarters, as keen as a vampire to avoid the unforgiving rays of dawn. Not so Ruth Lang. In the dimness I could see her bare shoulder and her crop of black hair, and I could tell by her irregular, almost inaudible breathing that she was as awake as I was, and lying there listening to me.

I reclined on my back, my hands folded across my stomach, as motionless as the stone effigy of a crusader knight on his tomb, shutting my eyes periodically as some fresh aspect of the mess occurred to me. On the Richter scale of bad ideas, this surely had registered a ten. It was a meteor strike of folly. After a while, I let one hand travel crabwise to the bedside table and feel for my watch. I brought it up close to my face. It was seven fifteen.

Cautiously, still pretending I didn't know that she was pretending, I slipped out of the bed and crept towards the bathroom.

'You're awake,' she said, without moving.

'I'm sorry if I disturbed you,' I said. 'I thought I'd take a shower.'

I locked the door behind me, turned the water up as hot and strong as I could bear, and let it pummel me – back, stomach, legs, scalp. The little room quickly filled with steam. Afterwards, when I shaved, I had to keep rubbing at my reflection in the mirror to stop myself from disappearing.

By the time I returned to the bedroom, she had put on her robe and was sitting at the desk, leafing through the manuscript. The curtains were still closed.

'You've taken out his family history,' she said. 'He won't like that. He's very proud of the Langs. And why have you underlined my name every time?'

'I wanted to check how often you were mentioned. I was surprised there wasn't more about you.'

'That will be a hangover from the focus groups.'

'I'm sorry?'

'When we were in Downing Street, Mike used to say that every time I opened my mouth I cost Adam ten thousand votes.'

'I'm sure that's not true.'

'Of course it is. People are always looking for someone to resent. I often think my main usefulness, as far as he was concerned, was to serve as a lightning rod. They could take their anger out on me instead of him.'

'Even so,' I said, 'you ought not to be written out of history.'

'Why not? Most women usually are. Even the Amelia Blys of this world are written out eventually.'

'Well then, I shall reinstate you.' I slid open the door of the closet so hard in my haste it banged. I had to get out of that house. I had to put some distance between myself and their destructive *ménage à trois*, before I ended up as crazed as they were. 'I'd like to sit down with you, when you have the time, and do a really long interview. Put in all the important occasions that he's forgotten.'

'How very kind of you,' she said bitterly. 'Like the boss's secretary whose job is to remember his wife's birthdays for him?'

'Something like that. But then as you say, I can't claim to be a proper writer.'

I was conscious of her watching me carefully. I put on a pair of boxer shorts, pulling them up under my robe.

'Ah,' she said drily, 'the modesty of the morning after.'

'A bit late for that,' I said.

I took off the dressing gown and reached for a shirt, and as the hanger rang its hollow chime, I thought that this was exactly the sort of miserable scene that the discreet nocturnal departure was invented to avoid. How typical of her not to sense what the occasion required. Now our former intimacy lay between us like a shadow. The silence lengthened, and hardened, until I could feel her resentment as an almost solid barrier. I could no more have gone across and kissed her now than I could on the day we met.

'What are you going to do?' she said.

'Leave.'

'That's not necessary as far as I'm concerned.'

'I'm afraid it is as far as I am.'

I pulled on my trousers.

'Are you going to tell Adam about this?' she said.

'Oh, for God's sake!' I cried. 'What do you think?'

I laid my suitcase on the bed and unzipped it.

'Where will you go?' She looked as if she might be about to cry again. I hoped not; I couldn't take it.

'Back to the hotel. I can work much better there.' I started throwing in my clothes, not bothering to fold them, such was my anxiety to get away. 'I'm sorry. I should never have stayed in a client's house. It always ends . . .' I hesitated.

'With you fucking the client's wife?'

'No, of course not. It just makes it hard to keep a professional distance. Anyway, it wasn't *entirely* my idea, if you recall.'

'That's not very gentlemanly of you.'

I didn't answer. I carried on packing. Her gaze followed my every move.

'And the things I told you last night?' she said. 'What do you propose to do about them?'

'Nothing.'

'You can't simply ignore them.'

'Ruth,' I said, stopping at last, 'I'm his ghostwriter, not an investigative reporter. If he wants to tell the truth about what's been going on, I'm here to help him. If he doesn't – fine. I'm morally neutral.'

'It isn't morally neutral to conceal the facts if you know something illegal has happened – that's criminal.'

'But I don't know that anything illegal *has* happened. All I have is a phone number on the back of a photograph and gossip from some old man who may well be senile. If anyone has any evidence, it's you. That's the real question, actually: what are *you* going to do about it?'

'I don't know,' she said. 'Perhaps I'll write my own memoirs. "Ex-Prime Minister's Wife Tells All."'

I resumed packing.

'Well, if ever you do decide to do that, give me a call.'

She emitted one of her trademark full-throated laughs.

'Do you really think I need someone like *you* to enable me to produce a book?'

She stood up then, and undid her belt, and for an instant I thought she was about to undress, but she was only loosening it in order to wrap the robe more closely around herself. She drew the belt very tight and knotted it, and the finality of the gesture somehow restored her superiority over me. My rights of access were hereby revoked. Her resolve was so firm I felt almost wistful, and if she had held out her arms it would have been my turn to fall against her, but instead, she turned and, in the practised manner of a prime minister's wife, pulled the nylon cord to open the curtains.

'I declare this day officially open,' she said. 'God bless it, and all who have to get through it.'

'Well,' I said, looking out at the scene, 'that really is the morning after the night before.'

The rain had turned to sleet and the lawn was covered with debris from the storm – small branches, twigs, a white cane chair thrown on its side. Here and there, around the edges of the door, where it was sheltered, the sleet had stuck together and frozen into strips, like bits of polystyrene packaging. The only brightness in the murk was the reflection of our bedroom light. It resembled a flying saucer hovering above the dunes. I could see Ruth's face quite clearly in the glass: watchful, brooding.

'I'm not going to give you an interview,' she said. 'I don't want to be in his bloody book, being patronised and thanked by him, using your words.' She turned and brushed past me. At the bedroom door she paused. 'He's on his own now. I'll get a divorce. And then *she* can do the prison visits.'

I listened to the sound of her own door opening and closing, and shortly afterwards the barely audible sound of a toilet flushing. I had almost finished packing. I folded the clothes she had lent me the previous evening and laid them on the chair, put my laptop into my shoulder bag, and then the only thing left was the manuscript. It sat in a thick pile on the table where she had left it, three sullen inches of it – my millstone, my albatross, my meal ticket. I couldn't make any progress without it, yet I wasn't supposed to take it from the house. It occurred to me that perhaps I could argue that the war crimes investigation had changed the circumstances of Lang's life so completely, the old rules no longer applied. At any rate I could use that as an excuse. I certainly couldn't face the embarrassment of staying here and running into Ruth every few hours. I put the manuscript into my suitcase, along with the package from the archive, zipped them up, and went out into the corridor.

Barry, the Special Branch man, was sitting with his Harry Potter novel in the chair by the front door. He raised his great slab of a face from the pages and gave me a look of weary disapproval, tinged with a sneer of amused contempt.

'Morning, sir,' he said. 'Finished for the night, have we?'

I thought, *He knows*. And then I thought: *Of course he knows, you bloody fool; it's his job to know*. In a flash I saw his sniggering conversations with his colleagues, the log of his official observations passed to London, a discreet entry in a file somewhere, and I felt a thrust of fury and resentment. Perhaps I should have responded with a wink, or a colluding quip – 'Well, Officer, you know what they say, there's many a good tune played on an old fiddle', or something of the sort – but instead I said, coldly, 'Why don't you just fuck off?'

It wasn't exactly Oscar Wilde, but it got me out of the house. I walked through the door and set off towards the track, only belatedly registering that unfortunately high moral dudgeon offers no protection against stinging squalls of sleet. I trudged on with an effort at dignity for a few more yards, then ducked for cover into the lee of the house. Rainwater was overflowing from the gutter and drilling into the sandy soil. I took off my jacket, and held it over my head, and considered how I was going to reach Edgartown. That was when the idea of borrowing the tan-coloured Ford Escape SUV popped helpfully into my mind.

How different – how very different – the course of my life would have been if I hadn't immediately gone running towards that garage, dodging the puddles, the tent of my jacket raised over me with one hand, the other dragging my little suitcase. I see myself now as if in a movie, or perhaps, more aptly, in one of those filmed reconstructions on a TV crime show: the victim skipping unknowingly towards his fate, as ominous chords underscore the portentousness of the scene. The door was still unlocked from the previous day and the keys of the Ford were in the ignition – after all, who worries about robbers when you live at the end of a two-mile track, protected by six armed bodyguards? I heaved my case into the front passenger seat, put my jacket back on, and slid behind the steering wheel.

It was as cold as a morgue, that Ford, and as dusty as an old attic. I ran my hands over the unfamiliar controls and my fingertips came away grey. I don't actually own a car – I've never found much need, living alone in London – and on the rare occasions I hire one, it always seems that another layer of gadgets has been added, so that the instrument panel of the average family saloon now looks to me like the cockpit of a jumbo. There was a mystifying screen to the right of the wheel, which came alive when I switched on the engine. Pulsing green arcs were shown radiating upwards from the earth to an orbiting space station. As I watched, the pulse switched direction and the arcs beamed down from the heavens. An instant later, the screen showed a large red arrow, a yellow path, and a great patch of blue.

An American woman's voice, soft but commanding, said, from somewhere behind me: 'Join the road as soon as possible.'

I would have turned her off, but I couldn't see how, and I was conscious that the noise of the engine might soon bring Barry lumbering out of the house to investigate. The thought of his lubricious gaze was enough to get me moving. I quickly put the Ford into reverse and backed out of the garage. Then I adjusted the mirrors, switched on the headlights and the windscreen wipers, engaged drive, and headed for the gate. As I passed the guard post the scene on the little satellite navigation monitor swung pleasingly, as if I were playing on an arcade game, and then the red arrow settled over the centre of the yellow path. I was away.

There was something oddly soothing about driving along and seeing all the little paths and streams, neatly labelled, appear at the top of the screen and then scroll down before disappearing off the bottom. It made me feel as if the world were a safe and tamed place, its every feature tagged and measured, and stored in some celestial control room, where softly spoken angels kept a benign vigil on the travellers below.

'In two hundred yards,' instructed the woman, 'turn right.'

'In fifty yards, turn right.'

And then:

'Turn right.'

The solitary demonstrator was huddled in his hut, reading a newspaper. He stood as he saw me at the junction, and came out into the sleet. I noticed he had a car parked nearby, a big old Volkswagen camper van, and I wondered why he didn't shelter in that. As I swung right, I got a good look at his gaunt grey face. He was immobile and expressionless, taking no more notice of the drenching rain than if he had been a carved wooden figure outside a drugstore. I pressed my foot on the accelerator and headed towards Edgartown, enjoying the slight sense of adventure that always comes from driving in a foreign country. My disembodied guide was silent for the next four miles or so, and I had forgotten all about her until, as I reached the outskirts of the town, she started up again.

'In two hundred yards, turn left.'

Her voice made me jump.

'In fifty yards, turn left.'

'Turn left,' she repeated, when we reached the junction.

Now she was beginning to get on my nerves.

'I'm sorry,' I muttered, and took a right towards Main Street.

'Turn around when possible.'

'This is getting ridiculous,' I said out loud, and pulled over. I pressed various buttons on the navigator's console, with the aim of shutting it down. The screen changed and offered me a menu. I can't remember all the options. One was 'ENTER A NEW DESTIN-ATION'. I think another was 'RETURN TO HOME ADDRESS'. And a third – the one highlighted – was 'REMEMBER PREVIOUS DESTINATION'.

I stared at it for a while, as the potential implications slowly filtered into my brain. Cautiously, I pressed 'SELECT'.

The screen went blank. The device was obviously malfunc-tioning.

I turned off the engine and hunted around for the instructions. I even braved the sleet and opened up the back of the Ford to see if they'd been left there. I returned empty-handed and turned on the ignition. Once again the navigation system lit up. As it went through its start-up routine, communicating with its mother ship, I put the car into gear and headed down the hill.

'Turn around when possible.'

I tapped the steering wheel with my forefingers. For the first time in my life I was confronted with the true meaning of the word predestination. I had just passed the Victorian whaling church. Before me the hill dipped towards the harbour. A few white masts were faintly visible through the dirty lace curtain of rain. I was not far from my old hotel – from the girl in the white mob cap, and the sailing prints, and old Captain John Coffin staring sternly from the wall. It was not yet eight o'clock. There was no traffic on the road. The sidewalks were deserted. I carried on down the slope, past all the empty shops with their cheery 'closed-for-the-winter-see-you-next-year!!' notices.

'Turn around when possible.'

Wearily, I surrendered to fate. I flicked the indicator and turned into a little street of houses – Summer Street, I think it was called, inappropriately enough – and braked. The rain pounded on the roof of the Ford; the windscreen wiper thudded back and forth. A small black and white terrier was defecating in the gutter, with an expression of intense concentration on its ancient, wise face. Its owner, too thickly swaddled against the wet and cold for me to tell either age or sex, turned clumsily to look at me, like a spaceman manoeuvring himself on a lunar walk. In one hand was a pooper scooper, in the other a white plastic scrotum of dog's crap. I quickly reversed back out into Main Street, swinging the wheel so hard I briefly mounted the kerb. With a thrilling screech of tyres, I set off back up the hill. The arrow swung wildly, before settling content-edly over the yellow route.

Exactly what I thought I was doing, I still don't really know. I couldn't even be sure that McAra had been the last driver to enter an address. It might have been some other guest of Rhinehart's;

it might have been Dep or Duc; it could even have been the police. Whatever the truth, it was certainly in the back of my mind that if things started to get remotely alarming, I could stop at any point, and I suppose that gave me a false sense of reassurance.

Once I was out of Edgartown and on to Vineyard Haven Road, I heard nothing more from my heavenly guide for several minutes. I passed dark patches of woodland and small white houses. The few approaching cars had their headlights on and were travelling slowly, swishing over the water-slicked road. I sat well forward, peering into the grimy morning. I passed a high school, just starting to get busy for the day, and beside it the island's set of traffic lights (they were marked on the map, like a tourist attraction: something to go and look at in the winter). The road bent sharply, the trees seemed to close in; the screen showed a fresh set of evocative names: Deer Hunter's Way, Skiff Avenue.

'In two hundred yards, turn right.'

'In fifty yards, turn right.'

'Turn right.'

I steered down the hill into Vineyard Haven, passing a school bus toiling up it. I had a brief impression of a deserted shopping street away to my left, and then I was into the flat, shabby area around the port. I turned a corner, passed a café, and pulled up in a big car park. About a hundred yards away, across the puddled, rain-swept tarmac, a queue of vehicles was driving up the ramp of a ferry. The red arrow pointed me towards it.

In the warmth of the Ford, as shown on the navigation screen, the proposed route was inviting, like a child's painting of a summer holiday – a yellow jetty extending into the bright blue of Vineyard Haven Harbor. But the reality through the windscreen was distinctly uninviting: the sagging black mouth of the ferry, smeared at the corners with rust, and, beyond it, the heaving grey swell and the flailing hawsers of sleet.

Someone tapped on the glass beside me and I fumbled for the switch to lower the window. He was wearing dark blue oilskins with the hood pulled up, and he had to keep one hand pressed firmly on top of it to prevent it flying off his head. His spectacles were dripping with rain. A badge announced that he worked for the Steamship Authority.

'You'll have to hurry,' he shouted, turning his back into the wind. 'She leaves at eight fifteen. The weather's getting bad. There might not be another for a while.' He opened the door for me and almost pushed me towards the ticket office. 'You go pay. I'll tell them you'll be right there.'

I left the engine running and went into the little building. Even as I stood at the counter, I remained in two minds. Through the window I could see the last of the cars boarding the ferry, and the car park attendant standing by the Ford, stamping his feet to ward off the cold. He saw me staring at him, and beckoned at me urgently to get a move on.

The elderly woman behind the desk looked as though she, too, could think of better places to be at a quarter past eight on a Friday morning.

'You going or what?' she demanded.

I sighed, took out my wallet and slapped down five ten-dollar bills, and was given a ticket and a few coins in change.

*

Once I'd driven up the clanking metal gangway into the dark, oily belly of the ship, another man in waterproofs directed me to a parking space, and I inched forwards until he held up his hand for me to stop. All around me, drivers were leaving their vehicles and squeezing through the narrow gaps towards the stairwells. I stayed where I was and carried on trying to figure out how the navigation system worked. But after about a minute the crewman tapped on my window and indicated by a mime that I had to switch off the ignition. As I did so, the screen died again. Behind me, the ferry's rear doors closed. The ship's engines started to throb, the hull lurched, and with a discouraging scrape of steel we began to move.

I felt trapped all of a sudden, sitting in the chilly twilight of that hold, with its stink of diesel and exhaust fumes, and it was more than just the claustrophobia of being below decks. It was McAra. I could sense his presence next to me. His dogged, leaden obsessions now seemed to have become mine. He was like some heavy, half-witted stranger one makes the mistake of talking to on a journey, and who then refuses to leave one alone. I got out of the car and locked it, and went in search of a cup of coffee. At the bar on the upper deck I queued behind a man reading *USA Today*, and over his shoulder I saw a picture of Lang with the Secretary of State. 'LANG TO FACE WAR CRIMES TRIAL' was the headline. 'WASHINGTON SHOWS SUPPORT.' The camera had caught him grinning.

I took my coffee over to a corner seat and considered where my curiosity had led me. For a start, I was technically guilty of stealing a car. I ought at least to call the house and let them know I'd taken it. But that would probably entail talking to Ruth, who would demand to know where I was, and I didn't want to tell her. Then there was the question of whether or not what I was doing was wise. If this *was* McAra's original route I was following, I had to face the fact that he hadn't returned from the trip alive. How was I to know what lay at the end of the journey? Perhaps I should tell someone what I was contemplating, or better still take a companion along as a witness. Or perhaps I should simply disembark at Woods Hole, wait in one of the bars, catch the next ferry back to the island, and plan the whole thing properly, rather than launch myself into the unknown so unprepared.

Oddly enough, I didn't feel any particular sense of danger – I suppose because it was all so ordinary. I glanced around at the faces of my fellow passengers: working people mostly, to judge by their denims and boots – weary guys who had just made an early-morning delivery to the island, or people going over to America to pick up supplies. A big wave hit the side of the ship and we all swayed as one, like rippling weed on the seabed. Through the brine-streaked porthole, the low grey line of coast and the restless, freezing sea appeared completely anonymous. We could have been in the Baltic or the Solent or the White Sea – any dreary stretch of flattened shoreline, where people have to find a means of turning a living at the very edge of the land.

Someone went out on deck for a cigarette, letting in a gust of cold, wet air. I didn't attempt to follow him. I had another coffee and relaxed in the safety of the warm, damp, yellowish atmosphere of the bar, until, about half an hour later, we passed the Nobska Point Lighthouse and a loudspeaker instructed us to return to our vehicles. The deck pitched badly in the swell, hitting the side of the dock with a clang that rang down the length of the hull. I was knocked against the metal doorframe at the foot of the stairs. A couple of car alarms started howling and my feeling of security vanished, replaced by panic that the Ford was being broken into. But as I swayed closer it looked untouched, and when I opened my case to check, Lang's memoirs were still there.

I switched on the engine, and by the time I emerged into the grey rain and wind of Woods Hole, the satellite screen was offering me its familiar golden path. It would have been a simple matter to have pulled over and gone into one of the nearby bars for breakfast, but instead I stayed in the convoy of traffic and let it carry me on – on into the filthy New England winter, up Woods Hole Road to Locust Street and Main Street, and beyond. I had half a tank of fuel and the whole day stretched ahead of me.

'In two hundred yards, at the roundabout, take the second exit.'

I took it, and for the next forty-five minutes I headed north on a couple of big freeways, more or less retracing my route back to Boston. That appeared to answer one question at any rate: whatever else McAra had been up to just before he died, he hadn't been driving to New York to see Rycart. I wondered what could have tempted him to Boston. The airport, perhaps? I let my mind fill with images of him meeting someone off a plane – from England, maybe – his solemn face turned expectantly towards the sky, a hurried greeting in the arrivals hall, and then off to some clandestine rendezvous. Or perhaps he had flown somewhere by himself? But just as that scenario was taking firm shape in my imagination, I was directed west towards Interstate 95, and even with my feeble grasp of Massachusetts geography I knew I must be heading away from Logan Airport and downtown Boston.

I drove as slowly as I could along the wide road for perhaps fifteen miles. The rain had eased, but it was still dark. The thermometer showed an outside temperature of 25 degrees Fahrenheit. I remember great swathes of woodland, interspersed with lakes, with office blocks and high-tech factories gleaming brightly amid landscaped grounds, as delicately positioned as country clubs, or cemeteries. Just as I was beginning to think that perhaps McAra had been making a run for the Canadian border, the voice behind me told me to take the next exit from the interstate, and I came down on to another big six-lane freeway which, according to the screen, was the Concord Turnpike.

I could make out very little through the screen of trees, even though their branches were bare. My slow speed was infuriating the drivers behind me. A succession of big trucks came lumbering up behind me and blazed their headlights and blared their horns, before pulling out to overtake in a fountain of dirty spray.

The woman in the back seat spoke up again.

'In two hundred yards take the next exit.'

I moved into the right-hand lane and came down the slip road. At the end of the curve I found myself in a sylvan suburbia of big houses, double garages, wide drives and open lawns – a rich but neighbourly kind of a place, the houses screened from one another by trees, almost every mailbox bearing a yellow ribbon in honour of the military. I believe it was actually called Pleasant Street.

A sign pointed to Belmont Center, and that was more or less the way I went, along roads which gradually became less populated as the price of the real estate rose. I passed a golf course and turned right into some woods. A red squirrel ran across the road in front of me, and jumped on top of a sign forbidding the lighting of campfires, and that was when, in the middle of what seemed to be nowhere, my guardian angel at last announced, in a tone of calm finality: 'You have reached your destination.'

Thirteen

Because I am so enthusiastic about the ghostwriting profession, I may have given the impression that it is an easy way to make a living. If so, then I should qualify my words just a little with a warning.

Ghostwriting

I pulled up on to the verge and turned off the engine. Looking around at the dense and dripping woodland, I felt a profound sense of disappointment. I wasn't sure exactly what I'd been expecting — not Deep Throat in an underground car park necessarily, but certainly more than this. Yet again, McAra had surprised me: here was a man reportedly even more hostile to the country than I was, and yet his trail had merely led me to a hiker's paradise.

I got out of the car and locked it. After two hours' driving I needed to fill my lungs with cold, damp New England air. I stretched and started to walk down the wet lane. The squirrel watched me from its perch across the road. I took a couple of paces towards it and clapped my hands at the cute little rodent. It streaked up into a nearby tree, flicking its tail at me like a swollen middle finger. I hunted around for a stick to throw at it, then stopped myself. I was spending far too much time alone in the woods, I decided, as I moved on down the road. I'd be happy not to hear the deep, vegetative silence of ten thousand trees for a very long while to come.

I walked on for about fifty yards until I came to an almost invisible gap in the trees. Demurely set back from the road, a five-barred electric gate blocked access to a private drive, which turned sharply after a few yards and disappeared behind trees. I couldn't see the house. Beside the gate was a grey metal mailbox with no name on it, just a number – 3551 – and a stone pillar with an intercom and a code pad. A sign said, 'THESE PREMISES ARE PROTECTED BY CYCLOPS SECURITY'; a toll-free number was printed across an eyeball. I hesitated, then pressed the buzzer. While I waited, I glanced around. A small video camera was mounted on a nearby branch. I tried the buzzer again. There was no answer.

I stepped back, uncertain what to do. It briefly crossed my mind to climb the gate and make an unauthorised inspection of the property, but I didn't like the look of the camera, and I didn't like the sound of Cyclops Security. I noticed that the mailbox was crammed too full to close properly, and I saw no harm in at least discovering the name of the house's owner. With another glance over my shoulder, and an apologetic shrug towards the camera, I pulled out a handful of mail. It was variously addressed to Mr and Mrs Paul Emmett, Professor and Mrs Paul Emmett, Professor Emmett, and Nancy Emmett. Judging by the postmarks it looked as though there was at least two days' worth uncollected. The Emmetts were either away, or – what? Lying inside, dead? I was developing a morbid imagination. Some of the letters had been forwarded, with a sticker covering the original address. I scraped one of the labels back with my thumb. Emmett, I learned, was President Emeritus of something called the Arcadia Institution, with an address in Washington DC.

Emmett . . . Emmett . . . For some reason that name was familiar to me. I stuffed the letters back in the box and returned to my car.

I opened my suitcase, took out the package addressed to McAra, and ten minutes later I'd found what I had vaguely remembered: P. Emmett (St John's) was one of the cast of the Footlights revue, pictured with Lang. He was the oldest of the group, the one whom I'd thought was a postgraduate. He had shorter hair than the others, looked more conventional: 'square', as the expression went at that time. Was this what had brought McAra all the way up here: yet more research about Cambridge? Emmett was mentioned in the memoirs, too, now I came to think about it. I picked up the manuscript and thumbed my way through the section on Lang's university days, but his name didn't appear there. Instead he was quoted at the start of the very last chapter:

> *Professor Paul Emmett of Harvard University has written of the unique*
> *importance of the English-speaking peoples in the spread of democracy*
> *around the world: 'As long as these nations stand together, freedom is safe;*
> *whenever they have faltered, tyranny has gathered strength.' I profoundly*
> *agree with this sentiment.*

The squirrel came back and regarded me malevolently from the roadside.

Odd: that was my overwhelming feeling about everything at that moment. *Odd.*

I don't know exactly how long I sat there. I do remember that I was so bemused I forgot to turn on the Ford's heater, and it was only when I heard the sound of another car approaching that I realised how cold and stiff I had become. I looked in the mirror and saw a pair of headlights, and then a small Japanese car drove past me. A middle-aged, dark-haired woman was at the wheel, and next to her was a man of about sixty, wearing glasses and a jacket and tie. He turned to stare at me, and I knew at once it was Emmett, not because I recognised him (I didn't) but because I couldn't imagine who else would be travelling down such a quiet road. The car pulled up outside the entrance to the drive, and I saw Emmett get out to empty his mailbox. Once again, he peered in my direction, and I thought he might be about to come down and challenge me. Instead, he returned to the car, which then moved on, out of my line of sight, presumably up to the house.

I stuffed the photographs and the page from the memoirs into my shoulder bag, gave the Emmetts ten minutes to open the place up and settle themselves in, then I turned on the engine and drove up to the gate. This time, when I pressed the buzzer, the answer came immediately.

'Hello?'

It was a woman's voice.

'Is that Mrs Emmett?'

'Who is this?'

'I wondered if I could have a word with Professor Emmett.'

'He's very tired.' She had a drawling voice, something between an English aristocrat and a southern belle, and the tinny quality of the intercom accentuated it: *'S'vair tahd.'*

'I won't keep him long.'

'Do you have an appointment?'

'It's about Adam Lang. I'm assisting him with his memoirs.'

'Just a moment, please.'

I knew they'd be studying me on the video camera. I tried to adopt a suitably respectable pose. When the intercom crackled again, it was an American male voice that spoke: resonant, fruity, actorish.

'This is Paul Emmett. I think you must have made a mistake.'

'You were at Cambridge with Mr Lang, I believe?'

'We were contemporaries, yes, but I can't claim to know him.'

'I have a picture of the two of you together in a Footlights revue.'

There was a long pause.

'Come on up to the house.'

There was a whine of an electric motor, and the gate slowly opened.

As I followed the drive, the big three-storey house gradually appeared through the trees: a central section built of grey stone, flanked by wings made of wood and painted white. Most of the windows were arched, with small panes of rippled glass and big slatted shutters. It could have been any age, from six months to a century. A short flight of steps led up to a pillared porch, where Emmett himself was waiting. The extent of the land and the encroaching trees provided a deep sense of seclusion. The only sound of civilisation was a big jet, invisible in the low cloud, dropping towards the airport. I parked in front of the garage, next to the Emmetts' car, and got out carrying my bag.

'You must forgive me if I seem a little groggy,' said Emmett, after we'd shaken hands. 'We just flew in from Washington and I'm feeling somewhat tired. I normally never see anyone without an appointment. But your mention of a photograph did rather stimulate my curiosity.'

He dressed as precisely as he spoke. His spectacles had fashionably modern tortoiseshell frames, his jacket was dark grey, his shirt was duck-egg blue, his bright red tie had a motif of pheasants on the wing; there was a matching silk handkerchief in his breast pocket. Now I was closer to him, I could discern the younger man staring out from the older: age had merely blurred him, that was all. He couldn't keep his eyes off my bag. I knew he wanted me to produce the photograph right there on the doorstep. But I was too canny for that. I waited, and kept on waiting, so that eventually he had to say, 'Fine. Please, do come in.'

The house had glossy wood floors and smelled of wax polish and dried flowers. It had an uninhabited chill about it. A grandfather clock ticked very loudly on the landing. I could hear his wife on the telephone in another room. 'Yes,' she said, 'he's here now.' Then she must have moved away. Her voice became indistinct, and faded altogether.

Emmett closed the front door behind us.

'May I?' he said.

I took out the cast photograph and gave it to him. He pushed his glasses up on to his silvery thatch of hair and wandered over with it to the hall window. He looked fit for his age and I guessed he played some regular sport: squash, probably; golf, definitely.

'Well, well,' he said, holding the monochrome image up to the weak winter light, tilting it this way and that, peering at it down his long nose, like an expert checking a painting for authenticity, 'I have literally no recollection of this.'

'But it *is* you?'

'Oh yes. I was on the board of the Dramat in the sixties. Which was quite a time, as you can imagine.' He shared a complicit chuckle with his youthful image. 'Oh yes.'

'The Dramat?'

'I'm sorry.' He looked up. 'The Yale Dramatic Association. I thought I'd maintain my theatrical interests when I went over to Cambridge, for my doctoral research. Alas, I only managed a term in the Footlights, before pressure of work put an end to my dramatic career. May I keep this?'

'I'm afraid not. But I'm sure I can get you a copy.'

'Would you? That would be very kind.' He turned it over and inspected the back. 'The *Cambridge Evening News*. You must tell me how you came by it.'

'I'd be happy to,' I said. And again I waited. It was like playing a hand of cards. He would not yield a trick unless I forced him. The big clock ticked back and forth a few times.

'Come into my study,' he said.

He opened a door and I followed him into a room straight out of Rick's London club: dark green wallpaper, floor-to-ceiling books, library steps, overstuffed brown leather furniture, a big brass lectern in the shape of an eagle, a Roman bust; a faint odour of cigars. One wall was devoted to memorabilia: citations, prizes, honorary degrees, and a lot of photographs. I took in Emmett with Bill Clinton and Al Gore, Emmett with Margaret Thatcher and Nelson Mandela. I'd tell you the names of the others if I knew who they were. A German chancellor. A French president. There was also a picture of him with Lang, a grin-and-grip at what seemed to be a cocktail party. He saw me looking.

'The wall of ego,' he said. 'We all have them. Think of it as the equivalent of the orthodontist's fish tank. Do take a seat. I'm afraid I can only spare a few minutes, unfortunately.'

I perched on the unyielding brown sofa while he took the captain's chair behind his desk. It rolled easily back and forth. He swung his feet up on to the desk, giving me a fine view of the slightly scuffed soles of his brogues.

'So,' he said. 'The picture.'

'I'm working with Adam Lang on his memoirs.'

'I know. You said. Poor Lang. It's a very bad business, this posturing by The Hague. As for Rycart – the worst Foreign Secretary since the war, in my view. It was a terrible error to appoint him. But if the ICC continues to behave so foolishly, they will succeed merely in making Lang first a martyr and then a hero, and thus,' he added, gesturing graciously towards me, 'a bestseller.'

'How well do you know him?'

'Lang? Hardly at all. You look surprised.'

'Well, for a start, he mentions you in his memoirs.'

Emmett appeared genuinely taken aback. 'Now it's my turn to be surprised. What does he say?'

'It's a quote, at the start of the final chapter.' I pulled the relevant page from my bag. '"As long as these nations" — that's everyone who speaks English — "stand together,"' I read, '"freedom is safe; whenever they have faltered, tyranny has gathered strength." And then Lang says, "I profoundly agree with this sentiment."'

'Well, that's decent of him,' said Emmett. 'And his instincts as prime minister were good, in my judgement. But that doesn't mean I know him.'

'And then there's that,' I said, pointing to the wall of ego.

'Oh, *that*.' Emmett waved his hand dismissively. 'That was just taken at a reception at Claridge's, to mark the tenth anniversary of the Arcadia Institution.'

'The Arcadia Institution?' I repeated.

'It's a little organisation I used to run. It's very select. No reason why you should have heard of it. The prime minister graced us with his presence. It was purely professional.'

'But you must have known Adam Lang at Cambridge,' I persisted.

'Not really. One summer term, our paths crossed. That was it.'

'Can you remember much about him?' I took out my notebook. Emmett eyed it as if I'd just pulled out a revolver. 'I'm sorry,' I said. 'Do you mind?'

'Not at all. Go ahead. I'm just rather bewildered. No one's ever mentioned the Cambridge connection between us in all these years.

I've barely thought about it myself until this moment. I don't think I can tell you anything worth writing down.'

'But you performed together?'

'In one production. The summer revue. I can't even remember now what it was called. There were a hundred members, you know.'

'So he made no impression on you?'

'None.'

'Even though he became prime minister?'

'Obviously if I'd known he was going to do that, I'd have taken the trouble to get to know him better. But in my time I've met eight presidents, four popes and five British prime ministers, and none of them was what I would describe as personally truly outstanding.'

Yes, I thought, and has it ever occurred to you they might not have reckoned you were up to much, either? But I didn't say that. Instead I said, 'Can I show you something else?'

'If you really think it will be of interest.' He ostentatiously checked his watch.

I took out the other photographs. Now I looked at them again, it was clear that Emmett featured in several. Indeed, he was unmistakably the man on the summer picnic, giving the thumbs-up sign behind Lang's back, while the future prime minister did a Bogart with his joint and was fed strawberries and champagne.

I reached across and handed them to Emmett, who performed his affected little piece of stage business again, pushing up his glasses so that he could study the pictures with his naked eyes. I can see him now: sleek and pink and imperturbable. His expression didn't flicker, which struck me as peculiar, because mine certainly would have done, in similar circumstances.

'Oh my,' he said. 'Is that what I think it is? Let's hope he didn't inhale.'

'But that is you standing behind him, isn't it?'

'I do believe it is. And I do believe I'm on the point of issuing a stern warning to him on the perils of drug abuse. Can't you just sense it forming on my lips?' He gave the pictures back to me and pulled his spectacles back down on to his nose. Tilting further back in his chair he scrutinised me carefully. 'Does Mr Lang really want these published in his memoirs? If so, I would prefer it if I weren't identified. My children would be mortified. They're so much more puritanical than we were.'

'Can you tell me the names of any of the others in the picture? The girls perhaps?'

'I'm sorry. That summer is just a blur – a long and happy blur. The world may have been going to pieces around us, but we were making merry.'

His words reminded me of something that Ruth had said: about all the things that were going on at the time the picture was taken.

'You must have been lucky,' I said, 'given that you were at Yale in the late sixties, to avoid being drafted to Vietnam.'

'You know the old saying: "If you had the dough, you didn't have to go." I got a student deferment. Now,' he said, twirling in his chair and lifting his feet off the desk. He was suddenly much more businesslike. He picked up a pen and opened a notebook. 'You were going to tell me where you got those pictures.'

'Does the name Michael McAra mean anything to you?'

'No. Should it?'

He answered just a touch too quickly, I thought.

'McAra was my predecessor on the Lang memoirs,' I said. 'He was the one who ordered the pictures from England. He drove up here to see you nearly three weeks ago and died a few hours afterwards.'

'Drove up to see *me*?' Emmett shook his head. 'I'm afraid you're mistaken. Where was he driving from?'

'Martha's Vineyard.'

'Martha's Vineyard! My dear fellow, *nobody* is on Martha's Vineyard at this time of year.'

He was teasing me again: anyone who had watched the news the previous day would have known where Lang had been staying.

I said, 'The vehicle McAra was driving had your address programmed into its navigation system.'

'Well, I can't think why that should be the case.' Emmett stroked his chin and seemed to weigh the matter carefully. 'No, I really can't. And even if it's true, it certainly doesn't prove he actually made the journey. How did he die?'

'He drowned.'

'I'm very sorry to hear it. I've never believed the myth that death by drowning is painless, have you? I'm sure it must be agonising.'

'The police never said anything to you about this?'

'No. I've had no contact with the police whatsoever.'

'Were you here that weekend? This would have been January the eleventh and twelfth.'

Emmett sighed. 'A less equable man than I would start to find your questions impertinent.' He came out from behind his desk and went over to the door. 'Nancy!' he called. 'Our visitor wishes to know where we were on the weekend of the eleventh and twelfth of January. Do we possess that information?' He stood holding the door open and gave me an unfriendly smile. When Mrs Emmett appeared, he didn't bother to introduce me. She was carrying a desk diary.

'That was the Colorado weekend,' she said, and showed the book to her husband.

'Of course it was,' he said. 'We were at the Aspen Institute,' he said flourishing the page at me. '"Bi-polar relationships in a multi-polar world."'

'Sounds fun.'

'It was.' He closed the diary with a definitive snap. 'I was the main speaker.'

'You were there the whole weekend?'

'I was,' said Mrs Emmett. 'I stayed for the skiing. Emmett flew back on Sunday, didn't you, darling?'

'So you could have seen McAra,' I said to him.

'I could have done, but I didn't.'

'Just to return to Cambridge—' I began.

'No,' he said, holding up his hand. 'Please. If you don't mind, let's *not* return to Cambridge. I've said all I have to say on the matter. Nancy?'

She must have been twenty years his junior, and she jumped when he addressed her in a way no first wife ever would.

'Emmett?'

'Show our friend here out, would you?'

As we shook hands, he said, 'I am an avid reader of political memoirs. I shall be sure to get hold of Mr Lang's book when it appears.'

'Perhaps he'll send you a copy,' I said, 'for old times' sake.'

'I doubt it very much,' he replied. 'The gate will open automatically. Be sure to make a right at the bottom of the drive. If you turn left, the road will take you deeper into the woods and you'll never be seen again.'

*

Mrs Emmett closed the door behind me before I'd even reached the bottom step. I could sense her husband watching me from the window of his study as I walked across the damp grass to the Ford. At the bottom of the drive, while I waited for the gate to open, the wind moved suddenly through the branches of the high trees on either side of me, laying a heavy lash of rainwater across the car. It startled me so much I felt the hairs on the back of my head stand out in tiny spikes.

I pulled out into the empty road and headed back the way I had come. I felt slightly unnerved, as if I'd just descended a staircase in the darkness and missed the bottom few steps. My immediate priority was to get clear of those trees.

'Turn around where possible.'

I stopped the Ford, grabbed the navigation system in both hands, and twisted and yanked it at the same time. It came away from the front panel with a satisfying twang of breaking cables and I tossed it into the footwell on the passenger's side. At the same time I became aware of a large black car with bright headlights coming up close behind me. It overtook the Ford too quickly for me to see who was driving, accelerated up to the junction and disappeared. When I looked back, the country lane was once again deserted.

It's curious how the processes of fear work. If I'd been asked a week earlier to predict what I might do in such a situation, I'd have said that I'd drive straight back to Martha's Vineyard and try to put the whole business out of my mind. In fact, I discovered, Nature mingles an unexpected element of anger in with fear, presumably to encourage the survival of the species. Like a caveman confronted by a tiger, my instinct at that moment was not to run; it was somehow get back at the supercilious Emmett — the sort of crazy, atavistic response that leads otherwise sane householders to chase armed burglars down the street, usually with disastrous results.

So instead of sensibly trying to find my way back to the inter-state, I followed the road signs to Belmont. It's a sprawling, leafy, wealthy town, of terrifying cleanliness and orderliness – the sort of place where you need a licence just to keep a cat. The neat streets, with their flagpoles and their four-by-fours, slipped by, seemingly identical. I cruised along the wide boulevards, unable to get my bearings, until at last I came to something which seemed to resemble the middle of town. This time, when I parked my car, I took my suitcase with me.

I was on a road called Leonard Street, a curve of pretty shops with coloured canopies set against a backdrop of big bare trees. One building was pink. A coating of snow, melted at the edges, covered the grey roofs. It could have been a ski resort. It offered me various things I didn't need – a real estate agent, a jeweller, a hairdresser – and one thing I did: an internet café. I ordered a coffee and a bagel and took a seat as far away from the window as I could. I put my case on the chair opposite, to discourage anyone from joining me, sipped my coffee, took a bite out of my bagel, clicked on Google, typed in '"Paul Emmett" "Arcadia Institution"', and leaned towards the screen.

*

According to www.arcadiainstitution.org, the Arcadia Institution was founded in August 1991 on the fiftieth anniversary of the first summit meeting between Prime Minister Winston S. Churchill and President Franklin D. Roosevelt, at Placentia Bay in Newfoundland. There was a photograph of Roosevelt on the deck of a US battle-ship, wearing a smart grey suit, receiving Churchill, who was about a head shorter and dressed in some peculiar rumpled dark blue naval outfit, complete with a cap. He looked like a crafty head gardener paying his respects to a local squire.

The aim of the institution, the website said, was 'to further Anglo-American relations and foster the timeless ideals of democracy and free speech for which our two nations have always stood in times of peace and war'. This was to be achieved 'through seminars, policy programs, conferences and leadership development initiatives', as well as through the publication of a bi-annual journal, *The Arcadian Review*, and the funding of ten Arcadia Scholarships, awarded annually, for postgraduate research into 'cultural, political and strategic subjects of mutual interest to Great Britain and the United States'. The Arcadia Institution had offices in St James's Square, London, and in Washington, and the names of its board of trustees – ex-ambassadors, corporate CEOs, university professors – read like the guest list for the dullest dinner party you would ever endure in your life.

Paul Emmett was the institution's first president and CEO, and the website usefully offered his life in a paragraph: born Chicago 1949, graduate of Yale University and St John's College, Cambridge (Rhodes Scholar); lecturer in international affairs at Harvard University, 1975–79, and subsequently Howard T. Polk III Professor of Foreign Relations, 1979–91; thereafter the founding head of the Arcadia Institution; President Emeritus since 2007; publications: *Whither thou Goest: The Special Relationship 1940–1956*; *The Conundrum of Change; Losing Empires, Finding Roles: Some Aspects of US–UK Relations since 1956; The Chains of Prometheus: Foreign Policy Constraints in the Nuclear Age; The Triumphant Generation: America, Britain and the New World Order; Why We Are In Iraq*. There was a profile in *Time* magazine, which described his hobbies as squash, golf and the operas of Gilbert and Sullivan, 'which he and his second wife, Nancy Cline, a defence analyst from Houston, Texas, regularly call upon their guests to perform at the end of one of their famous supper parties in the prosperous Harvard dormitory town of Belmont, MA'.

I worked my way through the first of what Google promised would eventually prove to be 37,000 entries about Emmett and Arcadia:

Roundtable on Middle East Policy – **Arcadia Institution**

The establishment of democracy in Syria and Iran . . . **Paul Emmett** in his

opening address stated his belief . . .

www.arcadiainstitution.org/site/roundtable/A56fL%2004.htm – 35k –

Cached – Similar pages

Arcadia Institution – Wikipedia, the free encyclopedia

The **Arcadia Institution** is an Anglo-American nonprofit organisation

founded in 1991 under the presidency of Professor **Paul Emmett** . . .

en.wikipedia.org/wiki/**Arcadia Institution** – 35k – Cached – Similar pages

Arcadia Institution/Arcadia Strategy Group – SourceWatch

The **Arcadia Institution** describes itself as dedicated to fostering . . .

Professor **Paul Emmett**, an expert in Anglo-American . . .

www.sourcewatch.org/index.php?title=**Arcadia Institution** – 39k –

USATODAY.com – 5 Questions for **Paul Emmett**

Paul Emmett, former professor of foreign relations at Harvard,

now heads the influential **Arcadia Institution** . . .

www.usatoday.com/world/2002-08-07/questions_x.htm?tab1.htm – 35k –

When I got bored with the same old stuff about seminars and summer conferences, I changed my search request to '"Arcadia Institution" "Adam Lang"' and got a news story from the *Guardian* website about Arcadia's anniversary reception and the prime minister's attendance. I switched to Google Images and was offered a mosaic of bizarre illustrations: a cat, a couple of acrobats in leotards, a cartoon of Lang blowing into a bag with the caption 'Soon to be humiliated'. This is the trouble with internet research, in my experience. The proportion of what's useful to what's dross dwindles very quickly and suddenly it's like searching for something dropped down the back of a sofa and coming up with handfuls of old coins, buttons, fluff and sucked sweets. What's important is to ask the right question, and somehow I sensed I was getting it wrong.

I broke off to rub my aching eyes. I ordered another coffee and another bagel and checked out my fellow diners. It was a light crowd, considering it was lunchtime: an old fellow with his paper, a man and woman in their twenties holding hands, two mothers – or, more likely, nannies – gossiping while their three toddlers played unheeded under the table, and a couple of young guys with short-cropped hair, who could have been in the armed forces, or one of the emergency services, perhaps (I'd seen a fire station nearby): they were sitting on stools at the counter and had their backs to me, engaged in earnest conversation.

I returned to the Arcadia Institution website and clicked on the board of trustees. Up they all came, like spirits summoned from the vast transatlantic deep: Steven D. Engler, former US Defense Secretary; Lord Leghorn, former British Foreign Secretary; Sir David Moberly, GCMG, KCVO, the thousand-year-old former British ambassador to Washington; Raymond T. Streicher, former US ambassador to London; Arthur Prussia, President and CEO of the Hallington Group; Professor Mel Crawford of the John F. Kennedy School of Government; Dame Unity Chambers of the Strategic Studies Foundation; Max Hardaker of Godolphin Securities; Stephanie Cox Morland, senior director of Manhattan

Equity Holdings; Sir Milius Rapp of the London School of Economics; Cornelius Iremonger of Cordesman Industrials, and Franklin R. Dollerman, senior partner of McCosh & Partners.

Laboriously, I began entering their names, together with Adam Lang's, into the search engine. Engler had praised Lang's steadfast courage on the op-ed page of *The New York Times*. Leghorn had made a hand-wringing speech in the House of Lords, regretting the situation in the Middle East but calling the prime minister 'a man of sincerity'. Moberly had suffered a stroke and was saying nothing. Streicher had been vocal in his support at the time Lang flew to Washington to pick up his Presidential Medal of Freedom. I was starting to weary of the whole procedure until I typed in Arthur Prussia. Then I got a one-year-old press release:

LONDON – The Hallington Group is pleased to announce that Adam Lang, the former Prime Minister of Great Britain, will be joining the company as a strategic consultant.

Mr Lang's position, which will not be full-time, will involve providing counsel and advice to senior Hallington investment professionals worldwide.

Arthur Prussia, Hallington's president and chief executive officer, said: 'Adam Lang is one of the world's most respected and experienced statesmen, and we are honoured to be able to draw on his well of experience.'

Adam Lang said: 'I welcome the challenge of working with a company of such global reach, commitment to democracy and renowned integrity as the Hallington Group.'

I had never heard of the Hallington Group, so I looked it up. Six hundred employees; twenty-four worldwide offices; a mere four hundred investors, mainly Saudi – and *thirty-five billion dollars* of funds at its disposal. The portfolio of companies it controlled looked as if it had been drawn up by Darth Vader. Hallington's subsidiaries manufactured cluster bombs, mobile howitzers, interceptor missiles, tank-busting helicopters, swing-wing bombers, tanks, nuclear centrifuges, aircraft carriers. It owned a company that provided security for contractors in the Middle East, another that carried out surveillance operations and data checks within the United States and worldwide, and a construction company that specialised in building military bunkers and airstrips. Two members of its main board had been senior directors of the CIA.

I know the internet is the stuff a paranoiac's dreams are made of. I know it parcels up everything – Lee Harvey Oswald, Princess Diana, Opus Dei, al-Qaeda, Israel, MI6, crop circles – and with pretty blue ribbons of hyperlinks it ties them all into a single grand conspiracy. But I also know the wisdom of the old saying that a paranoiac is simply a person in full possession of the facts, and as I typed in '"Arcadia Institution" "Hallington Group" CIA', I sensed that something was starting to emerge, like the lineaments of a ghost ship, out of the fog of data on the screen.

washingtonpost.com: **Hallington** jet linked to **CIA** 'torture flights'

The company denied all knowledge of the **CIA** programme of 'extraordinary rendition' . . . member of the board of the prestigious **Arcadia Institution** has . . .

www.washingtonpost.com/ac2/wp-dyn/A27824-2007Dec26language=-Cached – Similar pages

I clicked on the story and scrolled down to the relevant part:

The Hallington Gulfstream Four was clandestinely photographed – minus its corporate logo – at the Stare Kiejkuty military base in Poland, where the CIA is believed to have maintained a secret detention center, on February 18.

This was two days after four British citizens – Nasir Ashraf, Shakeel Qazi, Salim Khan and Faruk Ahmed – were allegedly kidnapped by CIA operatives from Peshawar, Pakistan. Mr Ashraf is reported to have died of heart failure after the interrogation procedure known as "water boarding".

Between February and July of that same year, the jet made 51 visits to Guantanamo and 82 visits to Washington Dulles International Air Force Base as well as landings at Andrews Air Force Base outside the capital and the US air bases at Ramstein and Rhein-Main in Germany.

The plane's flight log also shows visits to Afghanistan, Morocco, Dubai, Jordan, Italy, Japan, Switzerland, Azerbaijan and the Czech Republic.

The Hallington logo was visible in photographs taken at an air show in Schenectady, NY, on August 23, eight days after the Gulfstream returned to Washington from an around-the-world flight that included Anchorage; Osaka, Japan; Dubai, and Shannon.

The logo was not visible when the Gulfstream was photographed during a fuel stop at Shannon on September 27. But when the plane turned up at Denver's Centennial Airport in February of this year, a photo showed it was sporting not only the Hallington logo but a new registration number.

A spokesman for Hallington confirmed that the Gulfstream had been frequently leased to other operators, but insisted the company had no knowledge of the uses to which it might have been put.

Water boarding? I had never heard of it. It sounded harmless enough, a kind of healthy outdoor sport, a cross between wind-surfing and white-water rafting. I looked it up on a website.

Water boarding consists of tightly binding a prisoner to an inclined board in such a manner that the victim's feet are higher than the head and all movement is impossible. Cloth or cellophane is then used to cover the prisoner's face, on to which the interrogator pours a continuous stream of water. Although some of the liquid may enter the victim's lungs, it is the psychological sensation of being underwater which makes water boarding so effective. A gag reflex is triggered, the prisoner literally feels himself to be drowning, and almost instantly begs to be released. CIA officers who have been subjected to water boarding as part of their training have lasted an average of 14 seconds before caving in. Al-Qaeda's toughest prisoner, and alleged mastermind of the 9/11 bombings, Khalid Sheik Mohammed, won the admiration of his CIA interrogators when he was able to last two and a half minutes before begging to confess.

Water boarding can cause severe pain and damage to the lungs, brain damage due to oxygen deprivation, limb breakage and dislocation due to struggling against restraints, and long-term psyhological trauma. In 1947, a Japanese officer was convicted of using water boarding on a US citizen and sentenced to 15 years hard labour for a war crime. According to an investigation by ABC News, the CIA was authorized to begin using water boarding in mid-March 2002, and recruited a cadre of fourteen interrogators trained in the technique.

There was an illustration from Pol Pot's Cambodia, of a man bound by his wrists and ankles to a sloping table, lying on his back, upside down. His head was in a sack. His face was being saturated by a man holding a watering can. In another photograph, a Vietcong suspect, pinioned to the ground, was being given similar treatment by three GIs using water from a drinking bottle. The soldier pouring the water was grinning. The man sitting on the prisoner's chest had a cigarette held casually between the second and third fingers of his right hand.

I sat back in my chair and thought of various things. I thought, especially, of Emmett's comment about McAra's death – that drowning wasn't painless, but agonising. It had struck me at the time as an odd thing for a professor to say. Flexing my fingers, like a concert pianist preparing to play a challenging final movement, I typed a fresh request into the search engine: '"Paul Emmett" CIA'.

Immediately, the screen filled with results, all of them, at first sight, dross: articles and book reviews by Emmett that happened to mention the CIA; articles by others about the CIA that also contained references to Emmett; articles about the Arcadia Institution in which the words 'CIA' and 'Emmett' featured. I must have gone through thirty or forty in all, until I came to one which sounded promising.

The **CIA** in Academia

'The Central Intelligence Agency is now using several hundred American academics . . . **Paul Emmett** . . .

www.spooks-on-campus.org/Church/listKl897a/html – 11k

The web page was headed 'Who did Frank have in mind???' and started with a quote from Senator Frank Church's Select Committee report on the CIA, published in 1976:

The Central Intelligence Agency is now using several hundred American academics ("academics" includes administrators, faculty members and graduate students engaged in teaching), who in addition to providing leads and, on occasion, making introductions for intelligence purposes, occasionally write books and other material to be used for propaganda purposes abroad. Beyond these, an additional few score are used in an unwitting manner for minor activities.

Beneath it, in alphabetical order, was a hyperlinked list of about twenty names, among them Emmett's, and when I clicked on it, I felt as though I had fallen through a trapdoor.

Yale graduate Paul Emmett was reported by CIA whistleblower Frank Molinari to have joined the Agency as an officer in either 1969 or 1970, where he was assigned to the Foreign Resources Division of the Directorate of Operations. (Source: Inside the Agency, Amsterdam, 1977)

'Oh no,' I said quietly. 'No, no. That can't be right.'
I must have stared at the screen for a full minute, until a sudden crash of breaking crockery snapped me out of my reverie and I looked round to see that one of the kids playing under the nearby table had tipped the whole thing over. As a waitress hurried across with a dustpan and brush, and as the nannies (or mothers) scolded the children, I noticed that the two short-haired men at the counter

weren't taking any notice of this little drama: they were staring hard at me. One had a cell phone to his ear.

Fairly calmly – more calmly, I hoped, than I felt – I turned off the computer, and pretended to take a final sip of coffee. The liquid had gone cold while I'd been working and was freezing and bitter on my lips. Then I picked up my suitcase and put a twenty-dollar bill on the table. Already I was thinking that if something happened to me, the harassed waitress would surely remember the solitary Englishman who took the table furthest from the window and absurdly over-tipped. What good this would have done me, I have no idea, but it seemed clever at the time. I made sure I didn't look at the short-haired pair as I passed them.

Out on the street, in the grey cold light, with the green-canopied Starbucks a few doors down and the slowly passing traffic ('Baby on Board: Please Drive Carefully') and the elderly pedestrians in their fur hats and gloves, it was briefly possible to imagine that I'd spent the past hour playing some homemade virtual reality game. But then the door of the café opened behind me and the two men came out. I walked briskly up the street towards the Ford and once I was behind the wheel I locked myself in. When I checked the mirrors I couldn't see either of my fellow diners.

I didn't move for a while. It felt safer simply sitting there. I fantasised that perhaps if I stayed put long enough, I could somehow be absorbed by osmosis into the peaceful, prosperous life of Belmont. I could go and do what all these retired folk were bent on doing – playing a hand of bridge, maybe, or watching an afternoon movie, or wandering along to the local library to read the papers and shake their heads at the way the world was all going to hell, now that my callow and cosseted generation was in charge of it. I watched the newly coiffed ladies emerge from the salon and lightly pat their hair. The young couple who had been holding hands in the café were inspecting rings in the window of the jeweller's.

And I? I experienced a twinge of self-pity. I was as separate from all this normality as if I were in a bubble of glass.

I took out the photographs again and flicked through them until I came to the one of Lang and Emmett on stage together. A future prime minister and an alleged CIA officer, prancing around wearing gloves and hats in a comic revue? It seemed not so much improbable as grotesque, but here was the evidence in my hand. I turned the picture over and considered the number scrawled on the back, and the more I considered it, the more obvious it seemed that there was only one course of action open to me. The fact that I would, once again, be trailing along in the footsteps of McAra could not be helped.

I waited until the young lovers had gone into the jeweller's and then took out my mobile phone. I scrolled down to where the number was stored, and called Richard Rycart.

Fourteen

Half the job of ghosting is about finding out about other people.

Ghostwriting

This time, he answered within a few seconds.

'So you rang back,' he said quietly, in that nasal singsong voice of his. 'Somehow I had a feeling you would, whoever you are. Not many people have this number.' He waited for me to reply. I could hear a man talking in the background – delivering a speech, it sounded like. 'Well, my friend, are you going to stay on the line this time?'

'Yes,' I said.

He waited again, but I didn't know how to begin. I kept thinking of Lang – of what he would think if he could see me talking to his would-be nemesis. I was breaking every rule in the ghosting guide-book. I was in breach of the confidentiality agreement I'd signed with Rhinehart. It was professional suicide.

'I tried to call you back a couple of times,' he continued. I detected a hint of reproach.

Across the street, the young lovers had come out of the jeweller's and were strolling towards me.

'I know,' I said, finding my voice at last. 'I'm sorry. I found your number written down somewhere. I didn't know whose it was. I called it on the off-chance. It didn't seem right to be talking to you.'

'Why not?'

The couple passed by. I followed their progress in the mirror. They had their hands in one another's back pockets, like pickpockets on a blind date.

I took the plunge.

'I'm working for Adam Lang. I—'

'Don't tell me your name,' he said quickly. 'Don't use any names. Keep everything non-specific. Where exactly did you find my number?'

His urgency unnerved me.

'On the back of a photograph.'

'What sort of photograph?'

'Of my client's days at university. My predecessor had it.'

'Did he, by God?' Now it was Rycart's turn to pause. I could hear people clapping at the other end of the line.

'You sound shocked,' I said.

'Yes, well, it ties in with something he said to me.'

'I've been to see one of the people in the photograph. I thought you might be able to help me.'

'Why don't you talk to your employer?'

'He's away.'

'Of course he is.' He had a satisfied smile in his voice. 'And where are you? Without being too specific?'

'In New England.'

'Can you get to the city where I am, right away? You know where I am, I take it? Where I work?'

'I suppose so,' I said doubtfully. 'I have a car. I could drive.'

'No,' he said, 'don't drive. Flying's safer than the roads.'

'That's what the airlines say.'

'Listen, my friend,' whispered Rycart fiercely, 'if I was in your position, I wouldn't joke. Go to the nearest airport. Catch the first available plane. Text me the flight number — nothing else. I'll arrange for someone to collect you when you land.'

'But how will they know what I look like?'

'They won't. You'll have to look out for them.'

There was a renewed burst of applause in the background. I started to raise a fresh objection but it was too late. He had hung up.

*

I drove out of Belmont without any clear idea of the route I was supposed to follow. I checked the rear-view mirror neurotically every few seconds, but if I was being followed, I couldn't tell. Different cars appeared behind me, and none seemed to stay for longer than a couple of minutes. I kept my eyes open for signs to Boston, and eventually crossed a big river and joined the interstate, heading east.

It was not yet three in the afternoon but already the day was starting to darken. Away to my left, the downtown office blocks gleamed gold against a swollen Atlantic sky, while up ahead the lights of the big jets fell towards Logan like shooting stars. I maintained my usual cautious pace over the next couple of miles. Logan Airport, for those who have never had the pleasure, sits in the middle of Boston Harbor, approached from the south by a seemingly endless tunnel. As the road descended underground I asked myself whether I was really going to go through with this, and it was a good measure of my uncertainty that when — the best part of a mile later — I rose again into the deeper gloom of the afternoon, I still hadn't decided.

I followed the signs to the long-term car park and was just reversing into a bay when my telephone rang. The incoming number was unfamiliar. I almost didn't answer. When I did, a peremptory voice said, 'What on earth are you doing?'

It was Ruth Lang. She had that presumption of beginning a conversation without first announcing who was calling: a lapse in manners I was sure her husband would never have been guilty of, even when he was prime minister.

'Working,' I said.

'Really? You're not at your hotel.'

'Aren't I?'

'Well, are you? They told me you hadn't even checked in.'

I flailed around for an adequate lie and hit on a partial truth. 'I decided to go to New York.'

'Why?'

'I wanted to see John Maddox, to talk about the structure of the book, in view of the' – a tactful euphemism was needed, I decided – 'the changed circumstances.'

'I was worried about you,' she said. 'All day I've been walking up and down this fucking beach thinking about what we discussed last night—'

I interrupted. 'I wouldn't say anything about that on the phone.'

'Don't worry, I won't. I'm not a total fool. It's just that the more I go over things, the more worried I get.'

'Where's Adam?'

'Still in Washington, as far as I know. He keeps trying to call and I keep not answering. When will you be back?'

'I'm not sure.'

'Tonight?'

'I'll try.'

233

'Do, if you can.' She lowered her voice: I imagined the body-guard standing nearby. 'It's Dep's night off. I'll cook.'

'Is that supposed to be an incentive?'

'You rude man,' she said, and laughed. She rang off as abruptly as she had called, without saying goodbye.

I tapped my phone against my teeth. The prospect of a confiding fireside talk with Ruth, perhaps to be followed by a second round in her vigorous embrace, was not without its attractions. I could call Rycart and tell him I'd changed my mind. Undecided, I took my case out of the car and wheeled it through the puddles towards the waiting bus. Once I was aboard, I cradled it next to me and studied the airport map. At that point yet another choice presented itself. Terminal B – the shuttle to New York and Rycart – or terminal E: international departures and an evening flight back to London? I hadn't considered that before. I had my passport; everything. I could simply walk away.

B or E? I seriously weighed them. I was like an unusually dim lab rat in a maze, endlessly confronted with alternatives, endlessly picking the wrong one.

The bus doors opened with a heavy sigh.

I got off at B, bought my ticket, sent a text message to Rycart and caught the US Airways shuttle to La Guardia.

*

For some reason our plane was delayed on the tarmac. We taxied out on schedule but then stopped just short of the runway, pulling aside in a gentlemanly fashion to let the queue of jets behind us go ahead. It began to rain. I looked out of the porthole at the flattened grass and the welded sheets of sea and sky. Clear veins of water pulsed across the glass. Every time a plane took off, the thin skin of the cabin shook and the veins broke and reformed. The pilot came over the intercom and apologised: there was some problem with our security clearance, he said. The Department of Homeland Security had just raised its threat assessment from yellow (elevated) to orange (high) and our patience was appreciated. Among the business people around me, agitation grew. The man sitting next to me caught my eye above the edge of his pink paper and shook his head.

'It just gets worse,' he said.

He folded his *Financial Times*, placed it on his lap and closed his eyes. The headline was 'LANG WINS US SUPPORT', and there was that grin again. Ruth had been right. He shouldn't have smiled. It had gone round the world.

My small suitcase was in the luggage compartment above my head, my feet were resting on the shoulder bag beneath the seat in front of me. All was in order. But I couldn't relax. I felt guilty, even though I had done nothing wrong. I half expected the FBI to storm the plane and drag me away. After about forty-five minutes the engines suddenly started to roar again and the pilot broke radio silence to announce that we had finally been given permission to take off, and to thank us again for our understanding.

We laboured along the runway and up into the clouds, and such was my exhaustion that, despite my anxiety — or perhaps because of it — I actually drifted into sleep. I came awake with a jerk when I felt someone leaning across me, but it was only the cabin attendant, checking my seatbelt was fastened. It seemed to me that I had been unconscious for no more than a few seconds, but the pressure in my ears told me that already we were coming in to land at La Guardia. We touched down at six minutes past six — I remember the time exactly: I checked my watch — and by twenty past I was avoiding the impatient crowds around the baggage carousel and heading out of the gate into the arrivals hall.

It was busy, early evening, and people were in a hurry to get downtown or home for dinner. I scanned the bewildering array of faces, wondering if Rycart himself had turned out to greet me, but there was no one I recognised. The usual lugubrious line-up of drivers was waiting, holding the names of their passengers against their chests. They stared straight ahead, avoiding eye contact, like suspects in an identity parade, while I, in the manner of a nervous witness, walked along in front of them, checking each carefully, not wanting to make a mistake. Rycart had implied I'd recognise the right person when I saw them, and I did, and my heart almost stopped. He was standing apart from the others, in his own patch of space – wan-faced, dark-haired, tall, heavyset, early fifties, in a badly fitting chain-store suit – and he was holding a small blackboard on which was chalked 'Mike McAra'. Even his eyes were as I had imagined McAra's to be: crafty and colourless.

He was chewing gum. He nodded to my suitcase. 'You okay with that.' It was a statement, not a question, but I didn't care. I'd never been more pleased to hear a New York accent in my life. He turned on his heel and I followed him across the hall and out into the pandemonium of the night: shrieks, whistles, slamming doors, the fight to grab a cab, sirens in the distance.

He brought round his car, wound down his window, and beckoned to me to get in quickly. As I struggled to get my case into the back seat, he stared straight ahead, his hands on the wheel, discouraging conversation. Not that there was much time to talk. Barely had we left the perimeter of the airport than we were pulling up in front of a big glass-fronted hotel and conference centre overlooking Grand Central Parkway. He grunted as he shifted his heavy body round in his seat to address me. The car stank of his sweat and I had a moment of pure existential horror, staring beyond him, through the drizzle, to that bleak and anonymous building: what, in the name of God, was I doing?

'If you need to make contact, use this,' he said, giving me a brand-new cell phone, still in its polythene wrapper. 'There's a chip inside with twenty dollars' worth of calls on it. Don't use your old phone. The safest thing is to turn it off. You pay for your room in advance, with cash. Have you got enough? It'll be about three hundred bucks.'

I nodded.

'You're staying one night. You have a reservation.' He wriggled his fat wallet out from his back pocket. 'This is the card you use to guarantee the extras. The name on the card is the name you register under. Use an address in the United Kingdom that isn't your own. If there *are* any extras, make sure you pay for them in cash. This is the telephone number you use to make contact in future.'

'You used to be a cop,' I said. I took the credit card and a torn-out strip of paper with a number written on it in a childish hand. The paper and plastic were warm from the heat of his body.

'Don't use the internet. Don't speak to strangers. And especially avoid any women who might try to come on to you.'

'You sound like my mother.'

His face didn't flicker. We sat there for a few seconds. 'Well,' he said impatiently. He waved a meaty hand at me. 'That's it.'

Once I was through the revolving glass door and inside the lobby I checked the name on the card. Clive Dixon. A big conference had just ended. Scores of delegates wearing black suits with bright yellow lapel badges were pouring across the wide expanse of white marble, chattering to one another like a flight of crows. They looked eager, purposeful, motivated, newly fired up to meet their corporate targets and personal goals. I saw from their badges they belonged to a church. Above our heads, great glass globes of light hung from a ceiling a hundred feet high and shimmered on walls of chrome. I wasn't just out of my depth any more; I was out of sight of land.

'I have a reservation, I believe,' I said to the clerk at the desk, 'in the name of Dixon.'

It's not an alias I'd have chosen. I don't think of myself as a Dixon, whatever a Dixon is. But the receptionist was untroubled by my embarrassment. I was on his computer, that was all that mattered to him, and my card was good. The room rate was $275. I filled out the reservation form and gave as my false address the number of Kate's small terraced house in Shepherd's Bush and the street of Rick's London club. When I said I wanted to pay in cash, he took the notes between his finger and thumb as if they were the strangest things he had ever seen. *Cash?* If I'd tied a mule to his desk and offered to pay him in animal skins and sticks that I'd spent the winter carving, he couldn't have looked more nonplussed.

I declined to be assisted with my bags, took the elevator to the sixth floor, and stuck the electronic key card into the door. My room was beige and softly lit by table lamps, with a view across Grand Central Parkway to La Guardia and the unfathomable blackness of the East River. The TV was playing 'I'll Take Manhattan' over a caption that read 'Welcome to New York, Mr Nixon'. I turned it off and opened the minibar. I didn't even bother to find a glass. I unscrewed the cap and drank straight from the miniature bottle.

It must have been about twenty minutes and a second miniature later that my new telephone suddenly glowed blue and began

238

to emit a faintly ominous electronic purr. I left my post at the window to answer it.

'It's me,' said Rycart. 'Have you settled in?'

'Yes,' I said.

'Are you alone?'

'Yes.'

'Open the door then.'

He was standing in the corridor, his phone to his ear. Beside him was the driver who had met me at La Guardia.

'All right, Frank,' said Rycart to his minder. 'I'll take it from here. You keep an eye out in the lobby.'

Rycart slipped his phone into the pocket of his overcoat as Frank plodded back towards the elevators. He was what my mother would have called 'handsome, and knows it': a striking profile, narrowly set bright blue eyes accentuated by an orangey tan, and that swept-back waterfall of hair the cartoonists loved so much. He looked a lot younger than sixty. He nodded at the empty bottle in my hand. 'Tough day?'

'You could say that.'

He came into the room without waiting for an invitation, went straight over to the window and drew the curtains. I closed the door.

'My apologies for the location,' he said, 'but I tend to be recognised in Manhattan. Especially after yesterday. Did Frank look after you all right?'

'I've rarely had a warmer welcome.'

'I know what you mean, but he's a useful guy. Ex-NYPD. He handles logistics and security for me. I'm not the most popular kid on the block right now, as you can imagine.'

'Can I get you something to drink?'

'Water would be fine.'

He prowled around the room while I poured him a glass. He checked the bathroom, even the closet.

'What is it?' I said. 'Do you think this is a trap?'

'It crossed my mind.' He unbuttoned his coat and laid it carefully on the bed. I guessed his Armani suit would have cost about twice the annual income of a small African village. 'Let's face it, you do work for Lang.'

'I only met him for the first time on Monday,' I said. 'I don't even know him.'

Rycart laughed. 'Who does? If you met him on Monday you probably know him as well as anyone. I worked with him for fifteen years, and I certainly don't have a clue where he's coming from. Mike McAra didn't, either, and he was with him from the beginning.'

'His wife implied more or less the same thing to me.'

'Well, there you go. If someone as sharp as Ruth doesn't get him – and she's married to him, for God's sake – what hope do the rest of us have? The man's a mystery. Thanks.' Rycart took the water. He sipped it thoughtfully, studying me. 'But you sound as though you're starting to unravel him.'

'I feel as though I'm the one who's unravelling, quite frankly.'

'Let's sit down,' said Rycart, patting my shoulder, 'and you can tell me all about it.'

The gesture reminded me of Lang. A great man's charm. They made me feel like a minnow, swimming between sharks. I would need to be on my guard. I sat down carefully in one of the two small armchairs – it was beige, like the walls. Rycart sat opposite me.

'So,' he said. 'How do we begin? You know who I am. Who are you?'

'I'm a professional ghostwriter,' I said. 'I was brought in to rewrite Adam Lang's memoirs after Mike McAra died. I know nothing about politics. It's as if I've stepped through the looking-glass.'

'Tell me what you've found out.'

Even I was too canny for that. I hummed and hawed.

'Perhaps you could tell me about McAra first,' I said.

'If you like.' Rycart shrugged. 'What can I say? Mike was the consummate professional. If you'd pinned a rosette to that suitcase over there and told him it was the party leader, he'd have followed it. Everyone expected Lang would fire him when he became leader, and bring in his own man. But Mike was too useful. He knew the party inside out. What else do you want to know?'

'What was he like, as a person?'

'What was he like *as a person*?' Rycart gave me a strange look, as if it were the oddest question he'd ever heard. 'Well, he had no life outside politics, if that's what you mean, so you could say that Lang was everything to him – wife, kids, friends. What else? He was obsessive, a detail man. Almost everything Adam wasn't, Mike was. Maybe that was why he stayed on, right the way through Downing Street and all the way out again, long after the others had all cashed in and gone to make some money. No fancy corporate jobs for our Mike. He was very loyal to Adam.'

'Not that loyal,' I said. 'Not if he was in touch with you.'

'Ah, but that was only right at the very end. You mentioned a photograph. Can I see it?'

When I fetched the envelope, his face had the same greedy expression as Emmett's, but when he saw the picture, he couldn't hide his disappointment.

'Is this it?' he said. 'Just a bunch of privileged white kids doing a song-and-dance act?'

'It's a bit more interesting than that,' I said. 'For a start, why's your number on the back of it?'

Rycart gave me a sly look. 'Why exactly should I help you?'

'Why exactly should I help *you*?'

We stared at one another. Eventually he grinned, showing large, polished white teeth.

'You should have been a politician,' he said.

'I'm learning from the best.'

He bowed modestly, thinking I meant him, but actually it was Lang I had in mind. Vanity, that was his weakness, I realised. I could imagine how deftly Lang would have flattered him, and what a blow his sacking must have been to his ego. And now, with his lean face and his prow of a nose and those piercing eyes, he was as hell-bent on revenge as any discarded lover. He got to his feet and went over to the door. He checked the corridor up and down. When he returned he loomed over me, pointing a tanned finger directly at my face.

'If you double-cross me,' he said, 'you'll pay for it. And if you doubt my willingness to hold a grudge and eventually settle the score, ask Adam Lang.'

'Fine,' I said.

He was too agitated now to sit still, and that was something else I only realised at that moment: the pressure he was under. You had to hand it to Rycart. It did take a certain nerve to drag your former party leader and prime minister in front of a war crimes tribunal.

'This ICC business,' he said, patrolling up and down in front of the bed, 'it's only hit the headlines in the past week, but let me tell you I've been pursuing this thing behind the scenes for *years*. Iraq, rendition, torture, Guantanamo – what's been done in this so-called War on Terror is illegal under international law, just as much as

242

anything that's happened in Kosovo or Liberia. The only difference is: we're the ones doing it. The hypocrisy is nauseating.'

He seemed to realise he was starting on a speech he'd already made too many times before, and checked himself. He took a sip of water. 'Anyway, rhetoric is one thing and evidence is another thing entirely. I could sense the political climate changing: that was helpful. Every time a bomb went off, every time another soldier was killed, every time it became a little bit clearer we'd started another Hundred Years War without a clue how to end it, things shifted further my way. It was no longer inconceivable that a western leader could wind up in the dock. The worse the mess he'd left behind him got, the more people were willing to see it — wanted to see it. What I needed was just one piece of evidence that would meet the legal standard of proof — a single document with his name on it would have been enough — and I didn't have it.

'And then suddenly, just before Christmas, there it was. I had it in my hands. It just came through the post. Not even a covering letter. "Top Secret: Memorandum from the Prime Minister to the Secretary of State for Defence." It was five years old, written back in the days when I was still Foreign Secretary, but I'd no idea it even existed. A smoking gun if ever there was one — Christ, the barrel was still hot! A directive from the British prime minister that these four poor bastards should be snatched off the streets in Pakistan by the SAS and handed over to the CIA.'

'A war crime,' I said.

'A war crime,' he agreed. 'A minor one, okay. But so what? In the end, they could only get Al Capone for tax evasion. It didn't mean Capone wasn't a gangster. I carried out a few discreet checks to make sure the memo was authentic, then I took it to The Hague in person.'

'You'd no idea who it came from?'

'No. Not until my anonymous source called and told me. And just you wait till Lang hears who it was. This is going to be the worst thing of all.' He leaned in close to me. 'Mike McAra!'

Looking back, I suppose I already knew it. But suspicion is one thing, confirmation another, and to see Rycart's exultation at that moment was to appreciate the scale of McAra's treachery.

'*He* called *me*! Can you believe that? If anyone had predicted I'd ever be given help by Mike McAra, of all people, I'd have laughed at them.'

'When did he call?'

'About three weeks after I first got the document. The eighth of January? The ninth? Something like that. "Hello, Richard. Did you get the present I sent you?" I almost had a heart attack. Then I had to shut him up quickly. Because of course you know that the phone lines at the UN are all bugged?'

'Are they?' I was still trying to absorb everything.

'Oh, completely. The National Security Agency monitors every word that's transmitted in the western hemisphere. Every syllable you ever utter on a phone, every email you ever send, every credit card transaction you ever make – it's all recorded and stored. The only problem is sorting through it. At the UN, we're briefed that the easiest way to get round the eavesdropping is to use disposable mobile phones, try to avoid mentioning specifics, and change our numbers as often as possible – that way we can at least keep a bit ahead of them. So I told Mike to stop right there. Then I gave him a brand-new number I'd never used before, and asked him to call me straight back.'

'Ah,' I said. 'I see.' And I could. I could visualise it perfectly. McAra with his phone wedged between shoulder and ear, grabbing his cheap blue biro. 'He must have scribbled the number on the back of the photograph he was holding at the time.'

'And then he called me,' said Rycart. He had stopped pacing and was looking at himself in the mirror above the chest of drawers. He put both hands to his forehead and smoothed his hair back over his ears. 'Christ, I'm shattered,' he said. 'Look at me. I was never like this when I was in government, even when I was working eighteen hours a day. You know, people get it all wrong. It isn't having power that's exhausting – it's *not* having it that wears you out.'

'What did he say when he called? McAra?'

'The first thing that struck me was that he didn't sound his usual self at all. You were asking me what he was like. Well, he was a pretty tough operator, which of course is what Adam liked about him: he knew he could always rely on Mike to do the dirty work. He was sharp, businesslike. You could almost say he was brutal, especially on the phone. My private office used to call him McHorror: "The McHorror just rang for you, Foreign Secretary . . ." But that day, I remember, his voice was completely flat. He sounded broken, actually. He said he'd just spent the past year in the archives in Cambridge, working on Adam's memoirs, going over our whole time in government, and just getting more and more disillusioned with it all. He said that that was where he'd found the memorandum about Operation Tempest. But the real reason he was calling, he said, was that that was only the tip of the iceberg. He said he'd just discovered something much more important – something that made sense of everything that had gone wrong while we were in power.'

I could hardly breathe.

'What was it?'

Rycart laughed. 'Well, oddly enough, I did ask him that, but he wouldn't tell me over the phone. He said he wanted to meet me to discuss it face to face: it was that big. The only thing he would say was that the key to it could be found in Lang's autobiography, if anyone bothered to check – that it was all there in the beginning.'

'Those were his exact words?'

'Pretty much. I made a note as he was talking. And that was it. He said he'd call me in a day or two to fix a meeting. But I heard nothing, and then about a week later it was in the press that he was dead. And nobody else ever called me on that phone, because nobody else had that number. So you can imagine why I was so excited when it suddenly started ringing again. And so here we are,' he said, gesturing to the room, 'the perfect place to spend a Thursday night. And now I think you should tell me exactly what the hell is going on.'

'I will. Just one more thing, though. Why didn't you tell the police?'

'You are joking, are you? Discussions at The Hague were at a very delicate stage. If I'd told the police that McAra had been in contact with me, naturally they'd have wanted to know why. Then it would have been bound to get back to Lang, and he would have been able to make some kind of pre-emptive move against the war crimes court. He's still a hell of an operator, you know. That statement he put out against me the day before yesterday – "The international struggle against terror is too important to be used for the purposes of domestic political revenge." Wow.' He shuddered admiringly. 'Vicious.'

I squirmed slightly in my chair, but Rycart didn't notice. He'd gone back to inspecting himself in the mirror. 'Besides,' he said, sticking out his chin, 'I thought it was accepted that Mike had killed himself, either because he was depressed, or drunk, or both. I'd only have confirmed what they already knew. He was certainly in a poor state when he rang me.'

'And I can tell you why,' I said. 'What he'd just found out was that one of the men in that picture with Lang at Cambridge – the picture McAra had in his hand when he spoke to you – was an officer in the CIA.'

Rycart had been checking his profile. He stopped. His brow corrugated. And then, with great slowness, he turned his face towards me.

'He was *what?*'

'His name is Paul Emmett.' Suddenly I couldn't get the words out fast enough. I was desperate to unburden myself – to share it – to let someone else try to make sense of it. 'He later became a professor at Harvard. Then he went on to run something called the Arcadia Institution. Have you heard of it?'

'I've heard of it – of course I've heard of it – and I've always steered well clear of it, precisely because I've always thought it had CIA written all over it.' Rycart sat down. He seemed stunned.

'But is that really plausible?' I asked. 'I don't know how these things work. Would someone join the CIA and then immediately be sent off to do postgraduate research in another country?'

'I'd say that's highly plausible. What better cover could you want? And where better than a university to spot the future brightest and best?' He held out his hand. 'Show me the photograph again. Which one is Emmett?'

'It may all be balls,' I warned, pointing Emmett out. 'I've no proof. I just found his name on one of these paranoid websites. They said he joined the CIA after he left Yale, which must have been about three years before this was taken.'

'Oh, I can believe it,' said Rycart, studying him intently. 'In fact, now you mention it, I think I did hear some gossip once. But then that whole international conference-circuit world is crawling with them. I call them "the military-industrial-academic complex".' He smiled at his own wit, then looked serious again. 'What's really suspicious is that he should have known Lang.'

'No,' I said, 'what's *really* suspicious is that a matter of hours after McAra tracked down Emmett to his house near Boston, he was found washed up dead on a beach in Martha's Vineyard.'

*

After that I told him everything I'd discovered. I told him the story about the tides and the flashlights on the beach at Lambert's Cove, and the curious way the police investigation had been handled. I told him about Ruth's description of McAra's argument with Lang on the eve of his death, and about Lang's reluctance to discuss his Cambridge years, and the way he'd tried to conceal the fact that he'd become politically active immediately after leaving university rather than two years later. I described how McAra, with his typical, dogged thoroughness, had discovered all this, turning up detail after detail that gradually destroyed Lang's account of his early years: that was presumably what he meant when he said that the key to everything was in the beginning of Lang's autobiography. I told him about the satellite navigation system in the Ford and how it had taken me to Emmett's doorstep, and how strangely Emmett had behaved.

And, of course, the more I talked, the more excited Rycart became. I guess it must have been like Christmas for him.

'Just suppose,' he said, pacing up and down again, 'that it was

Emmett who originally suggested to Lang that he should think about a career in politics. Let's face it, someone must have put the idea into his pretty little head. I'd been a junior member of the party since I was fourteen. What year did Lang join?'

'Nineteen seventy-five.'

'Seventy-five! You see, that would make perfect sense. Do you remember what Britain was like in seventy-five? The security services were out of control, spying on the prime minister. Retired generals were forming private armies. The economy was collapsing. There were strikes, riots. It wouldn't exactly be a surprise if the CIA had decided to recruit a few bright young things and had encouraged them to make their careers in useful places – the civil service, the media, politics. It's what they do everywhere else, after all.'

'But not in Britain, surely,' I said. 'We're an ally.'

Rycart looked at me with contempt.

'The CIA was spying on *American* students back then. Do you really think they'd have been squeamish about spying on ours? Of course they were active in Britain! They still are. They have a Head of Station in London and a huge staff. I could name you half a dozen MPs right now who are in regular contact with the CIA. In fact . . .' He stopped pacing and clicked his fingers. 'That's a thought!' He whirled round to look at me. 'Does the name Reg Giffen mean anything to you?'

'Vaguely.'

'Reg Giffen – Sir Reginald Giffen, later Lord Giffen, now dead Giffen, thank God – spent so long making speeches in the House of Commons on behalf of the Americans, we used to call him the Member for Michigan. He announced his resignation as an MP in the first week of the nineteen-eighty-three general election campaign, and it caught everyone by surprise, apart from one very enterprising and photogenic young party member, who just happened to have moved into his constituency six months earlier.'

'And who then got the nomination to become the party's candidate, with Giffen's support,' I said, 'and who then won one of the safest seats in the country when he was still only thirty.' The story was legendary. It was the start of Lang's rise to national prominence. 'But you can't really think that the CIA asked Giffen to help fix it so that Lang could get into parliament? That sounds very far-fetched.'

'Oh, come on! Use your imagination! Imagine you're Professor Emmett, now back in Harvard, writing unreadable bilge about the alliance of the English-speaking peoples and the need to combat the communist menace. Haven't you got potentially the most amazing agent in history on your hands? A man who's already starting to be talked about as a future party leader? A possible prime minister? Aren't you going to persuade the powers-that-be at the Agency to do everything they can to further this man's career? I was already in parliament myself when Lang arrived. I watched him come from nowhere, and streak past all of us.' He scowled at the memory. 'Of course he had *help*. He had no real connection with the party at all. We couldn't begin to understand what made him tick.'

'Surely that's the point of him,' I said. 'He didn't have an ideology.'

'He may not have had an ideology, but he sure as hell had an agenda.' Rycart sat down again. He leaned towards me. 'Okay. Here's a quiz for you. Name me one decision that Adam Lang took as prime minister that wasn't in the interests of the United States of America.'

I was silent.

'Come on,' he said. 'It's not a trick question. Just name me one thing he did that Washington wouldn't have approved of. Let's think.' He held up his thumb. 'One: deployment of British troops to the Middle East, against the advice of just about every senior commander in our armed forces and all of our ambassadors who know the region. Two' – up went his right index finger – 'complete failure to demand any kind of quid pro quo from the White House in terms of reconstruction contracts for British firms, or anything else. Three: unwavering support for US foreign policy in the Middle East, even when it's patently crazy for us to set ourselves against the entire Arab world. Four: the stationing of an American missile defence system on British soil that does absolutely nothing for our security – in fact, the complete opposite: it makes us a more obvious target for a first strike – and can only provide protection for the US. Five: the purchase, for fifty billion dollars, of an American nuclear missile system, that we call "independent" but which we wouldn't even be able to fire without US approval, thus binding his successors to another twenty years of subservience to Washington over defence policy. Six: a treaty that allows the US to extradite our citizens to stand trial in America, but doesn't allow us to do the same to theirs. Seven: collusion in the illegal kidnapping, torture, imprisonment and even murder of our own citizens. Eight: a consistent record of sacking any minister – I speak with experience here – who is less than one hundred per cent supportive of the alliance with the United States. Nine—'

'All right,' I said, holding up my hand. 'I get the message.'

'I have friends in Washington who just can't believe the way that Lang ran British foreign policy. I mean, they were *embarrassed* about how much support he gave and how little he got in return. And where has it got us? Stuck fighting a so-called war we can't possibly win, colluding in methods we didn't use even when we were up against the Nazis!' Rycart laughed ruefully and shook his head. 'You know, in a way, I'm almost relieved to discover there might be a rational explanation for what we got up to in government while he was prime minister. If you think about it, the alternative's actually worse. At least if he was working for the CIA it makes sense. So now,' he said, patting my knee, 'the question is: what are we going to do about it?'

I didn't like the sound of that first person plural.

'Well,' I said, wincing slightly, 'I'm in a tricky position. I'm supposed to be helping him with his memoirs. I have a legal obligation not to divulge to a third party anything I hear in the course of my work.'

'It's too late to stop now.'

I didn't like the sound of that, either.

'We don't actually have any *proof*,' I pointed out. 'We don't even know for sure that *Emmett* was in the CIA, let alone that he recruited Lang. I mean – how is this relationship supposed to have worked after Lang got into Number Ten? Did he have a secret radio transmitter hidden in the attic, or what?'

'This isn't a joke, my friend,' said Rycart. 'I know something of how these things are done from when I was at the Foreign Office. Contact can be managed easily enough. For a start, Emmett was always coming to London, because of Arcadia. It was the perfect front. In fact, I wouldn't be surprised if the whole institution wasn't set up as part of the covert operation to run Lang. The timing would fit. They could have used intermediaries.'

'But there's still no *proof*,' I repeated, 'and short of Lang confessing, or Emmett confessing, or the CIA opening their files, there never will be.'

'Then you'll just have to get some proof,' said Rycart flatly.

'What?' My mouth sagged; my everything sagged.

'You're in the perfect position,' Rycart went on. 'He trusts you. He lets you ask him whatever you like. He even allows you to tape his answers. You can put words in his mouth. We'll have to devise a series of questions that gradually entrap him, and then finally you can confront him with the allegation, and let's see how he reacts. He'll deny it, but that won't matter. The mere fact that you're laying the evidence in front of him will put the story on the record.'

'No it won't. The tapes are his property.'

'Yes it will. The tapes can be subpoenaed by the war crimes court, as evidence of his direct complicity with the CIA rendition programme.'

'What if I don't make any tapes?'

'In that case, I'll suggest to the prosecutor that she subpoenas *you*.'

'Ah,' I said craftily, 'but what if I deny the whole story?'

'Then I'll give her this,' said Rycart, and opened his jacket to show a small microphone clipped to the front of his shirt, with a wire trailing into his inside pocket. 'Frank is recording every word down in the lobby, aren't you, Frank? Oh, come on! Don't look so shocked. What did you expect? That I'd come to a meeting with a complete stranger, who's working for Lang, without taking any precautions? Except that you're not working for Lang any more.' He smiled, showing again that row of teeth, more brilliantly white than anything in Nature. 'You're working for me.'

Fifteen

Authors need ghosts who will not challenge them, but will simply listen to what they have to say and understand why they did what they did.

Ghostwriting

After a few seconds I started to swear, fluently and indiscriminately. I was swearing at Rycart and at my own stupidity, at Frank and at whoever would one day transcribe the tape. I was swearing at the war crimes prosecutor, at the court, the judges, the media. And I would have gone on for a lot longer if my telephone hadn't started to ring – not the one I'd been given to contact Rycart, but the one I'd brought from London. Needless to say, I'd forgotten to switch it off.

'Don't answer it,' warned Rycart. 'It'll lead them straight to us.'

I looked at the incoming number. 'It's Amelia Bly,' I said. 'It could be important.'

'Amelia Bly,' repeated Rycart, his voice a blend of awe and lust. 'I haven't seen her for a while.' He hesitated: it was obvious he was desperate to know what she wanted. 'If they're monitoring you, they'll be able to fix your location to within a hundred metres, and this hotel is the only building where you're likely to be.'

The phone continued to throb in my outstretched palm. 'Well, to hell with you,' I said. 'I'm not taking my orders from you.'

I pressed the green button.

'Hi,' I said. 'Amelia.'

'Good evening,' she said, her voice as crisp as a matron's uniform. 'I have Adam for you.'

I mouthed, 'It's Adam Lang' at Rycart, and waved my hand at him to warn him against saying anything. An instant later the familiar, classless voice filled my ear.

'I was just speaking to Ruth,' he said. 'She tells me you're in New York.'

'That's right.'

'So am I. Whereabouts are you?'

'I'm not sure exactly where I am, Adam.' I made a helpless gesture at Rycart. 'I haven't checked in anywhere yet.'

'We're at the Waldorf,' said Lang. 'Why don't you come over?'

'Hold on a second, Adam.' I pressed MUTE.

'You,' said Rycart, 'are a fucking idiot.'

'He wants me to go over and see him at the Waldorf.'

Rycart sucked in his cheeks, appraising the options.

'You should go,' he said.

'What if it's a trap?'

'It's a risk, but it'll look odd if you don't go. He'll get suspicious. Tell him yes, quickly, and then hang up.'

I pressed MUTE again.

'Hi, Adam,' I said, trying to keep the tension out of my voice. 'That's great. I'll be right over.'

Rycart passed his finger across his throat.

'What brings you to New York, in any case?' asked Lang. 'I thought you had plenty to occupy you at the house.'

'I wanted to see John Maddox.'

'Right. And how was he?'

'Fine. Listen, I've got to go now.'

Rycart's throat-slashing was becoming ever more urgent.

'We've had a great couple of days,' continued Lang, as if he hadn't heard me. 'The Americans have been fantastic. You know, it's in the tough times that you find out who your real friends are.'

Was it my imagination, or did he freight those words with extra emphasis for my benefit?

'Great. I'll be with you as fast as I can, Adam.'

I ended the call. My hand was shaking.

'Well done,' said Rycart. He was on his feet, retrieving his coat from the bed. 'We have about ten minutes to get out of here. Get your stuff together.'

Mechanically, I began gathering up the photographs. I put them back in the case and fastened it while Rycart went into the bathroom and peed noisily.

'How did he sound?' called Rycart.

'Cheerful.'

He flushed the lavatory and emerged buttoning his flies. 'Well, we'll just have to do something about that, won't we?'

The elevator down to the lobby was crammed with members of the Church of Latter-Day Online Traders, or whoever the hell they were. It stopped at every floor. Rycart grew more and more nervous.

'We mustn't be seen together,' he muttered as we stepped out at the ground floor. 'You hang back. We'll meet you in the car park.'

He quickened his pace, drawing ahead of me. Frank was already on his feet — presumably he had been listening and knew of our intentions — and the two of them set off without a word: the dapper silver Rycart, and his taciturn swarthy sidekick. What a double-act, I thought. I bent and pretended to tie my shoelace, then took my time crossing the lobby, deliberately circling the groups of chattering guests, keeping my head down. There was something now so ludicrous about this whole situation that, as I joined the crush at the door waiting to get out, I actually found myself smiling. It was like a Feydeau farce: each new scene more far-fetched than the last, yet each, when you examined it, a logical development of its predecessor. Yes, that was what this was: a farce! I stood in line until my turn came, and that was when I saw Emmett, or at least that's when I thought I saw Emmett, and suddenly I wasn't smiling any more.

The hotel had one of these big revolving doors, with compartments that hold five or six people at a time, all of whom are obliged to lunge into it and shuffle forwards to avoid knocking into one another, like convicts on a chain gang. Luckily for me, I was in the middle of the outgoing group, which is probably the reason Emmett didn't see me. He had a man on either side of him, and they were in the compartment that was swinging into the hotel, all three pushing at the glass in front of them, as if they were in a violent hurry.

We came out into the night and I stumbled, almost falling over, in my anxiety to get away. My suitcase toppled on to its side and I dragged it along after me, as if it were a stubborn dog. The car park was separated from the hotel forecourt by a flower bed, but instead of going round it I walked straight through it. Across the parking lot, a pair of headlights came on, and then drove straight at me. The car swerved at the last moment and the rear passenger door flew open.

'Get in,' said Rycart.

The speed with which Frank accelerated away served to slam the door shut after me and threw me back in my seat.

'I just saw Emmett,' I said.

Rycart exchanged looks in the mirror with his driver.

'Are you sure?'

'No.'

'Did he see you?'

'No.'

'Are you sure?'

'Yes.'

I was holding on to my suitcase. It had become my security blanket. We sped down the slip road and pulled into the heavy traffic heading towards Manhattan.

'They could have followed us from La Guardia,' said Frank.

'Why did they hold back?' asked Rycart.

'Could be they were waiting for Emmett to arrive from Boston, to make a positive ID.'

Up to that point, I hadn't taken Rycart's amateur tradecraft too seriously, but now I felt a fresh surge of panic.

'Listen,' I said, 'I don't think it's a good idea for me to go and see Lang right now. Assuming that was Emmett, Lang must surely have been alerted to what I've been doing. He'll know that I've driven up to Boston and shown Emmett the photographs.'

'So? What do you think he's going to do about it?' asked Rycart. 'Drown you in his bathtub at the Waldorf-Astoria?'

'Yeah, right,' said Frank. His shoulders shook slightly with amusement. 'As if.'

I felt sick, and despite the freezing night, I lowered the window. The wind was blowing from the east, gusting off the river, carrying on its cold, industrial edge the sickly tang of aviation fuel. I can still taste it at the back of my throat whenever I think of it, and that, for me, will always be the taste of fear.

'Don't I need to have a cover story?' I said. 'What am I supposed to tell Lang?'

'You've done nothing wrong,' said Rycart. 'You're just following up your predecessor's work. You're trying to research his Cambridge years. Don't act so guilty. Lang can't know for sure that you're on to him.'

'It's not Lang I'm worried about.'

We both lapsed into silence. After a few minutes the night-time Manhattan skyline came into view, and my eyes automatically sought out the gap in the glittering façade. Strange how an absence can be a landmark. It was like a black hole, I thought: a tear in the cosmos. It could suck in anything – cities, countries, laws; it could certainly swallow me. Even Rycart seemed oppressed by the sight.

'Close the window, would you? I'm freezing to death.'

I did as he asked. Frank had turned the radio on low – a jazz station, playing softly.

'What about the car?' I said. 'It's still at Logan Airport.'

'You can pick it up in the morning.'

The station switched to playing the blues. I asked Frank to turn it off. He ignored me.

'I know Lang thinks it's personal,' Rycart said, 'but it's not. All right, there's an element of getting my own back, I'll admit – who likes to be humiliated? But if we carry on licensing torture, and if we simply judge victory by the number of the enemy's skulls we can carry back to decorate our caves – well, what will become of us?'

'I'll tell you what will become of us,' I said savagely. 'We'll get ten million dollars for our memoirs, and live happily ever after.' Once again, I found that my nervousness was making me angry.

'You do know this is pointless, don't you? In the end he'll just retire over here on his CIA pension and tell you and your bloody war crimes court to go screw yourselves.'

'Maybe he will. But the ancients thought exile a worse punishment than death – and boy, will Lang be an exile. He won't be able to travel anywhere in the world, not even the handful of shitty little countries that don't recognise the ICC, because there'll always be a danger that his plane may have to put in somewhere with engine trouble, or to refuel. And we'll be waiting for him. And that's when we'll get him.'

I glanced at Rycart. He was staring straight ahead, nodding slightly.

'Or the political climate may change here one day,' he went on, 'and there'll be a public campaign to hand him over to justice. I wonder if he's thought of that. His life is going to be hell.'

'You almost make me feel sorry for him.'

Rycart gave me a sharp look. 'He's charmed you, hasn't he? Charm! The English disease.'

'There are worse afflictions.'

We crossed the Triborough Bridge, the tyres thumping on the joints in the road like a fast pulse.

'I feel as though I'm in a tumbril,' I said.

It took us a while to make the journey downtown. Each time the car came to a stop in the Park Avenue traffic I thought of opening the door and making a run for it. The trouble was, I could imagine the first part well enough – darting through the stationary cars, and disappearing down one of the side streets – but then it all became a blank. Where would I go? How would I pay for a hotel room if my own credit card, and presumably the false one I'd used earlier, were known to my pursuers? My reluctant conclusion, from whichever angle I examined my predicament, was that I was safer with Rycart. At least he knew how to survive in this alien world into which I had blundered.

'If you're that worried we can arrange to have a fail-safe signal,' said Rycart. 'You can call me using the phone Frank gave you, let's say at ten past every hour. We don't have to speak necessarily. Just let it ring a couple of times.'

'What happens if I don't make the call?'

'I won't do anything if you miss the first time. If you miss a second, I'll call Lang and tell him I hold him personally responsible for your safety.'

'Why is it that I don't find that very reassuring?'

We were almost there by then. I could see ahead, on the opposite side of the road, a great floodlit Stars and Stripes, and beside it, flanking the Waldorf's entrance, a Union Jack. The area in front of the hotel was cordoned off by concrete blocks. I counted half a dozen police motorcycles waiting, four patrol cars, two large black limousines, a small crowd of cameramen, and a slightly larger one of curious onlookers. As I eyed it, my heart began to accelerate. I felt breathless.

Rycart squeezed my arm.

'Courage, my friend. He's already lost one ghost in suspicious circumstances. He can hardly afford to lose another.'

'This can't *all* be for him, surely?' I said in amazement. 'Anyone would think he was still prime minister.'

'It seems I've only made him even more of a celebrity,' said Rycart. 'You people should be grateful to me. Okay, good luck. We'll talk later. Pull over here, Frank.'

He turned up his collar and sank down in his seat, and there was pathos as well as absurdity in the precaution. Poor Rycart: I doubt if one person in ten thousand in New York would have known who he was. Frank pulled up briefly on the corner of East 50th Street to let me out, and then eased deftly back into the traffic, so that the last view I ever had of Rycart was of the back of his silvery head dwindling into the Manhattan evening.

I was on my own.

I crossed the great expanse of road, yellow with taxis, and made my way past the crowds and the police. None of the cops standing around challenged me: seeing my suitcase, they must have assumed I was just a guest checking in. I went through the art deco doors, up the grand marble staircase, and into the Babylonian splendour of the Waldorf's lobby. Normally I would have used my mobile to contact Amelia, but even I had learnt my lesson there. I went over to one of the concierges at the front desk and asked him to call her room.

There was no reply.

Frowning, he hung up. He was just starting to check his computer when a loud detonation sounded in Park Avenue. Several guests who were checking in ducked, only to straighten ruefully when the explosion turned into a cannonade of gunning motorcycle engines. From the interior of the hotel, across the immense expanse of the golden lobby, came a wedge of security men, Special Branch and Secret Service, with Lang enclosed among them, marching purposefully in his usual rolling, muscular way. Behind him walked Amelia and the two secretaries. Amelia was on the phone. I moved towards the group. Lang swept by me, his eyes fixed straight ahead, which was unlike him. Usually he liked to connect with people when he passed them: flash them a smile they'd remember always. As he began descending the staircase, Amelia saw me. She appeared flustered for once, a few blonde hairs actually out of place.

'I was just trying to call you,' she said as she went by. She didn't break step. 'There's been a change of plan,' she said over her shoulder. 'We're flying back to Martha's Vineyard now.'

'Now?' I hurried after her. 'It's rather late, isn't it?'

We started descending the stairs.

'Adam's insisting. I've managed to find us a plane.'

'But why now?'

'I've no idea. Something's come up. You'll have to ask him.'

Lang was below and ahead of us. He'd already reached the grand entrance. The bodyguards opened the doors and his broad shoulders were suddenly framed by a halogen glow of light. The shouts of the reporters, the fusillade of camera shutters, the rumble of the Harley Davidsons — it was as if someone had rolled back the doors to hell.

'What am I supposed to do?' I asked.

'Get into the backup car. I expect Adam will want to talk to you on the plane.' She saw my look of panic. 'You're very odd. Is there something the matter?'

Now what am I supposed to do? I wondered. Faint? Plead a prior engagement? I seemed to be trapped on a moving walkway with no means of escape.

'Everything seems to be happening in a rush,' I said weakly.

'This is nothing. You should have been with us when he was prime minister.'

We emerged into the tumult of noise and light, and it was as if all the controversy generated by the War on Terror, year after year of it, had briefly converged on one man and rendered him incandescent. The door to Lang's stretch limousine was open. He paused to wave briefly at the crowd beyond the security cordon, then ducked inside. Amelia took my arm and propelled me towards the second car. 'Go on!' she shouted. The motorbikes were already pulling away. 'Don't forget, we can't stop if you're left behind.'

She slipped in beside Lang, and I found myself stepping into the second limo, next to the secretaries. They shifted cheerfully along the bench seat to make room for me. A Special Branch man climbed in the front, next to the driver, and then we were away, with an accompanying *whoop whoop* from one of the motorbikes, ringing out like the cheerful whistle of a little tug boat escorting a big liner out to sea.

*

In different circumstances, I would have relished that journey: my legs stretched out before me; the Harley Davidsons gliding past us to hold back the traffic; the pale faces of the pedestrians, glimpsed through the smoked glass, turning to watch us as we hurtled by; the noise of the sirens; the vividness of the flashing lights; the speed; the *force*. I can think of only two categories of human being who are transported with such pomp and drama: world leaders and captured terrorists.

In my pocket, I surreptitiously fingered my new mobile phone. Ought I to alert Rycart to what was happening? I decided not. I didn't want to call him in front of witnesses. I would have felt too uncomfortable, my guilt too obvious. Treachery needs privacy. I surrendered myself to events.

We flew over the 59th Street Bridge like gods, Alice and Lucy giggling with excitement, and when we reached La Guardia a few minutes later we drove past the terminal building, through an open metal gate and directly on to the tarmac where a big private jet was being fuelled. It was a Hallington plane, in its dark blue livery, with the corporate logo painted on its high tail: the earth, with a circle girdling it, like the Colgate ring of confidence. Lang's limousine swerved to a halt and he was the first to emerge. He dived through the doorway of the mobile body scanner and up the steps into the Gulfstream without a backward glance. A bodyguard hurried after him.

As I clambered out of the car I felt almost arthritic with anxiety. It took an effort simply to walk over to the steps where Amelia was standing. The night air was shaking with the noise of jets coming in to land. I could see them stacked five or six deep above the water, steps of light ascending into the darkness.

'Now that's the way to travel,' I said, trying to sound relaxed. 'Is it always like that?'

'They want to show him they love him,' said Amelia. 'And no doubt it helps to show everyone else how they treat their friends. *Pour encourager les autres.*'

Security men with metal wands were inspecting all the luggage. I added my suitcase to the pile.

'He says he has to get back to Ruth,' she continued, gazing up at the plane. The windows were bigger than on a normal aircraft. Lang's profile was plainly visible towards the rear. 'There's something he needs to talk over with her.' Her voice was puzzled. She was almost talking to herself, as if I wasn't there. I wondered if they'd had a row during the drive to the airport.

One of the security men told me to open my suitcase. I unzipped it and held it up to him. He lifted out the manuscript to search underneath it. Amelia was so preoccupied, she didn't even notice.

'It's odd,' she said, 'because Washington went so well.' She stared vacantly towards the lights of the runway.

'Your shoulder bag,' said the security man.

I handed it to him. He took out the package of photographs, and for a moment I thought he was going to open it up, but he was more interested in my laptop. I felt the need to keep talking.

'Perhaps he's heard something from The Hague,' I suggested.

'No. It's nothing to do with that. He would have told me.'

'Okay, you're clear to board,' said the guard.

'Don't go near him just yet,' she warned, as I moved to pass through the scanner. 'Not in his present mood. I'll take you back to him if he wants to talk.'

I climbed the steps.

Lang was sitting in the very end seat, nearest to the tail, his chin in his hand, gazing out of the window. (The security people always liked him to sit in the last row, I discovered later: it meant no one could get behind him.) The cabin was configured to take ten passengers, two each on a couple of sofas that ran along the side of the fuselage, and the rest in six big armchairs. The armchairs faced one another in pairs, with a stowaway table between them. It looked like an extension of the Waldorf's lobby: gold fittings, polished walnut and padded, creamy leather. Lang was in one of the armchairs. The Special Branch man sat on a nearby sofa. A steward in a white jacket was bending over the former prime minister. I couldn't see what drink he was being served, but I could hear it. Your favourite sound might be a pair of nightingales in a summer dusk, or a peal of village church bells. Mine is the clink of ice against cut glass. Of this I am a connoisseur. And it sounded distinctly to me as if Lang had given up tea in favour of a stiff whisky.

The steward saw me staring and came down the gangway towards me.

'Can I get you something, sir?'

'Thanks. Yes. I'll have whatever Mr Lang is having.'

I was wrong: it was brandy.

By the time the door was closed, there were twelve of us on board: three crew (the pilot, co-pilot and steward), and nine passengers — two secretaries, four bodyguards, Amelia, Adam Lang and me. I sat with my back to the cockpit so that I could keep an eye on my client. Amelia was directly opposite him, and as the engines started to whine it was all I could do not to hurl myself at the door and wrench it open. That flight felt doomed to me from the start. The Gulfstream shuddered slightly, and slowly the terminal building seemed to drift away. I could see Amelia's hand making emphatic gestures, as if she were explaining something, but Lang just continued to stare out at the airfield.

Someone touched my arm. 'Do you know how much one of these things costs?'

It was the policeman who'd been in my car on the drive from the Waldorf. He was in the seat across the gangway.

'I don't, no.'

'Have a guess.'

'I genuinely have no idea.'

'Go on. Try.'

I shrugged.

'Ten million dollars?'

'*Forty* million dollars.' He was triumphant, as if knowing the price somehow implied he was involved in the ownership. 'Hallington have *five.*'

'Makes you wonder what they can possibly use them all for.'

'They lease them out when they don't need them.'

'Oh yes, that's right,' I said. 'I'd heard that.'

The noise of the engines increased and we began our charge

down the runway. I imagined the terrorist suspects, handcuffed and hooded, strapped into their luxurious leather armchairs as they lifted off from some red-dusted military airstrip near the Afghan border, bound for the pine forests of eastern Poland. The plane seemed to spring into the air and I watched over the edge of my glass as the lights of Manhattan spread to fill the window, then slid and tilted, and finally flickered into darkness as we rose into the low cloud. It felt as though we were climbing blindly for a long time in our vulnerable metal tube, but then the gauze fell away and we came up into a bright night. The clouds were as massive and solid as alps, and the moon appeared occasionally from behind the peaks, lighting valleys and glaciers and ravines.

Some time after the plane levelled off, Amelia rose and came down the aisle towards me. Her hips swayed, involuntarily seductive, with the motion of the cabin.

'All right,' she said, 'he's ready to have a word. But go easy on him, okay? He's had a hell of a couple of days.'

He and I both, I thought.

'Will do,' I said.

I fished out my shoulder bag from beside my seat and began to squeeze past her. She caught my arm.

'You haven't got long,' she warned. 'This flight's only a hop. We'll be starting to descend any minute.'

*

It certainly was a hop. I checked afterwards. Only two hundred and sixty miles separate New York City from Martha's Vineyard, and the cruising speed of a Gulfstream G450 is five hundred and forty-eight miles per hour. The conjunction of these two facts explains why the tape of my conversation with Lang lasts a mere eleven minutes. We were probably already losing altitude even as I approached him.

His eyes were closed, his glass still held in his outstretched hand. He had removed his jacket and tie, and eased off his shoes, and was sprawled back in his seat like a starfish, as if someone had pushed him into it. At first I thought he'd fallen asleep, but then I realised his eyes were narrowed to slits and he was watching me closely. He gestured vaguely with his drink towards the seat opposite him.

'Hi, man,' he said. 'Join me.' He opened his eyes fully, yawned, and put the back of his hand to his mouth. 'Sorry.'

'Hello, Adam.'

I sat down. I had my bag in my lap. I fumbled to pull out my notebook, the mini-recorder and a spare disc. Wasn't this what Rycart wanted? Tapes? Nervousness made me clumsy, and if Lang had so much as raised an eyebrow, I would have put the recorder away again. But he didn't appear to notice. He must have gone through this ritual so many times at the end of some official visit – the journalist conducted into his presence for a few minutes' exclusive access; the tape machine nervously examined to make sure it works; the illusion of informality over the relaxing prime ministerial drink. In the recording you can hear the exhaustion in his voice.

'So,' he said, 'how's it going?'

'It's going,' I said. 'It's certainly going.'

When I listen to the disc, my register's so high from the anxiety, it sounds as I've been sucking helium.

'Found out anything interesting?'

There was a gleam of something in his eyes. Contempt? Amusement? I sensed he was playing with me.

'This and that. How was Washington?'

'Washington was great, actually.' There's a rustling noise as he straightens slightly in his chair, drawing himself up to give one last performance before the theatre closes for the night. 'I got the most terrific support everywhere – on the Hill, of course, as you probably saw, but also the Vice President and the Secretary of State. They're going to help me in every way they can.'

'And is the bottom line that you'll be able to settle in America?'

'Oh, yes. If the worst comes to the worst, they'll offer me asylum, certainly. Maybe even a job of some kind, as long as it doesn't involve overseas travel. But it won't get that far. They're going to supply something much more valuable.'

'Really?'

Lang nodded. 'Evidence.'

'Right.' I hadn't a clue what he was talking about.

'Is that thing working?' he asked.

There is a deafening clunk as I pick up the disc recorder.

'Yes, I think so. Is that okay?'

With a thump, I replace it.

'Sure,' said Lang. 'I just want to make sure you get this down, because I definitely think we can use it. This is important. We should keep it as an exclusive for the memoirs. It will do wonders for the serialisation deal.' He leaned forwards to emphasise his words. 'Washington is prepared to provide sworn testimony that no United Kingdom personnel were directly involved in the capture of those four men in Pakistan.'

'Really?' *Really? Really?* I keep on parroting it, and I wince every time I hear the sycophancy in my voice. The fawning courtier. The self-effacing ghost.

'You bet. The director of the CIA himself will provide a

deposition to the court in The Hague, saying that this was an entirely American covert operation, and if that doesn't do the trick he's prepared to let the actual officers who were running the mission provide evidence in camera.' Lang sat back and sipped his brandy. 'That should give Rycart something to think about. How's he going to make a charge of war crimes stick now?'

'But your memorandum to the Ministry of Defence—'

'That's genuine,' he conceded with a shrug. 'It's true, I can't deny that I urged the use of the SAS. And it's true the British government can't deny that our special forces were in Peshawar at the time of Operation Tempest. And we also can't deny that it was our intelligence services that tracked down these men to the particular location where they were arrested. But there's no proof that we passed that intelligence on to the CIA.'

Lang smiled at me.

'But we did?'

'There's no proof that we passed that intelligence on to the CIA.'

'But if we did, surely that would be aiding and abetting—'

'There's no proof that we passed that intelligence on to the CIA.'

He was still holding his smile, albeit now with just a crease of concentration in his brow, as a tenor might hold a note at the end of a difficult aria.

'Then how did it get to them?'

'That's a difficult question. Not through any official channel, that's for sure. And certainly it was nothing to do with me.' There was a long pause. His smile died. 'Well,' he said. 'What do you think?'

'It sounds a bit' — I tried to find some diplomatic way of saying it — 'technical.'

'Meaning?'

My reply on the tape is so slippery, so sweaty with nervous circumlocutions, it's enough to make one laugh out loud.

'Well – you know – you admit yourself you wanted the SAS to pick them up – no doubt for, you know, understandable reasons – and even if they didn't actually do the job themselves, the Ministry of Defence – as I understand it – hasn't really been able to *deny* they were involved, presumably because they were, in a way, even if – even if – they were only parked in a car around the corner. And apparently British – you know – intelligence gave the CIA the location where they could be picked up. And when they were tortured, you didn't condemn it.'

The last line was delivered in a rush. Lang said coldly, 'Sid Kroll was very pleased with the commitment he was given by the CIA. He believes the prosecutor may even have to drop the case.'

'Well, if Sid says that—'

'But *fuck it*,' said Lang suddenly. He banged his hand on the edge of the table. On the tape it sounds like an explosion. The dozing Special Branch man on the nearby sofa looked up sharply. 'I don't regret what happened to those four men. If we'd relied on the Pakistanis we'd never have got them. We had to grab them while we had the chance, and if we'd missed them, they'd have gone underground and the next time we'd have known anything about them would've been when they were killing our people.'

'You really don't regret it?'

'No.'

'Not even the one who died under interrogation?'

'Oh, him,' said Lang dismissively. 'He had a heart problem – an undiagnosed heart problem. He could have died any time. He could have died getting out of bed one morning.'

I said nothing. I pretended to make a note.

'Look,' said Lang, 'I don't condone torture, but let me just say this to you. First, it does actually produce results – I've seen the intelligence. Second, having power, in the end, is all about balancing evils, and when you think about it, what are a couple of minutes of suffering for a few individuals compared to the deaths – the *deaths*, mark you – of thousands. Third, don't try telling me this is something unique to the War on Terror. Torture's always been part of warfare. The only difference is that in the past there were no fucking media around to report it.'

'The men arrested in Pakistan claim they were innocent,' I pointed out.

'Of course they claim they were innocent! What else are they going to say?' Lang studied me closely, as if seeing me properly for the first time. 'I'm beginning to think you're too naïve for this job.'

I couldn't resist it.

'Unlike Mike McAra?' I said.

'Mike!' Lang laughed and shook his head. 'Mike was naïve in a different way.'

The plane was beginning to descend quite rapidly now. The moon and stars had gone. We were dropping through cloud. I could feel the pressure change in my ears, and I had to pinch my nose and swallow hard.

Amelia made her way down the aisle.

'Is everything all right?' she asked. She looked concerned. She must have heard Lang's outburst of temper; everyone must have.

'We're just doing some work on my memoirs,' said Lang. 'I'm telling him what happened over Operation Tempest.'

'You're taping it?' said Amelia.

'If that's all right,' I said.

'You need to be careful,' she told Lang. 'Remember what Sid Kroll said.'

'The tapes will be yours,' I interrupted, 'not mine.'

'They could still be subpoenaed.'

'Stop treating me as though I'm a child,' said Lang abruptly. 'I know what I want to say. Let's deal with it once and for all.'

Amelia permitted herself a slight widening of her eyes, and withdrew.

'Women!' muttered Lang. He took another gulp of brandy. The ice had melted but the colour of the liquid remained dark. It must have been a very full measure, and it occurred to me that our former prime minister was slightly drunk. I sensed this was my moment.

'In what way,' I asked, 'was Mike McAra naïve?'

'Never mind,' muttered Lang. He nursed his drink, his chin on his chest, brooding. He suddenly jerked up again. 'I mean, take for instance all this civil liberties crap. You know what I'd do if I were in power again? I'd say, okay then, we'll have two queues at the airports. On the left, we'll have queues to flights on which we've done no background checks on the passengers, no profiling, no biometric data, nothing that infringed anyone's precious civil liberties, used no intelligence obtained under torture – nothing. On the right, we'll have queues to the flights where we've done everything possible to make them safe for passengers. Then people can make their own minds up which plane they want to catch. Wouldn't that be great? To sit back and watch which queue the Rycarts of this world would *really* choose to put their kids on, if the chips were down.'

'And Mike was like that?'

'Not at the beginning. But Mike, unfortunately, discovered

idealism in his old age. I said to him – it was our last conversation, actually – I said, if our Lord Jesus Christ was unable to solve all the problems of the world when He came down to live among us – and He was the son of God! – wasn't it a bit unreasonable of Mike to expect me to have sorted everything out in ten years?'

'Is it true you had a serious row with him? Just before he died?'

'Mike made certain wild accusations. I could hardly ignore them.'

'May I ask what kind of accusations?'

I could imagine Rycart and the special prosecutor sitting listening to the tape, straightening in their chairs at that. I had to swallow again. My voice sounded muffled in my ears, as if I was talking in a dream, or hailing myself from a great distance. On the tape, the pause that follows is quite short, but at the time it seemed endless, and Lang's voice when it came was deadly quiet.

'I'd prefer not to repeat them.'

'Were they to do with the CIA?'

'But surely you already know,' said Lang bitterly, 'if you've been to see Paul Emmett?'

And this time the pause is as long on the recording as it is in my memory.

Delivered of his bombshell, Lang gazed out of the window and sipped his drink. A few isolated lights had begun to appear beneath us. I think they must have been ships. I looked at him and I saw that the years had caught up even with him at last. It was in the droop of the flesh around his eyes, and in the loose skin beneath his jaw. Or perhaps it wasn't age. Perhaps he was simply exhausted. I doubt he could have had much sleep for weeks, probably not since McAra had confronted him. Certainly, when at last he turned back to me, there wasn't anger in his expression, merely a great weariness.

'I want you to understand,' he said, with heavy emphasis, 'that everything I did, both as party leader and as prime minister – everything – I did out of conviction, because I believed it was right.'

I mumbled a reply. I was in a state of shock.

'Emmett claims you showed him some photographs. Is that true? May I see?'

My hands shook slightly as I removed them from the envelope and pushed them across the table towards him. He flicked through the first four very quickly, paused over the fifth – the one that showed him and Emmett on stage – then went back to the beginning and started looking at them again, lingering over each image.

He said, without raising his eyes from the pictures, 'Where did you get them?'

'McAra ordered them up from the archive. I found them in his room.'

Over the intercom, the co-pilot asked us to fasten our seat belts.

'Odd,' murmured Lang. 'Odd the way we've all changed so much, and yet also stayed exactly the same. Mike never mentioned anything to me about photographs. Oh, that bloody archive!' He squinted closely at one of the river bank pictures. It was the girls, I noticed, rather than himself or Emmett, who seemed to fascinate him the most. 'I remember her,' he said, tapping the picture. 'And her. She wrote to me once, when I was prime minister. Ruth was not pleased. Oh God,' he said, and passed his hand across his face, 'Ruth.' For a moment, I thought he was about to break down, but when he looked at me his eyes were dry. 'What happens next? Is there a procedure in your line of work to deal with this sort of situation?'

Patterns of light were very clear in the window now. I could see the headlamps of a car on a road.

'The client always has the last word about what goes in a book,' I said. 'Always. But, obviously, in this case, given what happened . . .'

On the tape, my voice trails away, and then there is a loud clunk, as Lang leaned forward and grabbed my forearm.

'If you mean what happened to Mike, then let me tell you I was absolutely appalled by that.' His gaze was fixed on me unwaveringly: he was putting everything he had left within him into the task of convincing me, and I'll freely confess, despite everything I'd discovered, that he succeeded: to this day, I'm sure he was telling the truth. 'If you believe nothing else, you must please believe that his death had nothing to do with me, and I shall carry that image of Mike in the morgue until my own dying day. I'm sure it was an accident. But okay, let's say, for the sake of argument, it wasn't.' He tightened his grip on my arm. 'What was he thinking of, driving up to Boston to confront Emmett? He'd been around politics long enough to know that you don't do something like that – not when the stakes are this high. You know, in a way, he did kill himself. It was a suicidal act.'

'That's what worries me,' I said.

'You can't seriously think,' said Lang, 'that the same thing could happen to you?'

'It has crossed my mind.'

'You need have no fears on that score. I can guarantee it.' I guess my disbelief must have been obvious. 'Oh, come on, man!' he said urgently. Again, the fingers clenched on my flesh. 'There are four policemen travelling on this plane with us right now! What kind of people do you think we are?'

'Well, that's just it,' I said. 'What kind of people *are* you?'

We were coming in low over the treetops. The lights of the Gulfstream gleamed across dark waves of foliage. I tried to pull my arm away.

'Excuse me,' I said.

Lang reluctantly let go of me and I fastened my seat belt. He did the same. He glanced out of the window at the terminal, then back at me, appalled, as we dipped gracefully on to the runway.

'My God, you've already told someone, haven't you?'

I could feel myself turning scarlet.

'No,' I said.

'You have.'

'I haven't.' On the tape I sound as feeble as a child caught red-handed.

He leaned forwards again.

'Who have you told?'

Looking out at the dark forest beyond the perimeter of the airport, where anything could be lurking, it seemed like the only insurance policy I had.

'Richard Rycart,' I said.

That must have been a devastating blow to him. He must have known then that it was the end of everything. In my mind's eye I see him still, like one of those once-grand but now condemned apartment blocks, moments after the demolition charges have been exploded: for a few seconds, the façade remains bizarrely intact, before slowly beginning to slide. That was Lang. He gave me a long, blank look, and then subsided back into his seat.

The plane came to a halt in front of the terminal building. The engines died.

*

At this point, at long last, I did something smart.

As Lang sat contemplating his ruin, and as Amelia came

278

hurrying down the aisle to discover what I'd said, I had the presence of mind to eject the disc from the mini-recorder and slip it into my pocket. In its place I inserted the blank. Lang was too stunned to care, and Amelia too fixated on him to notice.

'All right,' she said firmly, 'that's enough for tonight.' She lifted the empty glass from his unresisting hand and gave it to the steward. 'We need to get you home, Adam. Ruth's waiting at the gate.' She reached over and unfastened his seat belt, and then removed his suit jacket from the back of his seat. She held it out ready for him to slip into, and shook it slightly, like a matador with a cloak, but her voice was very tender. 'Adam?'

He rose, trance-like, to obey, gazing vacantly towards the cockpit as she guided his arms into the sleeves. She glared at me over his shoulder, and mouthed, furiously and very distinctly, and with her customarily precise diction, 'What the fuck are you doing?'

And it was a good question. What the fuck *was* I doing? At the front of the plane, the door had opened and three of the Special Branch men were disembarking. A blast of cold air ran down the cabin. Lang began to walk towards the exit, preceded by his fourth bodyguard, Amelia at his back. I quickly stuffed my disc recorder and the photographs into my shoulder bag and followed them. The pilot had come out of the cockpit to say goodbye and I saw Lang visibly square his shoulders and advance to meet him, his hand outstretched.

'That was great,' said Lang vaguely, 'as usual. My favourite airline.' He shook the pilot's hand, then leaned past him to greet the co-pilot and the waiting steward. 'Thanks. Thanks so much.' He turned to us, still smiling his professional smile, but it faded fast; he looked stricken. The bodyguard was already halfway down the steps. There was just Amelia, me and the two secretaries waiting to follow him off the plane. Standing in the lighted glass window of the terminal

I could just make out the figure of Ruth. She was too far away for me to judge her expression. 'Would you mind just hanging back a minute?' he said to Amelia. 'And you, too?' he added to me. 'I need to have a private word with my wife.'

'Is everything all right, Adam?' asked Amelia. She had been with him too long, and I suppose she loved him too much, not to know that something was terribly wrong.

'It'll be fine,' said Lang. He touched her elbow lightly, then gave us all, including me and the plane crew, a slight bow. 'Thank you, ladies and gentlemen, and good night.'

He ducked through the door and paused at the top of the steps, glancing around, smoothing down his hair. Amelia and I watched him from the interior of the plane. He was just as he was when I first saw him — still, out of habit, searching for an audience with whom he could connect, even though the windy, floodlit concourse was deserted, apart from the waiting bodyguards, and a ground technician in overalls, working late, no doubt eager to get home.

Lang must also have seen Ruth waiting at the window, because he suddenly raised his hand in acknowledgement, then set off down the steps, gracefully, like a dancer. He reached the tarmac and had gone about ten yards towards the terminal when the technician shouted out, 'Adam!' and waved. The voice was English, and Lang must have recognised the accent of a fellow countryman because he suddenly broke away from his bodyguards and strode towards the man, his hand held out. And that is my final image of Lang: a man always with his hand held out. It is burned into my retina — his yearning shadow against the expanding ball of bright white fire that suddenly engulfed him; and then there was only the flying debris, the stinging grit, the glass, the furnace heat, and the under-water silence of the explosion.

Sixteen

If you are going to be the least bit upset not to see your name credited or not to be invited to the launch party then you are going to have a miserable time ghosting altogether.

Ghostwriting

I saw nothing more after that initial flash of brilliant light: there was too much glass and blood in my eyes. The force of the blast flung us all backwards. Amelia, I learned later, hit her head on the side of a seat and was knocked unconscious, while I lay across the aisle in darkness and silence for what could have been minutes or hours. I felt no pain, except when one of the terrified secretaries trod on my hand with her high heel in her desperation to get out of the plane. But I couldn't see, and it was also to be several hours before I could hear properly. Even today I get an occasional buzzing in my ears. It cuts me off from the world, like radio interference. Eventually, I was lifted away, and given a wonderful shot of morphine, that burst like warm fireworks in my brain. Then I was airlifted by helicopter with all the other survivors to a hospital near Boston – an institution very close, it turned out, to the place where Emmett lived.

Did you ever do something secretly as a child that seemed really bad at the time, and for which you were sure you were going to be punished? I remember breaking a precious old long-playing gramophone record of my father's, and putting it away in its sleeve again, and saying nothing about it. For days, I lived in a sweat of terror, convinced that retribution would arrive at any moment. But nothing was ever said. The next time I dared to look, the record had disappeared. He must have found it and thrown it away.

I had similar feelings following the assassination of Adam Lang. Throughout the next day or two, as I lay in my hospital room, my face bandaged, and with a policeman on guard in the corridor outside, I repeatedly ran over in my mind the events of the previous week, and it always seemed to me a certainty that I would never leave that place alive. If you stop to think of it, there's nowhere easier to dispose of someone than in a hospital: I should imagine it's almost routine. And who makes a better killer than a doctor?

But it turned out to be like the incident of my father's broken record. Nothing happened. While I was still blinded, I was gently questioned by a Special Agent Murphy from the Boston office of the FBI about what I could remember. The next afternoon, when the bandages were removed from my eyes, Murphy returned. He looked like a muscular young priest in a fifties movie, and this time he was accompanied by a saturnine Englishman from the British Security Service, MI5, whose name I never quite caught – because, I assume, I was never quite meant to catch it.

They showed me a photograph. My vision was still bleary, but I was nevertheless able to identify the crazy man I had met in the bar of my hotel, and who had staged that lonely vigil, with the biblical slogan, at the end of the track from the Rhinehart compound. His name, they said, was George Arthur Boxer, a former major in the British army, whose son had been killed in Iraq and whose wife had died six months later in a London suicide bombing. In his unhinged state, Major Boxer had held Adam Lang personally responsible, and had stalked him to Martha's Vineyard just after McAra's death had been reported in the papers. He had plenty of expertise in munitions and intelligence. He had studied tactics for suicide bombing on jihadist websites. He had rented a cottage in Oak Bluffs, brought in supplies of peroxide and weedkiller, and turned it into a minor factory for the production of homemade explosives. And it would have been easy for him to know when Lang was returning from New York, because he would have seen the bomb-proof car heading to the airport to meet him. How he had got on to the airfield nobody was quite sure, but it was dark, there was a four-mile perimeter fence, and the experts had always assumed that four Special Branch men and an armoured car was sufficient protection.

But one had to be realistic, said the man from MI5. There was a limit to what security could do, especially against a determined suicide bomber. He quoted Seneca, in the original Latin, and then helpfully translated: 'Who scorns his own life is lord of yours.' I got the impression everyone was slightly relieved by the way things had worked out: the British because Lang had been killed on American soil; the Americans because he'd been blown up by a Brit; and both because there would now be no war crimes trial, no unseemly revelations, and no guest who has overstayed his welcome, drifting around the dinner tables of Georgetown for the next twenty years. You could almost say it was the special relationship in action.

Agent Murphy asked me about the flight from New York, and whether Lang had expressed any worries about his personal security. I said truthfully that he hadn't.

'Mrs Bly,' said the MI5 man, 'tells us you recorded an interview with him during the final part of the flight.'

'No, she's wrong about that,' I said. 'I had the machine in front of me, but I never actually switched it on. It wasn't really an interview, in any case. It was more of a chat.'

'Do you mind if I take a look?'

'Go ahead.'

My shoulder bag was on the cupboard next to my bed. The MI5 man took out the mini-recorder and ejected the disc. I watched him, dry-mouthed.

'Can I borrow this?'

'You can keep it,' I said. He started poking through the rest of my belongings. 'How is Amelia, by the way?'

'She's fine.' He put the disc into his briefcase. 'Thanks.'

'Can I see her?'

'She flew back to London last night.' I guess my disappointment must have been evident, because the MI5 man added, with chilly pleasure, 'It's not surprising. She hasn't seen her husband since before Christmas.'

'And what about Ruth?' I asked.

'She's accompanying Mr Lang's body home right now,' said Murphy. 'Your government sent a plane to fetch them.'

'He'll get full military honours,' added the MI5 man, 'a statue in the Palace of Westminster, and a funeral in the Abbey if she wants it. He's never been more popular than since he died.'

'He should have done it years ago,' I said. They didn't smile. 'And is it really true that nobody else was killed?'

'Nobody,' said Murphy, 'which was a miracle, believe me.'

'In fact,' said the man from MI5, 'Mrs Bly wonders if Mr Lang didn't actually recognise his assassin and deliberately head towards him, knowing that something like this might happen. Can you shed any light on that?'

'It sounds far-fetched,' I said. 'I thought a fuel truck had exploded.'

'It was certainly quite a bang,' said Murphy, clicking his pen and slipping it into his inside pocket. 'We eventually found the killer's head on the terminal roof.'

*

I watched Lang's funeral on CNN two day later. My eyesight was more or less restored. I could see it was tastefully done: the Queen, the prime minister, the US vice president and half the leaders of Europe; the coffin draped in the Union Jack; the guard of honour; the solitary piper, playing a lament. Ruth looked very good in black, I thought: it was definitely her colour. I kept a lookout for Amelia, but I didn't see her. During a lull in proceedings, there was even an interview with Richard Rycart. Naturally, he hadn't been invited to the service, but he'd gone to the trouble of putting on a black tie and paid a very moving tribute from his office in the United Nations: a great colleague . . . a true patriot . . . we had our disagreements . . . remained friends . . . my heart goes out to Ruth and the family . . . as far as I'm concerned the whole chapter is closed.

I found the mobile phone he had given me and threw it out of the window.

The next day, when I was due to be discharged from hospital, Rick came up from New York to say goodbye and take me to the airport.

'Do you want the good news, or the good news?' he said.

'I'm not sure your idea of good news is the same as mine.'

'Sid Kroll just called. Ruth Lang still wants you to finish the memoirs, and Maddox will give you an extra month to work on the manuscript.'

'And the good news is?'

'Oh, very cute. Listen, don't be so goddamned snooty about it. This is a really hot book now. This is Adam Lang's voice from the grave. You don't have to work on it here any more: you can finish it in London. You look terrible, by the way.'

'His voice from the grave?' I repeated incredulously. 'So now I'm to be the ghost of a ghost?'

'Come on, the whole situation is rich with possibilities. Think about it. You can write what you like, within reason. Nobody's going to stop you. And you liked him, didn't you?'

I thought about that. In fact, I had been thinking about it ever since I came round from the sedative. Worse than the pain in my eyes and the buzzing in my ears; worse even than my fear that I would never emerge from the hospital, was my sense of guilt. That may seem odd, given what I'd learned, but I couldn't work up any sense of self-justification, or resentment against Lang. I was the one at fault. It wasn't just that I'd betrayed my client, personally and professionally: it was the sequence of events my actions had set in motion. If I hadn't gone to see Emmett, Emmett wouldn't have contacted Lang to warn him about the photograph. Then maybe Lang wouldn't have insisted on flying back to Martha's Vineyard that night to see Ruth. Then I wouldn't have had to tell him about Rycart. And then, and then . . . ? It nagged away at me as I lay in the darkness. I just couldn't erase the memory of how bleak he had looked on the plane at the very end.

'Mrs Bly wonders if Mr Lang didn't actually recognise his assassin and delib-erately head towards him, knowing that something like this might happen . . .'

'Yes,' I said to Rick. 'Yes, I did like him.'

'Well, there you go. You owe it to him. And besides, there's another consideration.'

'Which is what?'

'Sid Kroll says that if you don't fulfil your contractual obligations and finish the book, they'll sue your ass off.'

*

And so I returned to London, and for the next six weeks I barely emerged from my flat, except once, early on, to go out for dinner with Kate. We met in a restaurant in Notting Hill Gate, midway between our homes – territory as neutral as Switzerland, and about as expensive. The manner of Adam Lang's death seemed to have silenced even her hostility, and I suppose a kind of glamour attached to me as an eyewitness. I had turned down a score of requests to give interviews, so that she was the first person, apart from the FBI and MI5, to whom I described what had happened. I desperately wanted to tell her about my final conversation with Lang. I would have done, too. But in the way of these things, just as I was about to broach it, the waiter came over to discuss dessert, and when he left she announced she had something she wanted to tell me, first.

She was engaged to be married.

I confess it was a shock. I didn't like the other man. You'd know him if I mentioned his name: craggy, handsome, soulful. He specialises in flying briefly into the world's worst trouble spots and flying out again with moving descriptions of human suffering, usually his own.

'Congratulations,' I said.

We skipped dessert. Our affair, our relationship – our *thing*, whatever it was — ended ten minutes later with a peck on the cheek on the pavement outside the restaurant.

'You were going to tell me something,' she said, just before she got into her taxi. 'I'm sorry I cut you off. Only I didn't want you to say anything, you know, too personal, without telling you first about how things were with me and—'

'It doesn't matter,' I said.

'Are you sure you're all right? You seem — different.'

'I'm fine.'

'If you ever need me, I'll always be there for you.'

'There?' I said. 'I don't know about you, but I'm here. Where's there?'

I held open the door of her cab for her. I couldn't help over-hearing that the address she gave the driver wasn't hers.

After that, I withdrew from the world. I spent my every waking hour with Lang, and now that he was dead, I found I suddenly had his voice. It was more a ouija board than a keyboard that I sat down to every morning. If my fingers typed out a sentence that sounded wrong, I could almost physically feel them being drawn to the DELETE key. I was like a screenwriter producing lines with a particu-larly demanding star in mind: I knew he might say this, but not that; might do this scene, never that.

The basic structure of the story remained McAra's sixteen chapters, and my method was to work always with his manuscript on my left: to retype it completely, and in the process of passing it through my brain and fingers and on to my computer, to strain it of my predecessor's lumpy clichés. I made no mention of Emmett, of course, cutting even the anodyne quote of his which had opened the final chapter. The image of Adam Lang which I presented to the world was very much the character he'd always chosen to play: the regular guy who fell into politics almost by accident, and who rose to power because he was neither tribal nor ideological. I reconciled this with the chronology by taking up Ruth's suggestion that Lang had turned to politics as solace for his depression when he first arrived in London. I didn't really need to play up the misery here. Lang was dead, after all, his whole memoir suffused by the reader's knowledge of what was to come – that ought to be sufficient, I reckoned, to keep the ghouls happy. But it was still useful to have a page or two of heroic struggle against inner demons, etc, etc.

In the superficially tedious business of politics I found solace for my hurt.
I found activity, companionship, an outlet for my love of meeting new people.
I found a cause that was bigger than myself. Most of all, I found Ruth . . .

In my telling of his story, Lang's political involvement only really got going when Ruth came knocking at his door two years later. It sounded plausible. Who knows? It might even have been true.

I started writing *Memoirs by Adam Lang* on February the tenth, and promised Maddox I'd have the whole thing done, all 160,000 words, by the end of March. That meant I had to produce 3,400 words a day, every day. I had a chart on the wall, and marked it up each morning. I was like Captain Scott returning from the South Pole: I had to make those daily distances, or I'd fall irrevocably behind and perish in a white wilderness of blank pages. It was a hard slog, especially as almost no lines of McAra's were salvageable, except, curiously, the very last one in the manuscript, which had made me groan aloud when I read it on Martha's Vineyard: '*Ruth and I look forward to the future, whatever it may hold.*' Read that, you bastards, I thought, as I typed it in on the evening of the thirtieth of March: read that, and close this book without a catch in your throat.

I added 'THE END' and then, I guess, I had a kind of nervous breakdown.

*

I dispatched one copy of the manuscript to New York, and another to the office of the Adam Lang Foundation in London, for the personal attention of Mrs Ruth Lang – or, as I should more properly have styled her by then, Baroness Lang of Calderthorpe, the government having just given her a seat in the House of Lords as a mark of the nation's respect.

I hadn't heard anything from Ruth since the assassination. I'd written to her while I was still in hospital: one of more than a hundred thousand correspondents who were reported to have sent their condolences, so I wasn't surprised that all I got back was a standard printed reply. But a week after she received the manuscript, a handwritten message arrived on the red-embossed notepaper of the House of Lords:

> You have done all that I ever hoped you wd do – and more! You have caught his tone beautifully & brought him back to life – all his wonderful humour & compassion & energy. Pls. come & see me here in the HoL when you have a spare moment. It wd be great to catch up. Martha's V. seems a v. long time ago, & a long way away! Bless you again for yr talent. And it is a proper book!!
>
> Much love,
>
> R.

Maddox was equally effusive, but without the love. The first printing was to be four hundred thousand copies. The publication date was the end of May.

So that was that. The job was done.

It didn't take me long to realise I was in a bad state. I'd been kept going, I suppose, by Lang's 'wonderful humour & compassion & energy', but once he was written out of me, I collapsed like an empty suit of clothes. For years I had survived by inhabiting one life after another. But Rick had insisted we wait until the Lang memoirs were published — my 'breakthrough book', he called it — before negotiating new and better contracts, with the result that, for the first time I could remember, I had no work to go to. I was afflicted by a horrible combination of lethargy and panic. I could barely summon the energy to get out of bed before noon, and when I did I moped on the sofa in my dressing gown, watching daytime television. I didn't eat much. I stopped opening my letters, or answering the phone. I didn't shave. I only left the flat for any length of time on Mondays and Thursdays, to avoid seeing my cleaner — I wanted to fire her, but I didn't have the nerve — and then I either sat in a park, if it was fine, or in a nearby greasy café, if it wasn't; and, this being England, it mostly wasn't.

And yet, paradoxically, at the same time as being sunk in a stupor I was also permanently agitated. Nothing was in proportion. I fretted absurdly about trivialities — where I'd put a pair of shoes, for instance, or if it was wise to keep all my money with the same bank. This nerviness made me feel physically shaky, often breathless, and it was in this spirit, late one night, about two months after I finished the book, that I made what to me, in my condition, was a calamitous discovery.

I'd run out of whisky and knew I had about ten minutes to get to the little supermarket on Ladbroke Grove before it closed. It was towards the end of May, dark and raining. I grabbed the nearest jacket and was halfway down the stairs when I realised it was the one I'd been wearing when Lang was killed. It was torn at the front and stained with blood. In one pocket was the recording of my final interview with Adam, and in the other the keys to the Ford Escape SUV.

The car! I had forgotten all about it. It was still parked at Logan Airport! It was costing eighteen dollars a day! I must owe *thousands*!

To you, no doubt – and indeed to me, now – my panic seems ridiculous. But I raced back up those stairs with my pulse drumming. It was after six in New York and Rhinehart Inc. had closed for the day. There was no reply from the Martha's Vineyard house, either. In despair, I called Rick at home and, without preliminaries, began gabbling out the details of the crisis. He listened for about thirty seconds, then told me roughly to shut up.

'This was all sorted out weeks ago. The guys at the car park got suspicious and called the cops, and they called Rhinehart's office. Maddox paid the bill. I didn't bother you with it because I knew you were busy. Now listen to me, my friend. It seems to me you've got a nasty case of delayed shock. You need help. I know a shrink—'

I hung up.

When I finally fell asleep on the sofa, I had my usual recurrent dream about McAra – the one in which he floated fully clothed in the sea beside me, and told me he wasn't going to make it: *You go on without me*. But this time, instead of ending with my waking up, the dream lasted longer. A wave took McAra away, in his heavy raincoat and rubber-soled boots, until he became only a dark shape in the distance, face down in the shallow foam, sliding back and forth at the edge of the beach. I waded towards him and managed to get my hands around his bulky body and, with a supreme effort, to roll him over, and then suddenly he was staring up naked from a white slab, with Adam Lang bending over him.

The next morning I left the flat early and walked down the hill to the tube station. It really wouldn't take much to kill myself, I thought. One swift leap out in front of the approaching train, and then oblivion. Much better than drowning. But it was only the briefest of impulses, not least because I couldn't bear the idea of someone having to clean up afterwards. (*They found his head on the terminal roof . . .*) Instead I boarded the train and travelled to the end of the line at Hammersmith, then crossed the road to the other platform. Motion, that's the cure for depression, I decided. You have to keep moving. At Embankment I changed again for Morden, which always sounds to me like the end of the world. We passed through Balham and I got off two stops later.

It didn't take me long to find the grave. I remembered Ruth had said the funeral was at Streatham Cemetery. I looked up his name and a groundsman pointed the way towards the plot. I passed stone angels with vulture's wings, and mossy cherubs with lichened curls, Victorian sarcophagi the size of garden sheds, and crosses garlanded with marble roses. But McAra's contribution to the necropolis was characteristically plain. No flowery mottos – no 'Say not the struggle naught availeth' or 'Well done, thou good and faithful servant' for our Mike. Merely a slab of limestone with his name and dates.

It was a late spring morning, drowsy with pollen and petrol fumes. In the distance, the traffic rolled up Garratt Lane towards central London. I squatted on my haunches and pressed my palms to the dewy grass. As I've said before, I'm not the superstitious type, but at that moment I did feel a current of relief pass through me, as if I'd closed a circle, or fulfilled a task. I sensed he had wanted me to come here.

That was when I noticed, resting against the stone, half obscured by the overgrown grass, a small bunch of shrivelled flowers. There was a card attached, written in an elegant hand, just legible after successive London downpours: 'In memory of a good friend and loyal colleague. Rest in peace, dear Mike. Amelia.'

*

When I got back to my flat, I called her on her mobile number. She didn't seem surprised to hear from me.

'Hello,' she said. 'I was just thinking about you.'

'Why's that?'

'I'm reading your book – Adam's book.'

'And?'

'It's good. No, actually, it's better than good. It's like having him back. There's only one element missing, I think.'

'And what's that?'

'Oh, it doesn't matter. I'll tell you if I see you. Perhaps we'll get the opportunity to talk at the reception tonight.'

'What reception?'

She laughed.

'*Your* reception, you idiot. The launch of your book. Don't tell me you haven't been invited.'

I hadn't spoken to anyone for a long time. It took me a second or two to reply.

'I don't know whether I have or not. To be honest, I haven't checked my post in a while.'

'You must have been invited.'

'Don't you believe it. Authors tend to be funny about having their ghosts staring at them over the canapés.'

'Well, the author isn't going to be there, is he?' she said. She wanted to sound brisk, but she came across as desperately hollow and strained. 'You should go, whether you've been invited or not. In fact, if you really haven't been invited, you can come as my guest. My invitation has "Amelia Bly plus one" written on it.'

The prospect of returning to society made my heartbeat start to race again.

'But don't you want to take someone else? What about your husband?'

'Oh, him. That didn't work out, I'm afraid. I hadn't realised quite how bored he was with being my "plus one".'

'I'm sorry to hear that.'

'Liar,' she said. 'I'll meet you at the end of Downing Street at seven o'clock. The party's just across Whitehall. I'll only wait five minutes, so if you decide you do want to come, don't be late.'

*

After I finished speaking to Amelia, I went though my weeks of accumulated mail carefully. There was no invitation to the party. Bearing in mind the circumstances of my last encounter with Ruth, I wasn't too surprised. There was, however, a copy of the finished book. It was nicely produced. The cover, with an eye to the American market, was a photograph of Lang, looking debonair, addressing a joint session of the US Congress. The photographs inside did not include any of the ones from Cambridge that McAra had discovered: I hadn't passed them on to the picture researcher. I flicked through to the acknowledgements, which I had written in Lang's voice:

This book would not exist without the dedication, support, wisdom and friendship of the late Michael McAra, who collaborated with me on its composition from the first page to the last. Thank you, Mike – for everything.

My name wasn't mentioned. Much to Rick's annoyance, I'd forgone my collaborator credit. I didn't tell him why, which was that I thought it was safer that way. The expurgated contents and my anonymity would, I hoped, serve as a message to whoever might be paying atten-tion out there that there would be no further trouble from me.

I soaked in the bath for an hour that afternoon and contemplated whether or not to go to the reception. As usual, I was able to spin out my procrastination for hours. I told myself I still hadn't neces-sarily made up my mind as I shaved off my beard, and as I dressed in a decent dark suit and white shirt, and as I went out into the street and hailed a taxi, and even as I stood on the corner of Downing Street at five minutes to seven: it still wasn't too late to turn back. Across the broad, ceremonial boulevard of Whitehall, I could see the cars and taxis pulling up outside the Banqueting House, where I guessed the party must be taking place. Photographers' flashlights winked in the evening sunshine, a pale reminder of Lang's old glory days.

I kept looking for Amelia, up the street towards the mounted sentry outside Horse Guards, and down it again, past the Foreign Office, to the Victorian Gothic madhouse of the Palace of Westminster. A sign on the opposite side of the entrance to Downing Street pointed to the Cabinet War Rooms, with a drawing of Churchill, complete with V-sign and cigar. Whitehall always reminds me of the Blitz. I can picture it from the images I was brought up on as a child: the sandbags, the white tape across the windows, the searchlights blindly fingering the darkness, the drone of the bombers, the crump of high explosive, the red glow from the fires in the East End. Thirty thousand dead in London alone. Now *that*, as my father would have said, is what you call a *war* − not this drip, drip, drip of inconvenience and anxiety and folly. Yet Churchill used to stroll to parliament through St James's Park, raising his hat to passers-by, with just a solitary detective walking ten feet behind him.

I was still thinking about it when Big Ben finished chiming the hour. I peered left and right again, but there was still no sign of Amelia, which surprised me as I had her down as the punctual type. But then I felt a touch on my sleeve, and turned to find her standing behind me. She had emerged from the sunless canyon of Downing Street in her dark blue suit, carrying a briefcase. She looked older, faded, and just for a moment I glimpsed her future: a tiny flat, a smart address, a cat. We exchanged polite hellos.

'Well,' she said, 'here we are.'

'Here we are.' We stood awkwardly, a few feet apart. 'I didn't realise you were back working in Number Ten,' I said.

'I was only on attachment to Adam. The king is dead,' she said, and suddenly her voice cracked. I put my arms around her, and patted her back, as if she were a child that had fallen over. I felt the wetness of her cheek against mine. When she pulled back, she opened her briefcase and took out a handkerchief. 'Sorry,' she said. She blew her nose and stamped her high-heeled foot in self-reproach. 'I keep thinking I'm over it, and then I realise I'm not. You look terrible,' she added. 'In fact, you look—'

'Like a ghost?' I said. 'Thanks. I've heard it before.'

She checked herself in the mirror of her powder compact and

carried out some swift repairs. She was apprehensive, I realised. She needed someone to accompany her; even I would do.

'Right,' she said, shutting it with a click. 'Let's go.'

We walked up Whitehall, through the crowds of spring tourists.

'So, were you invited in the end?' she asked.

'No, I wasn't. Actually, I'm rather surprised that you were.'

'Oh, that's not so odd,' she said, with an attempt at careless-ness. 'She's won, hasn't she? She's the national icon. The grieving widow. Our very own Jackie Kennedy. She won't mind having me around. I'm hardly a threat; just a trophy in the victory parade.' We crossed the road. 'Charles the First stepped out of that window to be executed,' she said, pointing. 'You'd have thought someone would have realised the association, wouldn't you?'

'Poor staffwork,' I said. 'It wouldn't have happened when you were in charge.'

I knew it was a mistake to have come the moment we stepped inside. Amelia had to open her briefcase for the security men. My keys set off the metal detector and I had to be searched. It's come to something, I thought, standing with my hands up, having my groin felt, when you can't even go to a drinks party without being frisked. In the great open space of the Banqueting House, we were confronted by a roar of conversation and a wall of turned backs. I'd made it a rule never to attend the launch parties of my own books, and now I remembered why. A ghostwriter is about as welcome as the groom's unacknowledged love child at a society wedding. I didn't know a soul.

Deftly, I seized a couple of flutes of champagne from a passing waiter and presented one to Amelia.

'I can't see Ruth,' I said.

'She'll be in the thick of it, I expect. Your health,' she said.

We clinked glasses. Champagne: even more pointless than

white wine, in my opinion. But there didn't seem to be anything else.

'It's Ruth, actually, who is the one element missing from your book, if I had to make a criticism.'

'I know,' I said. 'I wanted to put in more about her, but she wouldn't have it.'

'Well, it's a pity.' Drink seem to embolden the normally cautious Mrs Bly. Or perhaps it was just that we had a bond now. After all, we were survivors – survivors of the Langs. At any rate, she leaned in close to me, giving me a familiar lungful of her scent. 'I adored Adam, and I think he had similar feelings for me. But I wasn't under any illusions: he'd never have left her. He told me that during that last drive to the airport. They were a complete team. He knew perfectly well he'd have been nothing without her. He made that absolutely clear to me. He owed her. She was the one who really understood power. She was the one who originally had the contacts in the party. In fact, *she* was the one who was supposed to go into parliament, did you know that? Not him at all. That isn't in your book.'

'I didn't know.'

'Adam told me about it once. It isn't widely known – at least I've never seen it written up anywhere. But apparently his seat was originally all lined up for her, only at the last minute she stood aside and let him have it.'

I thought of my conversation with Rycart.

'The Member for Michigan,' I murmured.

'Who?'

'The sitting MP was a man called Giffen. He was so pro-American, he was known as the Member for Michigan.' Something moved uneasily inside my mind. 'Can I ask you a question?' I said.

'Before Adam was killed — why were you so determined to keep that manuscript under lock and key?'

'I told you: security.'

'But there was nothing in it. I know that better than anyone. I've read every tedious word a dozen times.'

Amelia glanced around. We were still on the fringe of the party. Nobody was paying us any attention.

'Between you and me,' she said quietly, '*we* weren't the ones who were concerned. Apparently, it was the Americans. I was told they passed the word to MI5 that there might be something early on in the manuscript that was a potential threat to national security.'

'How did they know that?'

'Who's to say? All I can tell you is that immediately after Mike died, they requested we take special care to ensure the book wasn't circulated until they'd had a chance to clear it.'

'And did they?'

'I've no idea.'

I thought again of my meeting with Rycart. What was it he claimed McAra had said to him on the telephone, just before he died? *'The key to everything is in Lang's autobiography — it's all there in the beginning.'*

Did that mean their conversation had been bugged?

I sensed that something important had just changed — that some part of my solar system had tilted in its orbit — but I couldn't quite grasp what it was. I needed to get away to somewhere quiet, to take my time and think things through. But already I was aware that the acoustics of the party had changed. The roar of talk was dwindling. People were shushing one another. A man bellowed pompously, 'Be quiet!' and I turned around. At the side of the room, opposite the big windows, not very far from where we were standing, Ruth Lang was waiting patiently on a platform, holding a microphone.

'Thank you,' she said. 'Thank you very much. And good evening.' She paused, and a great stillness spread across three hundred people. She took a breath. There was a catch in her throat. 'I miss Adam all the time. But never more than tonight. Not just because we're meeting to launch his wonderful book, and he should be here to share the joy of his life story with us, but because he was so brilliant at making speeches, and I'm so terrible.'

I was surprised at how professionally she delivered the last line, how she built the emotional tension and then punctured it. There was a release of laughter. She seemed much more confident in public than I remembered her, as if Lang's absence had given her room to grow.

'Therefore,' she continued, 'you'll be relieved to hear I'm not going to make a speech. I'd just like to thank a few people. I'd like to thank Marty Rhinehart and John Maddox for not only being marvellous publishers, but also for being great friends. I'd like to thank Sidney Kroll for his wit, and his wise counsel. And in case this sounds as though the only people involved in the memoirs of a British prime minister are Americans, I'd also like to thank in particular, and especially, Mike McAra, who tragically also can't be with us. Mike: you are in our thoughts.'

The great hall rang with a rumble of 'hear hear'.

'And now,' said Ruth, 'may I propose a toast to the one we really need to thank?' She raised her glass of macrobiotic orange juice, or whatever it was. 'To the memory of a great man and a great patriot, a great father and a wonderful husband – to Adam Lang!'

'To Adam Lang!' we all boomed in unison, and then we clapped, and went on clapping, redoubling the volume, while Ruth nodded graciously to all corners of the hall, including ours, at which point she saw me and blinked, then recovered, smiled, and hoisted her glass to me in salute.

She left the platform quickly.

'The merry widow,' hissed Amelia. 'Death becomes her, don't you think? She's blossoming by the day.'

'I have a feeling she's coming over,' I said.

'Shit,' said Amelia, draining her glass. 'In that case I'm getting out of here. Would you like me to take you to dinner?'

'Amelia Bly, are you asking me on a *date*?'

'I'll meet you outside in ten minutes. Freddy!' she called. 'Nice to see you.'

Even as she moved away to talk to someone else, the crowd before me seemed to part, and Ruth emerged, looking very different from the last time I had seen her: glossy-haired, smooth-skinned, slimmed by grief, and designer-clad in something black and silky. Sid Kroll was just behind her.

'Hello, you,' she said.

She took my hands in hers and mwah-mwahed me, not kissing me but brushing her thick helmet of hair briefly against each of my cheeks.

'Hello, Ruth. Hello, Sid.'

I nodded to him. He winked.

'I was told you couldn't stand these kinds of parties,' she said, still holding on to my hands, and fixing me with her glittering dark eyes, 'or else I would have invited you. Did you get my note?'

'I did. Thanks.'

'But you didn't call me!'

'I didn't know if you were just being polite.'

'Being polite!' She briefly shook my hands in reproach. 'Since when was I ever polite? You must come and see me.'

And then she did that thing that important people always do to me at parties: she glanced over my shoulder. And I saw, almost immediately and quite unmistakably in her gaze, a flash of alarm, which was followed at once by a barely perceptible shake of her head. I detached my hands and turned around and saw Paul Emmett. He was no more than five feet away.

'Hello,' he said. 'I believe we've met.'

I swung back to Ruth. I tried to speak, but no words would come. 'Ah,' I said. 'Ah . . .'

'Paul was my tutor,' she said calmly, 'when I was a Fulbright Scholar at Harvard. You and I must talk.'

'Ah . . .'

I backed away from them all. I knocked into a man who shielded his drink and told me cheerfully to watch out. Ruth was saying something earnestly, and so was Kroll, but there was a buzzing in my ears and I couldn't hear them. I saw Amelia staring at me and I waved my hands feebly, and then I fled from the hall, across the lobby and out into the hollow, imperial grandeur of Whitehall.

*

It was obvious the moment I got outside that another bomb had gone off. I could hear the sirens in the distance, and a pillar of smoke was already dwarfing Nelson's Column, rising from somewhere behind the National Gallery. I set off at a loping run towards Trafalgar Square, and barged in front of an outraged couple to seize their taxi. Avenues of escape were being closed off all over central London, as if by a spreading forest fire. We turned into a one-way street, only to find the police sealing the far end with yellow tape. The driver flung the cab into reverse, jerking me forward and on to the edge of my seat, and that was how I stayed throughout the rest of the journey, clinging to the handle beside the door, as we twisted and dodged through the back routes north. When we reached my flat I paid him double the fare.

'The key to everything is in Lang's autobiography — it's all there in the beginning.'

I grabbed my copy of the finished book, took it over to my desk, and started flicking through the opening chapters. I ran my finger swiftly down the centre of the pages, sweeping my eyes over all the made-up feelings and half-true memories. My professional prose, typeset and bound, had rendered the roughness of a human life as smooth as a plastered wall.

Nothing.

I threw it away in disgust. What a worthless piece of junk it was: what a soulless commercial exercise. I was glad Lang wasn't around to read it. I actually preferred the original: for the first time I recognised something honest at least in its plodding earnestness. I opened a drawer and grabbed McAra's original manuscript, tattered from use and in places barely legible beneath my crossings-out and over-writings. *'Chapter One. Langs are Scottish folk originally, and proud of it . . .'* I remembered the deathless beginning I had cut so ruthlessly in Martha's Vineyard. But then, come to think of it, every single one of McAra's chapter beginnings had been particularly dreadful. I hadn't left one unaltered. I searched through the loose pages, the bulky manuscript fanning open and twisting in my clumsy hands like a living thing.

'Chapter Two. Wife and child in tow, I decided to settle in a small town where we could live away from the hurly-burly of London life . . .' 'Chapter Three. Ruth saw the possibility that I might become party leader long before I did . . .' 'Chapter Four. Studying the failures of my predecessors I resolved to be

different . . .' 'Chapter Five. In retrospect, our general election victory seems inevitable but at the time . . .' 'Chapter Six. Seventy-six separate agencies oversaw social security . . .' 'Chapter Seven. Was ever a land so haunted by history as Northern Ireland . . . ?' 'Chapter Eight. Recruited from all walks of life, I was proud of our candidates in the European elections . . .' 'Chapter Nine. As a rule, nations pursue self-interest in their foreign policy . . .' 'Chapter Ten. A major problem facing the new government . . .' 'Chapter Eleven. CIA assessments of the terrorist threat . . .' 'Chapter Twelve. Agent reports from Afghanistan . . .' 'Chapter Thirteen. In deciding to launch an attack on civilian areas, I knew . . .' 'Chapter Fourteen. America needs allies who are prepared . . .' 'Chapter Fifteen. By the time of the annual party conference, demands for my resignation . . .' 'Chapter Sixteen. Professor Paul Emmett of Harvard University has written of the importance . . .'

I took all sixteen chapter openings and laid them out across the desk in sequence.

'The key to everything is in Lang's autobiography — it's all there in the beginning.'

The *beginning* or the *beginnings*?

I was never any good at puzzles. But when I went through the pages and circled the first word of each chapter, even I couldn't help but see it — the sentence that McAra, fearful for his safety, had embedded in the manuscript, like a message from the grave: 'Langs Wife Ruth Studying In Seventy-six Was Recruited As A CIA Agent In America By Professor Paul Emmett of Harvard University.'

Seventeen

A ghost must expect no glory.

Ghostwriting

I left my flat that night, never to return. Since then a month has passed. As far as I know, I haven't been missed. There were times, especially in the first week, sitting alone in my scruffy hotel room – I've stayed in four by now – when I was sure I had gone mad. I ought to ring Rick, I told myself, and get the name of his shrink. I was suffering from delusions. But then, about three weeks ago, after a hard day's writing, just as I was falling asleep, I heard on the midnight news that the former Foreign Secretary, Richard Rycart, had been killed in a car accident in New York City, along with his driver. It was only the fourth headline, I'm afraid. There's nothing more ex than an ex-politician. Rycart would not have been pleased.

I knew after that there was no going back.

Although I've done nothing but write and think about what happened, I still can't tell you precisely how McAra uncovered the truth. I presume it must have started back in the archives, when he came across Operation Tempest. He was already disillusioned with Lang's years in power, unable to understand why something that had started with such high promise had ended in such a bloody mess. When, in his dogged way, researching the Cambridge years, he stumbled on those photographs, it must have seemed like the key to the mystery: certainly, if Rycart had heard rumours of Emmett's CIA links, it's reasonable to assume that McAra must have done so, too.

But McAra knew other things as well. He would have known that Ruth was a Fulbright Scholar at Harvard, and it wouldn't have taken him more than ten minutes on the internet to discover that Emmett was teaching her specialist subject on the campus in the mid-seventies. He also knew better than anyone that Lang rarely made a decision without consulting his wife. Adam was the brilliant political salesman, Ruth the strategist. If you had to pick which of them would have had the brains, the nerve and the ruthlessness to be an ideological recruit, there could only be one choice. McAra can't have known for sure, but I believe he'd put together enough of the picture to blurt out his suspicions to Lang during that heated argument on the night before he went off to confront Emmett.

I try to imagine what Lang must have felt when he heard the accusation. Dismissive, I'm sure; furious, also. But a day or two afterwards, when a body was washed up, and he went to the morgue to identify McAra – what did he think then?

Most days I have listened to the tape of my final conversation with Lang. The key to everything is there, I'm sure, but always the whole story remains just tantalisingly out of reach. Our voices are thin, but recognisable. In the background is the rumble of the jet's engines.

ME: Is it true you had a serious row with him? Just before he died?
LANG: Mike made certain wild accusations. I could hardly ignore them.
ME: May I ask what kind of accusations?
LANG: I'd prefer not to repeat them.

ME: Were they to do with the CIA?

LANG: But surely you already know, if you've been to see Paul Emmett?

[A pause, lasting 75 seconds]

LANG: I want you to understand that everything I did, both as party leader and as prime minister — everything — I did out of conviction, because I believed it was right.

ME: [Inaudible]

LANG: Emmett claims you showed him some photographs. Is that true? May I see?

And then there is nothing for a while but engine sound, as he studies them, and I spool forwards to the part where he lingers over the girls at the picnic on the river bank. He sounds inexpressibly sad.

'I remember her. And her. She wrote to me once, when I was prime minister. Ruth was not pleased. Oh God, Ruth—'

'Oh God, Ruth—'

'Oh God, Ruth—'

I play it over and over again. It's obvious from his voice, now that I've listened to it often enough, that at that moment, when he remembers his wife, his concern is entirely for her. I guess she must have called him late that afternoon in a panic to report I'd been to see Emmett, and shown him some photographs. She would have needed to talk to him face to face as soon as possible — the whole story was threatening to unravel — hence the scramble to find a plane. God knows if she was aware of what might be waiting for her husband on the tarmac: surely not, is my opinion, although the questions about the lapses in security that allowed it to happen have never been fully answered. But it's Lang's failure to complete the sentence that I find moving. *'What have you done?'* is surely what he means to add. *'Oh God, Ruth — what have you done?'* This, I think, is the instant when the days of suspicion abruptly crystallise in his mind, when he realises that McAra's 'wild accusations' must have been true after all, and his wife of thirty years is not the woman he thought she was.

No wonder I was the one she suggested should complete the book. She had plenty to hide, and she must have been confident that the author of Christy Costello's hazy memoir would be just about the least likely person on the planet to discover it.

I would like to write more, but, looking at the clock, I fear that this will have to do, at least for the present. As you can appreciate, I don't care to linger in one place too long. Already I sense that strangers are starting to take too close an interest in me. My plan is to parcel up a copy of this manuscript and give it to Kate. I shall put it through her door in about an hour's time, before anyone is awake, with a letter asking her not to open it, but to look after it. Only if she doesn't hear from me within a month, or if she discovers something has happened to me, is she to read it, and decide how best to get it published. She will think I'm being melodramatic, which I am. But I trust her. She will do it. If anyone is stubborn enough and bloody-minded enough to get this thing into print, it is Kate.

I wonder where I'll go next. I can't decide. I certainly know what I'd like to do. It may surprise you. I'd like to go back to Martha's Vineyard. It's summer there now, and I have a peculiar desire to see those wretched scrub oaks actually in leaf, and to watch the yachts go skimming out full-sailed from Edgartown across

Nantucket Sound. I'd like to return to that beach at Lambert's Cove and feel the hot sand beneath my bare feet, and watch the families playing in the surf, and stretch my limbs in the warmth of the clear New England sun.

This puts me in something of a dilemma, as you may appreciate, now that we reach the final paragraph. Am I supposed to be pleased that you are reading this, or not? Pleased, of course, to speak at last in my own voice. Disappointed, obviously, that it probably means I'm dead. But then, as my mother used to say, I'm afraid in this life you just can't have everything.